THE MEN

Lieutenant Hawkins, who learned how to kill and how to doubt . . . Sergeant LeBlanc, determined to run the platoon even if it was over the Lieutenant's dead body . . . the "Chief," an ex-hippie Indian who tried to forget the war in brothels . . . Wilson, a black man who just wanted to do his job and get home, if whitey would only let him . . . Carlysle, another black who decided to declare his private war. . .

These are some of the men you will live with, sometimes die with, and never forget in—

BODY COUNT

"Ultra-realistic . . . the action speaks for itself and packs a walloping message!"
—*The New York Times*

"This has to be one of the great novels dealing with the American Military Establishment, ranking with *From Here to Eternity* . . . accurate, intense, profoundly exciting, it will enthrall you every page of the way!"
—*Springfield Newspaper Syndicate*

BODY COUNT

❖❖❖❖❖❖❖❖❖❖❖❖❖❖❖❖❖❖❖❖❖❖

William Turner Huggett

A DELL BOOK

Published by
DELL PUBLISHING CO., INC.
1 Dag Hammarskjold Plaza
New York, New York 10017

Printed in the United States of America
First Dell printing—October 1974
Second Dell printing—December 1974

Contents

I

Operation Pegasus

1

Wilson

Deep in the elephant grass the wind never stirred. The dense stalks didn't shade the sun which baked down, searing the still air. If a man sat motionless with his pants stretched tight over his thighs he had to move or the cloth would burn. Slowly the point man inched his way up the mountain, hacking through the sea of grass with a long machete. Behind him Delta Company of the Third Marine Division was strung out single file, a long column snaking back over the smaller hills.

Corporal Robert Wilson dropped to one knee and flared his nostrils, sniffing intently. "I smell gooks." He snicked back the operating handle of his big M-14 and let the bolt snap home, pumping a round into the chamber. The noise seemed to hammer in his ears as he stared out to the flank. A quivering tenseness pricked at his stomach, and he half expected them to come charging out at him.

"Ih doan smell nothin'." Big John's voice came from five yards behind. Wilson looked up at the top of the peak, wondering if they were up there waiting. The man in front of him kept moving, so he hitched his pack and forced himself to climb on. But he left the round in the chamber.

He humped in wary silence for a few minutes until the man in front stopped again. Stop and start. Advance a little and hold it up. For the twentieth time since starting five hours ago, he faced down the hill, squatted, and rocked back awkwardly against the pack. He spread his legs and braced himself against a tree to keep from sliding downhill. It was the only way to sit comfortably on a steep slope.

Wilson opened his eyes and let out a deep sigh, forgetting the gook smell. Without moving, he unbuttoned his fly. With just his fingertips he took it out and skinned it back, idly watching the black head glisten wet in the sun.

No matter how hot it was, the sun always felt good in his crotch. In the half-reclining, half-standing position he emptied a few deep-yellow drops and felt intensely relieved. The gook smell was gone and his alertness slipped; his groin relaxed and the tiredness flowed away. Funny, he thought, how he had to piss so often when they humped in the sun; he only went a little each time. The sun and the weariness began to lull his mind when he caught a glimpse of the new lieutenant on the trail far below.

There, was trouble. Staff Sergeant LeBlanc had been platoon commander for months, almost the whole of the Pegasus Op. Now they were almost to the big base at Khe Sanh and sure to step in some bad shit when they got near those two NVA divisions. Wilson watched the lieutenant straining and sweating, his new green clothes standing out sharply against the dirt brown of everyone else's.

Wilson shook his head and lit a C-ration Marlboro. Well, if they stepped in it at the top of this hill, maybe the new lieutenant would get hit and LeBlanc would take over again. Wilson frowned—even though he didn't like LeBlanc, he felt safe with him.

Wilson blew out the smoke, took off his helmet, and religiously marked off another day. Getting short, he chuckled to himself. Only two hundred and twenty-eight days to go. Then he could get back on the Freedom Bird and fly to The World. The U.S.A. And after he was back just a couple more months, he would be out of the Crotch—really free. Even the anticipation made him feel good.

"Movin'."

The word cut through his thoughts and he forced himself to get up, reluctant to push against the pain of climbing. "Movin', Big John." He called back to the black giant behind him.

Wilson watched as Big John ambled to his feet with a sloshy grunt. He looked like a burly bear; the little M-16 rifle a toy against the huge naked arm. Big John Jackson could wear only a T-shirt or a flak jacket because the jungle shirts were too small for his shoulders.

The word echoed on down the line and the men staggered up under their assortment of gear: packs, rifles, grenades, ammo, extra ammo for the machine guns, Claymore mines, LAAW rockets, flak jackets, helmets, canteens, C-rats. They labored on up, sweating in the heat.

Again Wilson's eyes swept to the top as the column skirted a large B-52 bomb crater. There were scattered patches of jungle where the elephant grass thinned out. Not good, not good at all, he thought. Any minute now and he would hear shots. Any minute and the point man would be dead. The point man always got it.

Slowly, tentatively, the first platoon made it to the top and moved off to the left. Wilson motioned to Sedgewick, the lead man in the squad, to follow.

—"Two Bravo. Two Bravo. This is Two Assist. Over."—

He heard the radio crackle and reached back automatically. His radioman strained up and handed him the microphone without a word, knowing it was LeBlanc.

—"Two Assist, this is Two Bravo. Go."—

—"They've spotted some bunkers, move your squad to the right. We're gonna get on line. Over."—

—"Roger."—

—"Two Alpha will be on your right; don't move till I'm up. Over."—

—"Roger."—

Wilson gave the handset back, unconsciously relieved that the new lieutenant wasn't on the radio. LeBlanc was still running the show.

The terrain was open on top and Wilson fanned the squad out on a line, mentally checking the men; they were down to seven men. He watched Holton's squad move up on line beside his own. Sanders' squad was next. Then Sail, the Southerner, came over the crest leading one of two machine-gun teams.

"Sanders, keep your squad back on flank security," Sergeant LeBlanc yelled, and maneuvered close behind the second squad just as the new lieutenant struggled over the edge of the hill, soaked in sweat. Joseley, the platoon commander's radioman, was tagging along faithfully behind.

"Wilson, move it out," LeBlanc bellowed. Wilson jerked around and moved forward, low and cautious now; LeBlanc was still yelling.

"Chief, bring up one of the machine guns."

There was a small jungle patch before the hill dropped off on the other side—small but too dense to see through.

That's where the bunkers were; and they would have to check them before setting up for the night. Slowly they crept up toward the denser foliage. As the grass and heavy stalks came up between them, Wilson moved the men in tight to keep visual contact. They dropped their packs for the assault, but Wilson was sweating madly, waiting for the first distinctive pop of the gook AK-47 rifle. He flipped his big M-14 on automatic and hefted its weight. They had been issued the new M-16 at the beginning of this Op, but Wilson had scorned it and kept the older, heavier rifle.

Keep quiet, move low, he told himself. There must be nothing here or they would have fired by now. He sniffed. Was it his imagination? No. He could smell it. Gooks.

"Bunker!" Instantly they stopped and dropped down.

"Hold it up!"

"Frag it!" LeBlanc called. Wilson saw the Chief silently edging up. Damn, that Indian is good, Wilson thought, as the Chief began to move in a half-circle. Then Wilson saw it; just a little bump in the ground with a dark hole in one side. Sometimes the gooks would remain in the bunkers until the last minute and then come out firing like crazy. He flipped the safety off again just to make sure and felt the sweat rolling down his side.

Ta Tow Tow Tow Tow.

Sail, the machine gunner, was firing rounds into the opening as the Chief moved in from the side. The Chief seemed to slide along next to the ground. He sprang and darted forward, running unbelievably close to the orange tracers of the machine gun bullets. His arm flicked out. Wilson saw the frag, a grenade, sail into the opening. Chief whirled, darted back a few steps, then flattened himself to the ground. WHOOMP. The muted explosion shook the air. A little wisp of smoke came out.

The bunkers had been empty.

Wilson looked around and saw the new lieutenant crawling along behind LeBlanc.

LeBlanc

LeBlanc knew there wasn't anyone in the bunkers. If the gooks were going to hit, they'd have done it when the company was strung out down on the slope. Anybody who had been there was long gone by the time Second Platoon got up and got ready. Besides, the smell was old. The real worry now was mortars.

Staff Sergeant LeBlanc was a medium-sized man of twenty-six, with powerful shoulders and back. His hair was cropped close and carelessly, but his thick dark mustache was neatly trimmed. The eyes were hard and knowing beyond his years, and the voice was like a heavy whip.

LeBlanc was from Louisiana—part French, part Cajun, and part mean. His daddy had been a shrimper, and for a while LeBlanc had worked the boats, though he was always the striker and never a captain. Goddamn, that had been hard work: Start the winch, put out the nets, drop the doors, lower the tickler chain, check the tri-net. Then worst of all—pull off the heads before the shrimp went on ice. He hated that. After each drag, the striker sat there on the deck up to his ankles in a slimy bunch of wet shrimp, deheading each one.

His father had owned a boat, and for a while two boats; but they had lost the second one and one of his brothers with it. There had been a collision and the Coast Guard had ruled it accidental, although it would better be called a ramming. What could they do? Feuds between shrimpmen were settled by themselves.

Never in his life would he go back to that. He escaped, joined the Marines, and for tough LeBlanc the Crotch was good. He rose rapidly, making sergeant after his first tour in Nam. Rank came fast in a war.

Back in San Diego they made him an instructor. Damn San Diego and its lousy camp-following women. Well, he met one and married her. Fuck! After all he was getting it free—why get married? But she was hot—tough little tits and a hot box. Trouble was they were just alike—always fighting or loving.

"Drink, drink, drink, that's all you ever do anymore. Pretty soon you'll be nothing but a beergut and a mouth."

"Jesus Christ on a crutch, woman, I'll drink when I damn well please."

"Yeah, when you start raising that beer can, that's all you can raise."

He'd slapped her silly the first time she'd said it and they'd ended in gutty passion. They went at each other till their bodies were wet and drained, then lay still—the only time they didn't fight. And it went on like that till he left her. Only he really didn't leave her; he just volunteered to go back to Vietnam. So they developed a pattern; they fought and loved so hard that their reunions were good for only about two months, then he'd go off again. Oh, well, a woman on a military base is never alone, least of all a wife whose husband is away.

The platoon moved back to the crest of the hill and Le Blanc heard the captain call. He saw the new lieutenant jump and try to walk with a spring as if the climb up the mountain had been nothing. LeBlanc snorted in disgust. "Goddamn, not only is the SOB green, but looks like he gonna be a brown nose as well. Well, let him go suck ass; I'm gonna put these lines in."

Quickly LeBlanc noted the shape of the hill and the relative positioning of the other two platoons in the company. Each night the three platoons in the company grouped into a circle on the peak of the mountain. Foxholes were dug to form the perimeter, like covered wagons of old. To complete the circle, he placed the squads so each end of the platoon would join with the other two platoons. He noticed with satisfaction the Chief studying the ground to get the best place for the machine guns.

LeBlanc began designating each foxhole to get the maximum cover. He moved quickly now, worrying about mortars; the gooks mortared them almost every night, just about the time they were digging in. He looked around in irritation for Wilson's squad. Wilson and two others were pretending to be cleaning their gear while studiously watching the new lieutenant.

Unaware of the observation, the new lieutenant was carefully lacing his boots. With annoyance, LeBlanc's eyes searched over him. The lieutenant was an average-tall man, cleancut with light sandy hair. He had regular, even features and what might be called the All-American look. LeBlanc thought sarcastically it was the type that mothers liked their daughters to date; but right now he just looked exhausted.

The lieutenant plopped down his pack and shed his cartridge belt. He took out his handkerchief and wiped his face. LeBlanc watched in amused fascination as the lieutenant carefully wiped his neck, arms, and hands. Then, to LeBlanc's amazement, the lieutenant took out his canteen and poured some water on his hands and wrung them as if to wash.

Didn't this dumb ass know they never had enough water on a hill position? Well, he'd learn soon enough. But LeBlanc continued to stare as the lieutenant took off his shirt and wrung it out. He watched the new lieutenant sniff at it and saw him wrinkle his face in disgust. Christ, LeBlanc thought, if this dude thinks he's dirty now, man, he'd just better wait. "Wilson, quit your fucking eyeballing and get your ass over here." LeBlanc's voice pulsed with authority.

Looking up quickly, the lieutenant saw LeBlanc approaching and hastened to put his wet shirt back on.

"When was the last time the platoon had a bath, Sergeant?"

"Huh? Oh, about a week ago, sir. The company set up behind headquarters and we got to bathe in a stream."

"How long since you had clean clothes?"

LeBlanc thought back. "Well, most of the men rinsed theirs in the stream then but didn't have time to wash them."

"No. I mean when did you last have an opportunity to get new ones or have these washed? Don't you make them change regularly?"

"Men only got one set apiece, sir. Too heavy to carry more." LeBlanc saw the disbelief in the lieutenant's eyes as he bored on. "The gunny orders new ones every day, but only a few come in; the guys that got ripped ones get first go. But the last time we got a whole bunch was about two weeks ago, maybe ten days. Hard to remember. Chopper brought a whole box 'em, all medium-regular."

"What if they don't fit?"

"Well, men wear them regardless, sir. They're glad to get what they can."

The lieutenant seemed to ignore the reproach in the sergeant's voice and turned away. But LeBlanc called after him sharply.

"We'd better be settin' the lines in, Lieutenant, so's the men can start diggin' their holes."

Surprise and confusion momentarily replaced the embarrassment in the lieutenant's eyes. "Have you been placing the positions in already?" The lieutenant's voice rose, as if sensing the challenge to his authority.

"Just movin' them into tentative positions, Lieutenant. It's your job to set the men in." It galled LeBlanc to step down to any boot lieutenant, but usually they went along with suggestions.

"How did you know where to set them?"

"Saw the captain motioning and I just tied them into the ends of the First and Third platoons to complete the circle." Then he added, almost as a goad, "First and Third was already diggin'." Goddamn, if the boot-ass wanted to be stubborn, he'd show him. Maybe the lieutenant didn't think serving two tours in Nam meant anything.

"Well, let's go do it now." The lieutenant's voice was quiet.

Sergeant LeBlanc was surprised at the sudden energy in the lieutenant's voice, but he turned abruptly and stomped off toward the lines.

"That hole over there's the last of the Third Platoon. This'uns our first, part of Holton's squad."

The lieutenant looked nervously over to the other hole and down the line. LeBlanc could see it was confusing to him, and he knew exactly what the lieutenant was thinking. First thing, the SOB would try and set up the machine guns wrong. Hell, he ought to know—he'd taught officers just like this one. Ironic as shit. But the textbook solution for machine guns just didn't work in the northern mountain country of Vietnam.

All the troops heading for Vietnam, both new and old, enlisted and officer, had to go through a fifteen-day orientation course before leaving the States. They tried to cram about fifteen weeks of training into fifteen days. It looked impressive on paper and let the brass say to the administration, "Look, each man going to Vietnam has X number of refresher hours in the following courses. . . ."

LeBlanc's favorite class had been woods survival. He remembered teaching a class of fresh-faced young officers sitting on the bleachers around him.

LeBlanc had picked up the little white rabbit gently as he walked out in front of the class.

"Gentlemen, in this hour you are going to learn to survive in the woods—without equipment." (Preceded, of course, by a dirty joke to get attention.) "To survive you have to eat. Now I will show you how to prepare meat without tools of any sort." He cradled the rabbit gently in the crook of his arm. He could see by this time that the entire class was watching the rabbit—it was so cute.

"First, you must kill your game." Gently he grasped the rabbit by the hind legs and let the body hang down. It swayed to and fro just a little bit. The class collectively frowned at the "poor little rabbit" hanging so rudely by its feet.

"Now, gentlemen, I've never seen a rabbit in Vietnam, but any rat or rock ape will do." His voice crooned softly, and the rabbit continued to sway as if it weren't really uncomfortable at all. Suddenly, as the rabbit swung up, LeBlanc's free hand arced and slashed down in a vicious judo chop. The edge of his hand caught the rabbit at the top of the spine and the head snapped back, breaking the neck. The little body dropped lifelessly.

LeBlanc never ceased to delight in the gasp that went up when the rabbit's body hung dead and limp—what did they think he was here for, to plant Easter eggs?

"Now you have to skin it." Quickly he bit a piece out of the loose neck skin and inserted his fingers under the flap. Methodically and expertly he began to peel the whole skin back from the carcass.

"Just like peeling a stocking off a broad." At this point, he felt he had the full attention of the class.

"It is most important to see if the animal is diseased. Since you can't cook it, don't eat a diseased animal. The first thing to check is the liver."

His hard fingers probed and pulled out the soft pulpy meat from the rest. "If it's bright red with no spots, then it's okay, but you still must clean the rest of the animal."

With exaggerated care, he held the rabbit out and scooped the guts out of the stomach cavity.

"If you are careful, the intestines will pull right out without breaking. There are no ligaments holding the organs to the carcass." With the entire guts in one hand and the carcass in the other, he stopped and looked earnestly at the class. "You now have the carcass ready to eat."

Without a warning, he suddenly flung the entire mess of guts directly into the class. That was the part that always made his day. Invariably there was a violent upheaval, scrambling and screaming. The stiff, starched, haughty kids squealed and jumped. If some were unlucky enough to get hit, the mess was always passed on, so that others shared the discomfort.

"Just keeping the class awake, gentlemen. Don't forget—a mortar can drop on you at any time in Vietnam."

Only once or twice had he been questioned about his teaching methods: "Well, sir, the men have six one-hour classes today, each one covering a whole different subject. My class is the fourth one, right after lunch. The death hour. Everybody wants to sleep. But I'll bet a month's salary that if you find these same lieutenants one year from now and ask them which class they remember—I'll bet you get only one answer."

Yessir, LeBlanc was good in his field.

Now LeBlanc looked again at the new officer beside him. He was young, concerned, but there was a delicacy to him not found in most Marines. He watched as the lieutenant studied the positions.

They came to the middle of the line, which was the closest part to the little thicket of jungle which the platoon had searched earlier.

"This here's the first gun hole."

The lieutenant stopped and LeBlanc could see he was studying the ground, remembering how the school taught officers to place machine guns. The book said to fire the gun across the most likely avenue of approach so as to cut down wave attacks. According to that theory the bullet path should cross between the lines and the jungle, but that theory just didn't work in mountain jungle fighting. LeBlanc stared in angry silence as the lieutenant looked back and forth. Go on and say it, Lieutenant, I know what you're thinking: You want to move the gun.

"Where is your line of Final Protective Fire?"

"Huh?" The machine gunner looked plaintively at LeBlanc.

LeBlanc turned away to hide his grimace. Consciously he set his face before turning back. "We don't use none of that fancy stuff in Vietnam, Lieutenant."

"Oh, I see," the Lieutenant said quietly and moved on.

Pleased at shutting off the lieutenant so easily, LeBlanc started automatically to tell the men to dig in. He caught himself. "Okay with you, Lieutenant?"

The lieutenant looked up the line, dropped his eyes to the ground, and took a slow breath. "No, not yet. I want to check that machine gun again."

Every noise stopped. The whole platoon turned and stared at the two men. A look of impatience flashed on LeBlanc's face and he gritted his teeth but said nothing. The lieutenant turned from him and went back to the machine-gun position. He pointed to a man who was diligently cleaning the machine gun. "You there, walk out toward that jungle patch."

Sail, the rangy, raw-boned kid from the red-clay gulches of Gadsden, Alabama, looked up startled and unconsciously glanced at Sergeant LeBlanc. LeBlanc glowered, saying nothing but nodding affirmatively.

The man looked around and frowned, then carefully put on his helmet and flak jacket and picked up an M-16. The lieutenant moved to one side a bit and kneeled down. Raising his rifle, the man began to edge cautiously toward the jungle. The lieutenant watched as if sighting, until the man had slowed almost to a stop. "That's enough; come back."

The man flung a final look over his shoulder at the jungle and scurried back to the lines.

"What's your name?" the lieutenant asked.

"Sail, sir." The voice was relieved but angry as well.

"Good." The lieutenant turned to Sergeant LeBlanc triumphantly. "I think we have a better shot with the gun over here where I kneeled than where it is now."

LeBlanc looked down and kicked the ground a couple of times. Finally he looked up, striving to keep his voice calm. "Lieutenant, that ain't the way we do it over here. I know that's the way they teach it in the States, but it don't work in these mountains."

Both men were intensely conscious of the platoon, edging in to watch.

"Why not?" the lieutenant said slowly.

"Gooks ain't goin' to come running up like you think, Lieutenant. Too steep and there's no cover. If they're goin' to come in a wave like your plan here is for, they'd have to mass down there and run up this ridge. Gun would be better right up where it is."

The men were listening in a little circle, and the lieutenant was striving to keep his eyes on LeBlanc.

"Maybe. But the gun can still get more of them if it's over there. You saw him walk out. The man walked in the path of the most likely avenue of approach."

"Dammit!" Sergeant LeBlanc exploded. "The Chief picked that position himself; he's the right guide and the leader of the whole machine-gun section—both teams." He nodded toward the lean, copper-skinned man, but the Indian's face was impassive. "He's had a lot of experience. You can't just fire a machine gun over there in a stream like that. Gooks can come up on you all night. They just probe and pull back, probe and pull back. It just ain't going to work like you're trying to say, Lieutenant. Not in these mountains it ain't."

The lieutenant took a step back, and his eyes darted nervously around the group of men. The circle almost made an arena and the faces were eager in cruel anticipation, as if watching a bear baiting. "Well, I think it ought to go over there."

Sergeant LeBlanc glowered. He was incensed at the stubbornness of the officer, but to directly contradict was unthinkable. Marine discipline and obedience were fundamental to him, and he could not break that basic law. At length he shrugged his shoulders and turned aside. "It's your platoon Lieutenant; you can put the men wherever you want."

The lieutenant looked around him at the men. Their faces were angry and hostile. Sail looked at him with open disgust. LeBlanc moved off, but from the corner of his eye he saw the color drain from the lieutenant's face and the sweat break out on his upper lip.

"Well . . . well, go ahead and leave it there for tonight," the lieutenant stammered. Ashen-faced and avoiding their eyes, he spun around and rushed from the group.

Behind him, the faces didn't laugh but turned in unison to the Sergeant. LeBlanc nodded mutely, accepting their looks. For just a second he smiled to himself. "All right, quit your gawkin'! Get to diggin'. The Goddamn gooks will be poppin' mortars any minute now."

By instinct the men moved at the whip of the voice.

Hawkins

Lieutenant Hawkins walked away from the group and slumped down beside his pack. He felt defeated and drained. He watched the men and he wondered what he had gotten into. To run this platoon, he thought, I've got to do something about that sergeant. There's no doubt that he has their allegiance; but he's wrong about those guns and he's wrong to yell at the men.

Joseley came up and carefully laid his radio down beside the Lieutenant's pack. Joseley was a small man and the oversized pack and radio dwarfed him more. He spoke respectfully. "Where's the platoon CP going to be, sir?"

"CP?"

"Yes, sir. Command Post, CP, that's our position, the platoon headquarters."

"Oh, well, right here," the Lieutenant blurted out.

"Care for a cigarette, sir?" He held out a C-ration Winston and smiled.

"Yes, thanks." The officer took one while the radioman fished out a lighter and held the flame. He puffed out, sighed, and looked closely at Joseley, feeling a sudden affection for him. If he couldn't ask him about the machine gun, at least he was someone to *talk* to.

Stoically, Joseley accepted the talk. He took it as part of his job and spoke good-naturedly.

"Where you from, Joseley?"

"Portland, Maine, sir."

"Do you like carrying the radio?"

"Sure do, sir, best job there is."

"Why?"

"Well, sir, at first I was a snuffy, right out there in front. Oh, I didn't mind being in front, but I hated not *knowing* anything."

"What do you mean—knowing?"

"Sir, the snuffy on the line has no idea what's going on, particularly when we get in contact; everybody is screaming and yelling, people are shooting and running around, and he's lost, totally lost. But if you have a radio, you know everything that's going on; all you have to do is listen and there's the captain and the lieutenant and the squad leaders."

"I see."

"May I ask you a question, sir?"

"Sure."

"Do officers have to come to Vietnam?"

The Lieutenant laughed, "If they join the Marine Corps they do."

"Oh."

"Of course, they don't have to join, but then neither did you."

Lieutenant Chris Hawkins grinned at the little man, who nodded promptly. No, they don't have to join, he thought to himself, and *you* particularly didn't have to join. Tell this PFC that and see what he says. Yes, Christopher Hawkins, this is what you wanted. You volunteered. Well, here it is. You were graduated from Princeton, and you were halfway to a PhD. They all said you were crazy. By the time you got the degree you'd be over draft age. They called you a hawk. Chris Hawkins the hawk from Bucks County, Pennsylvania. The old country home in Bucks County was halfway between New York and Philadelphia, ideal because his father spent half his time in one or the other city. Then the old man had moved to Arlington, Virginia. Since he was in and out of Washington so often on his company's defense contracts, it was the only practical move to make. But the odd thing was that even with the Pentagon contacts, his father didn't want him to join the Marines.

Chris just couldn't understand this reaction, especially since the old flag-waver was always buddying around with half the generals in Washington and thought anybody under twenty-five should look like a cop. Chris remembered the day he'd brought home his roommate from Princeton. His father had been outright rude, implying that his roommate was effeminate and asking him if he read Marx. Of course that had been before long hair was really in vogue; but still, why didn't the old man want him to go to Vietnam?

Now he sat talking with a PFC. No, he didn't mind the old man. The only thing he minded was losing Poo. She'd cried and cried. Why join? Why the war? Why the *Marines?*

He thought back to that morning; it seemed an age. He had come incountry at Da Nang, been sent right on to Phu Bai and Quang Tri. He was assigned to Delta Company, Second Battalion, Seventh Regiment, Third Marine Division, known simply as Delta Two-Seven. They gave him his gear and helilifted him to his company. All he knew was that they were out on an operation called Pegasus which was moving to relieve the big base at Khe Sanh. And here he was only a few miles from the DMZ.

Then he had met his staff sergeant, who took over and assembled the men. God! He'd never forget that. They'd stood around in a stone-silent semicircle and stared at him. He'd never seen a field Marine before; only stateside, clean-shaven ones with close haircuts, neat uniforms, and quick salutes. But these—they slouched, dirty and ragged, with scraggly beards; each one had a different uniform. Some wore jungle blouses or T-shirts, some just wore flak jackets, others had all three or nothing at all. Most wore enemy souvenirs. He saw MARINE CORPS SUCKS in giant letters on one helmet. But it was the eyes that got him, cold and sullen, eyes totally lacking in mirth and warmth, just staring blankly. There seemed to be no life behind them, as if they had lost all caring.

A commotion near the company CP snapped him back. The company gunnery sergeant was running around yelling.

"What's all that?" Hawkins asked sharply.

"I think the chopper's coming in, sir. Resupply," Joseley said excitedly. "Maybe mail." He jumped up and started to run off, then flung back the words: "You'd better get down, sir. Sometimes they mortar us when the birds come in."

Hawkins sat on his pack feeling a little bewildered and watched the gunny direct the men in clearing an LZ, a helicopter landing zone. They knocked over some trees and stamped down the low brush and the grass until there was an open spot about twenty-five yards or so in diameter. A man with a radio stood watching the sky, and when the helicopter appeared as a speck on the horizon, he gave instructions guiding it toward the area. As it grew larger, he tossed what appeared to be a beer can in the opening. *Ssszzzt.* The can gave a little pop, and then thick bright smoke hissed out. The helicopter veered and came straight toward the smoke.

It hovered and whirred about twenty-five yards up with a dull *thap, thap, thap,* the smoke billowing everywhere. Then everything began to blow. The prop wash from the rotors was like a tornado. Dust, leaves, twigs, shirts, and jungle hats boiled up; poncho tents were ripped from their stakes and flapped viciously in the breeze. The men cursed and hid their faces from the flying dirt and hunched their backs into the wind.

The helicopter descended straight down, the co-pilot and crewmen anxiously watching the proximity of the blades to the nearby branches. Lowering its tail first as if to squat, it looked like a giant science-fiction grasshopper. As the chopper came lower, Hawkins could see stacks of five-gallon water cans suspended in a heavy net by a long cable from the bottom. When the net bundle was about three feet off the ground, the crewmen in the helicopter flipped a lever and the bundle dropped free. Abruptly, the helicopter shot straight up, then leveled off. Several Marines sprang out to set the water cans upright and whisk them away to clear the LZ for the next load. Hawkins stared in amazement. With all his training at Quantico, he'd never seen them land supplies with a net.

"Better get down. Might be mortars, sir."

Hawkins whirled around in surprise. A lean wiry man with copper skin and a deadpan face held out Hawkins' helmet.

For a moment Hawkins stood immobile, gawking at the figure, wondering if he might have hallucinated the sight. The man wore tight, tapered jungle utilities and a strip of camouflaged parachute silk tied as a scarf around his neck. Low on his hips was a wide leather belt fastened by a solid brass buckle engraved with a star—the kind worn by NVA officers. Under his left arm was a .38 revolver in a shoulder holster. But it was the hat that set him off. He seemed to have long hair, but an old jungle hat with a wide brim was pulled low over his ears and only the eyes peeked out. It looked like one of the floppy Stetsons a grizzled prospector in the movies might wear.

Recovering his presence, Hawkins took the helmet and eyed the high cheekbones and aquiline nose. "You're the one they call the Chief. Are you an Indian?"

"Yes, sir," the man answered proudly. "Full blood— one-half Chiricahua and one-half Blackfoot. I'm Corporal Eagle." He lay down, keeping his head up, listening as the next helicopter approached. "Hold your gear, sir. Here comes another one."

This time Hawkins turned his back away and held his gear tightly. The helicopter was bringing cardboard boxes of C-rations and a few miscellaneous objects. Again the chopper descended and again everything blew. The Chief turned his head from the LZ and looked out into the valley. "Listen for the tube, sir. Now is the time."

"Huh?" Hawkins strained to hear over the racket.

"The mortar tubes. Too much noise now. Look for the flash. . . ." The rest was drowned in the roar of the chopper. Again the wind blew and the dirt stung. But the Indian seemed to be concentrating on something else. He lay flat, staring out into the valley. Then the net dropped and the chopper was gone.

The Chief rolled up and sat cross-legged, his back arrowstraight, face still deadpan. He stretched his neck and turned his head, continuing to scan the valley. Then seemingly satisfied, he contemplated the Lieutenant.

"Did you think we were going to get mortared?" Hawkins asked.

"Never can tell, sir. They are in the area for sure, always best to be ready."

"How do you know they are around?"

"Smell 'em, sir."

"Smell them?"

"Yes, sir—on the way up and again on top, they definitely been on this hill within a week."

This guy is putting me on, Hawkins thought. People don't leave a *smell*. He decided to ignore it.

"You're the machine-gun section leader, aren't you?"

"That's right, sir. And right guide, too."

Hawkins considered discussing the emplacement of the guns but shied away. "You think we will be hit tonight?"

The Chief shrugged. "Maybe a probe. We haven't been here long enough to really get hit."

This guy might be a bit cocky, Hawkins thought, but he seems friendly and not at all like the others.

"You got all the gear you need?" the Chief asked. Hawkins cocked his head inquisitively. "Right guide—you know—supposed to get you what you need."

"Oh."

"Grenades?" Chief pulled up a vestlike thing and unhooked a couple of grenades. They were the smooth elliptical kind that looked like an overgrown green egg with a handle. Inside was a coil of wire niched in five hundred separate places, each making a little piece of shrapnel. They were far superior to the old metal pineapple chunk-type used in World War Two.

"Thanks."

"Maybe you'd like some of the new stuff, sir."

"Ah—what's that?"

The Chief looked closely at the Lieutenant for a minute. Hawkins, seeing the look, gave a wan smile. In return, the chief's face broke into a leering grin, then snapped back to normal.

"Okay, here's one of the new ones." He handed Hawkins a round grenade smaller and lighter than the other two. "You can throw these farther and they are more powerful, but they are hard to get. Mostly only the Army got 'em."

The Lieutenant wondered why he hadn't been shown these grenades back in training at Quantico.

"I haven't got any of the CS tear-gas grenades because they are too heavy, but I can give you a CN gas grenade." The Chief pulled out a round red grenade, a little larger than a baseball. "Only find 'em in d'Nam."

"Huh? Where's that?" Then, understanding the word, Hawkins added quickly, "Oh, yeah, go ahead."

The Chief stopped a minute, reexamining the Lieutenant as if he were uncertain, then once again the crazy grin came and went.

"Only Marvin is issued those; you got to trade for 'em, but I'll give you that one."

"Who's Marvin?" Hawkins asked, feeling foolish.

"Marvin the ARVN—you know, the South Vietnamese Army. Dig, sir?"

"Oh, yeah . . . well, thanks. But why is that . . . about the ARVN I mean?" Hawkins was fascinated but felt a growing annoyance at himself for the things he didn't know.

"You know, sir, we ain't supposed to use 'em. They'll make a man real sick, vomit and all."

"Oh, yes, I see. You ever used one?" Hawkins asked, hefting the little ball in his hand.

"That's a Rog—at Hue during Tet." Again the weird grin.

"Work good?"

Slowly the leering grin spread full across the copper face. "*Tree*mendous."

Hawkins puzzled at the violent changes of expression. But just then some helicopters began to swarm over a hilltop about a mile away. They were not the same as the Marine helicopters; these were plainly newer and faster. The Chief saw them and frowned briefly.

"Who's that?" Hawkins asked.

"Those are Hueys, sir. Hu-1's going to the Cav's helicopter parking lot.

Hawkins caught the cynicism. "Army?"

"That's them, sir. First Air Cavalry getting hot chow. We're on the same Op, but they get hot chow flown in to 'em twice a day." Abruptly he jumped up, and the mask came back. "I'd better go get our C's and water 'fore that fuckin' gunny goes ape-shit."

As Chief was silhouetted against the sky, Hawkins realized the man was really small; his hips were narrow, but he walked so straight he looked taller. What a crazy guy, Hawkins thought. His speech is a curious mixture of ain't's, Vietnamese slang, and some expressions that are surprisingly refined. Hawkins wondered what it was about the man that was so puzzling. He had liked the Chief at once and thought the feeling was mutual. Obviously he was experienced in fighting, but he had none of LeBlanc's hostility or brutality. There was something strange about his head, too, or was it his hair? He couldn't quite make it out. Even his M-16 was different: The plastic parts had been carefully covered with camouflage cloth; he had two magazines taped end to end. Hawkins shook his head in bewilderment, remembering a gold bracelet the man had on his wrist. A bracelet no less! Amazing. Yet at the time it had seemed normal.

He and the Chief could be a team, he knew—but Le Blanc. Why couldn't LeBlanc be more like the Chief?

After the choppers left, activities seemed to buzz all around him, yet he was alone. Joseley, Chief, Doc Smitty, and Little Doc began to set up the platoon CP around him. They got out their ponchos and strung them low to the ground forming a hooch. They had no tents, only the little stretches of rubberized canvas. He thought of the wooden huts he'd seen in the rear, then realized that he was in the bush and the poncho hooch was all he would

sleep under—for a year. Why had he come? When he
told his friends about his decision, it seemed that's all anybody could say. Why? Why? He never heard "That's a
fine thing" or "I envy you" or maybe even "That takes
courage." No, only why. Why was he going to Vietnam
when he didn't have to? Well, why did you, Hawkins?
Then he felt the indecision because he really didn't know.
Or did he?

He had been in graduate school, rooming with Arnie,
they had a great apartment. Arnold was going for a doc-
torate in philosophy and he looked the type. People were
always remarking on the physical contrast between the
two of them. The hippie and the Boy Scout, they said.
When Hawkins first told Arnie about joining the Marines,
his roommate was incredulous.

"The Marines? Look, Chris, you just have to be out of
your gourd." Arnie paced the floor, waving his hands, his
hair flying.

"What's wrong with that? I told you I was going to Vietnam, why the big deal about the Corps?" Chris felt himself
on the defensive.

"*The Corps.* Oh, now it's *the Corps.* I can understand
about having to go to Vietnam. But the Marines?"

"What do you understand?"

Arnie fell silent and then eased away. "Oh, you know. I
can get the picture about going to Vietnam—for you
that's okay—but the Marines! No way. A bunch of sadis-
tic egomaniacal killers."

"Wait a minute!" Chris sensed an undercurrent. "How
come you're suddenly so understanding about Vietnam
but not the Marines?"

Arnie, looking uncomfortable, abruptly sat down and
picked up a book.

"What is this, Arnie, what do you mean you 'get the
picture about my going to Vietnam'?" Chris strode across
the room and yanked the book away.

Arnie looked up slowly. "Look, Chris, you don't have
to bullshit with me. I've got a pretty good idea why you
have to join the military and get yourself over there."

Chris felt rather than saw the pained expression in Arnie's eyes. "Oh, you do, huh? Well, that's maybe just
more than I know."

"Cut the act, Chris. Most all your friends know, but they don't hold it against you. Hell, they know about your father and all that."

"What?" For the first time the import of Arnie's message began to leak through. "Now just a minute, Arnold, suppose you just tell me what everybody knows about my father."

"Hey, Chris, let's forget it—I'm sorry I said anything." He reached for the book.

"No! Tell me what's been said."

Slowly Arnie put the book down and stood up. The two stood face to face. "All right, Christopher, if that's the way you want it, I'll say it. You can adduce all the fancy reasons in the world, but you're going to Vietnam because your father wants you to."

Chris felt as if he'd been kicked. "Go on."

"Well, it's no big secret. I know he's got those defense contracts and he's friends with people in Washington. You told me yourself about the time he had dinner with the Secretary of Defense. It looks bad for his son to evade the military."

"You think I'm going to Vietnam just because the old man wants me to?"

"Well, he's paying you, isn't he? I know he's loaded and you never get any of it." Arnie blurted it out and turned away.

A look close to horror passed over Chris' face. There was a long silence, then Chris' voice was just a whisper. "You're kidding."

Immediately Arnie regretted what he had said. "I'm sorry, Chris. I know you're a man of principle; I know you wouldn't go if you were *opposed* to the war like I am."

Mutely Chris turned slowly away and stared out the window. Arnie hesitated and then moved after him, reaching for his sleeve. "Gee, Chris. I didn't mean it like you think. I know you think our presence in Vietnam is just, and you believe that. I know that and I respect you for it. I know you wouldn't go to Vietnam if you were basically against the war, but I don't think you're a hawk . . . or a killer, or anything crazy like that. But me, I'm against the war on basic principle, but I believe you and I respect your beliefs. But what the hell, I know you never have any money; you're still driving that old rattletrap Plymouth while your old man's loaded. The word is your father offered you fifty thousand as well as the deed to the house in the Bahamas as long as you . . ."

Chris spun from the window in a blur. *"Stop!"*

There was an instant of utter terror on Hawkins' face as they stared at each other.

"You don't really mean that, do you? Is that what people are saying?" Chris felt the blood rising. "Do—do *you* believe that, Arnie?" He stepped forward, the anger piling up in him, and grasped Arnie by the elbow.

"No, no!" Arnie shied away, watching Chris carefully. "Look, I didn't want to get into it in the first place, and, no, I don't believe it. Not me."

"What about the others?"

"Well"—Arnie looked apprehensive—"I think some do. Some do. But if you say no—then I believe you, Chris. It's just that . . . well . . ." He didn't finish.

The two moved stiffly about the room for a few minutes, trying to speak but feeling the gulf of awkwardness that had come between them.

At last Chris spoke lamely. "Arnie, it's just that *it's there*. And I want to experience it."

"I believe you, man. Knowing you, I really do."

Abruptly Chris went into his room and shut the door. He sat down and stared at the wall for a long time. He couldn't believe what he had heard. He was logical and reasonable. In prep school he had been captain of the debating team and had even won second place in the Middle Atlantic finals during his senior year. But he just couldn't believe it; this wasn't in any way logical.

He looked around the room vacantly, then took out the picture of his father and stared at it. "Do they really think that?" he whispered out loud. He felt an odd pressure behind his eyeballs and slowly shook his head. Ironic, really ironic. He looked at the picture once more. You don't even want me to go; he could hear his father's voice: *Stay in the Reserve, son. Finish your school and then think about the military.* He remembered the choking, shocked disappointment when his father had scorned him for wanting to go to Vietnam. But, even worse, was his father's outright anger when he said he was joining the Marines. Hawkins laughed without mirth as he thought of Arnie's words. Well, that was one rumor that was strictly a rumor.

Vacantly he put the picture back in a drawer, turned it face down. Dammit then, Hawkins, why did you join? Why couldn't they understand? Didn't anybody believe in anything anymore? He heard that at the outbreak of World War Two you had to stand in line to enlist. At his induction physical he found a line, all right. Only everybody else had some sort of paper in their hands. He had wondered what he was missing. They were reports from private doctors saying why so and so was physically unfit.

Was he the only one? Quietly he went to his old rolltop desk and slid up the top. He unlocked the inside drawer, then leafed through a pile of papers until he found it. A little paper. It was one of the few maxims he had ever kept. He had put it in a tiny frame. Slowly he read the quote. He didn't even know when the man had said it, or what the context was, but it told his story. He had never shown it to anyone. It would have embarrassed him, but now Hawkins set it out on the desk top. The printed words stood out boldly.

> The credit belongs to the man who is actually in the arena, whose face is marred by dust and sweat and blood . . . who knows the great enthusiasms, the great devotions; who spends himself at a worthy cause; who at best knows in the end the triumph of high achievement, and . . . if he fails, at least fails daring greatly so that his place shall never be with those cold timid souls who know neither victory nor defeat.
>
> —JOHN FITZGERALD KENNEDY

Well, I'm going. I'm going to get in the arena, he thought. He stood and faced the window. A light snow had begun. But Arnie's words echoed in his ears. *It's all right for you because you think it's right.* What if we are wrong? What if we are "imperialistic aggressors" as Arnie said? How in hell does Arnie know? How does anybody know? Weird, wasn't it? Kennedy himself had sent the first troops. Well, at least if I go over there and get in the arena, I'll know. Maybe I'll fail, but at least I'll have tried and *I'll know*.

One of the things which had come in on the chopper that night was some cans of dill pickles.

Hawkins watched the distribution of food but couldn't understand the great glee over the pickles.

"Joseley, how come everybody is talking about those pickles?"

"Well, sir, we haven't had anything but C-rations for a month now. Morning, noon, and night we eat C-rations. Only thing good about C's is the fruit, so when something a little different comes, no matter what it is, it's a treat."

"I see."

"Sometimes apples or oranges come and that's a banquet. But the best is onions."

"Onions?"

"Yep. Onions and sardines because you can take them and mix them with your other C-rations and then we get all kinds of new concoctions. Once, about three months ago, they flew out a load of fresh-cooked turkeys. They were cold by the time we got them, but nobody cared. Everybody just went wild eating them. The only thing was, we got hit by the gooks that night and now everybody thinks that whenever we get something special—some kind of goodies—then something is going to happen. Like we're going to get hit."

"Will pickles make us get hit?"

"No." He laughed. "No. Just pickles are safe."

After all the C-rations and water were distributed, the Chief as right guide ceremoniously opened the pickle can. It was a large can. The pickles were fat and covered with juice.

"Should be about two-thirds of a pickle per man," the Chief said. "Now how the hell are we going to divide these equally? Why can't they ever send a number that we can divide even? We always get the wrong number for the number of us."

"Well, since there ain't enough for all, we might as well pass them around the CP first," Sergeant LeBlanc said.

"Lieutenant, have a pickle," the Chief said. He held the

open can in his hand and extended it politely, giving the
Lieutenant first choice.

"No, thanks. You go ahead."

The chief looked surprised but didn't hesitate. He
plunged his hand into the juice, grabbed a pickle and
chomped into it.

Damn, thought Hawkins. No wonder they get sick. The
Chief's hand was ground-in dirty. The grit showed plainly
under the fingernails. They shouldn't do that; they'll
spread germs to everyone in the platoon. No doubt he's
wiped his ass with that hand and probably hasn't been
able to wash it in a week. Well, don't say anything, Chris.
You've already done enough today as it is.

But as he watched, he couldn't stop thinking. They
could *try* to be a little more clean. You've got to make an
extra effort to keep healthy in the bush. A knife could be
heated and used to pick each one out. *All right, but don't
say anything.*

Then Sergeant LeBlanc reached in. His hand sunk into
the can until the juice came up over his knuckles and he
pulled one out, holding it in his fist like a baseball bat.

"Chief, there should be enough for everyone to have
three-fourths a pickle." He grasped the pickle firmly with
both hands now, his thumbs meeting at the center. He
wrenched it cleanly in two and tossed part back into the
can carelessly. It gave a little plop and the juice splashed
out on the ground. The longer part he stuck in his mouth
like a big cigar and chomped down lustfully.

Hawkins felt the disgust rise up in him, and he couldn't
stand it any longer. It was his duty as platoon commander
to protect the men.

"Sergeant, don't take those out with your fingers. You'll
get germs on them for everybody else."

The grouped was stunned. Not a word was said. They
turned and looked up at the Lieutenant unanimously.
Someone snickered and Sergeant LeBlanc stopped chewing,
with the pickle still in his mouth. It puffed out his cheek,
and part stuck out like a fat green stogie. His eyes seemed
to bug out as if someone had slapped him. His jaw stopped
moving halfway through the pickle.

"Dammit, Lieutenant. How the hell do you expect us to
eat out here? We ain't got no way to wash." The Sergeant

glared in anger. He covered his outburst by attempting a laugh. "Anyway, we been doing it all along."

Hawkins hesitated, wishing he hadn't said it now because he saw the looks of incredulity on their faces, but he'd gone this far. "You can clean a knife and spear each one."

Grinning to cover his insolence and disbelief, the sergeant leaned over, stuck his hand in the juice and grabbed another pickle. "Ah, shit, Lieutenant. We're just a bunch of fuckin' animals. *Grrr*. See?"

Hawkins glanced at the men, his eyes tightening. All right, Sergeant, he thought—you win this time but not for long. Aloud, he said simply, "Okay."

He turned away slowly, moved off and sank down beside his pack, not really angry but unhappy with himself. Back by the pickles, eager hands reached forward toward the can.

Twilight came. The listening posts (LP's) were sent out and the lines were checked. Exhausted, Lieutenant Hawkins sat alone beside his pack. I should get up and string my poncho, he thought. But his muscles wouldn't move. Joseley had already dug a hole for both of them.

God, he felt dirty. He leaned over and took his toothbrush from his pack. Without getting up, he brushed his teeth, using the water from his canteen.

Jesus, I'll never sleep like this. His whole skin itched from the sweat and the dirt.

"Uh, sir, excuse me for saying so, but it's not a good idea to wash, with water like that. May need it for drinking later."

The Lieutenant looked up at Joseley in surprise, feeling a little ashamed. "Well, it's my water."

"I know that, sir, but the men won't like it."

"Why can't each man do what he wants with his own share? Surely we'll hit a stream tomorrow."

"Maybe, maybe . . . but we might have to stay on this hill and the resupply chopper might not get in. Never can tell, sir."

Hawkins realized it was so immediately, but his pride pricked him and he kept on doggedly. "Well, okay, but why should the men care how I use my share of the water?"

Joseley looked skeptical but explained patiently. "Sir, everyone knows that you're the platoon commander and can take more of the water if you want it, and they get pissed . . . ah, jealous . . . if you use yours to bathe in."

Hawkins was amazed at this open acknowledgment of his power. "Thanks, Jose. I appreciate your letting me know."

He lay back and watched as his radioman prepared to eat, and gradually he started to talk. Joseley opened a box of C-rations and sat quietly listening. It was canned turkey loaf, canned peaches, canned cheeses and crackers, with a plastic packet of cigarettes, sugar, salt, powdered coffee, toilet paper, and other stuff. Joseley took the fruit and cigarettes and threw the rest away.

"I'm glad you didn't like turkey loaf, Lieutenant," Joseley said casually.

"Why?"

"Because the platoon commander always has first choice and LeBlanc used to take the turkey loaf every time."

2

Red

Three days later Delta Company made enemy contact. Operation Pegasus had come within rifle-shot range of Khe Sanh, and the afternoon resupply chopper had brought some new men. One was a black guy from Texas called Banks, the other a white boy from Minneapolis, Minnesota. No one remembered his name, however; they just called him Red.

Red was a skinny little kid, barely turned eighteen. They made him wait three weeks at San Diego until he had his eighteenth birthday because it was the policy not to send seventeen-year-olds to Vietnam.

His strawberry hair was still close-cut and trimmed from the stateside military barbers, "white sidewalls" over his ears. To his great embarrassment, his face was smooth and unshaven. He didn't really need to shave, although they had made him do so at bootcamp at Parris Island; now the downy blond fuzz was struggling to grow over the mass of freckles.

Red walked around the foxhole to which he had been assigned and kicked a little dirt into it. Nervously he flipped a cigarette in his mouth and let it dangle from the corner of his lips. He did it out of habit, but he had started smoking that way because he thought it made him look tough. Gingerly he rubbed his bare forearm where the sun hit the fresh tattoo. He had the tattoo done in Diego one week before he left for Vietnam and the needle pricks were still enflamed. It was a picture of a mean-looking bulldog with a Marine hat on; under that was a dagger. In a semicircle over the top were the words: DEATH BEFORE DISHONOR. Sheepishly he thought of his mother and knew she would have a fit when she saw the tattoo. But by then it would be too late.

His mother worked in a department store as a cashier and had reared Red alone because his father had been killed in Korea. His mother had some very formal-looking pictures of his father on the mantel, but Red never thought of his dad except as he was in one particular picture. He had found the photograph in an old album at the bottom of a trunk. In the picture his dad was wearing a Marine uniform with the sleeves rolled up and his tie loose. He was leaning against a '46 Olds convertible with one arm around his mother's waist and a beer can in the other hand; his mother had a funny grin that Red had never seen before. The picture was not too clear, but it was clear enough for Red to see the bulldog and dagger on the forearm.

Again he walked around the foxhole. Some of the dirt was wet and stuck to his shoes. Why did they have to put Banks in the other squad? he thought. Now he didn't know anyone. Looking around, he wondered how long they'd be here. This was a miserable place. He glanced back at the spot where he was supposed to sleep. It was just a poncho strung out close to the ground. The other two guys in his hole had taken his poncho to put on the ground, and it was already tracked with mud. The ground sloped sharply, but the other men were asleep. One leg stuck out and lay in the half-dried mud.

Red shuddered and peered into the treeline, wondering what he'd do if the VC started to come. It was late afternoon. What time did they attack? What if they were getting ready right now? His chest felt squeezed and he had to breathe consciously to get any air. He looked intently at the trees and the jungle, thinking maybe he should go get his squad leader. What was his name?

"Hey, man, wha' you doin' lookin' out theah so sad fo'?"

Red whirled around and saw a huge black man with a warm smile; he felt immediately embarrassed because he had jumped. "Nothing, buddy, I'm not sad, just looking, that's all, just looking." Red purposely made his voice flippant, but his speech was precise and clear, like most native Minnesotans.

"Well, now, theah ain' much to look at out theah," the big man said. "You jus' come today, didn't you?"

"Did you see me here before?"

"No, doan reckon so." The big man chuckled and looked at the clean new clothes. His eyes went up to the freshly cut red hair. "You mus' be call Red. Eva'body call me Big John, but Ih doan know why."

Red looked over at the smiling face and saw the bright gold tooth in front. "Yeah, that's me." He relaxed a little and smiled weakly.

Big John's eyes examined the new equipment. "Say, man, you got a poncho-lina'?"

"What's that?"

"Ahhh—well, you gonna need one. Look up theah." He pointed back to the sleeping men. "See that camaflage lookin' blanket that dood's wrapped in?"

"Uh-huh."

"Tha's one—it doan weigh nothin', but it'll keep you warhm. They didn' give you one back in the reahr?"

"No, I remember now, they said they were out."

"Okay, man, you stay heahr, Ih'll get you one."

"Oh, thanks," Red mumbled, feeling a little ashamed of trying to be hard before.

"Man, lemmee see you' rifle."

Red handed him the M-16. Big John examined it briefly, looking under the forward part of the barrel and then pulling the cocking handle. He nodded and handed it back.

"What's the matter? Something wrong with it?" Red's voice was worried.

"No, man." Big John chuckled, but it was more of a high giggle. "It's a good one; see tha' li'l *C* theah unner the barrel? Tha' means it's one of the new ones—s'pose t'have a chrome chamba—won't jam like th'ole ones. But doan use no roun's wit'a red mark onna bottom. Make sure they have a blue mark; theah the good ones."

"What's the difference in the blue and the red?"

"Sahrgent LeBlanc say the red ones giv'off too much smoke and fuck up the chamba. Blue ones ahr new, got no smoke."

"Ah . . . okay." Red frowned, striving to keep his voice normal. "Hey, I read in the papers about that; this thing jams. Has yours ever jammed?"

"No man. Tha' useta be. These here okay now. Jus' kee'pit clean and doan use no roun's wit'a red mark."

Big John, like many Marines, had initially distrusted the new lightweight M-16 because, when first issued, it frequently jammed in combat. Many a Marine died while hiding behind a rice paddy dike trying to clear his rifle. Naturally, therefore, the men preferred the heavier old M-14—or even the Communist AK-47.

Public outcry over the "failure" of the M-16 finally caused a Congressional committee to make a detailed investigation. It was found, as the snuffies had long since known, that the most common fault was the failure of the bolt to extract the spent cartridge casing from the chamber after the bullet had fired. The main reason was the use of a powder which gave off an excessive amount of carbon and smoke. Because of the design of the rifle, the smoke was discharged directly into the chamber, causing dirt which gripped and held the cartridge, preventing it from being properly extracted. The fact that, in the rush to get the weapon onto the field, it was issued without cleaning equipment didn't help matters any.

Eventually they chromed the chamber, slowed the rate of fire, made a smokeless powder, and issued cleaning equipment—virtually eliminating the problem of jamming. And as the weapon began to prove itself, the snuffies gradually adopted it. But some Marines, like Wilson, still preferred the old M-14 and a few of them could always be found in every platoon.

Banks

The next morning Banks, the new man, struggled to get his gear together. Somebody shouted "Saddle up" and everyone started rushing around packing. Where were they going? Was this an operation? Christ, after last night he was ready to go back to the rear right now. This sleeping on wet, rocky, sloping ground was for the birds. Banks heard the Lieutenant shouting at the squad leaders.

He went over to Christian, his fire team leader, who was stuffing his pack. "Say, man, where we going?"

Christian glanced up at him scornfully and shrugged. "I don't know." He yanked the strap down and gave it a final tug. Christian was from LA, but he'd been born in Arkansas.

Banks looked around a minute, then returned to the fire team leader, who was the only person he knew. Christian was feverishly opening a C-ration can of chopped ham and eggs.

"When are they gonna tell us where we are going?"

"Christ, I don't know! They never tell us. Just shut up and get ready."

Banks backed off a few steps and coldly watched the man wolf his food. Why in hell are they eating all that now, he wondered. It would certainly be easier when they stopped. Typically Banks did what he was told and said little. He checked his gear again; he was ready. It might be his second day, but he knew how to pack his pack and get ready.

"Move it in here!" Corporal Holton, a square-cut Marine from Oshkosh, Wisconsin, returned from the CP and was calling the squad together. Before Vietnam, Holton had been on Embassy duty in New Delhi, India, where the Marine House was considered the best bar in town and the number of servants equalled the number of Marines. Banks and two others walked over; the rest just looked up. Now they would find out what was going on, Banks thought.

"All right, listen up," Holton yelled. "We got the point."

"Shit!" Christian spat.

"Goddamn that new lieutenant; we just had the point," someone else grumbled.

"Hold your bitchin'," Holton cut in. "We got it—we'll walk it, there ain't nothin' I can do."

"Did you tell him it wasn't our turn?" Christian asked accusingly.

"Yeah, I told him, but Chief was right there, wasn't nothing more I could say. Besides, it probably is our turn."

Christian looked down and went back to eating. "Ah, I meant it ain't our *platoon's* turn."

"And I suppose I should bitch to the captain?" Holton said.

"Go fuck yourself."

Holton turned back to the squad, ignoring Christian. "Captain probably wants to give the new lieutenant experience." He glanced at his watch. "We're heading up the same ridgeline as yesterday. Christian, your fire team will start up on point. Move it down that path on the far side in five minutes."

Christian glared up hotly for a moment, then violently flung his ham-and-eggs can in the hole. He grabbed up his pack and pulled on Banks' arm. "Come on, new boy, you're gonna learn some today."

There were three men in the fire team, and they went over to the edge of the perimeter where the trail began.

"Okay, new boy—what's your name?"

"Banks."

"Okay, Banks—you gotta walk point."

"Me—you mean walk first man in the column?" Even in the States Banks had heard that the point was the most dangerous position and was supposed to be walked by an experienced man.

"That's right."

"But I just came incountry. . . ."

"There ain't nobody else to do it."

"What about . . ." Banks started to protest but cut himself off.

"Look"—Christian's voice softened—"if we had more men I wouldn't put you on. But we only got you, me, and Bob. Bob's got the Bloop gun so he can't be on point."

"*Bloop* gun?"

"You know, an M-79 grenade launcher, best weapon in d'Nam. Breaks open and loads like an old shotgun but shoots a grenade instead of a bullet. Makes a 'bloop' when it fires."

"So?"

"So, it can't be on point because the round has to travel a ways before it explodes. Gooks might be too close. I'm the team leader and gotta listen to where Holton tells me to go. I walked point when I was new. That's just the way it is."

"Okay," Banks said calmly. If it was his duty, he'd do it. He didn't like this Chuck, but he'd do his job.

"Now, I'll be right behind you, telling you where to go. Start off just following the trail. Put a round in your chamber. Put it on full automatic. Anything suspicious, you stop. Anything *move,* you shoot."

Red

Red swore and pulled angrily at the strap. He had rearranged the two boxes of 7.62 machine-gun ammunition dozens of times, but they never carried right. They always banged around or fell off. But he stumbled on.

The platoon had been humping over three hours and Red was visibly tired. The pack straps cut into his shoulders. His left canteen was rubbing a sore spot on his hip, his feet and legs ached, but worst was that damn machine-gun ammo. Two hundred rounds! He wasn't supposed to be a fucking ammo humper.

They stopped again and he dropped to the ground panting. Water—it was all he could think about. He reached around, pulled out his canteen and fumbled with the cap. He turned it up eagerly, letting the drops run down his throat. *Aahhh,* nothing ever tasted so good. He couldn't get enough. He swigged again, tilting it higher. Empty. Without thinking, he shook it once, stuffed it back and reached for the other one. He had noticed that some guys carried four canteens; they had only given him two at the supply. He remembered thinking at the time that he would never need that many.

They moved again, now going up a long slope of elephant grass. Red looked ahead and saw the path disappear into a thatch of dense jungle woods at the top. His was the second squad in line and he wasn't far from the front.

Almost a whole company was behind them. He stumbled
on a root and looked down again. Don't look around, he
thought—too tiring—just follow the man in front of you.
The flak jacket in front of him read:

> YEA THOUGH I WALK THROUGH THE VALLEY OF THE
> SHADOW OF DEATH I WILL FEAR NO EVIL FOR I AM
> THE MEANEST MOTHERFUCKER IN THE VALLEY.

Red didn't feel mean; he just felt tired. He tried to open
his flak jacket and shirt, but the ammo box strapped across
his chest kept them closed. He constantly wiped the sweat
from his eyes. Now he understood why so many guys carried towels around their necks. The sweat from his back
wet the pants and made a dark splotch which extended below his buttocks. The sweat from his crotch had darkened
the whole inseam to the knee. He tore at the flak jacket.
"This thing is too hot," he said half aloud. He thought
about throwing it away. How far were they going anyway?
They'd come over so many damn hills.

BNOWP—BNOWP—BNOWP.

A heavy, distinctive popping sound thudded out and
jerked him upright.

"Jesus, what's that?"

Then everything around him seemed to erupt. There
was a lot of firing up ahead of him. Yelling—everybody
was screaming something. Then he heard the explosions,
heavy jarring *whumps.* He could feel the blasts. "What is
that? What is it?" he called aloud.

Confusion. The column had disintegrated. People were
running everywhere. By instinct Red got down. The firing
was up ahead. For just an instant he remembered his
friend Banks was up there where the firing was.

"Come on up!"

"Get down!"

"Look out!"

He heard more explosions. What were they? Then firing
began off to his right. That seemed close. Oh, Christ, I'd
better get out of here. Fear and panic rushed over him.
What will I do? *"Won't somebody tell me what to do?"*
He thought he heard his fire team leader yelling at him,
telling him to move. "What? What?" Where?

Then there were some distant poppings.

"Tube! Tube!"

"Get down."

People ran past him *downhill*.

They must be getting closer.

WHUUMPZT—WHUUMPZT.

Great blasting thuds shook him. He sprang up and ran back downhill. He ran blindly in terror, throwing off his gear.

"Get down!"

"Mortars!" someone screamed.

So that's what they are. Mortars. Got to hide. He saw a log and dove for it.

WHUUMPZT. A very close blast showered dirt and sticks all over him. He flattened himself to the ground and tried to burrow into it. He squeezed close to the log and tried to get under it. He pushed his face between the log and the ground, only dimly aware that his rear stood up. Suddenly he wanted to sleep. Go to sleep and it will go away. Sleep. Maybe it's all a bad dream. Dream! That's it. It's just a bad dream; I'll wake up and it'll be okay. For what could have been a second or an hour, Red seemed to freeze his mind, then he opened his eyes. It wasn't a dream. He wanted to cry.

He saw an ant right in front of his nose. Look at that ant minding his own business, he thought. The ant crawled along the underside of the log. It stopped, then meandered under some bark. Red's eyes followed it. Here I am going to get torn up, get killed, and that ant is just minding his own business.

"Red! Where's Red?" A voice cut through his thoughts. It sounded like Wilson, his squad leader. Somebody said to move. "Where?" He felt paralyzed.

Suddenly a figure slid down beside him. *"Aagh!"* He cringed and moaned aloud.

"Hey man, you okay?"

Red heard the words close to his ears. He knew that voice. He felt a big hand on his shoulder, then slowly he turned his head. He trembled with relief under the hand, his eyes looked up and he saw a massive face almost touching his own. It was black, grimy, and streaming with sweat; one cheek had a powder burn.

"Oh, Big John." Red thought it was the most beautiful

face he had ever seen. He grabbed the huge arm and held it tight. He didn't know if he was crying or not.

"Easy, man, easy theahr now." Big John patted his back. "Pull up, man. Pull up. You be okay. You not hit, ahr you?" Softly Big John ran his hand down Red's body and easily but gently lifted him over, examining, eyes looking for the blood.

"No, I'm not hit. I'm okay."

Big John saw the relief in Red's eyes as they pleaded up at him for help. He smiled almost as a mother and the gold front tooth winked out. "Come on li'l Red, we gotta move, you jus' keep with me. Keep right t'me."

"Okay, John, okay." The voice was quick but quavering.

They began to crawl up toward the firing, Red almost holding to the big man's shirttail.

The firing had slackened a bit as they moved up. Red saw a line of men, prone on the ground, firing up at the jungle. The lieutenant was yelling and moving back and forth. Jesus, Red thought, how can they do it?

Hawkins

When Hawkins heard the first shots on the hill above him, he thought it was a helicopter firing overhead. There was no other sound for a moment, so he took another step. The experienced men, however, immediately recognized the distinctive, heavy popping of the gook AK-47. Behind the Lieutenant someone was yelling, "Get down, sir, get down!" Hawkins dropped as firing and yelling erupted all around him. His first reaction was bewilderment. He couldn't see anything; all he knew was that they were just inside the edge of the jungle woods which covered the top of the hill. He squirmed up beside Holton the squad leader. The firing had stopped, but someone was up there screaming.

"Come on up here, you chicken-shits! Get up here, you chicken-shits." The voice was terrified but furious as well.

"It's Christian," Holton said. "I think they got the point."

Suddenly, almost by delayed reaction, it hit Hawkins. "This is it!" he thought, but somehow he couldn't believe it. He half stood and yelled, "Are you in contact?"

Holton looked at him as if he had gone mad. "Hell, yes, get down sir."

"Yes," a voice above screamed back in near panic, then pleaded, "Come on up, come on up!"

Zzzzzsssst. Something hissed through the air and plopped down in front of them.

"Chi-Com! Look out, sir," Holton bellowed. The Lieutenant gave him a blank look. "Grenade!" Holton pulled the Lieutenant down to the ground just as it went off, spraying them with dirt and twigs.

"*Lieutenant,* they're *caught* up there. We got to get 'em." The squad leader had said it loud, but his voice was imploring—asking.

Hawkins looked at him blankly a moment. "Well, why don't they . . . ?" he started to ask, then he felt the panic rise up and shake him. He's *asking* me, Hawkins thought. *What now, Lieutenant?*, a voice from training echoed in his ears. Jesus, somebody tell me what to do. LeBlanc. Where is LeBlanc? Sickeningly he remembered he had ordered LeBlanc to bring up the rear. He'd never be able to make his way through the whole long column on that narrow jungle trail.

Hawkins fought the panic rising and felt a tremendous pressure to do something, but he couldn't seem to move. Everything was rushing at his mind at once.

"Get down here," he yelled. "Can you get down?" he screamed up into the jungle.

"They got Banks," was yelled back at him.

"Oh, God," Hawkins muttered. He looked around frantically. "Holton, tell your people to fire. Fire up there." Then he yelled up. "Get down here. Get down anyway." For some reason he felt he had to get his men lined up in a row. Subconsciously he remembered that's what LeBlanc had done the day he cleared the bunkers. But here it was all this steep slope and the jungle was everywhere. What could he do here? The men began to fire up the hill into the trees, not seeing anything, just firing.

Suddenly Christian seemed to fly out of the trees above. He plunged down the slope, arms flailing wildly and dropped down beside the Lieutenant. "They got him, sir. They shot the point man Banks. He's still up there." Christian was gasping and his eyes were crazed.

"Is he dead?" Hawkins asked.

"I don't know, sir, I don't know. They are hidden in bunkers. Just all of a sudden they opened up, and he dropped. I jumped back into a bomb crater."

From somewhere behind, Wilson's voice screamed out, "You put the *new man* on point?! Christian, you son of a bitch!"

Hawkins looked back at Wilson vacantly, then at Holton. Wilson's words had no meaning to Hawkins.

"Captain calling, sir." It was Joseley, pulling on Hawkins' arm. He had forgotten about Joseley and the radio. Hawkins took the handset.

—"Delta Six. Delta Six, this is Two—Go."—

—"Two, this is Six. Stay next to that radio. What have you got up there? Over."—

The voice was unbelievably cool and calm.

—"Ah . . . Six . . . We got ah . . . gooks are on the top. They hit the point. The rest of us are back a bit. Over."—

—"Is he dead? Over."—

—"We don't know, can't see him. Over."—

—"Can you get him back? How many gooks are there? Over."—

—"Ah . . . I don't know yet. Over."—Jesus, what does he think I am, Hawkins thought; but it cut through to him that he had to find out. The captain would be mad as hell. He had to get that man back or attack—or something. — "Six, we're trying to get him now. I'm not sure how many there are up on top. I'm trying to envelop some men around to the right. Over."—he lied.

The voice came back irritatingly calm. —"Okay. That sounds good. Try to get him back. Let me know. Six out."—

Hawkins gave the handset back and began to crawl around. His mind was racing. He had to maneuver and get that man. What would that sergeant do?

Barely conscious of what his actions would lead to, he began to move.

"Wilson! Move your squad up. Go around to the right, try to come up on the flank." Wilson looked at him for a moment as though stunned, and then nodded and moved out.

"Sir, don't yell. Use the radio." Joseley tugged at

Hawkins' arm. Hawkins grabbed the radio without thinking.

—"Two Alpha, Two Alpha, this is Two."—He was calling Sanders' squad. —"Two Alpha, Two Alpha, this is
Two, do you read me? Over."—

—"Two, this is Two Alpha. Wait for the actual."—

Hawkins gritted his teeth and felt the surge of annoyance at the radio procedure. Hawkins peered up through
the jungle trying to see the hit man. It was impossible.

Wilson crawled to the right and slowly disappeared into
the jungle.

Nothing seemed to happen, and Holton's squad began
to slow their fire.

"Fire. Keep up a cover fire," Hawkins yelled angrily.
There was a heavy burst of fire, and then gradually it
slackened away to nothing. Dammit, what's the matter
with these people; didn't they teach them anything in
training? "Fire uniformly. Slower," he yelled again. A few
nearby turned and looked at him uncomprehendingly.

Just then his eye caught a lean figure sliding easily up
the hill on his left. The jungle growth seemed to part and
flow around him.

"Chief!" Hawkins' face broke into something resem-
bling joy. The Indian silently motioned the three men behind him to continue toward the scattering of men firing,
and then he moved over quickly to the Lieutenant.

"Sir?" His face was calm as a canal.

"There's a man trapped up there."

"I know, sir." Chief eyed the jungle which slanted up
sharply. The gooks were almost overhead. He studied the
small clearing made by the big bomb.

"Our man just above that bomb crater?"

"Yes. I sent Wilson around there to envelop."

"What? To envelop?" Chief moved instantly, shoving a
machine-gun team over to the right and began to fire a
slow burst of fire across the far corner of the crater.
Hawkins watched, feeling useless. He took the radio and
tried calling Wilson's squad.

—"Two Bravo, Two Bravo, this is Two. Two Bravo,
Two Bravo, this is Two."—

There was no answer.

BNOWP—BNOWP—BNOWP.

Firing came from the left flank. Hawkins flattened to

the ground and yelled to Joseley, "What's that?"

"I don't know, sir, but it sounds like AK's on the flank." There was no other sound like that.

"Gooks?"

Joseley nodded.

—"Delta Two, Delta Two, this is Delta Six, over."—

"Oh, stay off the net," Hawkins yelled aloud, without depressing the handset key.

—"Delta Two, I hear a lot of firing. Have you got targets? Over."—

—"No, we can't see a thing. Over."—

—"What are you shooting at then? Over."—

Hawkins couldn't reply.

—"Delta Two, repeat: Have you got to the man yet? Over."—

—"Not yet."—

—"Keep trying, but I can't give you much longer. We are going to have to call in air strikes on the hill if we can't make it. Over."—

The Lieutenant looked at the radio with obvious incomprehension. He dropped the handset and bellowed, "Sanders, put your people out to the left." He began to crawl madly back and forth, yelling to everyone.

Sssssszzzzzt.

"Look out, Chi-Com."

WHAMP!

The grenade seemed to come right for the Lieutenant, but he squirmed back and yelled again to the line, "Keep firing, keep on firing."

Another grenade blasted near the Lieutenant. He didn't even notice.

Joseley finally worked his way up to him. "Lieutenant, use the radio. *Please* use the radio! They are throwing grenades at your voice."

Hawkins just glanced at him blankly. "Stay there." He kept on yelling and running back and forth. One thought had seized his mind—he had to get Banks back before the captain ordered the platoon to come down. They couldn't retreat without him; Banks might still be alive. He shouted over to Wilson's squad—the damn radio seemed too slow. *Goddamn,* he just couldn't make the platoon move. It was like driving a big clumsy machine. He had the feeling he was in a dream, running, running, but getting nowhere. What would LeBlanc do?

He lay with his chest on the jungle floor but kept his head up, watching the men. Amazement and frustration built up in him. He had to do it himself. He would get Banks. He glanced back once more, then yelled for fire cover. Getting to his hands and knees, he crawled off after Wilson's squad.

"Lieutenant, Lieutenant," Joseley called, "sir, come back; you can't leave the radio!"

Hawkins never turned around and disappeared into the jungle.

The Platoon

Joseley sat almost sick with indecision. The Lieutenant had told him to stay where he was, yet he knew it was his duty to carry the radio wherever the Lieutenant went. The Lieutenant shouldn't have gone off like that.

Without direction the other Marines soon slackened their fire. They darted little glances at each other and began to edge backward. They couldn't see anything, and there wasn't really any returning fire aside from an occasional grenade.

—"Delta Two, Delta Two, this is Delta Six."—

The radio sounded in Joseley's hands and he looked at it blankly.

"Lieutenant, Lieutenant Hawkins," Joseley screamed into the jungle, then started to run after him.

—"Delta Two, Delta Two, this is Delta Six"—

Joseley stopped. Ordinarily he would have answered immediately, but he knew it was Captain Calahan, and the captain would want to speak to the Lieutenant. How could he tell the captain the Lieutenant wasn't near the radio—should he cover for the Lieutenant—or should he not answer? Slowly he put the microphone to his mouth.

—"Delta Six, this is Delta Two. Go."—

"Delta Two, pull your platoon back immediately. Air strikes will hit in ten minutes. Over."—

Joseley went white and looked down at the set. Almost in horror, he knew that the captain hadn't recognized his voice.

—"Roger."—He whispered. His mind whirled. He had to relay the message. Where was LeBlanc? Immediately he began to push back through the jungle toward the machine guns.

"Chief, Chief."

The Chief spun around as Joseley crawled up gasping.

"Where's the Lieutenant?"

"I don't know; he went off by himself. He's going to try to reach Banks, but you've got to find him. The captain's calling air strikes in ten minutes."

For just a second a trace of something frightful passed over the Chief's face, then it went back to the stone mask.

"Go find him! Find the Lieutenant and stay with him! Try to get Wilson's squad on the radio and get them back. I'll start the others down."

Chief spun around to the machine guns above him. "Sail, keep firing till I get Alpha and Charley squad down." He started moving off through the brush, then he turned and called back. "Sail!"

"Yeah."

"If the gooks assault before we get down, you've got to hold 'em."

Suddenly from the far side of the hill his ears picked up the little poops.

"Tube! Tube!" he yelled.

"Tube! Tube!" was picked up down the line.

"Inncommmming!"

He flattened himself to the ground.

"Inncommmming!"

"Get down! Get down!"

Then he heard the awful whistle and the crash.

WHUUMPZT. WHUUMPZT. WHUUMPZT.

Chief held his breath, waiting for the crash, but his mind already raced ahead. The gooks must have a mortar tube up on the far side of the hill—perfect setup for a mortar.

A mortar is so simple. It's just a three-foot lead pipe closed at one end. The closed end is mounted on a flat plate which sits on the ground. The open end is held up in the air by two legs. The shell, or round, looks like a miniature bomb and is dropped by hand, tail first into the raised open end of the tube. When the shell hits the bottom, a small charge in the tail fins explodes, throwing the round out and high into the air. That's what makes the warning "poops." The gook tube had to be on the back side of the hill, and they were shooting an arc right over the hilltop, sort of like a skyrocket.

Then he heard the awful whistle and the crunch.

WHUUMPZT. WHUUMPZT. WHUUMPZT.

Chief jumped up—they were off—but all they had to do was adjust the angle of the tube to the ground in order to reaim.

Chief knew then the wounded man was bait. That's why they held off firing at first; it was a trap. The mortars on top meant there were probably a lot of gooks. He guessed their plan was to pin them down with mortars while they tried to slip some men in behind the platoon. They would try to come between the platoon and the rest of the company down the hill. He remembered seeing some old foxholes off the trail; if just one or two gooks got in those holes, it would be all over for the rest of the platoon. The main gook force would assault from the top, leading with RPG rockets. "Hell," he muttered aloud, "they don't even need to assault us." Without leadership, the men would dash down the hill and get mauled by those in the holes. In shooting them, we'd have to fire on our own people down the hill. He knew LeBlanc was tail-end-Charlie, but he had a suspicion the captain probably told him to hang back and let the new lieutenant get bloodied. Experience—yeah.

As Chief began to move Alpha and Charley squads down, he thought of the Lieutenant and shrugged his shoulders. Too late now.

Hawkins

Hawkins had crawled to a spot just beyond the crater; the body lay on the far side. He stood up behind a tree until he could see a portion of the body. "Hey," he yelled— what was his name—Banks, yeah.

"Banks! Can you hear me?"

No answer. No movement.

"Banks," he shouted louder. He could hear the Chief's machine guns on the other side of the crater. They were firing regular bursts.

Something kept pounding in his head. It seemed to be

from an old movie—*Marines never leave their buddies.*
He yelled again. No answer. He didn't move. If the man
was dead, it would be okay; they could leave him then.
He eased back down to the dirt and his eyes searched the
jungle curtain.

Slowly Hawkins' mind began to shut down. He wasn't
afraid or unknowledgeable—for he'd been too well
trained—just stunned. His head drooped to his forearm.
His last thought was of LeBlanc. It was LeBlanc who had
beaten him, not the gooks. He'd failed. That stupid sergeant had beaten him. The SOB was laughing.

"Lieutenant, Lieutenant." Joseley's voice cut through
the jungle. Finally the little man saw the Lieutenant and
ran over, bent low under the radio. "Sir, we've got to pull
back. The captain's calling for air strikes; they'll be here
any minute."

Hawkins stared at him blankly. "What about Banks?"

"Sir," Joseley was frantic, "we've only got about six
minutes till this hill is gonna be bombed." His voice was
rising now, beginning to get panicky. "Lieutenant! Air
strikes!"

Hawkins looked across the crater. "Gotta get Banks."

"Lieutenant! Lieutenant!" Joseley grabbed his arm and
shook it violently. "They're gonna bomb here in just six
minutes—airplanes—bombs—this hill will be leveled—
blown away."

"Air strikes? Here? Oh. . . ." Hawkin's voice was
wrenched and he rose to his knees, giving a final glance
up the hill. "Okay, let's go down." They began to crawl
out around the bottom lip of the crater. "Call the squads;
tell them to start down."

"Chief is already moving Alpha and Charley."

"Can you get Wilson on the radio?"

"Not yet."

"Wilson," Hawkins screamed, "come back."

"Coming"—a cry came through the jungle.

Moving as fast as the jungle would allow, the squads
and the Lieutenant moved down the trail. Sail and Chief
on the machine guns were the last ones left. There was
only an occasional shot from the top of the hill. The last
man in the squad to pass was Big John. Hawkins was in a
daze, but Joseley was yelling and pushing him along.

"Move it out; get down fast! Lieutenant, the bombers will be coming any minute; we've got to get off this hill." His voice was panicky.

Still Hawkins wavered.

"Sir, it's *four minutes* till Air Time! Let's go!" Joseley's voice was screaming now.

Somehow Hawkins began to understand and he hollered out, "Sail, get back, pull on back."

"Go, Lieutenant. Go on back. I'll stay and cover," Sail yelled. Then they all began to fall back. Hawkins started to run when a motion caught his eye. He saw Big John throwing off his pack. He had a crazed look in his eye and Hawkins immediately knew what he was going to try. "No! Don't try it. Get down the hill," he screamed.

"Ih ain't leavin' a brother!"

Hawkins sat transfixed, unable to move. Before the pack hit the ground, the big man had charged. He shot out of the jungle wall and into the crater like a monstrous bull into a ring. Low to the ground, legs pounding high, he hurtled across the ground. Joseley and Hawkins could only stare. Hawkins had never seen such a big man move so fast. He barely touched the ground as he went up the far side of the crater, yet it seemed to take an eternity. The two watched, holding their breath. Big John came to the lip; his hand went out. His speed was incredible, but it seemed as if he were running in slow motion. He was up. The arm was shooting out. The fingers grasped an arm of the man. Big John spun backward and the crumpled body was literally jerked into the air as if by levitation. Big John whirled halfway around and started back. The body was on his shoulder.

BNOWP—BNOWP—BNOWP. WHUUMPZT.

The Chi-Com grenade went off and the two figures seemed to hang suspended for just a moment, then flew apart. Big John was tumbled over and rolled back. He hit the bottom of the crater but bounced up and barreled into the jungle. He didn't stop, just kept right on going downhill, making a new path.

Joseley shook his head as if he couldn't quite believe the sight, then looked at his watch. "Two minutes till Air Time; get down the hill. They're gonna bomb here in two minutes! Move, sir!" This time he turned and fled, the handset dangling from the radio as he ran.

Hawkins stared after him, not quite believing what he saw.

Then for the first time, he realized what it really meant. *Bombs.* Our own bombs. He leaped up and ran blindly, wildly, running back toward the trail. He crashed into Sail just as there was a volley of firing from the top of the hill. The bullets whipped down around them.

"Lieutenant, we've got to keep up our fire while we are going down or they'll ding us for sure."

For an instant, in a kaleidoscope of noises, firing, and flashes, two men were etched into Hawkins' mind. Dodging backward, firing as they went, Chief and Sail were the last cover, struggling to protect the rest of the platoon. If no one fired back, the gooks would just sit up and zero in on the whole fleeing target. Hawkins' paralysis vanished. He joined them.

Feverishly now, they worked their way back down the hill, one constantly firing while the others dodged back. Equipment was strewn along the trail. Hawkins picked up an M-16 and began firing bursts on automatic. Sail fired, ran back, and dropped to one knee. Then Chief moved down, and Hawkins felt the rifle bucking against his own shoulder. He was covering. For the first time that day he felt really good. At last he knew what he was doing.

The three men leap-frogged backward, covering one another, running and firing; then they realized there was no firing from the top.

"Hey, they quit."

"Let's get outta here."

They raised up and ran, slipping, tripping, sliding, careening straight down. They were just about one hundred and fifty yards from the edge of the jungle when the first Phantom Jet roared over.

"Look ooout!"

The Lieutenant was running full-tilt and never heard the plane until the first two-hundred-and-fifty-pound bomb hit. It seemed as if the whole earth shook. The blast rolled over the three like a great cresting ocean swell and flung Hawkins to the ground. He lay flat as the second blast shook him. For a few moments he was stunned, then up and running again. The trail was strewn with gear—packs, machine-gun ammo, mortar rounds. He leaped over a gas mask and was dimly aware of being angry that the men should leave so much behind.

Then he saw the silver glint flashing toward the hill. It rolled into a high arc, crested over, and dove straight down toward them. This time Hawkins knew the power of the bomb. He flung himself down and hugged the ground, trying to burrow his every pore and sinew into the dirt. The plane roared in, straight over his head and pulled up right over the top of the treeline. Hawkins watched the two little snake-eye bombs drop away from the plane just at the bottom of its dive path. Curiously, it seemed an age as they fell—so close, he could see them plainly against the sky. Each bomb had a four-pronged tail that spread out and caught the wind, slowing the bomb to give the plane time to climb to safety before it exploded. Hawkins couldn't tear his eyes away; he wanted to see the bombs hit—explode—and watch the orange balls send the trees flying. Something unknown, training perhaps, finally tore his eyes away and he rammed his face into the earth.

THWOOM. THWOOM.

The planes passed and all was quiet.

They stumbled on down the hill and came upon the company. Hawkins burst into a little clearing and stopped in his tracks. The captain, the gunny, and LeBlanc stood eyeing him, calm and unperturbed.

LeBlanc! What was he doing there so calm, as if nothing had happened; where had he been before? Hawkins stood covered with sweat and dirt, eyes red and glaring. For a moment they stared across the clearing at one another, and he felt as if he were on exhibition. To his surprise he saw disgust and even anger in their eyes. In Le Blanc's he saw contempt.

The feelings of remorse vanished in an instant and anger swept in behind them. He took the empty magazine out and jammed in another; then he spat and stomped past them without a word.

"Lieutenant Hawkins." The captain's voice cracked out and whipped him around.

"Sir?" Exhaustion crept over him as he turned back; but the captain was on the radio. Slowly Hawkins dropped his pack, conscious of his growing thirst, and he pulled out his canteen and took a long swallow. Aching fatigue gnawed at him and he plodded back to where the captain

was. It had been only a few seconds and he felt the thirst
again. Hawkins glanced at the top. It was quiet. The captain and the gunny were standing beside the mortar tubes.
LeBlanc was off to one side casually watching the activity.
They were surrounded by the company CP radiomen.
There was one for the company radio net, one for the battalion net, one for the artillery and one for the air net. At
that moment one of the radiomen had out the special little
high-frequency radio set that meant they were in direct
contact with the airplanes. Hawkins looked up and saw
the tiny spotter plane circling overhead. A little single-engine Piper-Cub type which was used to spot the enemy
positions and guide the big bomber jets in. The radio
stopped and Hawkins stepped over to the captain, conscious
of LeBlanc's stare.

"Where's your men?" The captain asked sharply.

"The platoon? Well, they're back along the trail."

"Saddle up."

"*What?*" Hawkins was dumbfounded.

"Get ready, you're going back up."

Hawkins stood stricken. The men were exhausted. Why
in hell doesn't he send another platoon? We'll never make
it without water and a rest. "Sir, the men. . . ."

"We're waiting for another air strike," the captain cut
in. "They'll be along any minute. Get your platoon ready
and stand by to move out as soon as the planes come
over."

That's insane, Hawkins thought. Can't he see how tired
they are? Why doesn't he send another platoon? Why us?
He glanced at LeBlanc and saw the contempt on the hard
face, and the hate flashed up in him again. Well, I'll be
damned if they'll call my platoon chicken. In a rage, he
turned back to get the men.

"Lieutenant"—the captain's voice stopped him—"keep
Sergeant LeBlanc with you this time. He's experienced
and can give you some good pointers."

Red

Red flopped flat on the ground, his body exhausted.
There was no shade and he dropped his arm over his eyes
to cut the searing sun. Jesus Christ, it was a good thing he
had taken cover and stayed behind that log. Otherwise he

would have been almost at the top when the airplanes came. As it was, he'd barely been able to get back as soon as they passed the word to retreat.

He didn't know who was left up there, but he hoped they wouldn't have to go up again. The Lieutenant had been yelling and running and directing everybody; maybe they got the guy. How did that lieutenant do it? Red wondered. Didn't he get thirsty? Almost in agony, Red lifted his arm and turned his head. He saw the Lieutenant talking to the captain and pointing to the top. "Oh, shit," he moaned aloud and sat up. "Why don't we just rest here?"

Red noticed that many of the men were eating fruit, and it made him thirsty again. His mouth was so dry and furry that the water didn't seem to help at all. He needed a swallow every two minutes. Taking his canteen, he gauged what was left and then looked up at the hill. If we have to fight, I'll never make it, he thought. It's my mouth that's making me so thirsty. If I could only brush my teeth, I'd be okay. He sucked his teeth and realized that it had been almost two days since he had brushed them. Longingly, he looked down at his pack sitting at his feet; his toothbrush was right there in the pocket. Well, I've got time. No! Can't brush my teeth *now*. Everybody will think I'm crazy. He took another little swig and put the canteen back, running his tongue over his teeth. I'll just have to last, he thought.

Then another plane came over. He lay down while it made a pass, resting until the next one came. Lying on his elbow, he watched Wilson eating C-ration peaches. He chewed slowly, savoring each bite. Red had heard the story: The men ate their fruit just before a fight because they didn't want to take a chance on dying without getting the only good thing they had. He hadn't believed the story when he heard it.

But Red didn't have any fruit, and it made his own mouth more thirsty. His tongue was beginning to feel like a dry sponge. Damn my mouth, he thought. If I could just brush my teeth, I'd be okay. Well, you can't brush here. What would everybody think? Yes, but if you don't brush, you're not going to make it up that hill, he told himself. Finally, with a last exasperated look up at the hill, he reached for his pack. Oh, to hell with it. He tried to turn into the bushes. Very carefully he took out his toothbrush,

Colgate toothpaste, and proceeded to brush his teeth. He used just one and a half swallows from the canteen and still tried to keep his back to the platoon.

Hawkins

Hawkins hoisted his gear and trudged slowly back down the trail to collect his men. For a moment he thought about ordering LeBlanc to assemble them, but the very idea hardened his determination.

He found the platoon sprawled along the trail, lying in the bushes, exhausted and uncaring. Sweat washed the dirt in streaks from their cheeks and necks, leaving brown smudges for noses. Shocked red eyes stared out beneath grimy lids.

Doc Smitty had cut Sail's pants' leg off and was tying battle dressings to two long red grooves in his thigh. Holton sat nearby, blood trickling from one ear. Hawkins watched in reticence as the corpsman worked, but his mind was spinning. How had he escaped unhurt with no wounds? Wounds? Those weren't even wounds; they were caused by our own bombs. He'd never *seen* the enemy.

Sail held up a frayed gas mask which had been strapped to his leg. He lay propped on his elbows with his legs stretched in front of him. Hawkins saw the eyes—they were hard and drained yet not quite cold. For a rural Southerner, Sail had an odd quirk; he had a sophisticated cynicism—nothing was ever right.

"You did a fine job, Sail," Hawkins said.

"Thanks." The voice bored into Hawkins; it had no emotion—neither relief nor anger—yet there was something. It might have been defeat. Hawkins was confused; he felt rebuffed. He wanted Sail to feel his appreciation, and unconsciously he wanted the same in return. But there was silence.

He left them and hurried on down the path anxiously, stopping at each man, not speaking but asking and ministering with his eyes. They would glance up with blank, far-off expressions. Anger and sadness were somehow mixed, but he could also see frustration. Hawkins felt a deep bond with them, but there was no joy. Did they think he had done wrong? Was he a failure to them?

More seeking than giving, he went on. He found Red
holding an empty canteen.

"Are you out of water?"

"Huh? Ah . . ." Red looked up startled at the officer.
"Ah, naw. No, sir, I'm okay."

Hawkins reached out and shook the canteen then
smiled, and he dropped his pack. If there was anything he
did know it was the importance of a reserve supply of
water; he had been an Eagle Scout. With a certain self-
satisfaction, he fished in his pack for the extra canteen—a
round flat plastic one. He had bought it especially to bring
to Vietnam.

"Here, give me your canteen," he said to Red.

"That's okay. I don't need any, sir," Red said stiffly.

Silently Hawkins took the canteen and poured in a few
inches. "How's that?"

"Thank you, sir," Red said and turned away, sitting
down formally.

Hawkins watched perplexed as Red looked away, then
he frowned and went on down the trail.

He was looking for the face that would smile and reas-
sure. Then he saw him sitting on a stone, bent over, head
down in hands, elbow on knees.

"Big John, are you okay?" he whispered.

The man didn't even look up. Hawkins went over questioningly and stood directly in front of him.

"Jackson, are you okay?" His voice cracked a little.

"He can't hear you, Lieutenant—concussion got his
eardrums," someone said heavily.

"Oh." The Lieutenant's hands went out and touched the
shoulder, and immediately the head came up.

"Wha'? Oh—'tenant, wha' say, suh?"

"I said, are you. . . ." He stopped, seeing the blank
incomprehension.

"He can't hear a thing, Lieutenant. It was one of those
Chinese grenades; they got no shrapnel in 'em—just concussion. He'll get over it in a few days."

"Yes, I understand," Hawkins said and gently put his
hand on top of the nappy head.

Big John put out his arm and grasped the Lieutenant's
knee. "We tried, 'tenant." The big hand patted the leg ten-
derly, "We ready t'go."

Moving steadily now, Hawkins called the squad leaders and lined up the machine-gun teams, one at the head and one at the tail of the column. *God damn it, his platoon would make it.*

The platoon went back up the hill. They entered the jungle, fanned out on line and began to sweep the area. The bombs had pulverized the jungle, turning it into a chaotic tangle of vegetation. There was a tree, over a foot thick, which had been snapped off at the base, not a clean snap but torn like a frayed rope; the stump stuck up at an angle, cracked and jagged. The trunk lay off to one side, branches down, base thrown up, with the end disintegrating into splinters like chewed toothpicks. They fought their way through the mess, expecting the fusillade of an ambush at every step.

They found the bunkers almost invisible. Each one had to be cleared: A covering fire was shot into the entrance, then a frag was thrown in. This was sufficient for the first sweep. A later platoon had the job of crawling in with a .45 pistol to check each one. But Hawkins' platoon found no one, not even bodies, only the gear the gooks had left. Hawkins struggled forward, almost shaking with tenseness. LeBlanc walked easily, keeping the line even, ordering the squad leaders with low barks. But the gooks had gone.

Then it began, before they were even halfway through the sweep. The men dropped out for a moment, ran to a hole, then scampered back.

"Get away from that gear," Hawkins shouted. The man dropped the pack but stuffed something in his pocket.

"Dammit, leave that alone! You can worry with it later." Hawkins was appalled. Packs and equipment were strewn everywhere, and the men were dropping out of line to scoop up souvenirs.

"Leave that stuff be! Stay in line!" Hawkins was furious. How could they be bothered with *souvenirs* when the platoon might get hit at any minute. They had to keep going. The gooks might be just ahead.

"It's good to let the men take souvenirs, Lieutenant," LeBlanc said coolly.

"Are you crazy, Sergeant—not when we could make contact at any minute."

"I believe the gooks are gone, sir; most likely all ran when the first plane came over—even left their gear. If we go on and the men don't get 'em, the other platoons will pick the bunkers clean before we get back."

The man can't be serious, Hawkins thought. How could the men want that stuff anyway? It disgusted him. He faced LeBlanc squarely. "Well, my order is to move on; we can't be bothered now."

"Sir, it does the men *good* to get souvenirs. They feel proved. Platoon will have good spirit. Particularly when there is no bodies."

"I said MOVE ON."

"All right, sir." LeBlanc shrugged casually and turned away.

Somehow Hawkins made them keep moving. They pushed on and passed the area of the bunkers and gear. Finally they swept the entire hill. But the gooks had left. There wasn't even a single body from the bombs.

They swept through to the end of the hill, and the men sank down, drained of emotion and energy. Exhausted, they trudged back to the top to join the rest of the company. The other platoons had taken all the souvenirs.

Banks' body was found under a pile of uprooted brush. There were two small round holes in his chest. He had died instantly. Hawkins looked down at the body, horrified. He had never seen a dead man before. The face was an odd chalky white for a black man, and the eyes stared out in fixed blankness. But the mouth was the worst—it hung open stiffly, showing the immobile tongue.

Hawkins stared and felt a prickly revulsion. It made him quiver to think of *touching* the body, but he could not take his eyes away. He felt he would be sick even while the terrible fascination of the mouth rooted him to the spot and held his eyes. They yanked the body to free it from the brush, and it bounced on its side. The head bobbed back, drawing the mouth further open.

He wrenched himself away, but the sight of the gaping mouth stuck in his mind. He clamped his jaws together, suddenly conscious that everyone was close by and there was no place to go. Not here. He had to get away. He moved just as a sound caught him.

"Ooohh," somebody moaned.

Unable to keep from turning, he looked back and glimpsed the body just as it was pulled free from the

brush. Part of the stomach had been ripped open by the
bomb and the smell rushed up and hit him in the face. He
recoiled and ran wildly into the trees, savagely biting his
teeth together. As the jungle enveloped him, he felt the
vomit rushing up, blasting his teeth apart. Mercifully it
was quick.

3

Chief

The Chief stood with his nose and face into the wind.
His whole body appeared taut and stretched like a full sail
on a windy day. The uplift of the wild face served to ac-
centuate the ramrod erectness of his whiplike body. He
sniffed deeply, then cupped his ears. Finally satisfied, he
turned from the trail and slipped silently into the lines. He
started for his hooch, but as he passed the poncho-wrapped
body of Banks, his nostrils quivered and he hesitated, frowning slightly. Then the frown passed and his face slid into a
stone mask as he stepped directly toward the Lieutenant's
hooch.

When the Chief prowled the lines at night, no one asked
questions. But the men only knew the Chief in the here and
the now; he never spoke of his past.

The Chief had been raised for the first seven years of
his life in the wilds of the Utah-Wyoming border. His father had wanted him to learn the old ways of their people,
so Screaming Sky Eagle and his father had spent many
long months in the open, tracking game, living on the
land. Then a small silver lode was discovered on the com-
munal lands, and his father was killed in the rush to mine
it. The money was just enough to send little Eagle to live
with a cousin, his mother's niece, in Los Angeles.

Screaming Sky was a little much of a name for modern
LA, so his new white father had changed it to Randolph,
which he called "a good American name." And after a
few years the little Indian boy grew right into the California scene—surfing and sun, The Malibu Kid. In the ninth

grade they moved to San Francisco and Randy went to South San Francisco High. That was fine, too; as small as he was, he made varsity football. It was his speed, they all said. Then came the magic age—sixteen—a car. Freedom. Hot rods and motorcycles. Speedy Randy with his proud good looks and long black hair had girls. California girls. Wherever he was—skiing, surfing, football, dancing—there were always girls—and pot.

But even in San Francisco all the doors were not open to an Indian. In his senior year Randy met a girl from the Pacific Heights section. A cheerleader, her hair was long and blond, parted in the middle and hanging straight down. It was the golden spring before graduation, and there they were—on top of Telegraph Hill with red wine and the whole of San Francisco Bay spread below them; gliding through the soft night air in the convertible, their long straight hair streaming behind them, blue black and snow blond; riding the big surf at Malibu, their lean bodies glistening wet in the sun; standing, hanging ten, streaking for shore, reaching out and touching fingertips; taking the Powell Street cable car at midnight to Fisherman's Wharf for Irish coffee.

That fall they headed for Berkeley, still together. He took an apartment, and she started out in the dorm but soon moved in with him. They called them live-ins; their favorite game was to get stoned, really stoned on Acapulco Gold, lie naked in bed, put on the dual set of earphones from his stereo, and groove. Just groove to the *Sergeant Pepper* album.

But Charlene's mother had other ideas.

"Charlene, dear, your father and I think it would be good for you to attend school in the East."

"But Mother, I don't. . . ."

"Your father has already inquired if you can enter Vassar next semester."

"No, I won't go. You're just trying to get me away from Randy. I won't do it."

"Now, dear, you know I like Randy, but it's just that . . . well, I'm sure you'll meet some wonderful boys in the East."

She knew the reason, of course; they'd been through it before. They wanted her to go with the "right" boys, like the ones at the Burlington Country Club.

"Mother, Randy's not like his parents; he's unique."

"Charlene, you *do* want to go abroad for your sopho-more year, don't you? At the Sorbonne?" Her mother's eyes were cold and Charlene knew they meant it.

Randy didn't believe her, didn't believe it right up until she moved out. She told him a tearful line, but he knew the reason, and he knew the decision had been hers. She was an only child.

After that they began to call him the crazy Indian, and the next semester he busted out. He became a flaming rad-ical, an advocate of the downtrodden red man. He went to New York's Greenwich Village and thought he had found IT. They organized a United Protest Parade and marched right through Sheridan Square along Christopher Street and Seventh Avenue. The blacks, the faggots, and one Indian. He remembered the chant; they had sung it out right in the middle of the street.

> Black Black Power to the Black Black Man.
> Red Red Power to the Red Red Man.
> Gay Gay Power to the Gay Gay Man.
> FUUUCK THE PIGS!

But that was sick, too. He found Manhattan life, with all its professed freedoms, to be just as uptight as any-where else. It was more cliquey, more narrowminded in its own way than California ever was.

So he went back to Berkeley and became a real Indian with long hair. He was as "in" as he could get, or so he thought. He dissented and he demonstrated, but something went wrong. He didn't like the Establishment and he didn't like society, but he didn't like the students either. After one more semester he left; and the next day he went to the courthouse and changed his name back to Scream-ing Sky Eagle.

For a while he considered going to the Himalayas and studying Hindu in Katmandu, but that would really be more of the same—phony. Once he even went back to the reservation, but he had changed too much for that. He didn't really know what he wanted, except not to be a phony. In the end he joined the Marines and asked for Vietnam.

Chief moved toward the platoon CP where he knew the Lieutenant was sleeping. It was still—no breeze, no birds, no animal sounds, not even cricket noises. There never were after a bombing attack. Chief spotted the dark mound off from the rest of the men, and he could see the Lieutenant lying on his rubber lady, staring straight up at the leafy ceiling. It was a dark tangled net across the moonlit sky.

"Lieutenant?" he whispered.

Hawkins answered without moving, his voice hollow. "Yes."

"Mind if I come over for a minute?"

"No."

"Sir, I'd . . . ah . . . I'd like to talk to you a little bit if I may."

No answer.

"Sir . . . about today."

"Yes?"

"Thank you, sir, ah, Lieutenant, I know I'm only a corporal." He stopped, awaiting the reaction. "But sometimes even a PFC who's been in the bush a long time knows a lot." He paused again. "Everybody is green at one time and has a lot to learn. A guy just can't come over here and know all there is to know." Chief stopped. The Lieutenant had said nothing. The gulf of rank in the Marine Corps stood between them.

Finally Hawkins spoke. "Go on."

Chief smiled and lay down in the dark. "Like I say, I know I'm only a corporal, but I've been incountry a long time and learned a few things." He took off his hat and lit a cigarette, carefully shielding the light. He knew the officer couldn't see his hair in the dark.

"I'm listening," Hawkins said, staring up into the leaves.

"Well, first thing is, you know the gooks tried to flank us today. There was some firing off to the side and Wilson's squad reported movement to their right. . . ."

"They did?"

"Yes, sir—on the radio."

Hawkins clenched his teeth, almost with a snap.

Chief cupped the cigarette in his fist and sucked on the tip protruding between his fingers. "Well, I'm sure they were trying to get in between us and the company."

"How do you know that?" Hawkins blurted.

"That's an old gook trick. Get between two units and fire a few shots each way. Each unit will think that the other one is the enemy and they will commence to blow each other apart. It works better at night between two different companies, but this time I would guess that they wanted to cut us off from the rest of the company. When the platoon retreated down the hill, the gooks between us and the company would have cut us down. Of course we would have killed those few, but they don't care. A couple of them to get five or ten or twenty of us. That's great. You see, they counted on us to retreat."

"Why?"

"They know how we fight, sir. We hit and pull back, then call in artillery or air almost every time. Then again, the new man, Banks, was up there wounded and he was serving as bait. They wanted us to think there were only a few. You remember how they held their fire; but from the gear we found up there, I would say there were at least thirty or forty. It was a trap."

"It was?" Hawkins voice was hushed.

"Sir, you just have to know . . . about the flanking, I mean. You just have to know what they are likely to do." Chief paused, wondering why he liked this new lieutenant; he felt sure he need say nothing more about the radio. "Sir, there's one more thing I've gotta tell you. The men, the snuffies on the line, they learn by experience, but they depend on somebody smarter to tell 'em what to do. They'll never admit it, sir, but in the bush and most important of all in combat, they *need* to be *led*, sir. And they need somebody with brains that's got their head and their ass wired together to tell them what to do."

Hawkins said nothing but sat up and peered intently through the dark.

The Chief felt the Lieutenant focus on him. "Sir, the snuffies in this outfit or . . . or, hell, the snuffies in any Marine outfit, they'll follow you across the 'Z' into the north if you lead 'em right."

A heavy silence grew between them and the Chief sensed that the Lieutenant had shifted imperceptibly forward. "It takes somebody the men respect but at the same time who will kick ass."

"You mean somebody like LeBlanc?" Hawkins' voice was a hiss.

"Well, sir, LeBlanc's good. He's been around a long time, he's savvy." Chief knew he must tread cautiously. "But that doesn't mean his way is the only way."

"Well, the men all do what he says."

"Sir, they all respect him, but it isn't because he slaps them around. It's because they know he's got his shit together."

"So you're telling me that the way to . . ."

"No, sir," Chief cut in, "that's the point. It isn't the way he handles the men; it's that they feel safe with him. But there's more. You need to have that. . . ." Chief paused, reaching for the right word.

"That what?"

"Lieutenant, his methods are different than your methods, but that doesn't mean yours won't work."

"My methods?" Hawkins' voice rose sharply.

"Yes, sir—logic, concern, example." The Chief hesitated, conscious again of the rank between them. He thought of the Lieutenant leaving the radio and trying to get to Banks himself. He didn't know why, but he suspected the Lieutenant had that unique ability for combat. Or was he just hoping, projecting? Chief felt an uneasy disquiet at the thought. "Lieutenant, if you can learn the gook ways . . . well, it's more than that."

"Corporal, what are you saying?"

"Hard to put in words, sir. It's . . ." Chief stopped abruptly and reached into his pocket, pulling out a lighter. "The best I can say is that it's like it is here, sir." He leaned forward, holding his cigarette close to the inscription on the lighter and inhaling sharply.

IF YOU'RE NOT AFRAID TO DIE
YOU NEVER WILL.

"What does that mean?" Hawkins' voice rose.

Chief jerked his head back and put his lighter away stiffly. "Nothing, Lieutenant." His voice had an edge. "Just something you get once you been in combat . . . and kicked ass."

"Kicked ass?" Hawkins' voice softened quickly.

"Yeah, if you lose and get a lot of men killed, it can

sour a guy. But if you win—man, it's something that just gets in your blood."

"What about today? What about LeBlanc?"

"I don't know about that, sir." In the dark, Chief's face cracked and the leering grin came out as the Chief felt the old irreverence rise in him. "I got to get on the guns, Lieutenant, but"—he turned back and leaned close to Hawkins—"you'll get it, Lieutenant. It's just something you get in your blood."

Hawkins

Hawkins watched the figure disappear into the darkness. What brought that on? he wondered. Angrily Hawkins rolled and shifted uneasily on his air mattress. The folded poncho-liner caught under his legs and he jerked to free it; finally he spread it smooth and, settling back, began to focus his mind. Hawkins felt a curious sense of dissatisfaction. The gooks had gone; he hadn't seen so much as a glimpse of one. Yet they had shot one of his men. Making the sweep, he had been tense, primed, ready to fight. Then he had been acutely relieved when it was over—that no one else was hurt—but he still felt oddly cheated. It was like making love but not being able to reach a climax.

As his mind went back over the fight, he suspected Le Blanc had hung behind for some reason, but the nagging thought remained that he didn't want LeBlanc to help. Yet it had been painfully obvious that he had needed the Sergeant. Slowly Hawkins' thoughts converged on what he must do—indeed must become—in order to master the platoon and the Sergeant. Once again the quote flowed to him: *The credit belongs to the man in the arena.*

He realized he was sweating heavily, and jerking his arm, he wiped his face angrily, suddenly remembering the hurt when he had told his father he was going to join the Marines. Somehow he had expected the old man to be proud.

"The Marines?" The older man's fierce head snapped around and his voice rose sharply, bellowing out the way it did whenever he was angry.

Chris looked down and fidgeted, his father's anger catching him by surprise.

"Yes, sir."

"Why the *Marines?*"

"Well, I don't know. . . ." He did know, of course, but he couldn't say it.

"Look, son"—the old man cooled a little, trying reason now—"it's one thing to go to Vietnam; I understand that. That's very patriotic and your mother and I are pleased; but don't go as a Marine. . . ."

"Why not, Dad?" He looked up imploringly, hoping but knowing it was futile.

"What about the Air Force? You can learn something there. There are some fine people in the Air Force, and I am sure I could get you a job in Intelligence or. . . ."

"Well, I don't want you to get me anything!" Chris jumped to his feet.

"Chris, sit down and be reasonable." The power and the pulse came back to the older voice. "You go over a Marine, and you may get killed."

"I can take care of myself," Chris said coldly.

"What do you know? What are you going to *do* when they drop a mortar on your head? You don't have to fight like an animal to do your duty. With your education you could be more effective in the Air Force or even the Army. What makes you want to be a Marine?"

"Because they're the best!"

For a moment there was a silence and then his father almost laughed; he pulled his head back in a gesture of sarcasm. "The best? The best *what?*"

Chris shrugged. "Well, you know. . . ."

"Oh, son. Look, I know the Air Force has tremendous education programs. All the research money is flowing into Air Force projects. A man in the right spot in the Air Force has great opportunities to get some terrific experience. Chris, the Marines have nothing. Why, the Army is getting all the funds for equipment. Do you have any idea of the difference between mechanical support of an Army and a Marine division?"

"So?" Chris asked sullenly.

"So! What in hell are Marines best for? Marines are no match for the Army." His father bored in as Chris sat mutely. "The only thing Marines are best at is being animals."

"They're not animals!" Chris shot out violently and flung the poncho-liner back, wiping his sweating brow. He looked around in the dark and slowly sank back to the ground, staring up at the jungle leaves overhead.

II

Khe Sanh

Hawkins

At dusk they filed into the great base; and every man felt the awesome hush. So many had died here. The bunkers seemed to stretch on and on into the gloom, a zigzagging trench between each bunker. In silence they passed rows of rusted coils of sagging concertina wire stacked five and seven rolls high. Beyond that were the crosswoven patterns of straight barbed wire, knee and waist high. Between these was the thatch row of German barbed tape, tangled fields of metal strips edged with razorlike flanges instead of barbs. Beyond that, scattered through the wires, were the Claymore mines, a load of buckshot plastered onto the front of a curved block of TNT, with electric detonating cords running back into the bunkers. There was one last row of concertina wire and finally the misty valley stretched out to the hills where the NVA made the final circle.

"Christ, it's big!"

"Gives me the creeps."

It had been three weeks since the contact at Banks' Hill, and the company was assigned to perimeter guard duty at Khe Sanh even though the base was largely evacuated.

They moved on toward the COC, Command of Camp, bunker and waited. The COC and the medical bunkers were deep in the ground, only the top making a little bulge on the surface. It looked like a big boil, crudely bandaged with tarps and canvas. Here and there was a little wooden appendage for air.

Along the runway great hulks of twisted metal bore witness to the inferno it had once been. Grotesque trucks with jagged, deformed bodies lay everywhere. Burned-out airplane frames reared into the sky like weird sculpture. Open trash pits stank. Everything lay discarded and rusting as if it were a city abandoned before a plague. Now it

was only quiet and still. A ghost town—deserted and old.
Rats manned the dilapidated bunkers.

A sergeant came to show them to their positions. The
perimeter seemed endless as they filed past bunker after
bunker.

"You've got that sector. It's the sector One-Nine used
to have."

"One-Nine *Battalion*," Hawkins exclaimed; "we're only
a company!" He began to count the bunkers and realized
that there would only be two men to a bunker with
several empty bunkers in between, fifty percent watch all
night.

Their platoon section was so long it would take Hawkins an hour to check the lines—even in the daytime. He
stumbled along the trench and stopped at the yawning
hole of the bunker he and Joseley would man.

"Let's see what we got." He struck a match and timor-
ously poked his head through the hole. Immediately there
was a scurrying of little bodies; but it was the odor that
hit him—of old urine, rotten C-rations, and moldy dank-
ness. Something like putrid Camembert cheese.

"Whew! People slept in there." He lit another match
and stepped in again. It was a hole about five and a half
feet high; three feet dug into the ground, and two feet
above the ground level piled up with sandbags to complete
the structure. Odd strips of metal and crooked wooden
poles formed the frame for the roof. Hawkins' eyes
lighted as he saw a bed, a hospital stretcher. The poles
were stuck into the dirt wall at one end and propped on
sandbags at the other. He put his hand down, testing. The
canvas was slick wet. His hand jerked away.

"Let's sleep outside, Lieutenant."

Hawkins laughed cynically. "Maybe they'll let us sleep
in the daytime."

The next day they did nothing. Hawkins sat beside a
bunker in the late afternoon sun, leaning against the sandbags. It had been eighteen days before he got his first letter from the States and he was anxious to write. His fingers flew over the soiled little pad:

> What bothers me the most is being dirty. I was
> two weeks in the bush before I had a bath. Now and
> then I was able to rinse my face in a stream, but that

was it. We only have one set of clothes, and we wear them till they rip off. I thought about carrying an extra pair at first, but it would be a wasted luxury—too heavy. Everything you own is carried on your back. So you wear the same clothes and hope resupply will bring you new ones. Sometimes they do and sometimes they don't.

Each day my shirt gets completely soaked with sweat. Each night I sleep on the ground. If it rains, I'm muddy. If it's dry, I'm dusty. At first I couldn't stand it, practically went crazy looking for water to wash, but there is hardly enough water to drink. All water is for drinking.

The men say we usually bathe about once a week in a stream, but only if the security situation allows. So far we've only bathed twice. But like everything else, you get used to it. After three weeks here, it doesn't bother me at all.

His pen stopped. Three and a half weeks? Had it really been that long? Yet in a way it seemed like forever, as if he'd never done anything else. He looked down at two of the letters he had received, one from his mother, the other from one of the girls he had been dating in Washington during training. He felt a wisp of sorrow; he knew whom he'd like to get a letter from. Unconsciously he touched the Omega watch she had given him. It had been so long ago, yet he could see her perfectly.

He remembered that day on Easter vacation when he'd told Poo he was going to join the Marines and go to Vietnam. She had come with him on the yearly spring migration to the South. The year before he had flown to the Bahamas, but this year, with Poo along, he'd gone to Miami. They went up to Fort Lauderdale for a day of *Where the Boys Are;* but it was a mob scene, and mostly high school students. Somebody said Daytona Beach was better—supposed to be an older group—but Hawkins had had enough. He wanted to get away from all that; he had to be alone.

He got the twenty-foot Bertram inboard-outboard his father kept for fishing and headed for Bimini, the British island straight off the coast of Miami. In the early morning the water is very calm, and a fast boat can make the run in a couple of hours or less. By the time the sun was up they were out of the bottle green of the coast waters and into the ink blue of the Gulf Stream.

Poo wasn't really a pretty girl, but she had everything else in triplicate. The two were at the stage where they had started to think alike and knew exactly how to please each other. Sometimes too well. Once they had gone to church with his folks. The church was overly warm, boring as usual, and Poo had seen him nodding. Very easily she had moved her leg, just an inch, until it touched his. The pew was crowded and it seemed quite normal, except that she could send waves to him without any apparent movement. He tensed immediately and had to struggle not to reach right out and caress her. Next she draped her hand over her pocketbook so her fingertips just brushed her own thigh. Finally she breathed, just breathed—all this with an angelic gaze at the minister. Chris got the message, even with his mother sitting right next to him. He began to sweat a little and kept his hands folded discreetly in his lap. He was sure his mother would notice and he kept trying to stare daggers at Poo. The only time she looked at him it was as if she were taking communion. But he *knew* it was a front and he was livid—also very excited. By sheer luck he had his coat, and after the sermon, he shook hands with the minister and kept the coat clamped to his front. All the while Poo looked angelic. As soon as they were alone in his car, however, she howled with laughter. Within a minute they were both panting to find a place to be alone.

They explored along the water's edge until they found the perfect spot. The rocks and sand dunes cut back in a tiny inlet, leaving about fifteen feet of sandy beach. The sand was foamy and white, and it ran up under the scrub pine which formed a sort of half shelter. The water was clear as air. They spread their blanket, and the dunes and trees made it a private beach for two.

Chris reached for a cigarette and watched her kneel beside him, pursing her mouth in a little *o*. He put the cigarette to her lips and saw her eyes shut as her cheeks sucked in; then he put the cigarette back in his own mouth.

"Oh, the water's wonderful." She reached for a towel and briskly rubbed her hair.

"Yeah." He watched her quietly, struggling to bring himself to say what he had rehearsed for weeks.

"What's the matter with you, silly Bear?" She leaned up and gave him a wet kiss. They were Poo and Pooh Bear in their private world. "You must be thirsty." She fished a beer from the cooler and carefully wiped the top before she gave it to him.

"Thanks." He smiled, seeking a way out of what he had to say. She reminded him of three things together—a puppy cuddling to its mother, a frisky colt exploring a pasture on a sunny day, and warm honey.

She hummed and stood up, looking around. "Do you think anyone will come?"

"Here? Not a chance."

She smiled slyly over her shoulder and took his hand and put it on the back of her bikini top.

He unhooked it, and she demurely laid it on the blanket. Then she leaned back in the sun, propping her head on his hip, and closed her eyes.

His fingers trailed over her bare shoulder, and he felt the love flow out to her. Something was tearing at him to put it off. Tell her later.

"Honey." He had to start *now*. His voice was foreign to him.

"Yes, Pooh Bear?" She reached up and patted his leg.

He forced his voice to speak. "I've got to talk to you."

He felt the shudder go through her. She sensed something immediately and got up to look at him.

"What?" Her face had just a trace of worry—almost hope.

Chris dreaded his next words. "I . . . I'm going to go away for a while." He dodged.

"Go away? Where?"

He knew he had to make it fast. "I'm going to go to Vietnam. I'm going at the end of this semester. I think I can get a special deal and I should be back in about two years."

For an awful moment she stared at him, her face contorted. He saw her anguish. Then she whirled away violently and buried her face in her hands.

"I'm sorry, Poo. Don't . . ." He reached for her shoulder.

"No!" She wrenched away violently. "Go *away*. Oh, I

knew it. I knew it." She sobbed into her hands.

He jumped to his knees, reaching out. "Look, honey, with my Reserve time, I'll only have to serve two years as a Marine and just one year in Vietnam."

"A *Marine?* Oh, *no no;* God, *no.*" She looked at him with something close to hate, sobbing hard. "Why? Why? Why do you want to do this?"

He tried to hold her, but she shook him away. Impulsively she snatched her bikini top and put it on.

"Now stop that!" He grabbed her roughly and dragged her to him, but she struggled free.

"Why? Why this?" she sobbed. "Don't you love me?"

"Don't say that! Ever!" Angrily he knocked her hands aside and pulled her tight. For a second she struggled, then sagged against his chest as deep sobs wracked her body. He felt her tears on his chest as she clung to him.

After a while she dried her eyes and gave him the hardest look he had ever known. "Don't you ever make me cry again."

He caught his breath. The words struck him like a hammer, and something told him it was all over. Only it would never really be over for them. There is a certain love that can never be destroyed.

He tried to explain how he wanted to go because he wanted to learn firsthand what was going on. So he could work to prevent more Vietnams. So in some small way he would be better prepared to avoid fighting in the future. She said nothing. He tried to explain he wanted to go because of the challenge of it, the self-satisfaction of mastering the art of leading men and winning over the competition of the enemy. She glared and said the two contradicted each other.

"Please, Poo, I'm *trying* to explain."

"You haven't said anything about *us.*"

He winced and felt the bitterness. "All right, there is another reason. I believe that Vietnam is *the* thing going on in the world today. In other words it's where the action is. Ten, twenty, thirty years from now, history will look back and say that the big event. . . ."

"But it's a terrible event, it's horrible . . ." she broke in. "*It's wrong* killing those innocent people. Do you want to be a killer?

"Please, whether it's bad or good, it's the great thing happening. By great I mean in terms of affecting people's lives. That doesn't mean I think it's good—at all—but it's the biggest thing going. I want to be a part of it, to experience it, to be in the movement of life. No war is ever good, but they are great—great in the sense of affecting lives and people, and I want to experience it, good or bad, to be able to tell my grandchildren, 'Yes I was there. It was like this.'"

"That's insane!" she cried. "You want to experience it because it's great and glorious and a big challenge and at the same time you say you want to learn to prevent war." She was crying again.

He could only shrug. "No, that's not true. . . ."

"What about your PhD?" she said in desperation.

"It'll wait."

"Oh, Pooh Bear, why do you have to go as a Marine? You're crazy—crazy."

A spasm of pain squeezed his stomach, bringing him back to Khe Sanh. He grimaced and threw down the pen as the pain, like a cramp, worked its way down his gut. "Ooohh," he moaned. It seemed he either had the GI runs or else was stopped up and couldn't go at all—nothing in between. He held his stomach and wound his way along the trenches between the bunkers. The trench sides were eroded and had begun to fill up the bottoms and become V-shaped. Many of the sandbags placed along the top had broken. Still, a man was half-hidden as he walked along.

Finally he found what he was looking for, a trench that ran back away from the others, dead-ending inside a little box hut. He went back and peered in, squinting his eyes in the darkness. There were two boards about five inches apart over a half barrel.

Well, at least they have a sit-down shitter he thought to himself.

It was like all heads in Vietnam, a wooden outhouse with seats built over half barrels. The barrels were cut from empty oil or tar drums. Periodically, the half barrels were removed from the outhouses, kerosene or Diesel fuel was added and the contents burned. The method required upkeep but was more sanitary and required far less initial effort than digging a deep pit. It also stank like hell when burning.

It was so dark Hawkins could barely see, but he clutched his C-ration toilet paper and gingerly lowered his bare rear to the boards.

"Beats squatting on your haunches over the ground," he said aloud to himself.

But he wasn't convinced. He had that ticklish, tight feeling that some unknown bug would crawl up and touch him. He carefully stacked his pants on his boot tops so they wouldn't touch the sliminess of the wet dirt. He longed for a clean flush toilet where he could sit down and relax.

Eventually, he did his business, but something was warm beneath him. He could feel a slow heat radiating up to him.

That's odd. One guy could warm the boards but not the whole barrel. He looked around, but it was too dark to see anything. He got up and hitched his pants. Curiously, he put his hand near the seat. It *was* warm; he was sure now.

Striking a match, he gently lowered it toward the slit in the boards and then froze in horror. The barrel was teeming, packed wall-to-wall with maggots. They worked furiously over one another in a sea of motion. He shrank back and clutched his rear. It had been only five inches from that horrifying mess. Ohhh, what if they had come up the sides and crawled on him. He backed away, fearing to turn lest the maggots jump up and touch him. "*Ooaagh.*" A shudder went through his body and he fled.

Sedgewick

Sedgewick was from Detroit. He was short, stocky, black, and wore glasses. His nickname was Pimp. His MOS was motor transport, but when he arrived in Da Nang, they didn't need any drivers so they made him a grunt. He'd been in the bush carrying a rifle for more than four months and he wanted out.

"Shee-it," he said aloud, "I'm supposed to be a driver not a Goddamned ammo humper." And he kicked the box of machine-gun bullets he had to carry. He looked at his short-timer calendar and frowned again. "Sheeeee-it." One hundred and twenty-five days he'd been out here—except for the time when he'd gotten himself to the rear as a guard for the Exec. That was good, but it didn't take him long to figure out why he couldn't get a permanent job in the rear.

But now he *really had* to get to the rear. He'd broken his glasses. He'd told them, he'd asked them, he'd begged them, but they still wouldn't let him go. How in the hell those muthafuckers expect him to shoot a rifle if he couldn't even see.

"Shee-it!" All he wanted was the chance to go to the Med Center and get a new pair made, but they all thought he was just trying to skate.

For a while he busied himself with his calendar: numbering the days backward to one, the day he rotated and went home. Then it hit him—the new lieutenant. The very thought made him feel better. Maybe, just maybe, he could get that new lieutenant to help him. But he'd have to do it right. Official, strictly by the book. Immediately he squared away his blouse and went to find his squad leader.

Wilson was humming and cleaning his M-14 when Sedgewick came up. Sedgewick mentally shook his head; he would never understand why Wilson voluntarily carried the heavier weapon.

"Hey, Wilson, you gotta help me, man."

"Whadda ya want?" Wilson's voice was irritated and he didn't look up.

"I gotta get outta the bush, Wilson; I broke my glasses."

"Get outta here, boy. You know you already seen the captain 'bout that and he said no."

"Aw, he's a beast."

Wilson looked up at the word "beast." "So he's a beast—ain't nothing I can do about gettin' you to the rear." He glanced over at his own short-time calendar ornately drawn on his helmet. " 'Sides, you ain't been here much longer'n me."

"Hey man, I can't see. I'm getting headaches."

"So?" Wilson went back to wiping the oiled parts of the M-14.

"Look, Wil"—Sedgewick's voice became soft and plaintive—"at least go see the Lieutenant for me."

"Lieutenant Hawkins?" Wilson jerked up and stared hard at Sedgewick. "Go see him yourself. I already told him."

"Naw, Wilson, I got to do it right. You're my squad leader, and I got to go through you to make it official."

Wearily Wilson leaned back against the bunker and scratched his head. "Yeah?"

"Yeah, Wil. Please help me out. I can't see."

"All right, all right. Just slide off the heat, man." Wilson sighed and began carefully wrapping the rifle parts, stashing them in his pack. "I'll take you to the damn lieutenant, but you do your own talking."

The two walked down the long row of bunkers to the CP.

"Lieutenant, can I speak to you a minute?" Wilson called into the bunker.

The Lieutenant put on his helmet and went out.

"Um-hum?"

"Sir, you know Sedgewick in my squad," Wilson said, indicating the man with him. The Lieutenant nodded. "He's the one I told you about who broke his glasses."

"Oh, yes, I remember."

"He would like to talk to you, sir. He's been having a bad time, and he can't see too well and he gets headaches without his glasses.

"Yeah, sure, sit down." The Lieutenant sat on an ammo box and motioned Sedgewick to sit.

"I'll go on, sir, and let you talk in private." Wilson turned immediately and left.

"Okay, Wilson, thanks." The Lieutenant turned to Sedgewick and leaned forward, smiling. "I understand you broke your glasses."

"Yes, sir, I did and I need to get another pair." Sedgewick saw the eager face and was sure this would be one of the officer's first "problems." His idea had been right.

"Well, that shouldn't be too hard."

Sedgewick frowned. "No, except we're in the bush, sir, and I can't get out to the rear."

"Oh." The Lieutenant laughed slightly. "That shouldn't be a problem. They probably have your prescription in the rear. Have you tried to get another set?"

"Yes, sir, you see, that's what I want to talk to you

about—I been trying, but the gunny and the captain won't let me go and . . . well, I can't see too good, sir, and . . . I wanta see the major," he blurted abruptly.

"The major?" Hawkins stood up. "You mean the CO of the battalion?"

"Yes sir." Sedgewick hurried on, desperately sincere. "I get headaches and I'm afraid bein's I can't see that . . . and, well, you know, sir, it's dangerous in the bush in the fighting zone, and if you can't see—well, I'm afraid I'll get hit because I can't see, but the captain won't let me go to the rear and get some more so . . . well, that's why I gotta see the major."

The Lieutenant leaned back and let out his breath in a silent whistle. "You mean you want to request mast."

"Yes sir."

Hawkins' eyebrows knitted together. Requesting mast was a most serious procedure. It was the right of every person in the Armed Services to have a private interview with any of his superiors in the chain of command. In theory, under the Uniform Code of Military Justice, any private had the absolute right to talk to the commanding general. Hawkins remembered that the applicant had to first take his request to each subordinate commander. This meant he must stop at every rung in the ladder. But certainly any man had the right to request mast; he'd heard it over and over in basic training. But he couldn't understand why the captain had not sent the man to get the glasses. That would seem routine, the practical thing to do.

"Well"—the Lieutenant exhaled sharply—"that's absolutely your right and if you're ah . . . really serious, I'll certainly push the matter on through." The confrontation with a real-life request for what Hawkins viewed as a fundamental right made him a little giddy.

Sedgewick was elated. He almost whooped—he was really going to get to the rear. Quickly he looked down, hesitated a moment, then spoke with conviction. "Yes, sir, I . . . I am. I think I must."

"All right. You better tell me what happened though."

"Well, we was going up a hill and I slipped and fell; the glasses came off and broke on a rock."

"I mean what have you done about trying to get another pair? Did you see the gunny?"

Sedgewick strained to say it right. He'd tried so many times; this had to work. "Yes, sir . . . 'fore you came."

"What'd he say?"

"Oh, he acted like I was fuckin' off, and said they'd see about it later and that I should have been more careful; and they wanted to know where my other pair was."

"And you saw the captain, too?"

"Yes, he said it wasn't important enough to send me to the rear for, because we were short on men."

"Do you have another pair?"

"No, sir." His voice was indignant and he looked straight into the Lieutenant's eye. "Lieutenant, I can't see! How can I fight? All I want is a chance to get another pair."

The Lieutenant stood up and thrust his hands into his pockets, avoiding Sedgewick's stare. "Well, look, Sedgewick . . . I don't know about the gunny's or the captain's reasoning or anything else, but let me go see the captain first and I'll see if I can't smooth it over and get you some glasses."

"Tha'd be good, sir. Thank you, sir."

"Now you do want to see the major if the captain refuses and I can't work it out. Is that correct?"

"Yes, sir, I'm . . . I'm having trouble with headaches, you know."

"All right, I'll talk to the captain tonight." Hawkins absentmindedly scratched the unaccustomed stubble on his chin, and a troubled frown creased his face.

"Thank you, sir." Sedgewick turned, and as he walked away his whole insides smiled. At last he would get out of the bush.

Captain Calahan

Captain Calahan and the Gunny hovered about the tiny flame from the heat tablet, patiently waiting for the water to become hot enough for coffee. Around them were scattered the radiomen and their antennas, the mortar squads and their tubes, the artillery forward observer, and all the paraphernalia of the company CP group. At twilight each was busy, completing his own private affairs—eating, writing, cleaning gear—before the dark came.

"Gunny, I'm going to need a new bodyguard next week. Gonzalez is due to rotate."

"I've already got one picked out, Skipper. I think you'll like him. He doesn't say much." The Gunny looked directly at the Captain. "Do you want to see him?"

"No. The less he says the better; that's what I want." Calahan smiled. "Just so long as he digs a good foxhole."

"Oh, he will, Skipper," the Gunny said quickly. "I've told him all he has to do. He wants the job."

The Captain looked over at his gunnery sergeant and their eyes met in a mutual camaraderie. They two alone were the Old Corps. Calahan knew the men called the Gunny the vulture, but not in disrespect. Rather because he was skinny, with stooped, bent-over shoulders and a permanent hump in his back. His long neck craned up to his face, which was beaked and hooked. The short prickly gray stubble on his chin flowed even into the same gray-flecked stubble on his head.

Their eyes held an instant, each seeing a worthy supplement to the command of his company.

Abruptly the moment passed and Calahan looked off to the mountains toward the north. "It's about time for them to lob a few shells."

The Gunny watched the Captain crawl into the bunker, then poured the coffee packet into the water and stamped out the little flame. As he sipped gently, his gaze automatically checked down along the zigzag of the bunkers. Unexpectedly, the leathery face squinted and a flash of disdain crossed the face. He saw the new lieutenant picking his way along the trench line, steadily approaching the CP.

Calahan, too, saw Hawkins, and he sensed a confrontation. He couldn't make up his mind about his new lieutenant. The man had the ability; he was smart, but could he handle the troops in a real fire fight? There was something about him Calahan couldn't put his finger on. He was trained, but did he have the blood or breeding or guts, or whatever it was, that made a real combat leader? Calahan watched him approach and unconsciously thought of his own background.

Oliver Calahan was from Atlanta, Georgia, actually from Decatur in the area toward Stone Mountain. His fa-

ther had been the head of the highway patrol in DeKalb
County. Like so many officers in the Corps, Calahan had
originally enlisted. After a four-year hitch he had gone
back to get his degree at the University of Georgia; but he
was a career man, it was in his blood, and he went to
OCS. Now at thirty-two, his thick muscular body had just
begun to turn heavy, but the months in Vietnam had taken
off the fat and he was trim and hard. Even in the bush he
kept himself neat, his hair always bristle-short.

"Hello Gunny. Captain around?" Hawkins asked, taking off his helmet.

The Gunny turned and his eyes had that deceptively
wide-eyed look, as if he had just seen Hawkins coming for
the first time. "Evening, Lieutenant." His voice was overly
solicitous. "I believe the Captain is in his bunker."

The Lieutenant approached the bunker just as the Captain stepped out. "Yes, Chris." Calahan straightened lan-
guidly from the low entrance and placidly began to take a
C-ration fruitcake out of its can.

"Sir, I need to talk to you about one of the men."

"All right. What is it?" Calahan contemplated Hawkins
evenly but started in on the fruitcake.

"I have a man named Sedgewick. I think he may have
spoken to you or the Gunnery Sergeant before. He seems to
have broken his glasses."

"Yes." Instantly Calahan guessed the purpose of Hawkins' visit, but he kept on chewing the fruitcake, with no
change of expression.

"Well, apparently he can't see too well without them, and
he is getting headaches. I spoke to the man and his squad
leader today, and I know he has been having headaches for
some time."

"Um-hum." Calahan carefully broke another piece of
fruitcake and looked straight into Hawkins' eyes.

"The man would like to get another pair, sir . . . if he
could." The Lieutenant began to twitch his fingers a little.

Calahan said nothing. He was angry but disappointed;
his new lieutenant had been taken in. Well, he'd make this
a lesson. Calahan glanced briefly at the Gunny and received a slight affirmative nod. Then he looked squarely
back at Hawkins and took another bite.

The Lieutenant shifted his weight uneasily. "I don't
know the procedure for going about getting a new pair,

but I'm sure the prescription must be in his health record. I'd like to do whatever is necessary to help him get them." He glanced over and saw the gunny listening intently. "He said he had spoken to you and the Gunny already. I—I don't know what was said but—he's quite concerned about getting another pair."

"Yes, I think I can remember some man complaining about his glasses."

The Lieutenant's face brightened. "Would it be possible to send him to the rear for a day or two?"

"Yup, that's just what I recall—he wanted to get to the rear," Calahan said dryly, then he turned casually to the Gunny, "Am I thinking of the right one, Gunny?"

"That's the one, sir." The Gunny moved forward at once, his voice firmly solicitous of the Captain. "The Captain spoke to him; the colored boy with the chipped tooth." The Gunny used the "Old Corps" form of address in the third person to signify excessive respect.

"Yeah, that's the one I thought," the Captain drawled slowly, eyeing the Lieutenant. Hawkins' naïveté angered him. That lazy black son of a bitch was just trying another trick to get out of the bush. It was a constant problem, but he would not tolerate his officers being a party to it. "Didn't you ask to see where the other pair was, Gunny?"

"That's correct, I did, sir. The man only had one pair," Gunny said.

"Captain," Hawkins began politely, "regardless of the reason, the man can't see properly now and he shouldn't be out in the. . . ."

"*Lieutenant*"—Calahan cut in harshly—"the Gunny talked with this man and told him another pair would be sent for but that he was required to have two pairs, and since our strength was down, he couldn't be sent to the rear at this time."

Hawkins glanced around him, then took a deep breath and tried to hold his eyes on Calahan's face. "The man indicated he had talked with you and the Gunny already, but that he's still very adamant about it and he says that if he can't get to the rear to secure his glasses, he wants to request mast with the major."

Everyone in the area fell silent and looked directly toward the two officers. Calahan was conscious of the reaction. He knew the whole CP group was edging in to hear. Slowly he bent over and set his fruitcake down, using the seconds to organize his reply. "So he wants to go see the major, does he? In other words, if I don't send him out of the bush, he's going over my head."

The Lieutenant winced. "Oh, no, sir, I don't think he meant it that way at all. I think he just felt he had done all that he could here, and he was concerned about his inability to see, and he wanted to go through all the channels available to him."

Calahan's eyes narrowed at Hawkins. The Lieutenant surprised him. He did not like men who tried to go over his head to get out of the bush, nor did he like his junior officers to support such attempts. The trouble with this new lieutenant, Calahan thought, is that he just isn't hard enough on his men. This was a war, not a picnic. If you let one lazy man get away with a story like this, they'd all be on your neck.

He turned back to Hawkins and his voice was much lighter. "Did you talk to this man? He has to go through the chain of command to get to the major, you know."

"Oh, yes—I spoke to him and his squad leader." Hawkins relaxed a little.

"Did you ask where his second pair was? He is supposed to have two."

"Ah, no, sir. He has no other; I presume he broke those, too."

"Did you know how they got broken?"

"He fell, sir."

"What kind of man is this Sedgewick? Good man?"

"Yes, I think so. I haven't known him too long, but he seems all right."

"Do you believe him or do you think he might just be trying to get out of the bush?" He could see Hawkins was getting nervous, and he kept his voice up so the whole group could hear.

"Yes, I believe him. I have seen him several times with a headache, and his squad leader has spoken to me also."

"Who is the squad leader?"

"Lance Corporal Wilson."

"Wilson, Wilson—colored boy? Tall? Thin mustache?" Again Calahan glanced at the Gunny.

"Yes, sir."

"That's what I thought."

"Sir, I understood the man had already spoken to you and therefore I didn't think I had much to say about it."

Calahan made an elaborate motion of crushing the cake can and throwing it away. Then he swung back and his voice was cold but even. "Lieutenant"—he paused—"did you *encourage* him to say this? Don't you know we need all the men we can get? Don't you know you have a duty to interrogate the men before sending them to me?"

The Lieutenant stepped back confused. "No, sir, I didn't encourage him. He told me, and you agreed, sir, that he had already spoken with you. My thinking was that the matter had already gone over to your level and was out of my hands. I don't understand the problem, sir."

"He *talked* with the Gunny; *I* just spoke to him casually, along the line at night or something. Now you come up here and say he demands to see the major. The first I've heard about *that* is through you!" His voice had risen sharply, and he thrust his face menacingly toward Hawkins.

"Captain, I really didn't have anything to do with it. The man came to me to request mast with the major. They taught us at the Basic School that the man has a *right* to do that. I assumed it was my *duty* to bring the matter to you."

The twilight flickered over the two faces, and the little muscles at the back of Callahan's jaw twitched. Hawkins was much more than he realized. "Okay, Lieutenant, he *does* have that *right*." Suddenly the voice exploded. "Gunny, get Sergeant LeBlanc." He yelled to the side, then swung back like a bulldog. "But he also has some Goddamn *obligations*. That man was given an order to have two pair of glasses. If he didn't have two, he is violating an order."

Abruptly Callahan turned away, forcing the Lieutenant to follow.

"Sir, I'm sure he had two pair to start with and I didn't intend to. . . ."

"Look, Lieutenant"—the Captain swung around, shoving his face only inches from Hawkins, his voice thundering—"I *don't* like men who come up to me and say 'If I don't get such and such, then I'm going over your head.'

Nobody in this company is going to threaten me. Now if he had come and asked to see me and we had sat down and talked it over and afterward if he still wasn't satisfied, then he could have said, 'Well, thank you, sir, but I'd like to speak to the major.' That would be what I expect. That's the way a *good* Marine would do." He glared at Hawkins.

The Gunny came up with Sergeant LeBlanc. LeBlanc's eyes darted over the group and his face set in a hard mask, eyeing the Lieutenant coldly.

"Sergeant LeBlanc, you had Second Platoon when we left Quang Tri on this operation. Did you or did you not order every man who wore glasses to have two pair?"

"Yes sir, I did." His voice was hard and sure.

"Was PFC Sedgewick in the platoon at that time and did he receive that order?"

"Yes sir, that's affirmative." The three men stood in a tight triangle. LeBlanc's eyes flicked over to Hawkins and then back to the Captain. If he wondered what was going on, his expression betrayed none of it.

"Do you know if he had two in his possession when we left?"

This time there was just a moment's hesitation before the Sergeant spoke. "Far as I know he did, sir."

The Captain bored in. "Did you check?"

The hesitation was longer. "I checked the squad leaders and they checked the men."

"Goddamn it, Sergeant, don't give me that shit! Did you yourself see two pair on him or not?"

"Ah . . . no, sir." LeBlanc lowered his eyes and he scuffed the dirt with his toe. "But I asked the whole platoon if everyone had all their gear and if not to step forward." His voice was low and apologetic.

Hawkins' mouth almost dropped and he stared at LeBlanc in amazement. His head swung from LeBlanc to Calahan and back to LeBlanc.

"All right." Calahan's voice dropped the threat. "But you did give him a direct order to get two pair?"

"Yes, sir." The Sergeant spoke quietly.

Abruptly Calahan whirled away from LeBlanc. "Gunny, did you ask this man about his extra pair?"

"Yes, sir, I did."

"What did he say?"

"The man said he'd never had a second pair."

"That does it! The man has violated a direct order," Calahan's voice became savage. "Lieutenant, if this man wants to see the major, we'll send him. But he should have thought about disobeying orders before he runs off giving me an ultimatum. Shouldn't he have, Lieutenant?"

"Ah . . ." Hawkins had been staring openly and unbelievingly at LeBlanc, now he snapped back to the Captain. "Ah . . . well, yes, sir," Hawkins mumbled.

"Any son of a bitch that starts giving his officers ultimatums can't be much good. Right, Gunny?"

"Right, sir."

Calahan looked directly at Hawkins. "Gunny, prepare the charge sheets; we'll send this man up to see the major. He can talk to him about disobeying a direct order."

For a moment the two eyed each other coldly; then Calahan walked off and sat by the bunker, once again starting on his fruitcake. "Bring the man to see me at eight fifteen in the morning. I'll take care of him then."

After they had gone, the Gunny and Calahan sat alone in the bunker, slowly sipping their coffee.

"Skipper, I don't think that Hawkins is going to make it."

Calahan stared at his coffee without answering, then looked absently up at the sandbags. "What do you mean, Gunny?"

"You know what I mean, sir. I don't think he can hack it in a real fire fight. And LeBlanc thinks the same."

"What'd LeBlanc say?" Calahan cut in quietly.

"Just that. LeBlanc said he's too wishywashy with the men. Tries to reason with 'em. If you don't mind me sayin' so, sir, we both think he ought to be in the rear somewhere."

"Why, Gunny? What's your reason? Specific."

"Well—just a feeling, sir, really, I guess. Some men are fighters and some aren't."

For a long moment there was silence. The Gunny frowned and peered anxiously across at the captain. Calahan took out his lighter and began thumping it in his hand.

"You're wrong, Gunny. You're both wrong."

"Sir?" The voice was incredulous. "You remember that

day on Banks' Hill when he came running down during
the air strike."

"That was his first time, Gunny." Calahan thumped the
lighter rhythmically.

"Well, LeBlanc had to. . . ."

"Yes, Gunny; we'll keep LeBlanc with him for a
while." Calahan cut in. "But Hawkins is going to change.
LeBlanc will help that change; matter of fact, he already
has."

The Gunny knew when to keep silent, and the Captain
continued to thump his lighter.

"Gunny, I'm going to kick his ass till he either . . .
makes or breaks."

"He'll break, sir," the Gunny said flatly.

"He might, Gunny. Or he might"—Calahan stopped his
thumping and gazed long out the low entrance—"or he
just might become too good."

Logan

A few days later, sometime before dawn, the night rain
had slowed to a fine drizzle. A fog was creeping up. The
night had been typical of those when they expected an attack. But now the danger seemed remote and the men on
guard duty tended to doze.

Second Platoon lines stretched a long way in the dark.
There were still two men only to a bunker, with empties
in between. And as the men peered out into the foggy
darkness, they knew they were isolated. LeBlanc was on R
'n' R, but Lieutenant Hawkins was picking his way along
the decrepit trenches in an attempt to check the lines. He
could barely see and at the moment wished he had stayed
in his bunker. He had just passed two empty bunkers and
was groping to find the next one, which should be manned.

Inside the bunker that Hawkins was approaching were
Martin Logan and Sedgewick, both of Wilson's squad.
Neither had been outside for several hours.

"When I get out of here, I'm going back to my father's
ranch and raise cattle," Logan said decisively.

"What?" Sedgewick's voice was bored.

"That's right, by God. I'm gonna build up that ranch
till I've got more cattle than the King ranchers."

"I thought you lived in Houston."

"My mother lives in Houston, but it's my dad that's got the ranch. He spends most of his time out there. I've been out there almost every summer riding herd."

Sedgewick had heard Logan's stories before, and he didn't know why he listened.

"Yep, and when I get out of this fucking Corps, I'm going home and really make some money. Listen, Sedgewick, maybe you'd like to come with me. Say, that'd be great. How 'bout you could get a job on the ranch, and we'd work together—just like now."

"Oh, come off that shit, muthafucker, you ain't got no ranch."

Martin Logan drew back as if he had been slapped. "My dad does too!" he asserted righteously. "As soon as we get back to the rear, I'll show you the pictures."

"Uh-huh, las' time he was an officer in the Marines."

"He *was*. He was a colonel and fought in World War Two, but he retired."

"Okay, man, lettit go, jus' lettit go."

The two men wrapped their poncho-liners tighter and huddled against the cold; the bunker was total darkness. Most of Vietnam was hot, but at night, in the mountains, when everything is wet, it is cold.

Logan lay quietly fingering a jungle sore on his hand, but it was impossible for him to stay silent long. "Thad"— his voice was confidential and whispery. There was no answer. "Thaddeus!"

"Yeah, muthafucker." Sedgewick's voice was harsh and wary. Now what's this Chuck-dude want, he wondered. Nobody ever called Sedgewick by his first name unless they were after something. Very few in d'Nam even knew it.

"How 'bout we smoke some shit?"

"You got herb?" Sedgewick's voice was much friendlier.

"Well, no, I thought you did."

"I don't." This was a lie because Sedgewick knew he had two in his pack, wrapped in a C-ration accessory pack wrapper, but he was saving those. " 'Sides, I wouldn't get stoned here anyway. Too dangerous."

"Aw boo-shee-it, you'd smoke in a fire fight."

"I might, but I-fuckin'-doubt-it."

"You sure dee-deed off that hill three weeks ago when we caught the shit."

"*Dee-Dee,* my ass, don't give me that Slope talk. I went when Chief said to."

"Yeah, 'fore that you was rootin'."

"Okay, tell me you wudn't scared. I damn sure wudn't smokin'."

They shivered in silence a while and Logan pulled his flak jacket over him. "Goddamn, but it's cold up here," Logan said. "I thought d'Nam was supposed to be hot."

"Not in the mountains. The Hawk is out."

Logan suddenly sat up. "I tell you what; let's pop some Darvon."

"All right, *my man.* You got 'em?" Sedgewick said, chuckling.

"Yep."

"Where you get 'em? Doc Smitty?"

"Aw, you're so fulla shit. Smitty's straight . . . I bought them from a Doc at Delta Med."

"Think anybody'll come around?"

"Checking lines? *Who?* LeBlanc ain't here."

"Maybe the Lieutenant."

"Shit, Sedgewick, that dipshit ain't about to check lines this time of night. It's misty, been raining; even if he did, he ain't got no way of knowing. An' what can he do if he does know?"

"All right, lemme hold some." He laughed.

"How many you start with?" Logan asked.

"Six."

"Six? Jesus. Three or four gets me going." Logan fumbled in the dark for his pack, rummaging till he found the plastic vial of red and gray capsules, pain killers. Sedgewick flicked his lighter and they leaned forward together, sorting the pills. The light fell onto the shiny capsules as they spilled into Sedgewick's hand.

"Wow, look at them."

They gulped them without water and sat back in silence, eager for the flight from the cold and the stink of the bunker.

"How long's it take you to feel it?"

" 'Tween twenty—thirty minutes."

"Say, Sedgewick, whatever happened when you went to

see the Captain 'bout your glasses? I heard you ast to see the major."

"Aw, nothing much." Sedgewick looked down.

"Gonna get your glasses?"

"Shit, no."

"What'd the Captain say?" Logan asked.

"Aw, the cocksucker chewed my ass, gave me a lotta bullshit about a second pair and disobeying some order, you know, the usual crap."

"Anything come of it?"

"Naw, they let it slide."

"How 'bout Hawkins—he believe your story?"

"Yeah, I sucked that dipshit right in."

Meanwhile Lieutenant Hawkins slowly felt his way along. He could barely see the ground in the mist, but he was following the trench line counting bunkers. At the third bunker he stopped and looked about him. He leaned over to make sure it was actually a bunker. His foot kicked the M-16 lying on the ground. He froze, then drew his .45 and ducked into the trench line, drawing back the hammer silently.

"Hello," he called softly, "hello, anybody here?" He waited and listened. He thought he heard a furtive rustling in the bunker. He listened again. Slowly he stepped out of the trench line and eased over to the entrance of the bunker. He flattened himself beside it and then called again, "Anybody . . ."

"Evening, Lieutenant. How are you?" Logan came out of the bunker nonchalantly, glanced at Hawkins' dark outline and smiled oddly. He casually moved over and sat on the far side of the bunker. His hand groped for a moment, then he moved toward the trench line and picked up the rifle.

Hawkins' body sagged and the pistol lowered to his side. "Who's on duty here?"

"Sedgewick is, sir. I just went in to wake him up."

"Who's been on till now?" Hawkins' voice became harsh.

"I have, sir. My watch has been over a while, but I let him sleep some extra. He was pretty beat. I went to get him just as you come up."

Hawkins stood silently, staring in the dark from Logan to the bunker.

Logan mutely hunched over his rifle and looked out intently toward the wire.

"Well, where is Sedgewick now?"

"Oh, he's getting ready, sir." Logan's voice was cheery and confident. "He's had a pretty bad time with his stomach lately"—he chuckled—"you know what I mean, sir." Without stopping, he raised his voice a little and called to the bunker, "Hey, Sedge, let's go, boy, I'm ready for some sack time."

Sedgewick emerged. "H'lo, Lieutenant." He yawned and sat down on the bunker.

Hawkins stroked the stubble on his chin, eyeing the two figures, then eased down the hammer on his .45 and snapped the pistol into its holster. He moved to the figure and lightly touched Logan's hair and ran a finger across the top of his shoulder. Dry. Logan didn't move. Then Hawkins wiped his finger across the top of a sandbag. Wet. Finally, holding his hand up high, he rubbed the moisture between the finger and thumb. "Where have you been sitting while you were on watch?" Hawkins asked calmly.

"Right here, sir." Logan's voice became a little reedy.

For a full minute the Lieutenant stared at both men, his head turned from one to the other. They remained impassive, holding their rifles, eyes fixed out toward the barbed wire.

Finally Hawkins thrust his hands in his pocket and turned toward the trench line to the next bunker.

"Logan, Sedgewick"—he spoke over his shoulder— "keep a good watch. I'm counting on you." Then he moved on down the line and in three steps disappeared into the fog.

"Oooooo shit." Sedgewick whistled softly.

"Think he knows? Do you think he knows?" Logan whispered anxiously.

"I don't know." Sedgewick squinted after the Lieutenant and rubbed his forehead. "I just don't know."

"But . . . how come he. . . ." Logan's voice trailed off and for once he had nothing to say.

Wilson

The Lieutenant groped on, counting the bunkers as he went. Down the line others also sat awake in the isolation of the fog.

Lance Corporal Robert Wilson stared out into the blackness unable to sleep. The bunker was damp and smelled unclean; it reminded him of an underground dungeon. A rat squeaked and Wilson twitched. The rats began to fight and scurry around. "God damn it." Wilson sat bolt upright. He ripped off the poncho-liner in anger and grabbed his lighter. "I can't sleep in here," he muttered aloud, "even if it's raining outside!" He dragged the cot outside and flung it down beside Big John. "Goddamn rats."

He heard Big John chuckle.

"Come out heahr, Sonny Boy Wilson, an' sit by me." Big John patted the cot beside him.

Wilson hesitated a second, then slid over and leaned up against Big John's shoulder.

"Theahr you ahr, Sonny Boy." Big John shifted his rifle and patted Wilson's thigh. "Now sing me a li'l."

Wilson smiled and relaxed back against the warm bulk. He let his head rest against the big shoulder and began to hum. His mind slipped away to his home in Chicago.

Going to get back to the world and get the group going again and maybe they will even get a shot at Rush Street instead of just the black nightclubs.

Wilson was a tall handsome black man of twenty-one. He had those narrow lithe antelope hips and broad shoulders characteristic of some of his race, those seen on the streets in highwaisted trousers and red silk cutaway T-shirts. His muscles, lean and ropy, moved under his skin like ripples under silk. Walking was more of a liquid glide with natural rhythm. Even in the bush he kept his pencil-line mustache; and when he could, he parted his hair and trimmed the temple line with a razor. His close buddies called him Sonny Boy.

"How I wish that it would rain." He sang softly in a high, wavering alto voice. Singing always cheered him and his spirits bubbled up; his slender body began to sway with that lithe grace found in athletes or dancers. His cocoa-brown skin was smooth and unblemished. Once, out on patrol, Wilson pretended that he was back on the high school track team; he had hurdled a log like a deer, even in his combat boots. But the captain had seen, and the same night Wilson had to dig a latrine and trash pit.

Thinking back, he wished now he had gone to college as his father had wanted. There had been some terrible scenes. His father was a mailman and had saved for years so he could go to Loop Junior College. But Wilson wanted to sing. He loved singing and the feeling of the audience, the soft lights and the shiny clothes. Everybody had said he could make it big, so he skipped college and started singing full time after high school. Then came the draft notice. Damned if they'd draft him.

"Gotta cigarette, Wil?" Big John's throaty chuckle cut into his thoughts.

"Yeah, but you can't smoke now," Wilson said without thinking.

"Aw, fo' shit's sake, Wil—jus' cause the 'tenant said no smokin'!" Big John sat up quickly and Wilson tumbled away. The motion accented the difference in the two bodies.

"The Lieutenant doesn't have anything to do with it. You know how easy it is to spot a cigarette glowing in the dark. We're too close to Injun country."

"Nobody eva see nothin' in the fog."

Wilson looked about suddenly, as if seeing the mist and fog for the first time. It *was* foggy. Couldn't see ten feet down the line. He glanced at his watch . . . 5:15. "Good," he muttered half aloud, feeling relieved that it would soon be light. Wonder if they had all this fog during the siege. Once the planes got socked in, they would never have been able to hold this place. He hefted his big M-14 and snapped the bolt. "They might," he said in answer to Big John, "they might be crawling up to the lines right now."

"Wha're you turnin' into, a lif'a, since you made squad leader?"

"Cut out that crap."

"You always sayin' the brothers got t'stick tugethur. Then you made squad leader and stahrt bein' a hahrd ass jus' to impress the 'tenant and the cap'n."

"Shut up, motherfucker. With all those white girls you

write to, you can just kiss my black ass. . . ." Wilson knew Big John was baiting him, but anytime someone accused him of being anything close to an Uncle Tom he was furious.

"Shee-it. You tryin' to tell me you ain' never had none. Up theahr in big Chicago wheahr you hang out, oughta be easy."

"Chicago is better than Chittlin' Switch, North Carolina, where you live. I hear they have to fly daylight in there." Wilson laughed derisively at his own joke.

"Aw, man, you are a sorry muthur. Up theah tryin' to sing to make bread."

"Hulk, you haven't got any room to talk. How about that football contract?"

Big John squirmed a little but said nothing. He'd been reared near Raleigh, North Carolina, where his father had worked for a white man and there'd never been any trouble. Mr. Sanders had always been good to the Jacksons. Big John had gone to an integrated high school and figured all North Carolina was the same. He'd never graduated, but still he'd gone to a Midwest university to play football, before his straight F average had disqualified him. The Marines had told him he could play ball for them and so he had, for a year. Just how he got to Vietnam he wasn't sure. But he was sure that the Miami Dolphins had offered him a contract as soon as he was out.

"The trouble with you, Big John, is you just don't care. You're going to play pro ball and make a lot of money. You'll be rich and famous and all the rest won't matter to you anymore. I think you got a kindly father-image of all the Chuck officers."

Big John frowned and wished Wilson wouldn't talk that way. He had no idea what "father-image" was, but he just couldn't understand all the fuss Wilson and the others made about Chucks. When he got out of the Corps he would play ball. What if he did make a lot of money?

"Alla time you in a hassle, Sonny. Out inna bush doan make no difference what color you ahr. Next thing Ih heahr you gonna be same as Carlysle."

At the word "Carlysle," Wilson's mood changed abruptly. "John, Carlysle is a good man, but he's got the fire in him, too much fire. We're never going to get anywhere his way."

"Well, Ih doan need all that hassle. Ih just doan *need* it; Carlysle's fucked up tha' way."

Wilson's smooth face creased in a frown. He stroked his pencil mustache as he remembered the last time he had seen Carlysle. It was back in the rear at Quang Tri, the day before they had gone on the Pegasus Op.

They must have been waiting for him because it was just after dark and Wilson was walking toward the slop chute for a last beer. Carlysle's high, fast voice whipped out at him. "Hey man, where ya goin'?"

Wilson looked between the rickety wooden hooches where the troops slept and saw the dark figures loafing against the bunker, pinpointed by the red glow of their cigarettes. He sensed the mood and started to move away, but Carlysle slid toward him quickly and started the motions of the black power handshake.

"Gimme some power, Wilson."

Wilson had to stop, to refuse to give power was unthinkable in d'Nam. It was a solemn rite and Wilson raised his clenched fist. Carlysle's fist rose to meet it and they hit twice head on against the knuckles, then once against the back of the hand, and swinging over once against the palm side. In unison then, each raised his fist to his mouth and blew into the hollow of the hand as if wishing luck to dice. Finally with their fists slightly uncurled, they grasped hands with just the fingertips going into the curve of the other man's fingers; lastly two short shakes.

Wilson gave power to each man silently and deliberately. Two were from Hotel Company, two he didn't know. Wilson detested Carlysle, but all the brothers in d'Nam gave power, except some of the old sergeants.

Carlysle was small and wiry with light, almost yellow skin. He wore no cover in defiance of regulations, and his hair, though still Marine-short, was combed high in the Afro style. It puffed from his head in an arch, dark brown with a slightly reddish tinge. He had thin lips for a black man, and they curled in a constant snarl over a set of perfect, gleaming teeth. The teeth always surprised those seeing him for the first time because they were in sharp contrast to the rest of his otherwise ugly features. A slight scar ran along the sharp angle made by his chin and jawline. Carlysle spoke rapidly with the staccato-popping of the northern big-city black.

"We're going out there tonight, Sonny Boy; we're going to get the beast. We're going to catch him an' mess him up good." The hard bony face leaned up and peered close into Wilson's handsome face. "We want ya ta go with us, man. We're goin' to catch that muddafukka tonight. Maybe even catch that muddafukka top. Maybe put a frag in the top's hooch."

Wilson recoiled inwardly, as much from the senseless violence as from the venom of hatred in Carlysle's voice. "No, man. I ain't goin'. I'm going to drink some beer."

Carlysle moved closer, his slightly bugged eyes sneering directly into Wilson's face. Wilson tried to back off, but Carlysle caught his arm. "I've been watchin' you, man, and you ain't with us."

Wilson's mind raced hard and a fine line of sweat broke out on his thin mustache. He felt very strongly about black power, but fighting and rioting wasn't the way. "Hell, you say. I just don't feel like going tonight. I'm going to drink a beer and get some sleep. We're movin' out tomorrow. You just slide on off without me."

He jerked away and turned to go, but the others blocked his way. Just then, two big-bellied top sergeants walked by. Since they had been drinking since four o'clock, they didn't notice the group. But instinctively the other four backed slowly toward the deeper shadow. Only Carlysle held his ground. Wilson saw the chance and turned abruptly. "I gotta go now."

Wilson hastened off, relieved to be free of the situation. Then he heard Carlysle mutter after him.

"Fukkin' Tom."

Wilson slowly shook his head and spat on the ground as though trying to clear away the ugly remembrance. He had been enraged, but he hadn't turned back. Why? Damned if he was an Uncle Tom. What had kept him from going after Carlysle? Was he afraid? What was the spell Carlysle had over him?

He was the only lance corporal who made squad leader and, with the exception of Moore in the Third Platoon, the only black squad leader in the company. And he was proud of that. Why did they mock his efforts to work hard? He had no great love for any Chuck, but damned if throwing grenades in the staff NCO hooch was going to accomplish anything.

The first pale tinting of light began to creep into the air and Wilson's hand slipped for his cigarettes; then he checked himself and he dropped his hand. For a while the two men sat in silence watching the blackness of the mist begin to blush with just a wisp of light. No rays, no pinkness, no horizon—the fog just got lighter. They watched objects grow out of the darkness around them; but Wilson's mind couldn't rest and it skipped back and forth.

"Big John, how about the Lieutenant?"

"Wha' 'bout him?"

Slightly exasperated, Wilson looked over at Big John. "Sometimes, motherfucker, you just too damn dumb." Wilson leaned forward. "What about him and LeBlanc? Which one you rather have for platoon commander?"

"Aw, Ih dunno. They both okay." Big John hunched his giant shoulders and put his hands between his thighs for warmth against the dawn chill.

"Listen, Big John, before long there's going to be a fight between those two."

"Well, Ih dunno nothin' 'bout that, but 'tenant's fo' the men," Big John said determinedly.

"Ah, Hulk, you just say that because he stood up for you to the Captain when the Captain found you asleep on post," Wilson shot back.

"Maybe, maybe. But tha' showed me he be definitely fo' the men; an' Ih think he got his shit tugethur anyway."

Wilson paused, unable to make up his own mind. "I'll tell you this, Big John, before long there's gonna be trouble between him and LeBlanc."

Big John shrugged and said nothing.

"Long as the company's all together and the Captain's right there, won't be any trouble. But someday them two is gonna go at it."

"You fo' LeBlanc?" Big John asked.

"Well, I sure as hell don't *like* LeBlanc, but I feel *safe* with him."

"'Tenant's jus' green. We all boot once."

"Maybe, maybe, but this one's too stubborn. He don't seem to hear; he bucks everything LeBlanc says."

"Hey, Sonny, whyn't you slide offa that. You jus' gettin' uptight 'bout somethin' you cain't do nothin' 'bout."

Suddenly Wilson's body went stiff and alert. There was just the slightest noise of a rock rolling. His hand instinctively moved toward the rifle. He wasn't sure, maybe he just imagined it. Big John didn't move. He felt, rather than saw or heard, Wilson's senses go on the alert.

There was the sound of a step. They seized the rifles and both bodies spun toward the sound.

"Who's there?" Wilson cried out before his mind could even think. His voice was taut from the surging adrenaline. He and Big John crouched, peering intently into the misty darkness, their guts shaking.

The voice came quickly out of the void, low but clear and distinct. "Lieutenant."

"Aahhha." They stood up, flooding with relief, almost giddy.

The Lieutenant stepped out of the fog. He bent closely to recognize the faces and smiled when he saw the broad features of Big John.

Wilson and Big John sagged down on the cot, both minds racing over the things they could have been doing wrong: sleeping, drinking, smoking pot. Had the Lieutenant heard them talking? Simultaneously they glanced at each other, then their faces broke into a sheepish grin.

The Lieutenant squatted down in front of them. "How's it going?"

"Okay, sir." They answered in unison, their voices still shaking.

"Hear anything out there?"

"No, suh."

"No, sir."

The Lieutenant cocked his head. "You two okay?"

"Yes, suh," Big John said, grinning. "You jus' scarud us a li'l and weahr glad t'see it was you."

Wilson shot Big John a dark look.

"Well, to tell the truth, I was glad to see you, too," the Lieutenant said huskily, grinning broadly. He leaned back as if to settle down. "Both of you awake?"

Wilson was surprised to feel himself relax. Hawkins had been as scared as they were. "I couldn't sleep because of all the rats, so I just came out to talk with Big John."

"Yeah, they're in my bunker, too." The Lieutenant laughed tentatively. "Most of the time they just squeak and run around, but tonight they started fighting. What a racket! Flick on the flashlight, they'd stop. Turn it off, and they'd start again."

"Hee hee hee," Big John laughed, the huge shoulders shaking incongruously against his high giggle. "They'us gettin' some in our bunker. Man, they'us huffin' and scuffin'. Tha' boy rat must 'a turned tha' girl rat ev'way but loose."

The Lieutenant laughed out loud, and Big John laughed his funny little giggle again at his own words.

Wilson scowled sheepishly.

The light was growing and the Lieutenant's eyes studied Big John. "How tall are you, Big John?" he asked abruptly, curious.

"Li'l mo' than six-fi', suh."

"Jesus! How much do you weigh?"

" 'Bout two-fo'ty or two-fi'ty." Then as he heard the Lieutenant's whistle, he added quickly, "But Ih don los' fi'ty pounds since Ih been in Vee-et Nam."

The Lieutenant shook his head and whistled again.

"Suh, can Ih ask *you* a question?"

Wilson looked over sharply at Big John. He never understood how Big John could be so casual with officers.

"Sure, go ahead." The Lieutenant was pleased at the directness.

"This place be almos' empty, Ih heard weahr goin' to aba'non it altugethur. Tha' be right, suh?"

"Yeah, I think so, Big John."

Big John hesitated, scratched his head, then took a deep breath. "Suh, wha' Ih cain't unnerstan' is, if we fought so hahrd to keep it befo', why we givin' it up now?"

Wilson looked quickly to the Lieutenant and saw him frowning, rubbing his temples. Hawkins was obviously searching.

"Well, Big John"—the Lieutenant began slowly—"last year this area was considered to be a strategic location for interdiction." He glanced at Big John. "I mean it was an *important* base. The valley was a main supply route for the NVA going south, so they put the base here to block the flow of supplies. After the siege, the NVA shifted most of their forces elsewhere. They shifted to the south around Saigon. They bypassed this area; that is, they went around this area. They began using the Ho Chi Minh Trail over toward the west . . . you know, over in Laos. We couldn't go into Laos and the brass figures it wasn't worth it to keep the base here."

"Ih doan unnerstan', suh, if we goin' to leave now, how come we didn't leave befo' eva'body had t'die?"

The Lieutenant shifted uncomfortably and Wilson watched both men with mounting curiosity.

"We got tied to a fixed position, which was in range of the big Russian guns in the mountains at Co Roc, over in Laos. I don't think they'll try to keep a big base that far out again."

"Jus doan seem right to make a stan' like that and then jus' walk away an' giv'it back to 'em. Jus' like that."

Wilson saw Hawkins stop and knew the officer was searching for words, for thoughts; and then he glanced back at Big John. He was surprised—Dumb Big John was asking penetrating questions. But even more amazing was that the officer replied.

"But now General Davis is using a more mobile defense along the DMZ than we did before. You know how we keep having to move the company."

"You can say that again," Wilson piped in despite himself.

"These fire support bases we're building are so we can rush troops around wherever they're needed and still have artillery support. Choppers fly the artillery in once the base is made, and they are ready to fire half an hour later."

"*Still,* suh, it jus' doan seem right to fight so hahrd and then give it up. My cousin los' a leg heahr and now they're goin' to forgit about it. Aba'non it. Give it back to the gooks."

"I agree with you, but I guess they know what they're doing."

Wilson watched the Lieutenant closely, and he knew Hawkins was striving to give an answer, even when there was no answer. But he had never heard an officer really try to explain the war strategy in intelligent terms. Wilson didn't know why, but he felt a strange compelling urge to talk to this lieutenant. "You know, that's the way we always seem to do in Vietnam." Wilson's voice came eagerly. "Fight to take a place, then fight like hell to keep the place, and then we walk away and give it back to them. They get it back and then we got to go and take it all over again. Happened on Hill 881. Had to take the son of a bitch two times. Now I hear they're going to give up

Hamburger Hill, too. Happened to us too—on Banks'
Hill."

"Banks' Hill, Banks' Hill." The Lieutenant whispered
aloud. Big John and Wilson looked at him squarely, but
he stared off into the fog, seemingly unaware of their
stares, his lips moving silently. *It was the macabre Marine
way of naming the hills for the men that had died there.
We took Banks' Hill. Actually we destroyed it; and a man
died and . . . and we didn't even see a gook. They slipped
away. And then we abandoned it. They could have come
right back.*

"Then we're fighting just to *kill* gooks . . . is that it,
sir?" Wilson asked hesitantly.

"Yes, that's it . . . to kill the . . . I mean . . ." The
Lieutenant snapped his mouth shut. "You see," he began
again, "in this type of war, we're trying to preserve a way
of life we think right, and to 'win' here we have to wear
them down while keeping strong ourselves."

"I know about that, sir. Always got to have the body
count so we know the kill ratio."

"Kill ratio." Big John spoke suddenly. "Is tha' wha'
weahr heahr fo'? Seems t'me like weahr jus' fighten to be
fighten; jus' killen t'be killen."

Sssssssssszzzwwwwhhhoo.

It was a high sighing that seemed to come faster and
faster as it approached, and then became a rush of air,
ending suddenly just a second before the explosion, as if a
lid had been clamped on the sound. Wilson knew it was
the sighing of artillery, like the whistling of mortars.
Sometimes it seemed as if the explosion began before the
sighing stopped. Then the explosion was followed by what
sounded like a sickle cutting weeds. Before he got used to
it, the *whump* and the sickle sounded together but the
sickle was actually the shrapnel cutting into the surrounding dirt and bush. It was the one sure way Wilson could
tell the difference between incoming and outgoing. Sometimes the incoming *whump* would be the same as the outgoing *boomp* of their own artillery—but the outgoing
noises never had the sickle. The worst part was to feel the
blast as well as to hear it.

WHUUMPZT. WHUUMPZT. WHUUMPZT.

They dived for the bunker and the dreaded cry rang
down the line.

"Innncomming! Innncomming!"

There was a frantic pushing, stumbling, and banging of elbows, heads, and feet as they all tried to get in the door at once. They stumbled into the little chamber, ready to lie flat and bury their faces if the shells came closer.

Wilson felt an immediate relief, almost pleasure, not to have been hit and to have made the bunker. It was followed at once by anxiety. He'd waited silent and tense; automatically his eyes went up and searched the walls and ceilings, testing, gauging the strength. He cringed as another round went over and he looked up as if he could see the shells themselves.

"They're going right over us."

"I think they are landing down in the First Platoon area."

The rounds began to hit farther down and the sigh became softer and higher. Now it would build and fade away, without the rush of air, just the sigh coming and fading and then the *whump* of the rounds.

The tension drained slightly and they stole little glances and grinned at each other. A deep bond jumped between them.

"Whew." The Lieutenant laughed nervously. "Those first ones were pretty close." The relief from the sudden strain always left him a little lightheaded, and he reached for his C-ration cigarettes. "Want a smoke?" He pushed them toward the other two.

Big John grinned and reached out immediately. "Yes, suh, thank you."

Wilson looked shyly at the Lieutenant for a moment, surprised at the smile and the offer; even in a bunker together officers weren't usually that way.

"Uh, yes, thank you, sir." He fished for his lighter and then felt a wave of embarrassment.

The Lieutenant was holding a match for him! No officer had ever done that. He pushed his head forward awkwardly. He got his light as quickly as he could and drew back his head.

The Lieutenant moved the match over to a candle and their faces glistened slightly with sweat.

They puffed in silence, listening for the swish; each face glowing in turn as they dragged on their cigarettes. They were totally without masks. As they waited for the next shell, their faces were like windows.

The white face with lines of responsibility beginning to etch around the eyes showed anxiety beyond the shelling—anxieties over his own abilities, intentions, and his reasons. The handsome chocolate face, its thin mustache twitching, showed conflicts beyond the war. The tired strain of the eyes told of pressures and worries and uncertainties. The last face, like a huge chunk of ebony, was the calmest and showed only the path of each round as it went over.

III

Monsoon

Wilson

"Make three lines. Fifteen men to each line," the Lieutenant was yelling. Overhead there came a distant hum and then the *Dhup Dhup Dhup* sound, as the old Marine helicopters approached.

The Lieutenant and Sergeant LeBlanc started shoving people and getting them into line for the chopper. The first chopper dropped into the LZ and the line of waiting men grasped their helmets firmly, bent low against the blasting wind of the prop wash and ran for the lowering tailgate. Sergeant LeBlanc went in with the first, the Lieutenant in with the last.

Chief and Wilson pounded up the ramp, and the crewmen pushed them to the back. There were no seats. It was an empty hulk, just the outer skin covered the frame; inside, the wires and hydraulic tubes were all exposed; an old twin rotor CH-46, it could carry only ten to fifteen men in combat gear. The two crewmen manned M-60 machine guns mounted to fire out through big square holes cut in the side. The plastic of the portholes had long since been knocked out so the troops could fire out, too.

"Move in tight. Sit down."

They slumped on the steel floor, backs at odd angles because of their packs and bundles of gear.

The back ramp came up and the *Whap Whap Whap* of the blades increased to a steady roar. Inside, the helicopter had a totally different sound. The roar became louder until eardrums ached; the wind buffed and rushed in the windows and wrapped each man in a cocoon of air and noise. Wilson looked to the Chief, but there was no talking. Nothing could be heard except the droning whine of the engine. It became a shriek, a wailing in and out, a rising and falling. Even the wind couldn't be heard, only felt as it tore at clothes and skin. Each man lapsed into his own thoughts. Communication except by sign language was impossible. None was necessary. They had done this many times before.

And then the fear came. A hot LZ.

Wilson stared down at his boots and thought about the rain. It had rained on and off the whole week they spent at Khe Sanh; but even the crumbling, putrid bunkers were better than going to some platoon outpost. They would have nothing but muddy foxholes and ponchos. This was mountain country and cold. Wilson remembered being cold even as they had waited for the choppers.

"The rice-paddy daddies will never know about this shit," Chief had said. "It's gonna raaain in the mountains."

"So what else is new," Wilson grunted sarcastically, thinking of his socks which were still damp despite the special ventilating holes in the boots. They told him the boots were specially designed for Vietnam, with nylon uppers and special quick-dry soft leather around the feet. They were good, he thought, comfortable and dried right out. Then why in hell couldn't they improve those old World War Two socks made for cold weather and shoes that didn't fit.

"Whatsamatta, Dude"—Chief sang out—"no dry socks in your pack?"

Wilson looked up surprised: the damn crazy-grinning Indian had read his thoughts.

"Monsoon's coming, Dude. It's gonna rain old Mr. Charles right outta his tennis shoes," Chief chortled, taking off his floppy jungle hat, with the all-around brim which he always wore pulled down, and shaking out his hair. It tumbled around his ears, shiny and black.

"You better put that hat back on before Gunny sees you," Wilson said, watching Chief first comb, then tuck up the hair and put on his helmet.

"Never happen."

"Someday, they're gonna catch you without a cover and you're gonna get shaved on the spot and I hope I'm there to laugh."

The Chief just chuckled. He always wore either his helmet or the jungle hat. Only at night or when there were no officers or lifers around did he take it off or roll up the brim. "They'll never catch me d'Nam."

"Oh, no?"

"That's right—it don't exist."

Wilson looked again at the helmet. Not a hair showed. "Well, *we*, meaning just this one platoon, are going on some helo op and nobody knows where. It's probably the start of the op over to Laos that everybody is talking about."

"Take it easy, Wil." Chief finished with the helmet and hunched his arm to adjust the shoulder harness of the .38. "We never know where we're going; sometimes we get there and we still don't know."

But when it was time for the choppers to come, Wilson noticed the Chief eating his peaches.

Wilson looked out the chopper window; there was nothing below but jungle mountains and maybe gook gunners. Involuntarily his hands went down to cover his rear. Would the LZ be hot? He had visions of running off the chopper and seeing machine-gun bullets exploding into the back ramp.

Even in the cold blast Wilson began to sweat. He fingered the big M-14 and remembered the time when they were sent to find the bodies of a platoon that landed by mistake in the middle of a gook regiment. The story was that the gooks let two loads get in, then opened up. Foolishly a captain and a lieutenant were together on the same bird. He always wondered why they found only twenty-five men when it was supposed to be a company landing. The same answer always came back to him. Someone had seen the carnage and, knowing it was hopeless, aborted the rest of the drop. He shuddered involuntarily. He could never believe they had intentionally left twenty-five men without help—to fight their way out or die. But Wilson had seen the bodies with his own eyes.

They were about a week old; most were dead from the fighting but a few had been captured alive. They found them strung up in the trees with knife gashes and strips of skin pulled off. Wilson would never forget the expression of pure horror that remained on the faces even in death. The worst were the ones they found with their balls in their mouths. Forget it! Wilson shook his head to clear the picture away.

And always the droning, shrieking whine drowned out all other sound. The noise and the whine made the fear. It became an association. Pavlovian. The tan, taut faces

were ashen and drawn. Each man looked *at* the other, but
no one looked *into* another's eyes.

The chopper began to circle, and the crewmen cocked
the machine guns and stared out intently, eyes searching
every piece of ground. Even the Chief began to sweat.

Up! Wilson faced the rear, ready to run. He felt the
bump; they were down and the ramp began to drop. Suddenly hands were pushing on his back. They were pointing left and two men were out before the ramp was all the
way down. Wilson ran out and saw the tree line. He could
almost hear the bark of the machine guns. He dropped in
the elephant grass and slammed the bolt. But it was quiet.
A cold LZ.

LeBlanc

The road ran parallel to the DMZ. The northernmost
road in South Vietnam. North of the road was a river,
then a flat land area covered with high bamboo clumps
and scattered elephant grass. Behind that the mountains
rose up. And on one of these, between the Witches Tit
and Mudders Ridge, they dropped the Second Platoon of
Delta Company, Two-Seven.

LeBlanc's eyes swept the area in a glance. The road was
the closest contact—for help or escape. The river was
only thigh deep but wide, deadly if it had to be crossed
under fire.

He didn't know why they had dumped one platoon way
out here, but it wasn't a bad place to defend. They'd have
to spread thin though; the hill needed eight or nine holes
to cover it right, machine gun on each end. His eye fell
on a cluster of trees, and for a second he smiled. That's
where they would come from, but the gun would
murder 'em. The decision made him feel confident.
Quickly he threw down his gear and stretched his hooch
in minutes. He'd dig a fighting hole as soon as the lines
were in. Then he saw Hawkins. Caught up in the landing
and the rush, he'd almost forgotten; now the bitterness returned. He watched in frustration as Hawkins walked
back and forth. LeBlanc knew the Lieutenant was studying the terrain and trying to plot the machine-gun positions. Well, how long was it going to take him, he won-

dered. LeBlanc's eyes flicked to the north, then back to the cluster of trees. "Hey, Lieutenant, somebody's gotta be puttin' the lines in."

For an instant the Lieutenant didn't move, then he spoke curtly over his shoulder, "That's exactly what I'm doing."

"Well, we'd better hurry, sir, this is a bad place to be just sittin' around."

The Lieutenant swung around and LeBlanc saw the eyes blazing for a second, but he held his own gaze level and hard.

"Sergeant"—the voice had a conciliatory edge—"I am planning the positions, do you have a suggestion?"

LeBlanc's face went stiff with impatience. "Well, Lieutenant"—he dragged the word out and made it sound degrading—"You just put 'em in a circle; machine guns on the likely avenues of approach. And then you put out an LP."

"LP?" Hawkins' voice seemed surprised.

"Yes, sir. LP, Listening Post"—LeBlanc's voice intoned the classroom sing-song—"comprised of three or four men, placed outside the line in the likely avenues of approach. Its mission is to give warning by radio of approaching enemy forces." Out of the corner of his eye he saw the Chief covering his laugh, and LeBlanc knew he shouldn't have said it.

"Thank you, Sergeant," Hawkins said coldly. "I am aware of that, and that you were once an instructor in such. I was asking *where* you thought it should be placed."

"In those trees over there"—LeBlanc tossed his head. He had enjoyed the impertinence, but orders were not to be mocked. It nagged at him that he would have severely punished any of the men for doing the same.

"How about the machine guns?" Hawkins asked dryly.

"Put one right here."

"Why?"

"Lieutenant"—LeBlanc was conscious of his words—"if they rush us, they're going to mass in the trees over there." He pointed down the slope to where the trees came up closer to the perimeter line. "And the LP will be in there to warn. The gun has to be here to cover."

The Lieutenant said nothing but paced about, eyeing the trees and the slope, finally settling on a spot to the right.

LeBlanc curled his lip and spat openly. "Lieutenant, I've been fighting in these hills for two tours now. I've told you before, the textbook way don't work here."

"Sergeant."

"Sir?" LeBlanc's voice was stone.

"If there's going to be an LP in the woods, and if they have to run back to the lines in the night, the machine gun can put cover fire behind them from this position. But in the first position, your position, the gun would have to wait until the LP got back into the lines to fire cover, or they would hit our own men."

Immediately LeBlanc knew the Lieutenant was right. "Okay, Lieutenant, either Goddamn place you pick. *You* pick it." He whirled away.

"Tell them to start digging here, then spread five watch holes between the guns."

"Five! Lieutenant, that ain't enough," LeBlanc exploded back. "This is fucking Injun country. Ain't nothin' between us and North Vietnam except a couple of hills and the Ben Hai River. We need at least nine for protection!"

Hawkins glanced around nervously and saw the men turning to stare. "I'm talking about *watch* positions, not fighting holes. I agree we need nine holes to fight from, but I think five watching positions are enough. If the gooks come, everyone will be up anyway. But if they don't come, then there is no need to man so many positions. That way the men get more sleep."

"Goddamn, sir! Men ain't gonna worry about *sleep* when the gooks are around. We need them eight or nine holes," the hoarse voice bellowed out, and he fought against his temper.

"Well"—Hawkins looked down—"let's try seven."

"Lieutenant, I'm telling ya." LeBlanc stopped short; he was used to orders either to him or from him. He had served under plenty of green officers, but they usually went along with him if he pushed the matter or just laid it out. But to stand and argue was wrong. Orders were orders, not debates. His eyes burned intensely.

"All right, Sergeant, make it eight." Hawkins turned his back and walked off.

"Well, it's about time," LeBlanc said under his breath. He felt a surprised satisfaction, but conscious of the men's stares, he looked down and said nothing more, knowing that such behavior would spread quickly to the men.

The Chief came up and the two walked slowly around the hill.

"That son of a bitch pisses me off," LeBlanc muttered.

"He's right though, about the gun being to the right."

"Shit, I would have done the same." The Sergeant spat upon the ground and looked away.

"He asked you, didn't he? I heard him ask for your suggestion."

"Ah, fuckit. Let's get some C's."

Joseley

The Lieutenant walked back to his gear and flopped down. "We got communication with company and battalion?" His voice was drawn and heavy.

"Yes, sir, loud and clear."

"Well, that's good." He sighed.

Joseley looked at Hawkins earnestly. "I heard you ask him about the lines, sir."

"Yeah?" Hawkins looked up warily.

"The men will like that," Joseley said brightly. Joseley was staunchly loyal but believed in constructive suggestions when he thought they would help.

The Lieutenant exhaled his breath sharply, sort of a laugh and sort of a snort. He relaxed and Joseley could see the tension slip.

"I'm glad they will."

Joseley knew what he could say and what he couldn't and he pressed on. "Sometimes they think you think they don't know anything, sir."

"Well, Joseley, let's put it this way. Captain is not here now. When he is here, he always checks and he can change it if he likes. We're alone now and it's all on me. I need help. I have my own ideas, but it's good to get advice."

Joseley looked at Hawkins incredulously.

The Lieutenant saw his expression and smiled. "I see you are surprised, but I always listen to what they say. I may not agree, but I take it all in." Joseley's face showed open amazement and disbelief. "There's no need for me to argue or agree with each man. But don't think I don't listen."

"But do you do any of what they say, sir?" Joseley asked openly. Then realizing immediately he might have gone a little too far, he smiled quickly. "Well, I mean . . .I . . ."

The Lieutenant chuckled. "I like to hear all sides, but you'd be surprised at how many different ways I hear to do the same thing. If I took everybody's advice, we'd be going in twenty different directions."

Joseley was impressed but laughed politely. He turned to his pack and busied himself changing the batteries. Joseley was a great radioman and as deeply conservative as the Maine he came from. He carried the twenty-five-pound radio inside his own pack to hide it from snipers, tying his own gear on the outside. The only incongruous thing about him was the ring he wore on the dog-tag chain around his neck. It was made from the puller ring of a grenade pin. Trip flare wire had been carefully twisted and stretched across the diameter in the form of a Y. The result was a perfect ban-the-bomb peace symbol.

The Lieutenant opened his pack and fished out a can of meatballs and beans and a can of cheese and crackers.

"Let me borrow your opener, Jose."

Joseley shook his head but grinned and pulled out one and tossed it over.

"You don't need a radioman, Lieutenant, you just need someone to carry a can opener."

Joseley smiled to himself. Openers came in every carton of rations, but the Lieutenant somehow always lost his. So the Lieutenant always borrowed one from Joseley. And Joseley always made a fuss—it was a little game they played.

"One of the privileges of being an officer is to have your own C-ration-opener carrier." They both laughed.

"But, sir, aside from the machine guns . . ." Joseley began tentatively and paused.

The Lieutenant didn't look up from the food but Joseley could sense he was listening. "Sir, remember the time they asked if you needed choppers and you said no, we could walk it?"

The Lieutenant nodded lightly but busied himself emptying the cheese and crackers can. He then punched holes in the side of the can and took the foil off a heat tablet. It was a disk of compressed fuel about the size of two Alka-Seltzers. Joseley watched in silence a moment because he knew it was Hawkins' favorite meal and Joseley wanted his full attention. The Lieutenant took the meatballs and beans and put that can on top of the makeshift stove can. Nonchalantly he flipped a match and the heat tab caught instantly, giving a tiny flame with no smoke and hardly any light. When he leaned back and gazed out to the river, Joseley spoke again. "Well, sir, LeBlanc advised you to ask for them. Refusing made the men real mad."

Joseley watched the Lieutenant jiggle his beans and look purposely at the river. Joseley remembered the incident quite clearly; they had to walk about two and a half hours to reach the battalion. The operations officer told them he would send the choppers if the men were in bad shape. Hawkins had denied the ride because he felt the helicopters were needed elsewhere. Now Joseley was watching the Lieutenant closely, but he couldn't decide whether he'd said too much or not.

"What else did the men say, Jose?"

Joseley knew when to stop. "Oh, that's about all."

A flash of irritation crossed the Lieutenant's face, but he said nothing, merely turned back to his beans and meatballs and added the cheese. Just as the heat tab burned out, the cheese melted and oozed down into the beans. Then Hawkins stretched over to get his canteen and his foot accidentally hit the can of beans, knocking it over. The carefully made concoction spilled into the dirt.

"Damn!"

Joseley looked up sharply and almost giggled seeing Hawkins staring angrily at the spoiled dinner.

The Lieutenant watched the beans flow into the dirt; for a long moment he looked about, perplexed. "Oh, to hell with it," he muttered. "Joseley, gimme your K-Bar." Without waiting, he reached over, snatched the big jungle knife and began scooping the beans back into the can. With most of the beans back in the can, he jabbed the blade into the ground, picked a twig out of the beans and flicked it away. Finally, with grim determination, he took a plastic spoon and began to wolf down the beans.

Joseley had been watching intently and his mouth

dropped in amazement when Hawkins started to eat. He quickly shut his mouth and turned away to hide his grin.

The Lieutenant finished the beans and flung the can aside. For a minute Joseley was tempted to remind him of the pickle incident, but he held his tongue.

That night the Lieutenant didn't put up a hooch. The clouds had gone and the stars had come out. He lay on his air mattress, wrapped up in his poncho-liner. If it rains, he thought, he'd just pull the poncho over himself and the rubber lady would keep him off the ground.

Chief, however, carefully made his hooch. He and Doc Smitty buttoned their ponchos together and, with a couple of sticks, stretched them tight, making a two sided pyramid shape, similar to a regular puptent. They spread the cardboard from a C-ration carton over the dirt floor.

Joseley ordinarily slept with the Lieutenant and he waited silently by the radio. But after seeing that Hawkins was not going to pitch a two-poncho hooch, he joined the Chief and Doc Smitty. Joseley's poncho was strung over the open end and tucked tightly to the ground. The three ponchos together made a snug hooch.

Toward dawn the rain started and the Lieutenant pulled the poncho over himself and hoped the rain wouldn't last long. As long as the poncho was over him and the rubber lady underneath, he would stay dry. It worked—for a while.

His body made a little tent, and he squirmed to keep the edges of the poncho spread out, knowing that if he got up he would be drenched. Ponchos are supposed to be waterproof, but he could feel the rain pounding on it. Wherever the poncho touched his skin, the sensation was the same as if the rain were dropping on his face. Soon the poncho began to sweat. Struggling against the encroaching wetness, he put the poncho-liner between himself and the poncho, trying to go back to sleep. But the rain increased and in a few minutes the wetness seeped through. He felt the water on his leg and squirmed to avoid it. Then the poncho pulled up and water got on the mattress and ran down the groove as a stream.

"*AAAUGH*. Shit!" His hip was in a puddle. "Enough! Enough!" He ripped off the covers and jumped up. The rain drenched him immediately.

"Joseley!"

There was no answer to his cry. He stood shivering in the rain and looked stupidly over at the tight dry tent of the Chief.

"Joseley!" he yelled again.

Inside the tent, Joseley automatically reached out to the radio—almost before he woke. He heard the splattering of the rain on the roof and raised himself on one elbow. For a moment he looked at the radio in silence; Smitty was on watch. They waited, but the voice bleated again.

"Sir?" he called over the rain.

"I want to make a hooch. Come on. Let's get it done."

For thirty seconds there was no sound. Joseley eased back the poncho-liner, sat up, and peered at Doc Smitty. Chief lay motionless, only his eyes turned to Joseley.

The Chief shrugged. Slowly Joseley looked down at his hands, then he sighed, checked his watch, and began to worm into his raincoat.

"Coming, sir."

Hawkins

The rain fell steadily, gradually increasing in tempo. First it soaked the earth; then the ground became full and puddles formed in the bottom of the foxholes. The wind came and drove the rain in blasts and sheets; it drove it in the cracks of the hooches, drove it around the open places, drove it across the muddy floor; and the men scrambled to patch up the flopping holes. Anything was used—packs, stones, flak jackets, cardboard from C-ration boxes. Sometimes the rain would slow to a fine drizzle, almost stop, and the men would peep out, hoping to build their hooches a little bit tighter. But it never quite stopped and they never got quite dry.

The rain came back in cycles; each time it seemed to pour harder and harder. Wet bodies shivered in the cold, flimsy shelters blew down, and still it increased in tempo. Finally it was as if someone were taking a giant bucket of water and sloshing it over the camp.

Hawkins listened to Joseley make the radio checks and stared out into the falling gray mist. No airplane could go out in this. If the river rose, they would be totally cut off. The crackle of the radio filled the hooch. He looked at the radio and knew it was their link, their bridge back to security and safety. He reached over and patted it.

"Got enough batteries, Jose?"

"I think so, sir."

—"Delta Two. Delta Two. This is Northtide. Over."—

Hawkins was startled to hear his own call sign as if in answer to his thoughts. He sat up immediately.

Being alone, they were on the battalion net, not the company net. Radio procedure was strict. Their contact was the battalion operations officer, known as the Three, Captain Tolson, soon to be major.

—"Northtide, this is Delta Two. Go ahead. Over."— Joseley answered.

—"Delta Two, this is Northtide. Put on your Actual for Northtide Three. Over."—

The Lieutenant reached for the handset. "Actual" meant the unit commander personally, not the radio operator.

—"Northtide Three, Northtide Three, this is Delta Two Actual. Over."—

—"Delta Two Actual, this is Northtide Three. Be advised that all birds are grounded and weather reports rain for at least twenty-four hours. Interrogative. Do you have sufficient chow at this time? Over."—

—"Northtide Three, this is Delta Two. That is affirmative. Over."—

—"Delta Two, this is Northtide Three. Very good. Hold your pos, and report any change of status. Northtide Three out."—

Hawkins handed the handset back slowly and the two stared at each other. "We're cut off, sir." Joseley's voice was hushed. Hawkins lay down again; there was nothing else to do.

By afternoon Hawkins had stripped to his tiger-striped shorts and T-shirt; he lay immobile on the rubber lady wrapped in his poncho-liner. To go out was to be immediately soaked; it would take hours to get even partially dry again. After a while the hooch was only damp, not wet. Any movement from the tiny island of dryness brought instant wetness.

Hawkins shrank down on the air mattress, knowing he should do something about the perimeter; but he could

only gaze blankly at the canvas above him, unable to
force himself to move. He thought about the river and
wondered how high it would rise. Go and look, he told
himself, but he couldn't budge. He realized that if the rain
kept up, the river would rise and cut them off from the
road.

The water in the foxholes rose to three or four inches.
Hawkins worried about the line, and it nagged at him that
he didn't have a fighting hole himself. He hated even to
think about the LP for the night. Twice he called over to
Chief's tent to ask about the watches and the lines; and
twice the Chief went out to check them. Then Joseley
went over to visit in Chief's tent.

By late afternoon Hawkins had to urinate, but he didn't
want to go out. He tried to kneel at the flap, but he fell
over. The hooch was too low. He sat back. His bladder
ached. Well, I could pee in a can and pour it out, he
thought. Joseley was over in the Chief's tent. Quickly
Hawkins looked around and found an empty B-3 can in
the corner. Hunching over awkwardly, he filled the can
and then leaned over toward the open end of the tent.
Sticking just his hand and wrist into the hated downpour,
he emptied the contents onto the ground. The relief was
fantastic, and he lay back hoping no one had seen.

LeBlanc

Sergeant LeBlanc and the Chief stood in the rain along
the ridge of the hill looking down at the river. The river
hadn't risen, but it looked darker and fuller. The two men
moved from hole to hole checking depth and calculating
the strength of their position against the possibility of attack. They slogged past the Lieutenant's tent.

"That boot son of a bitch still hasn't dug a hole! Probably expects Joseley to dig it for him," LeBlanc said.

"Joseley will dig it for him if he asks, but not on his
own initiative," Chief said flatly.

"Wonder where that bastard's going to be if we get hit?
Sure as hell won't be in my hole."

"Think we should have a hole dug for him?"

Something close to horror passed over Sergeant Le
Blanc's face. "Hell, no. He can dig his own fucking hole."

"Maybe we should suggest it to him or talk to Joseley."

Sergeant LeBlanc looked at Chief and spat out his cigar stub. "Fuckit, let him learn for himself."

Hawkins

At first light, Hawkins took off everything but his shorts, struggled into the damp boots, and went to check the river. He came to the edge and recoiled in shock. The river had risen at least two or three feet. Dark, muddy water whirled and gushed along the bank. Sticks and branches were racing downstream. Even as he stood, the river seemed to creep up the bank and spill out, flooding the lowlands. The overflow of water had worked its way back from the riverbed and isolated little clumps of bamboo and elephant grass. He rushed for the radio.

—"Request to speak to Northtide Three. Over."—

—"Roger. Delta Two. Wait one."—

There was a pause and then a sleepy voice answered.

—"Northtide Three, this is Delta Two. Blue line between our position and the brown line is swollen and rising. Appears to have risen two to three feet already. If rain continues may become impossible to cross. Over."—

—"Roger that, Delta Two. Can you cross at this time? Over."—

—"Ah, Northtide, uncertain. It's pretty misty. Over."—

—"Is it rising now? Over."

—"Can't tell yet. With the dark and the rain we've just now been able to see it. Over."—

—"I roger that, Delta Two. Stand by one."—

The water ate away at the bank and the bushes. It cut the dirt from their roots, and slowly the bushes were dragged down, one by one, like deer by a pack of wolves. The swirling water sucked them under, and they rolled over as they picked up speed, slowly tumbling down into the surging mass.

—"Delta Two, this is Northtide Three, you are to attempt to reach brown line to the Dixie of your pos, if possible. If blue line cannot be broken, maintain present pos. Do you copy—over."—

Hawkins frowned. What did "if possible" mean?

—"Roger that Northtide Three. Break. Interrogative. Shall I attempt to reach brown line now?"—

There was a pause, then a different voice came over, clear and calm.

—"Delta Two, this is Northtide Six. Over."—

The colonel! The battalion commander! Hawkins stood up by reflex.

—"Northtide Six, this is Delta Two. Go ahead. Over."—

"Delta Two, obviously we do not have knowledge of the field conditions there. *You* will make the decision to attempt the blue line or maintain present position. Six out."—

Hawkins swallowed hard.

—"Delta Two, this is Northtide Three again; stay in constant contact. If you make it, we will send six-bys with a pig escort. Do you copy all. Over."—

Pigs? Pigs! Code slang meaning they were sending an ONTOS to escort the trucks that were to pick them up. Hawkins knew an ONTOS was a small, light tanklike vehicle which fired six 106-mm recoilless rifles. That could only mean the gooks were near, probably had ambushed the road.

The colonel's words began to jell. *You will make the decision.* Quietly he went back to look at the river again. Should they stay or should they try it?

Instantly he forgot the rain, and his mind began to function: If there were gooks near the road, they could easily ambush the river. Murder. They would know the platoon's destination the minute they left the hill. If the gooks saw the chopper come in, they knew their strength. As he watched, the fog began to clear from the river; Hawkins squinted; the river had risen in the ten minutes he had been talking. Suppose they left the hill and tried but failed to get across. . . . He shook his head. Better to dig in and wait.

LeBlanc

"Lieutenant! What are we going to do?" It wasn't a question; it was a demand.

LeBlanc had kept his radio on battalion net, switching on and off. He had heard the colonel, and he had watched the Lieutenant standing numbly at the edge of the hill. The Lieutenant had angered him before, but now LeBlanc began to sense something was wrong. He feared it was more than a conflict of method; he suspected Hawkins was cracking under the strain of the rain. It would be up to him to protect the men. As he spoke, Joseley came up and took the radio body from the Lieutenant's hand, dried it, and put it back in his pack.

"What do you mean, what are we going to do?"

"Battalion left it up to us, didn't they, Lieutenant?"

"How'd you know that?" The Lieutenant blurted out and glanced at Joseley.

LeBlanc knew the words had slipped before Hawkins could stop them. "Had my squad radio on battalion, Lieutenant. Heard you talkin'." He spoke flatly with no denial or explanation, knowing that he must work through the Lieutenant.

The Lieutenant fidgeted and ducked his head against the rain. Only Joseley and Chief were out, but LeBlanc was conscious that some of the men could hear from their hooches.

"LeBlanc, I . . . we." The Lieutenant turned toward the river and looked down at the handset; unconsciously he dried it against his shirt.

LeBlanc could tell that the Lieutenant was wavering. He was right—Hawkins couldn't hack it in the rain. Le Blanc stood pillar-still. The water dripped off his nose, but his eyes burned straight ahead at the Lieutenant as his mind bore down. He knew they had to get off the hill. "Lieutenant, I'll tell ya. I don't know about you, but I'm fer gettin' outta here. We got to give it a try." LeBlanc's voice was still calm, but there was an intense power in it.

"Sergeant, we'd never make it across that river unless we had a rope already stretched across. Some men would drown; we're better off here." The Lieutenant seemed to regain his poise, but his voice was questioning.

The possibilities raced through LeBlanc's mind. If they left now—quickly—they could make it, he was sure. Maybe some would drown but most would make it. But if they stayed they would be short of food; the rain could go on for days, even a week. They were sure to be attacked. How long could they hold? There wouldn't be any air support, only artillery, and if the river continued to rise there could be no relief. And no retreat . . . "Look Lieutenant,"—his voice was still quiet but began to pulse with an edge of irritation—"we got to give it a try. We stay here, we're sittin' ducks. But if we try the river at least we got a chance."

"Suppose we don't make it. If they've got just two snipers on that river they could murder us when we go across that water." The Lieutenant's voice was stronger.

"It's a chance we gotta take, Lieutenant." The veins on LeBlanc's neck were beginning to stand out. "We'll return fire and call for arty, but if we stay that's another two days at least. The gooks will know we're stuck here, and they'd have plenty of time to wipe us out."

"Yeah but. . . ."

"Lieutenant, I'm telling you we gotta get out of here." LeBlanc's voice was booming. It had a cold, threatening tone.

"Well, I'm sorry, I think we should stay here."

"Lieutenant, I ain't staying here! It's crazy to stay here." He paused and purposely glanced around, knowing that the men were listening in their hooches. "And I'll tell ya, Lieutenant, the *men* wanna get out of here too."

He'd said it. He'd laid it out in the open. He'd pitted the men against the Lieutenant. The idea rebelled against his training, but he had to get the platoon out. He must; this officer was nuts.

"Sergeant."

Hawkins was looking him in the eye, and LeBlanc felt a sharp doubt of surprise at the calm insistence of the voice.

"Sergeant LeBlanc, it is our duty to stay here. We've been assigned to be an outpost. There's NVA in the area and we're supposed to be a forward screen. Doesn't that mean anything to you?"

The words slapped into LeBlanc's face, and for a moment he felt the stun of command. His mind went to the men—his men—and his lips drew back in a snarl. "Ha"—he gave a short snorting laugh and flipped his head, flinging the water from his mustache—"I ain't seen you doin' much observing, Lootenant." LeBlanc spun around sharply, feeling his senses rage at the insanity of staying on the hill. He strode to the Lieutenant's hooch, paused, pointed at a B-3 can, then kicked it scornfully. Just as abruptly he strode back and looked directly into Hawkins' face. "And if we get hit, Lieutenant—where you gonna fight from?"

Hawkins gulped and nervously handed the receiver to
Joseley. LeBlanc could see the red flush creep up toward
the Lieutenant's ears. The officer looked furtively to Joseley then to the Chief.

"I still think . . ."

"Lieutenant"—LeBlanc pushed his voice to a sneering
blast—"the Chief thinks we ought to be outta here." Le
Blanc held his gaze straight to the Lieutenant's face, but
he felt the Indian's eyes. He couldn't stop now. "We gotta
go quick!"

"I—I . . . ah, all right . . ." The Lieutenant's eyes
drooped and he turned for the radio. "Ah, I'll tell bat-
alion we're going to give it a try."

2

Hawkins

Hawkins was with the point squad going down, but he
was wondering if he should put Sergeant LeBlanc there.
Finally he decided that since finding the best path across
the flatland and river was critical he should stay on point
himself.

As they came to the flat basin, the odd forest of bamboo and elephant grass clumps closed over their heads.
Hawkins checked his compass and bore straight to the
river, but within minutes they were walking in patches of
water. They pushed on through the weird forest, and the
water spread out like a lake or swamp until all the ground
was covered and only isolated patches of grass or bamboo
stuck up. Hawkins paused to check his compass and the
water swirled to his ankles, engulfing them on all sides.
Then Hawkins noticed the water was flowing. Numbly he
looked down; this wasn't standing rainwater. It was the
overflow from the river! He tried to see forward, but the
grass blocked him in. He estimated they were at least a
hundred and fifty meters away from the actual riverbed;
and with a rising sense of horror he realized that this
water must be the *level of the river.*

Wilson's squad was on point, with Red being the absolute point man. Hawkins pushed up to him. "Have you seen the river yet?"

"Not yet, sir."

"Red"—Hawkins' voice was hollow as he counted the contour lines on the map.

"Sir?"

"If this is the same level as the river, how deep do you think the bed will be?"

"Jees, sir"—Red gulped—"I don't know."

They began to slosh, heading down toward the river. The elephant grass and bamboo clumps cut his vision to about fifteen yards and the rain and mist shut off the sky, hazing the mountains. It looks like the Everglades or the Okefenokee, Hawkins thought.

Red was feeling for the trail with his feet. The ground was still firm, but the water was over his boots, almost to his knees. It sucked on his pants and boots, and he had to drag his legs in exaggerated slow motion.

Red could hear the rushing roar of the river and he was guided forward by the sound. Suddenly Red clutched for a bamboo stalk and his eyes stared wide.

"Lieutenant! Come up!"

Hawkins splashed forward, and as he came through the last screen of bamboo his face went white in a slow, sinking horror.

The main river stretched out before them. The top level of the water was the same as where they stood, but the ground obviously dropped off into the riverbed no more than ten feet out. A clump of bamboo bent slowly as the current forced it down. The branchy tops sank under as the swirl angrily shucked off the leaves; stripped bare, the naked poles whipped up again. But slowly the stream ate into the roots, until finally, ripped free, the clump somersaulted into the torrent.

A log shot by and they stared hypnotized. The forbidding power in the water seemed to compel their eyes as it boiled and gushed.

"That's evil," Joseley whispered.

We've got to try, Hawkins thought to himself. "Red, go down there and see how deep it is. Slowly!"

Red nodded, tight-lipped. Carefully he eased himself out, holding onto the bushes, feeling his way on the bottom. The water swirled up to his hips, then up to his ribs. Without warning he stepped down and the water tugged greedily around him.

"Come back!" Hawkins yelled.

Red scrambled up, his face ashen. "Never make it, Lieutenant." He was shaking, eyes wide. His words came in a gush. "I went in to my chest and the ground was still falling away. I know it'd be over my head. I could hardly stand up in the current."

The column had halted, but the little point group stood gaping from Red to the river. For a moment there was silence except for the gurgling swirl.

"Looks like it's gonna get purty deep," a bullfrog voice boomed. Sergeant LeBlanc burst into the group and in one movement glanced at the river, dropped his pack, and whipped out his map.

The others stepped back in deference to the two leaders. Instantly Hawkins considered sending him back down the column.

"It's too deep here, Lieutenant. We'll never make it," LeBlanc said flatly.

"I can see that."

For a moment neither said a word, but each studied his map intently. Hawkins smoothed the map in the plastic battery bag—their position was everything. His mind was racing, but he wanted to be certain before he spoke. He was committed to trying the crossing now, but the question was where. Finally he drew his breath and tried to look straight into LeBlanc's face. "Yes, I think it's too deep to cross right here; we'll have to go downstream a ways."

"Downstream? Lieutenant, it's got to get shallower if we go upstream." LeBlanc's face had a look of indignant, outraged surprise.

Hawkins thrust his map forward, pointing. "Here, about a klik and a half downstream." LeBlanc glanced around at the ring of men, then looked at the map impatiently.

The rain was still coming down steadily, but it was ignored; the two felt it no more than as sweat to be wiped away.

"See there"—Hawkins spoke, trying to keep his voice hard—"the map shows that the river widens considerably at this point. I'm sure you know that the wider it is the shallower it is. I expect that it's probably shoals at that point and we can ford it easily; also the river is much closer to the road there. Battalion will send trucks and an ONTOS. It would be easier to make contact there and we could get protection and security. If the current is too swift, I can request a rope. With the rope across, it would be no sweat, as long as it wasn't over our heads." Hawkins looked inquiringly into LeBlanc's face, then averted his eyes. He couldn't match the stare.

LeBlanc watched the Lieutenant's eyes, then reached down for his pack. "Okay, we'll follow the bank upstream then." He said it as a statement, acting as if the decision was made, but he lingered just a fraction of a second.

"No."

None of the men had spoken, but the air had become charged with a pregnant silence. Only the gurgling rush of the river could be heard.

LeBlanc whirled back on the Lieutenant, "Dammit all, Lieutenant, nobody's gonna cross that river downstream; it'll only get worse."

"Let's call battalion and see what they say."

"Fuck battalion! Battalion's not here! We're here, Lieutenant. The longer we sit here, the worse it's gonna get." The outburst poured from him uncontrollably.

Hawkins took a step backward. He felt himself cringing. His eyes darted to the men around him, out over the river, and back to the hard man who stood solidly in front of him. He felt as if the rain were pushing in on him and he began to sweat in spite of the cold. He fought a twinge of fear and his mind tried to call back reason and logic. "LeBlanc, don't you agree that the wide place in the river indicates that there would be shoals?"

"God damn it, sir, the wider it is, the more chance the gooks would have to shoot at us. We gotta go up, don't you realize that?" His voice was ringing, but then his Marine discipline held him in check. He glanced down at the map and said aloud, "Lieutenant, it's no good. There'll be no telling if it's deep or not. Can't trust a map like that. But you go upriver and it's bound to become more shallow."

Hawkins studied the map, trying to concentrate on the situation of the river and not on his resentment of Le

Blanc. The river was narrow above; he knew it would be deep and swift. It forked several times.

"Look here, Lieutenant." Now LeBlanc was shoving his map at Hawkins. "We go upriver here and you see the river forks. Between here and there is a stream that comes in from the right. That stream is adding to the water in this river. Once we cross that, the river will be shallower. Just above the stream the river forks and there is an old broken-down aqueduct bridge on the right-hand tributary. If we can get there and cross that old bridge, then we can push on to the other branch of the river, and at that point it'll only be one-third as big as it is here. We'll take the river by parts. Somewhere we'll be able to find a place to cross."

Hawkins studied the map. It sounded good, but something was wrong. He saw the old bridge marking, but the military map showed that it had been partially destroyed. It might be half under water anyway, and it was probably submerged now.

Suddenly Hawkins frowned and he looked back to the hill from which they had come, then at his compass. *They were already above the stream LeBlanc said was on the map.*

"Sir, battalion is calling for our pos again." Joseley pushed forward, holding out the handset.

Hawkins didn't move. He looked again to the misty hill, to his compass, then to the sergeant. Slowly he reached for the microphone and stared LeBlanc full in the face. "Sergeant, what's our position?"

The Sergeant shifted his wet cigar impatiently, but he knew it was essential to send higher-up a pos rep. Grudgingly he shoved the map out and jabbed his finger. "There."

LeBlanc was wrong. Hawkins knew it immediately. They were above that stream from the right, and LeBlanc had pointed downhill from it! But more important, it meant that the water would be too deep at the old bridge.

"You're wrong, Sergeant. We're above that stream." His voice was terse.

LeBlanc said nothing but sighted again with his compass and studied the map. Watching him double-check, Hawkins felt a glow of satisfaction. For the first time in a long while he knew within himself he was right. He smiled and reached for the handset, picking the code coordinates marked as soft drinks.

—"Northtide, Northtide, this is Delta Two. Our pos is from Coca-Cola down 2.3, left 1.6. Over."—

Hawkins watched with self-righteous disdain as LeBlanc methodically traced the position with his plodding finger. *Down 2.3, left 1.6.* His head snapped up, and for an instant Hawkins thought he saw doubt in LeBlanc's eyes, then it flicked away. Smugly he gave the handset back to Joseley.

"LeBlanc, we're above that stream; we're here." He took his pen and carefully pointed to a spot downstream from the bridge near the fork, but above the stream from the right.

LeBlanc didn't move and Hawkins pushed the map forward holding it practically beneath the Sergeant's nose. "Look. We're here," he said insistently.

"Don't make no difference, Lieutenant." LeBlanc shrugged.

Awkwardly Hawkins pulled his arm back. "Well, it certainly does. It means that bridge is more likely to be submerged." He knew he was right and he expected confirmation from LeBlanc. "Finding that bridge is critical to your plan. We'll be lucky if we don't pass it and get lost altogether in the mist." Hawkins' voice was rising.

"So what, Lieutenant. It's still better than going downstream." LeBlanc spoke matter-of-factly.

Hawkins was stunned. He'd been so sure of himself in LeBlanc's error. He had somehow felt that his triumph with the map would turn them around. "Look, uh. I still think we ought to go downstream and try for the shoals."

"Christ's sake, Lieutenant," LeBlanc bellowed with impatience. "Listen to me, will ya. I've been walking these hills for almost two years and I know a shit pot lot more about 'em. . . ."

He halted abruptly and Hawkins cringed at the outburst, knowing LeBlanc had almost said, "a shit pot lot more than you."

"Lieutenant, we can't count on battalion. Even if we can make contact at them shoals, they may not have a rope. We go upstream, we gotta chance. We know we gotta chance." His voice was yelling over the water's roar.

Hawkins glanced around him and saw the men staring

with hostile eyes. He looked at the surging current and felt an overwhelming helplessness. "All right, let's go upstream." His words came out in a hush.

Perceptibly the group let out their breath.

"Yes, now that I studied the map, I think that bridge might be a good idea," Hawkins mumbled. He had no idea what he was saying. He felt only the pain of the men's stares.

The Sergeant hoisted his pack and moved back down the column.

"LeBlanc, you take the point."

For one instant LeBlanc looked surprised. Then he shrugged and, turning abruptly, walked off in the other direction. "Move it out, Red," he barked. His lips had just a hint of a smile.

LeBlanc

Sergeant LeBlanc waded into the water, oblivious of the rain. He moved into position, three men behind the point. His first action was to ascertain who was on all sides of him.

Red on point, good. It was Wilson's squad, Cater on the radio, that's okay. "Shit," he said out loud. Logan, the most worthless man in the platoon, was three men behind Cater. He shrugged his shoulders and slung his shotgun, muzzle down to keep the rain out of the barrel, hitched up his pants, and wished he had a dry cigar. "Move it out, Red."

That damn lieutenant, he thought. Is he ever stubborn! Here I am with six and a half years in the Corps and two in Nam. And that boot-ass is gonna tell me about this fuckin' river. Christ, I fought all the way from Chu Lai to the Z, and that SOB has only been here a month or two.

As he walked, the rain reminded him of his father's shrimp boats, the salt spray and the wind. He thought of his two brothers. They were still bustin' their asses off and for what? Christ, they'd been poor.

Yes, sir, the Corps had been good to him. He'd been offered a combat commission but turned it down. He was gonna stay in and make sergeant major. Yep—then he'd really have it made. Prestige. If he'd taken the commission, that would have been fine—good pay as long as the

war went on. He might even have made captain. He'd
sure done plenty of lieutenant's jobs. If it wasn't for this
fuckhead, he'd be platoon commander now. But the war
would eventually end, and then the big cutback would
come. Mustang officers without an education, particularly
without high school education, would be first to go. He'd
be out. Might not even revert to an enlisted man. If he
was lucky, maybe back to sergeant. But this way with promotion so fast—yep, sergeant major.

He sighted in on the hills with his compass and tried to
figure out how far they were from the fork in the river.
What the hell's the difference if we're above or below the
stream? If they could find that bridge, he was sure they
could make it.

As the water got deeper, the men began to function as
a whole. They knew the danger of going back. In the deep
spots they held hands, bracing against the swift current. In
spite of the grave situation, or maybe because of it, the
mood was high. They felt that they would be back in
Camp Carroll soon in a dry hooch with hot food.

"Red, get the lead out of your ass. What do you think
this is, a fuckin' picnic?"

Red turned, looked back but said nothing. LeBlanc saw
the look. "You know what'll happen if we have to go
back, don't you? Fuckin' gooks will spot us for sure and
know we're cut off. Slope-headed bastards will see just one
platoon and then whap, we'll get waxed, so keep that ass
movin' upstream."

Red nodded, hitched his pack a little higher but said
nothing.

Red had tried more than once to cross. Once he had
slipped to his neck and come very close to being washed
away. He knew he'd sink like a rock with all the heavy
gear he had on.

LeBlanc looked again to his map. He couldn't be sure,
but he thought the water had gotten worse. It had risen to
his thighs. He didn't think that the water level had risen
that much. They were probably just in a deeper part. He
looked again and again for the stream to the right.

They went on for about an hour. The water became
deeper, and they had to move farther and farther away
from the river. They ran into a mist that shrouded the
mountains that he sighted his compasses on. In spite of

himself LeBlanc began to worry. He had convinced the
Lieutenant to go along with him upstream—all it had
taken was a little yelling—but he wasn't sure of their location.

"Sarge," Red suddenly called, "there's deeper water
here. It's a current flowing down toward the river."

"Let me see." LeBlanc pushed his way to the front and
shouldered past Red. The water lay all around them up to
their thighs, but in front of them there was a noticeable
current. It flowed across their path and headed down
toward the main river.

Could this be the stream? he wondered. Sure as hell
couldn't be the fork. He studied his map and tried to get a
bearing on one of the mountains, but it was almost impossible. Nothing was the same. As they had moved upstream
the land changed, sometimes a ridge ran out toward the
river, making a high spot to cross. The water had spread
all over and he couldn't even see the hills through the
bamboo and mist. There was nothing to sight on. Naw,
this was nothing, he decided. "Red, just keep movin' forward; you can hear the noise of the river rushing over to
your left. All you gotta do is keep following that noise."

They waded in; the water crept up to their thighs with
each step. Finally they came to a place where they had to
step down. *Oooooooooooo*—they sucked in their breath as
the water came up around their testicles. They wore no
underclothes in the bush and the water caught them with
an icy shock.

"*Go-od da-mum.*" LeBlanc caught his breath. "Man,
that's cold on my balls." The water tugged angrily at him
and pulled at his hips, but a few steps later it dropped
back to his knees. He splashed on in silence.

Suddenly a scream and then hoarse yells rent the air
from back down the line.

"Where ya goin'?"

"Hey, come back here."

"Logan. Hey, Logan."

LeBlanc stopped dead. "What the shit is that?" He
looked around, but the bamboo clumps blocked his vision.
"Red, hold it up some." He ran back, lifting his knees
high to break the drag of the water. He came to the place
where he'd crossed the deeper water and found Wilson,
Big John, and some of the others looking up toward a lit-

tle hillock about fifteen yards away. There sat Logan in a
dry patch of bamboo and high grass. His face was white
and his eyes were jumping around in their sockets like
those of a wild animal caught in a cage. He was sitting
with one arm around some bamboo stalks.

"What the fuck are you doing over there, shithead?"
LeBlanc yelled.

Logan started to tremble. He shook his head back and
forth violently. His mouth was open as if to speak, but he
was saying nothing.

"He's gone crazy or something," Wilson said. "He hit
that deep part and then ran off like a wild man."

LeBlanc eased his way back across the deep water and
stood looking at Logan.

"I ain't going on, Sergeant." Logan broke his silence.
The voice was high and screechy, but there was a note of
fatal insistence in it.

"What do you mean, you ain't going on? Get over
here!" LeBlanc bellowed.

"I quit. I've had enough. I don't care what you do to
me. I don't care. I ain't going back. I ain't going on, and I
ain't going in no deeper water. You can do anything you
want to me, I don't care. I ain't going."

Logan's face had gone chalk-white. As he spoke, he
trembled so violently that the water shook from his chin
and hands.

The rest of the men stood in a group, as if spooked by
the hysterical voice.

LeBlanc looked back and forth between Logan and the
men standing watching him. Then he shrugged out of his
pack and tossed it to Wilson. He didn't say a word but
turned and splashed straight across the swampy water
toward Logan. Logan sat frozen, but his face twisted grotesquely.

LeBlanc sprang onto the grassy hillock with his fingers
hooked out like talons. Logan flinched away and tried to
squirm but the claw had seized his shirt. LeBlanc jerked
the shaking body to its feet as if it were a weed; his free
hand swung up from his waist and cracked Logan across
the cheek in a back-handed slap, snapping his head over.
LeBlanc changed hands on the shirt and drew back with
his other hand; he held a fist just a second so Logan could
see it coming. The frightened eyes squinched shut just be-

fore LeBlanc's knuckles smashed into the cheek.

Logan wrenched violently, but LeBlanc shook him with both hands. "What are you trying to do?" he yelled, shoving Logan's head against the bamboo and viciously slapping him half a dozen times. Logan screamed and went limp. LeBlanc stepped back, breathing hard, lips still curled over his teeth. A trickle of blood ran down from the corner of Logan's mouth.

"All right. All right, Sarge. Don't hit me again," he sobbed.

Bending briefly, LeBlanc picked up Logan's rifle and slammed it into the man's chest. Logan's arms flapped awkwardly around the rifle and he stumbled backwards from the force of the blow. LeBlanc jerked him forward by the shirt and flung him in the direction of the platoon. Logan staggered forward, flouncing through the water.

"Get over there you motherfuckin' maggot," LeBlanc yelled.

As he slopped back, the men turned their heads away. A wounded man would be nursed, coaxed, even carried until everybody fell dead from exhaustion. But they thought of Logan as a quitter, a weakling. Logan didn't have to see their faces to know their thoughts, but he was too tired to care.

Sergeant LeBlanc walked directly behind the slouching man. His eyes burned straight into Logan's back. LeBlanc felt no elation, no brotherhood, and certainly no pity. It was all part of his job. He only felt that he had made a mistake by not checking on the man before. He should have had somebody pushing on Logan all the time.

Logan feebly began to move on. Wilson went across ahead of him, and gingerly Logan stepped into the deeper water. It came to his knees; he stepped again and sank sickeningly to his thighs. He took another step and it swirled higher.

"No, no, I can't." Terrified, he leaped back and scrambled up the bank, then he saw the towering figure above him. "*Aaugh.* Sergeant, no, please," his voice screamed in agonizing shrillness.

LeBlanc was ready; he knew it might take a little more to get the man across. His boot, lashing out, smacked Logan squarely in the chest, spun him around and sent him reeling into the water.

Instantly LeBlanc stepped forward and picked him up, grabbing the pack off and tossing it to Wilson. Then he slung the shaking body over his shoulder as if it were a sack of wheat and waded across to the other side. With a contemptuous shrug he let the man drop to the ground.

"Are you ready now?" LeBlanc asked calmly.

"Yes, Sergeant. Yes, sir. Please let me go. Let me go." He sputtered water and struggled to his feet.

LeBlanc looked at him closely, wondering if the man was okay. Then he looked over his shoulder and barked to Big John, "Be sure he doesn't fall down again. Be sure he makes it. You walk right behind him and take care of him."

"Yeah, Sarge."

LeBlanc moved back to the point as the radio crackled.

—"Two Assist. Two Assist. This is Two."—

"God damn it, what's that motherfuckin' green Looie want now?" LeBlanc whirled around and grabbed the handset from the radioman. Immediately he knew he shouldn't have said it in front of the other men.

—"Two Actual. This is Two Assist. Go."—

—"What's up there? Over."—

—"Ah some kid, you know the one, don't want to go on. I got him movin'. Over."—

—"Assist, this is Two. Go ahead, let me know if something else comes up. Out."—

—"Two Assist, this is Two Actual again. Give me a pos rep. Over."—

What the hell, LeBlanc thought. The stupid guy's right behind me. But he shrugged his shoulders and pulled out his map. The Looie probably has to send a position report to battalion and doesn't even know where he is.

For a good three minutes LeBlanc studied the map, checking his compass and trying to see the mountains, then he reached for the handset. He picked the code coordinates marked as cars.

—"Two. This is Assist. From Ford up 2.3, right 1.6."—

With a gnawing doubt, LeBlanc waited for acknowledgment and glanced at the shrouded mountains.

—"Two Assist. I make us out three-quarters of a klik *up* blue line from your stated pos. Should be near bridge. Over."—

—"Roger,"—LeBlanc acknowledged, staring at his map. Maybe, he thought. Who could tell in this shit?

LeBlanc had already handed back the receiver and dismissed it from his mind when the set crackled again.

—"Two Assist, you'd better find that bridge. Two Actual, out."—

"What?" LeBlanc's head jerked around. For an instant he thought Cater the radioman had said it, but Cater's face was equally surprised. A flash of concern crossed Le Blanc's strong features, then he snorted and turned back to the front. "Get off your ass, Red. Keep moving forward."

LeBlanc splashed angrily as they moved again. Straightening out Logan had been simple, and he congratulated himself on the way he'd handled it; there was a satisfaction in that, but his anger was with the Lieutenant. Wonder what that damn Brown-bar would have done, he asked himself. Probably have the men carry the damn weakling across. Logan was just a skater. Logan and his kind had been getting away with all sorts of shit under the Lieutenant—just like that Sedgewick trying to get out of the bush with that cock-and-bull story about his glasses. Le Blanc nodded in grim satisfaction. Logan got just what he needed—a good kick in the ass. *Better find that bridge.* "Shit." He muttered aloud at the Lieutenant's words.

They moved on and the rain continued to pour. They fought and waded their way upstream, moving as if in a maze, guided only by the sound of the rushing torrent to their left. It came up over their hips.

"Red, move it farther away from the river. Move back to higher ground but keep going upstream."

They had to move farther and farther away from the river. Now and then a finger ridge would lead down to the river, forcing them out of the water. When they came to one of these ridges LeBlanc would order Red to go toward the river because they could get closer to the riverbed and still be on high ground.

"Sarge, don't you think that we should look for that bridge again?" Red called back. They'd just crossed a ridge and the current was running swiftly to the left, although they couldn't distinguish a separate channel.

"Just keep moving where I tell ya," LeBlanc said.

"That might have been the fork back there, Sarge."

"Shut your yap," LeBlanc yelled harshly, but he took out his map and checked it again.

As they moved on, LeBlanc's map was almost constantly in his hand. He concentrated more and more on the bends in the river and the lay of the land. He was looking down at his map and listening for the river when the sound came.

It was a scream—a horrifying eerie scream lancing out over the murky water.

Hawkins

Big John had been carrying Logan's rifle and walking about four yards behind him. They were on one of the little ridges, and Logan had gone around the bend in the dense bush and started down the steep slope just out of sight. The second he heard the scream Big John rushed forward and saw Logan hit the water.

Others rushed up and watched in horror as Logan sank from the weight of his pack and was sucked out into the mainstream. He struggled frantically, then the current caught him and they saw his screaming face go under. He rolled and turned like the other debris that was rushing by.

When Hawkins heard the scream and the splash, he guessed immediately what had happened. He shrugged off his pack and dropped the heavy cartridge belt and helmet. The urge *to do, to act himself*, propelled him past the column of startled men. As he ran, he flipped out of his flak jacket and shirt and burst into the stunned group. It was like the time he had come tearing off Banks' Hill. The action, the feeling of motion, *of entering the arena*, replaced the indecision and frustration of following in a line of men.

"Where is he?" he cried. He saw their looks and didn't wait. Bare-chested but booted, he leaped free of the ridge and sliced into the boiling waters. As he went under, he knew that it must be Logan. He let the current sweep him along, guiding himself as if he were a canoe in white waters. He saw the rolling body rise and kicked with all his power. He reached out and caught a pack strap.

Sickeningly he felt himself being pulled down as the weight of Logan's gear rolled them both under in the mass

of turbulent water. He summoned all his strength to pull
the pack off. They were going down toward the deeper
water. His lungs were bursting. He had to let go. Frantically he burst to the surface. He sucked in a fresh lungful
of air, then saw Logan about two feet away. He grabbed
the hair, but he knew he'd never be able to get the pack
off. If he could just maneuver them over to the shore and
catch hold of a branch. The water surged over him. He
came up sputtering and coughing. His body strained at
full strength, gliding with the water yet frantically kicking
to get to the side. Then his skull cracked. Something solid
and large. Pain shot through his head and he felt the
water seep over him. His grip relaxed and the body slipped
away. His mind reeled. For a second he blacked out.

The current boiled him up as the water surged over
some obstacle. It forced him up and rolled his head into
the air. His mouth opened and he gulped water, choked,
coughed, and his head cleared. He looked once but the
body was gone. Slowly he struggled toward shore, his
strength sapped and his boots dragging him. Treading
water against the current, he swung up to grab an overhead branch. He missed and sank back, bouncing off a
rock and feeling the water catch at him again. Panic began to choke his mind. He flailed at the water, but then,
from nowhere, a hand grabbed his wrist; he felt himself
slow, stop, and the current swirled around him.

The Chief was strung far out over the water holding to
a branch. The Indian's face contorted with the strain. Inch
by inch he pulled against the suction of the water, his
body almost horizontal. The helmet fell off and the long
hair blew free. Then Hawkins' feet hit bottom and he
sank down in the shallow overflow. Slowly the exhaustion
faded and he became aware that the men had come up
and surrounded him. They were pointing upstream. He
raised his eyes and followed their directions. Then he
knew what had hit his head. It was the bridge.

Hawkins sat in a bamboo patch, holding the handset.
He dreaded what he would have to report to battalion. In
silence he cursed himself. He knew he should have taken
the point. He knew they should have gone downstream.
He knew if he had been on point, they would have found
the bridge. *He knew if he had any guts they would have*

stayed on top of the hill to begin with.

LeBlanc came up and sat down a short distance away on another clump of grass. He put his pack behind him, propped up his shotgun, and bent to tie his boots. Then he leaned over and rested his head on his arm.

Hawkins saw the mustache droop from the water. The Sergeant looked just like any other tired man. Somehow he didn't seem like the same sergeant. The Lieutenant gazed around and saw they were all exhausted—exhausted and waiting. They were waiting for him to report to battalion. Only he could report to battalion. He moved his thumb to squeeze the transmit button and suddenly he laughed.

"Fuck it." He looked at LeBlanc; he looked at the men. He thought of all the other times that day when he had looked back and forth between these two. He thought about the new boy, Banks, killed back on that hill. And he thought about Logan. They wouldn't even find his body.

"Fuck it," he whispered. What did it matter now? He couldn't understand why, but he felt as if a great weight had been lifted from him.

—"Northtide, Northtide, this is Delta Two."—

The Three was calm. Captain Calahan came on. He was not calm. Later the colonel came on.

They all said the same thing. What had *he* done? It was *his* platoon. *He* was in charge. He was in for a lot of explaining. How had it happened? Why had he done this? Why hadn't he done that? But nothing was said about Sergeant LeBlanc.

For long moments he sat, just sat and stared at the water. He looked at LeBlanc drooped over his pack.

He'd come here because it was his duty. He'd come to do a job, because somebody had to do that job. Yes, Arnie, that's why he'd come. Because there was a job to do. This was the arena.

"Fuck it. Just plain fuck it all." He said it loud, laughing. Abruptly he stood and yelled it as loud as he could. *"FUCK IT!"*

The faces turned up in surprise. Joseley looked up and Hawkins caught his eye. A quick glance went between them; Joseley turned his face and looked over to the Chief. Chief was grinning. For a moment Hawkins stood

looking at the faces surrounding him. He saw fear and
weariness. But he saw they were waiting, waiting for
whatever he would decide.

"We're going back up! Pass the word and move out."
He swung on his pack and walked off. Joseley had to
scramble to collect the radio and catch up. Somehow the
Lieutenant never even bothered to look at LeBlanc.

As Hawkins splashed back down the stream his decision
swelled up in him like a great freedom. It filled his belly
like food; he felt good, intensely good, as keen as a knife.

What was it? he wondered. It was nothing. He tried to
figure what was different. The men moved at once; they
scrambled. And he could see it in their eyes. LeBlanc had
simply stood up and started moving the men into line.

When they reached the base of the hill, Hawkins gave
orders to cock rifles and move upwards. As he heard the
bolts slam, he could see their confidence. And he knew it
had flowed from himself. Then he looked up and waved
his hand. The platoon moved forward.

Wilson

When they returned to the hill, there were no gooks at
the top—only foxholes full of water. But the Chief went
to each hole, sniffing intently. Finally he shrugged. "I
don't know, Lieutenant. It's too wet to smell 'em." The
men gathered and stood in a half circle as the rain continued to fall. They were scared, and they watched the Lieutenant wearily.

Hawkins read their feelings, but his voice came like a
chisel. "Take your same holes. You all know we're in
trouble. If the gooks are here, they're sure to have seen us
go down and come back up. They'll know we're cut off. I
want you to bail the water out of the foxholes with your
helmets, and I want you to start digging. I'm going to
surround this place with a ring of artillery fire so close
you can kiss the shrapnel. I want *deep* holes. Any questions?"

There was silence.

"Get it done." He turned abruptly and started to dig.

By the end of the following day the rain still fell, and
the men had shared their last cans of peanut butter. For
once there was no thirst, but now hunger rumbled with

the fear of the night. Even during the day visibility had been bad in the mist and low clouds; and the men huddled in their hooches and stared over the gunsights down into the treeline. They waited.

In the late afternoon the Lieutenant called the squad leaders and told them he would bring night defensive artillery even closer that night. They nodded mutely and moved away through the mist to their muddy hooches. Only Wilson lingered a moment.

"Lieutenant, sir. Could I speak to you a moment?"

Hearing the tone in Wilson's voice, the Lieutenant instinctively knew there was a problem, and he nodded silently. They crawled into the hooch, and the Lieutenant tried to ease the distance between them. "What's on your mind?" Hawkins' voice was open.

"Well, I . . . uh . . . gotta little problem," he stammered, crawling into the bunker.

Hawkins saw the troubled face and heard him grope for words. He felt in his pocket and found his one unopened C-ration cigarette pack. "Wanna smoke?"

"Yes, sir." Wilson reached eagerly since his were gone, remembering their night in Khe Sanh.

"Last dry ones."

Jesus. Why can't all Chucks be like this? Wilson thought. He lit the cigarette nervously, stalling for time, then exhaled sharply. "Sir, you know I'm married and I gotta little baby, a girl."

Wilson saw the Lieutenant nod, but his words stuck.

"Yeah, I'm not married." Hawkins was speaking. "Almost was before I came over, but that's finished now." Hawkins smiled.

"Oh, I'm sorry, sir." Wilson was amazed. The officer was telling him about *his* problems.

"Sir, I don't wanna bother you. Maybe I'd better get on. . . ."

Hawkins held up his hand. "Gotta picture of your little girl?"

"You wanna see, sir?" Wilson was genuinely surprised. Fumbling eagerly, he pulled out his wallet and carefully unwrapped the plastic case. With great pride he took out a picture of an infant on a rug. "Isn't she cute?"

The Lieutenant took it, glancing briefly but noting the beaming pride in Wilson's face. "Real nice, looks just like her old man—she's a beauty."

Wilson took the picture back and gazed lovingly for a long minute. Finally he kissed the picture and put it back in his wallet. "My pretty little girl, Brenda. Brenda's her name. She's the greatest in the world—smart, too."

"Is that your wife?" Hawkins pointed at the open wallet.

Wilson seemed to sag visibly at the words. "Yes, sir."

It was a high school graduation photo. In the white cap, mortar board, and gown, the girl looked sweet and demure. She had pretty features and light-caramel skin, and her hair hung straight with only a slight curl at the shoulder.

"Nice."

Wilson looked shyly at the Lieutenant. "Thank you, sir."

"Now what's the problem?"

Wilson looked down. "Well, uhhh, you see she's been writing me that she's not getting her allotment check."

"Did you take one out?"

"Yes, sir. I most certainly did. Back at Camp Pendleton, before we came over. And I even had it checked at Phu Bai when we got here."

"But she's not receiving it?"

"No, sir."

"What have you done to check on it?"

"Sir, I tried everything. I reminded the paymaster in Quang Tri before we left. I asked the Gunny at least a dozen times. When Top came out to the bush I asked him to check, but she still hasn't got it."

"Did you write her?"

"Oh, yes, I did." Then the dam broke and the words rushed out. "But, you see, she thinks it's me. She thinks that I'm the one who's not sending her money. I've asked Top to check when he's come out to the bush, but she still hasn't gotten it. Lieutenant, she thinks I'm doing it on purpose. I don't know; I just don't know what's happening." He paused and his eyes dropped sadly. "She's already taken the baby and she's gone back to live with her mother. She says she doesn't have the money to keep our place. I've tried everything, and they still don't send it. There just ain't nothing more I can do out here in the bush and on the road." His voice caught and he paused a second. "I ain't had a letter in a long time but her last one—she . . . she says I don't love her anymore." Wilson turned his face away and put his hand over his eyes.

"Top Goresuch?"

"Y . . . yes, sir." Wilson's voice quivered.

Hawkins turned his head, remembering the stories about Top Goresuch, the company first sergeant. He came to the bush all smiles, asking about the men's problems but then never did anything. The Lieutenant reached out and put his hand on Wilson's shoulder. "Wilson, as soon as we get off this duty, I promise I'll send you to the rear to get your allotment straightened out. And if they don't square it away, I'll go back and see about it myself. I swear I will."

"Thanks, sir." Wilson's moist eyes wavered to the Lieutenant's hand. "Well, I better be going, sir."

"Why don't you have some coffee with me? I've got a packet left."

"That's all right, sir. I better go." He said it quickly to hide his embarrassment. The officer had touched him. No officer or NCO in the whole Marine Corps had ever done that.

"Aw, hold off." Hawkins covered the hooch opening to hide the light, lit a heat tab, and shook the coffee packet into an empty B-3 can, one of the old type that had cookies and cocoa in it. Wilson smiled faintly.

They squatted in silence as the coffee heated. The smell filled the little hooch, and Hawkins took out a pocket flask and poured a dab of bourbon in the coffee.

"Man!" Wilson gulped, staring unbelievingly.

"What I'd like right now," Hawkins said as he leaned back, "is a great big breakfast like my grandmother used to fix." He looked off dreamily. "These big eggs, sunny-side up. My grandmother was the only person I ever knew who could cook eggs sunny-side up without them tasting greasy, and still have them done on top. And then there'd be a big piece of East Tennessee smoked ham with red-eye gravy and grits with lots of butter."

"Grits! You eat grits, Lieutenant?"

Lieutenant saw the look of amazement on his face and laughed. "Sure, I love grits. Nothin's gooder'n grits."

The coffee bubbled and Hawkins gingerly picked up the can and took a sip, blowing first and sipping in to cool it.

"Ahhhhh, that's good." He passed the can-cup over to Wilson. The heavy aroma filled his nostrils and Wilson felt his head swim.

The mustached lip pursed and blew gently on the dark muddy liquid. "Man that's good." Wilson felt the rich warmth slide down. He dropped the wallet and cupped the can with both hands, savoring its warmth.

Hawkins looked down and picked up another picture which had slipped from the wallet. He started to look at it.

Instantly Wilson jumped and snatched the picture from the Lieutenant's hand. "Oh!" His hands froze and his eyes shot up to Hawkins. "Oh, sir, I'm sorry . . . I—I didn't mean to. . . ." The whites of his eyes showed wide and he gulped twice.

Hawkins laughed nervously. "That's all right, it's none of my business. I'm sorry."

"No, no, sir, please." Wilson hesitated and looked down at the picture. Then, biting his lip, he awkwardly thrust it at Hawkins.

Slowly Hawkins raised his hand. Out of curiosity he struck his lighter to see better. It was a three-quarter shot of a beautiful girl in a miniskirt. She was tall and slim, but her hips flared gracefully and her breasts were high and proud. Her hair was in the natural Afro style and it set off her large doe eyes. Her face didn't smile but it showed glistening white teeth. It was barely recognizable as the same girl. The Lieutenant slowly let out a low whistle.

"Do you like it?" Wilson was amazed.

"I think she's beautiful," Hawkins said sincerely.

"Wow," Wilson murmured involuntarily and rocked back. This Chuck, this white officer, likes Sylvia like that. Then, before he could think, he spoke again. "Sir? You like the *Afro?*"

Hawkins looked up sharply and frowned. Immediately, embarrassment welled up in Wilson, and he was horrified at what he had said.

"Yes, I do." The Lieutenant paused and looked off. "She's tough. Reminds me of a girl I used to know." He glanced at the Omega and then once again looked at the picture. "I like it very much. You're lucky. We'd better get that allotment." Abruptly, he handed the picture back

and peered out of the hooch into the fading twilight.
"Look, the clouds have broken. Come on, time to start the
arty." He squirmed out from under the low canvas.

Suddenly an orange flash on the horizon to the north
caught their eye. Then long minutes before they felt the
tremor, the orange flashes blossomed into a line. One after
another in rapid staccato, they winked and lit the sky until
there was a row of orange flashes outlining the mountains.

"Oh my God!" Wilson's voice quivered in alarm.

The Lieutenant stood mute, as if in a trance, and then
the burgeoning thunder washed over him in long rolls.
Unconsciously he glanced up, knowing they would be invisible at 30,000 feet but looking by instinct anyway.
Abruptly he gasped; the moonlight had etched out three
tiny vapor trails against the darkening sky.

"Sir, is that . . . ? Is it . . . ?"

"Yeah," Hawkins breathed, turning slowly to Wilson,
"That's them all right."

"Oooh! That means the gooks are . . ."

Hawkins

Later Hawkins stood on the crest of the hill, clad only
in his tiger shorts. The rain drizzled around him. Handset
in hand, he yelled, "Put on your flak jackets and helmets.
Get down in your holes. I'm bringing it in close. There'll
be a solid ring of fire around us." Then he spoke into the
handset. A few minutes lapsed and the radio spoke back.
"Rounds out," Hawkins yelled and jumped down into the
hole he had dug with Joseley.

WHOOMZT WHOOMZT WHOOMZT.

The rounds were more than two hundred and fifty
yards away, but the men cringed and huddled as the blasts
echoed around them. Hawkins had just started to call it
closer when LeBlanc came up. Each man paused for a
moment and looked intensely at the other.

"Lieutenant, you're not going to bring that in any closer
right now, are you?"

Hawkins hesitated, feeling the old pressure, then looked
away. "Why not?"

"Well, Lieutenant, I'm all for bringing it right in when
you need it, but there ain't no need now. Just needlessly
endangering some lives."

For a long time Hawkins didn't reply. The two men looked at each other. He had been flushed with the action on the trail below, but now he'd begun to wonder anew.

"Sergeant, the closer it is the quicker we can get it going when we need it."

"Look, Lieutenant, you can register it out there and then bring it in close when the time calls for it. Just don't make any sense to bring it in here right now."

For an instant he stared at the Sergeant, then suddenly all the pent-up anger and frustration burst forth.

"SHUT THE FUCK UP." His eyes blazed. "God damn it, Sergeant, I run this Goddamn platoon! If you've got advice, state it and get the fuck out!"

The relief was exquisite. Then he felt an onrushing realization that he had lost his temper, yelled a senseless obscenity, and the Sergeant would be angry and hostile. Slowly the relief gave way and dismay welled in his brain as he anticipated the sergeant's reaction.

But LeBlanc dropped his eyes and fidgeted in the mud with his toe. "I . . . I'm sorry about that, sir. Sometimes I guess I'm pretty hot-headed, I say things I shouldn't."

Hawkins stared at him in amazement. Finally he found his voice. "Ah . . . that's okay . . . no sweat."

"Yes, sir." For some reason Hawkins nodded. Immediately LeBlanc turned and walked rapidly away.

Hawkins sat dumbfounded at the Sergeant's reaction. It was almost anticlimactic. He had felt an exhilarating satisfaction at his outburst, as if he had lanced a long-painful boil. But as the passion of the moment passed, he began to realize the power of anger. But it troubled him. Was this what it took to be a Marine? It occurred to him that this was how the Captain would have handled LeBlanc. And this was how LeBlanc handled the men. Hawkins held the handset and stared out across the mist. Would he become like them?

The crackle of the radio snapped him back. He stood up and saw Joseley grinning. Hawkins' face broke wide.

"Get down in those holes! This is coming in close!"

IV

In the Rear

1

Hawkins

Three days later they made it across the river. The truck came and took them to Camp Carroll. The whole starved platoon crowded into the back of the two open six-bys and yelled at everybody that went by.

"Hot dog, we're gonna get some hot chow!"

"Look at them wooden hooches."

"Jesus H. Christ. There it is. A mess hall."

"*Yaaaaahooo.*"

The filthy, muddy, ragged Marines leaped off the truck and whooped for joy.

"Let me at it."

"Sarge, have them stack their gear over there by that hooch and I'll check on the chow. Bring them on up to the mess hall as soon as you're ready."

The Lieutenant looked questioningly at the big mess hall and then finally went around to the enlisted side. He grinned at the separate dining room for officers. Really back in the rear here, he thought. He glanced down at the Omega. Just six. Should be able to feed them okay. He was about to push through the door when a fat man in white cook's T-shirt stopped him.

"Secured, buddy."

"Wha . . ." Hawkins stopped as if someone had slapped him.

"I said 'secured.' Chow's over."

"I'm just going in to check on. . . ."

"You ain't going *nowhere* in there, buddy." The fat man leaned over menacingly. "Now shut the fucking door and get out."

Hawkins was doubly shocked. He'd been in the bush for so long that he'd forgotten he wouldn't be recognized. He unconsciously stepped back, then realized what he must look like. He grinned to himself. He could handle the fat man, but he had a sinking feeling that the fat man wasn't going to be the trouble. He took off his helmet and carefully pulled out his soft cover with the bar on it and put it on his head. "What did you say, Marine?"

"Oh, uhh, excuse me, sir. I didn't know. The officers' mess is over on the other side. If the Lieutenant will go over there, I'm sure they will have some chow."

"I'm not interested in feeding myself just yet. I've got a whole platoon. Where's the NCO in charge?" He went in and found an old salty staff sergeant.

"You the NCOIC?"

"Yeah, Lieutenant, what can I do for you?" he asked flippantly.

"I've got forty men outside just come in from the bush. Haven't even had C's for five days. Can you feed them?"

The staff sergeant looked at the door as the dirty, drooling mob swirled up against the screen. They had smelled the food and were just about to go wild. The sergeant's mood changed radically; his face went sour. "No, we can't."

"Why not?" Hawkins had begun to get angry. He looked down at his watch and around the mess hall; it was only a few minutes past six. He knew that six must be the cutting-off time, but there were some men still eating.

The sergeant saw his look. "No food on the line at all. And besides some of your men ain't got on blouses."

"Ain't got blouses! This is a *bush* platoon!"

"Sorry, sir. Orders from the colonel himself. Everyone must have a blouse on in this mess hall."

Hawkins' anger was rising rapidly and he struggled not to blow his cool. He thought quickly, Well, we can eat in shifts. The ones who have shirts can eat first, and then they'll come out and give their shirts to the ones who haven't got any. "Okay, okay, I'll get the blouses. Now how about cooking up some soup or something for them."

"Sorry, sir, it's against the regulations; I only have the fixed rations for the regular meals."

The Lieutenant spotted a pile of sandwiches. "What about that stuff?" His voice had lowered a decibel or two.

"Oh, no, sir, those are the mid-rats for the officers on night watch in the command bunker."

"Are you shitting me?" Suddenly he felt that yelling was just the Marine Corps way. "Get me the Goddamn mess officer!"

Hearing the voices, Chief had slipped in the door and now grabbed the Lieutenant's arm. "It's okay, sir, let him go."

Hawkins fixed Chief with an incredulous stare.

"We've run into this before. As a matter of fact, I expected it. Don't worry, we'll get some chow," Chief said.

"But where? How? This is where all the food is."

"Come on, sir, I'll show you," Chief said hesitantly.

The troops were already running away in the twilight and Chief and Hawkins followed.

"What is this, Chief? Where are we going?" Out of the corner of his eye, he saw LeBlanc going into the Staff NCO section.

"You'll see, sir, just wait. The men appreciate your trying to get us chow, and they're pissed, too, but that mess hall route is hopeless, and besides they couldn't wait even if you did get the mess officer to order more food cooked."

They walked down to a large open pit which was piled with rubble of all sorts. The men were swarming over it like ants, rummaging, tossing things in the air and yelling.

"Hey, a can of beans!"

"Man, cheese and crackers."

Chief looked hesitantly at Hawkins. "It's the garbage dump, Lieutenant. You can always find a lot of unopened chow here."

Hawkins' mouth hung open for a minute in disbelief, then his face gave way to bitterness. "Jesus Christ. The United States' finest fighting men. We can send men to the moon and give every First Cavalry private a helicopter, but we can't feed the Marines in Vietnam. The U.S. Marine Corps picking over a garbage dump."

Chief nudged the Lieutenant. "Ah, excuse me, sir. I'm a little hungry myself, and in a minute it's going to be picked clean."

Hawkins shook his head and forced his gaze from the dump to the Chief. Then he grinned. "What are we waiting for?"

The Platoon

After Khe Sanh was abandoned, the company's new duty was convoy security, guarding the supply trucks that rolled every day between Da Nang and the far outposts. The usual run was along Route 9 from the Rockpile (later known as Camp Vandergrift, which replaced Khe Sanh as the westernmost base) to Dong Ha or Quang Tri. Normally they slept at the Rockpile but sometimes anywhere along the way: Quang Tri, Dong Ha, Cam Lo, Camp Carroll, the Rockpile, LZ Stud, Ca Lu, LZ Hawk, and at the end of the line Khe Sanh.

The company technique was to load a couple of squads onto an open truck. Machine guns over the cab to the front or to the rear. Men sat in the middle, facing out, ready to fire. The troop trucks were spread out at intervals through the convoy, hopefully a radio with each. If the situation was bad and one was lucky, a tank or an ONTOS would come along and precede the lead truck. If the convoy was hit, SOP was to floorboard it, go like hell, and fire everything like crazy. If a single truck was knocked out, the next one just shoved it aside and kept on rolling. Should the whole convoy become halted, the troops immediately dismounted and the fight was on.

Most of the time the runs were uneventful, the hardship being the crowded, cramped bed, the jarring ride, and worst of all the dust or rain from which there was no escape. The dust rose in thick choking clouds powdering the men an even tan. But the nights were good. Quang Tri and Dong Ha had regular mess halls, beer, marijuana, even *women*. But the Rockpile was pretty far out. It was a primitive outpost, which took its name from a nearby mountain of rock. The rock was a weird-looking thing, almost perfectly round at the base with the sides rising straight up from the flat ground around. Another formation about a klik away was called the Witch's Tit.

Chief and Wilson, Big John and Red, wound their way through the bunkers and tents, which were also covered with dust, and joined the end of a long line.

"Shit, it'll take us forever to get through this line," Wilson muttered.

"You want to eat, you got to wait. That's the way it is," Chief replied, pulling his jungle hat brim down to make sure no officer saw his hair.

They shuffled along, joking and talking, slowly creeping toward the mess tent.

On impulse, Chief bent down and peered into a low

tent. It was large and covered a square room which was
cut about five feet down into the earth. The canvas was
rolled up from the ground and left about a foot and a half
of space for the air to blow through. Inside were tables
and chairs. A crude bar had been set up at one end. "Hey,
looky there."

The others bent to see but couldn't make it out for a
moment because of the darkness of the tent. Then they let
out a soft low curse.

"Man, that piss me *ouff*."

"Goddamn, look at that. Stateside liquor served up for
the high and mighty officers by one jolly ass-lickin' PFC."

"Can you believe that?"

"Cocktails before dinner."

Wilson turned away and they moved on, not wanting
to see. "That's the kind of thing that really gets me. Here
we stand in line, fucking shit-bird peons, enlisted dogs,
waiting to eat, and the officers are getting iced drinks for
twenty-five cents. And our fucking captain limited us to
two beers to be graciously issued. That back-stabbin' Gunny's in there too. That motherfucker was acting like he
was doing us such a great big favor getting us two lousy
beers. Shit. Hot beer."

"Gunny is a sorry motha."

Wilson's anger kept rising. "That's the Marine Corps for
you, real justice, real equality. Enlisted dogs can't buy no
liquor. Officers can get it; NCO's can get it. And all the
fuck we get is beer. Even in the Goddamn rear at Quang
Tri—just beer."

"Knock off that shit, willya. There ain't nowhere in all
Vee-et Nam that a Marine below sergeant can buy liquor,"
Chief said. "So forget about it and let's go and eat. That's
the way it is; that's the way it's going to be and it ain't
gonna do any good getting mad."

"Least I didn't see Lieutenant Hawkins in there," Wilson
muttered.

Chief looked over his shoulder. Hawkins was just walking into the tent; Chief turned quickly, saying nothing to
the others.

After about a twenty-minute wait, they came to the serving area and picked up a paper plate and cup.

"Getting real fancy. Paper plates and paper cups."

"Yeah, just like a fuckin' picnic," Wilson said.

The mess hall consisted of two tents, one partially covering the stacks of boxes and cans of food and the other serving as a galley. The front was open and in the back were
four gasoline-burning stoves. There was a motley assortment of large pots and kettles.

In front, empty wooden crates had been stacked on end
in a row, forming a serving line. The first server was a
greasy man in a soiled T-shirt. He was sweating profusely.
The day was normal for Vietnam, about ninety degrees in
the shade. But what made him sweat was the great ball
of heat which rolled out from the tent where the four
gas stoves were burning steadily.

"Must be nice to be a cook in Korea," the Chief said,
with a wide grin.

The man flung a piece of nondescript meat on his plate
and said, "Just get your chow and keep moving, wise
guy."

Chief's eyes grinned, but apparently the man was too
tired or too hot to respond.

"Hey, man, what is that stuff?" Wilson asked.

"Beef—what do you think?" the man answered irri-
tably.

"Sort of thought it looked like fried waterboo shit to
me," Chief sang out from down the line.

They all laughed, but the sweaty cook just grumbled,
"Take it or leave it."

"Ih'll eat it, man. Ih'll eat all you got," Big John said
quickly. "Doan pay no 'tention to them doods, they jus'
razzin'. We all so hungry after C's tha' this'll be a feace'."

The greasy T-shirted cook flickered at the appreciation
and gave Big John an extra piece.

They received canned boiled potatoes, runny corn, and
thick hunks of bread. At the end of the line were two gal-
lon-sized cans, one of jelly and one of peanut butter. An
assortment of knives and spoons stuck out of each and
were laying messily around the wooden-crate top. Each of
the cans was about half empty, and it was hard to tell
which was which because the spoons had been dipped
back and forth so many times that they had effectively
mixed the top inch-and-a-half layers of the two.

They had their choice of watery coffee or watery cocoa.

The eaters fanned out through the area, sitting on what

they could: bunkers, crates, the ground. The hoods of several trucks were very popular because they made nice stand-up tables.

An empty oil drum served as a garbage can, and it was mounded over with empty plates and garbage. The ground around it was rapidly assuming the place of the garbage can.

Chief's eyes scanned the area. Noting the crowd around the coffee pot, he moved around to the far side of a bunker.

Wilson and Red followed him automatically.

"Wha' you come clear ovhur heahr fo'?"

They sat down and attacked the food fanatically. For a while nothing was said. They all were absorbed in their eating. Finally Big John slowed and said again, "Hey, Chief, why'd you come clear ovhur heahr? Now Ih go' t' go all the way back fo' coffee." He got up and left.

Chief looked without mirth at Wilson. "When you gonna teach him?" he asked sharply.

Wilson looked blank.

Chief read the face. "Didn't you hear that they been shelling this place every day about dinner time? Ever wonder what they're aiming at?"

Wilson dropped his eyes. "Yeah, I heard, Chief. But uhh . . . but, well, there hasn't been any since we came and I didn't really think much about it."

Chief's face fell into the Indian mask. "Forget it."

Big John came back and attacked his plate again. "This chow wouldn't be much back in the worl' but shur seems like a feace' now."

"You said it, Hulk. Seems like I never tasted anything so good," Red said.

After finishing, they walked back contentedly through the throng of eaters and tossed their plates in the general direction of the garbage can.

"Hey Red-Top, you gotta cig'rette?" Big John drawled at Red who slouched along picking his teeth.

"Um-hum," Red murmured.

"Well giv' it t'me, then."

"Fuck you, Hulk. I only have one left."

"Man, you betta gimme tha' cigarette."

"I am not about to give you this cigarette. In fact I am

going to smoke it myself, right now." Red reached in his jungle shirt and pulled out the five pack of C-ration cigarettes, flipped the last one in his mouth, and threw the empty box at Big John.

"Why, you li'l mothafucka'."

Big John jumped up and charged Red. But Red was waiting and he danced aside, chopping Big John in the ribs, laughing insanely. Big John let out a roar and, as if the sudden pain speeded his reflexes, whirled and reached out for Red.

Maybe because he was laughing, Red was a split second too slow in leaping back. Big John's hand smacked around Red's forearm, and in one motion Red stopped, changed directions, and was yanked into the air as if he were a rag doll. Big John's free hand zipped out and snatched the cigarette from Red's mouth as he flew by. Big John let go, pulled out his Zippo, and was inhaling before Red hit the ground.

But Red was no longer a "newboy," and picking himself up, he immediately looked for a weapon. He sprang up, seized a helmet, and hurled it with all his might at the back of the head which was blowing out the smoke. The helmet thunked into the head with the same sound as if it had hit a tree—and about the same effect, except to knock the cigarette to the ground. Big John shook his head once and looked down for the cigarette, but Red was already scooting away, howling.

Chief stood watching, with the leering grin from ear to ear, when Big John started to charge again. "Hey, Jackson."

"Huh?" Big John swung around.

"Here, 'fore one of you idiots kills somebody." Chief flipped his wrist sidearm and shot another pack at the big man.

"Thanks, Injun." Big John caught the cigarettes against his belly and made a face at Red.

"Wil, you see that ARVN battery over by the far gate?"

"You mean the South Vietnamese artillery? Yeah, I saw them."

"Well, let's go pay them a visit."

Wilson looked at Chief, saw the wild faraway look. "Oh . . . here we go again."

"If yoah'r thinkin' 'bout smokin'—forget it. They ain't got any." Big John's voice cut in from behind.

Chief jerked around to Big John. "How do you know?"

"Ih already tried."

"Well, shit. They got any liquor?"

"Colt Fo'ty-fiv."

"Ahh, that fucking gook whiskey is made out of turpentine and formaldehyde."

"Yeah, but it'll still curl your toes," Wilson stuck in, laughing.

"Colt Forty-five," Red said. "That's beer. I wonder how they ever got that name and gave it to the whiskey they make."

"Same way they got 'boo-coo,' or *beaucoup*, from the French, I suppose," the Chief said half to himself. Then he turned and spoke directly to Big John. "Those South Vietnamese always got grass. You sure they ain't got any?"

"Pos'tiv'. They done sold it all to the doggies," Big John replied.

"Doggies? Oh, yeah, I *do* remember. They got those one hundred and fifty-five self-propelled . . . let's go see what we can steal from the doggies."

The other three faces lighted immediately at the prospect of fleecing the Army.

"They got boo-coo geahr," Big John said.

They ambled casually into the Army area, trying to look as though they were just passing through. All the time their eyes were darting, looking for choice objects, their minds planning avenues of approach and escape routes. One of the oldest rules of the Marine Corps is "Thou shalt steal from the Army." Suddenly all four stopped, rooted to the ground, their eyes fixed on one Army private who walked past them with a segmented metal tray. It was several moments after he passed before they could speak.

"Did you see that chow!"

"Holy Christ. That dood had *fryad chicken*."

"And mashed potatoes with gravy."

"Green peas and salad."

"Tha' son of a bitch even had col' milk. Man, tha' pisses me ouff."

"I can't believe that. I just can't believe that one little

artillery battery eat so good and we eat so bad," Wilson muttered aloud.

"Ih though' we ate pretty good till I saw that," Big John said mournfully.

Chief

Chief came up to the wire around the Vietnamese artillery camp and called softly to the closest man.

"Hey, hey, Papa-san."

The little man was squatting on his heels, knees up, rear end about two inches from the ground. He and three others held little bowls to their mouths and raked their chopsticks with quick furtive motions. Between them an overturned helmet was filled with cooked rice; several dishes lay around it. One appeared to be some kind of spinach and the other fishheads. Then Chief's nose wrinkled at something that smelled like a cross between dead fish and rotten olive oil. *Nuoc Mam.* Chief knew what that was: the foul-smelling sauce that the Vietnamese eat on everything—morning, noon, and night.

The men looked up warily.

"Chow Ong," Chief said.

Their faces brightened instantly. "Ah, *Chow Ong.*" They began to babble.

With his slender hips, long black hair, dusky skin, and high cheekbones, the Chief was often mistaken for a Vietnamese. The fact that he wore tapered ARVN pants because the Marine issue were too big, reinforced the impression. Even when it became apparent that he was an American soldier the Vietnamese still regarded him with special interest, a fact Chief never failed to exploit.

"Hey, Papa-san, *Ong có* whiskey?"

The man grinned and motioned to the back of his hooch. Chief waited and the man returned with two fifths wrapped in tissue paper.

"You got P?" the man whispered.

This guy's really playing all the tricks, Chief thought, looks like I'm going to have to bargain.

Chief snorted to himself: The trick was to ask for P, Vietnamese piasters, because all the bush Marines had was MPC, Military Payment Script. When the GI said no, the Vietnamese would fake dismay, claiming MPC was no good, but as a favor the Vietnamese would take it—thus giving him a start to jack the price up. Of course, he actually preferred the MPC because the official rate of exchange was 118 P for one U.S. MPC dollar, but the black market exchange rate in Da Nang was 145 P for one MPC dollar, and 210 for one U.S. real green dollar.

MPC was used exclusively by American forces "incountry" to pay the troops so they could purchase from the PX, the purpose being to control black market inflation. The black market demand for MPC arose because the Vietnamese could give the MPC to the Koreans in Vietnam who had access to the American PX. With the MPC the Koreans would then buy the stuff for the Vietnamese charging the Vietnamese about double what it cost in the PX. Because of the shortage of retail goods, particularly electrical, optical, and electronic, the Vietnamese could either keep it or more likely sell it again for three or four times the original price.

Chief knew all this but feigned ignorance. "Ah, yes, I have P," he lied.

The man's face twitched a little, but Chief's was frozen in the deadpan Indian mask.

"Maybe you want MPC?" Chief asked innocently.

"Okay, MPC numba one."

"How much?"

"Ten dolla."

"Ten dollars!" Chief shrieked in mock amazement. *"Suc Moi.* Never happen." The Chief's face looked very sorrowful. "Give you fifteen dollars for two. I have tee-tee money."

"No. American GI got boo-coo money. Twenty dollars for two."

"Colt Forty-five number ten."

"No, no, numba one."

Chief pulled out his wallet, from which he had already extracted all but the fifteen dollars. He held it open for the man to see. "Fifteen dollars MPC for two bottle."

The man hesitated. "No can do."

"Papa-san want Salem?"

The Vietnamese eyes opened just a little wider, and the Chief smiled to himself.

"I give you fifteen dollar and two pack Salem."

"Okay. Can do."

They bent and completed their little transaction underneath the barbed wire.

Calahan

Captain Calahan called the three platoon commanders and their platoon sergeants to his CP. He liked to gather them all once a day and pass on the orders; but in the bush it was dangerous to get all the leaders close together at once. One mortar.

Calahan had the lifer's fetish about keeping his hair short. When he had his chance he would have the sides skinned down practically to the bone with just a little brush left on the top. With blond hair the result was like a round bullet sticking from the shoulders. Had his manner been a little lighter, however, his square jaw and blue eyes would have made him almost good-looking.

"We got some trucks and we're going to get a bath," Calahan said to the group.

Immediately smiles broke all around.

"Hoo Boy. A whole week of convoy security dust and haven't had a bath."

"Jesus, that's great. I been a dustbag long enough."

"First," Calahan held up his hand, "I'm going to make some changes."

A hush fell at once and Calahan secretly smiled at the quick anticipation in the faces. "You know Lieutenant Diandre is going to rotate next week." He glanced at Diandre and saw the ear-to-ear grin. "And since he's got short-timers' fever so bad, I'm sending him on incountry R 'n' R." Slowly Calahan smiled. "Today."

"Thanks, Skipper." Diandre grinned even wider. He'd been First Platoon commander his whole tour and in the bush most of that time. He'd even gone through Hue during Tet. He was good, but he had become bitter. Now he only wanted to get home.

"That leaves us with only two officers in the company." Calahan's face was solemn as he looked at Hawkins. "Le Blanc."

"Sir?"

"I'm shifting you over to First Platoon. You'll take over as platoon commander."

"Hey, baby. They're *all* yours," Diandre crooned happily. "Every last fucking one of 'em."

"Lieutenant Hawkins"—Calahan's voice was dry—"I reckon you've had a nursemaid long enough. You're broke in now." Calahan heard the group laugh, but his eyes fixed on Hawkins without mirth. *More than broke in,* he thought. Calahan had monitored the platoon radio occasionally during the period when Hawkins had been stuck on the hill, and he had begun to feel an uneasy caution about the Lieutenant.

"Okay, listen up." Calahan's voice cut hard across the laughter and his own thoughts. "The truck will take us down to the bend in the river below LZ Stud. First and Third platoons will bathe first while Second is on security. Now get this straight. I want every man well shaven. No sideburns."

LeBlanc stirred uneasily and Calahan read his thoughts. "And *only* neat, trim military mustaches." His fingers jabbed out and punched each word. They were hostile to haircuts he knew, but if he let up, there would be Fu Manchus and Beatle sideburns all over.

"Captain, the men like a little face hair." LeBlanc spoke quietly.

"No!" Calahan cut him off sharply. "You know my policy. I will not tolerate any more excess hair than the regulations allow. You're out in the bush; it only gets dirty and draws lice. On this duty we pass through rear areas and Colonel Ryan or anybody may see us. We *will* be neat." Calahan bristled, and he glanced at the group, daring an objection. "Now then, any questions?" Calahan paused, looking inquiringly. No one spoke.

"And make sure your Nigras wash," he said flatly. The others merely nodded, but the Captain saw an immediate flash of resentment on Hawkins' face. Calahan never ceased to wonder at the people from liberal Eastern backgrounds; they were all so pretentious about race. "If you don't keep after them, they'll skip right out," he added, looking directly at Hawkins.

"Sir, I don't. . . ."

"Don't tell me, Lieutenant Hawkins. I know. I've seen them all my life. They're naturally dirty."

"Wha . . . that's ridiculous," Hawkins muttered under his breath.

"Lieutenant Hawkins, I'm not going to belabor the

point, but for your benefit and because you don't know, I'll explain. When you get to the water, you watch. You will see, number one, that most Nigras can't swim. Number two, of those that go into the water voluntarily, almost everyone will keep his trousers on. Why, I don't know; but the white boys will strip immediately and begin to wash."

Hawkins started to protest, but Calahan raised his hand. "Just watch. I'm not trying to be a racist. You just watch for yourself." Calahan stopped making his point; now he let it sink in. Then he flicked his hand. "Okay, that's all—let's move."

The group scrambled off. LeBlanc and Lieutenant Diandre left together, laughing. Hawkins showed no emotion but left quietly, and the Captain followed him with his eyes.

"Lieutenant Hawkins," Calahan called.

Hawkins half-turned, and Calahan beckoned with his head. "I see you've taken to not wearing your forty-five."

"Oh." Hawkins looked down in surprise. He wore only a cartridge belt with a canteen. "I keep it in my pack now."

"I see. Any particular reason?"

"Well, I started out with one, but I never use it. In a fire fight it's my job to be on the radio and directing the troops. If I were to start firing, I couldn't be near as efficient, and we'd fall apart in confusion. Somebody's got to coordinate."

"What happens if a gook gets through and starts to shoot at you?"

"By that time, sir, I'd have the forty-five out of the pack."

"Yes, but suppose something happens to it and the gooks are closing in on you?"

"Captain"—Hawkins looked straight into Calahan's eyes—"if they ever get that far, there'll be plenty of rifles to pick up."

There was a long silence as they stared hard at each other. Finally Calahan nodded, and the Lieutenant turned and left in silence. As he moved off, Calahan felt the nagging worry again. He'd seen Hawkins' type before—usually they got killed. Slowly he rubbed the bristles on his head. But sometimes, sometimes, they became too good. Calahan stared after him. Before long, he knew, Hawkins would want the company.

2

Hawkins

At first, convoy security had been fun, the men just sat in a truck and watched the country go by. Little girls were along the road, selling pop, booze, marijuana, and themselves. Almost every day the platoon had been through Cam Lo, but they had never spent the night at the district headquarters there, which was really a small fort for United States' advisers and Vietnamese military personnel outside the village. The compound had deep bunkers, layers of barbed wire, and more than yards of mines around it. As the men looked at the rows of barbed wire, they knew they would get plenty of sleep.

Hawkins was blowing up his air mattress when he saw First Lieutenant Jim Ragland. He had met this man several times before at battalion rear in Quang Tri; he had some sort of skate job in Intelligence or civil affairs or something like that. The man had a fresh "white sidewall" haircut, and his utilities were clean and pressed. He'd never been in the bush, yet he was always telling some war story. Hawkins didn't like him and couldn't understand why Ragland would be spending the night at this primitive place.

In spite of his dislike, Hawkins went up to speak. "Hello, Jim." He stuck out his hand.

" 'Lo." The freshly starched man sat in his jeep and continued to fiddle with some papers. He appeared not to notice the hand.

Hawkins withdrew his hand awkwardly and wished he hadn't come. "What brings you out here?"

"Oh, fucking investigation. That's the trouble with being on battalion staff—you're always getting stuck with some investigation or trial." He continued to appear absorbed in the work.

Oh, break my heart, Hawkins thought. "Yeah? What are you investigating?"

"Accident," Ragland replied curtly.

"Well—what happened?"

Ragland looked up disdainfully and studied Hawkins as if deciding whether it would be a break of security to tell such a lowly person; then with a bored sigh, he said, "One of our drivers ran over a kid."

"Oh, was he hurt?"

"Killed him."

Hawkins decided to drop the whole affair and go back to the platoon.

Abruptly Ragland looked up at the setting sun and checked his watch, apparently deciding it was time to quit for the day. "You want a drink?" he asked amiably, putting his papers in a plastic case.

Hawkins looked back, cocked his head quizzically. "You got a bottle?"

"No, come on. I'll show you a regular mixed drink with ice."

"You must be nuts."

"Well, I think we can get some. I used to know a guy named Mel Northcutt who worked in this area. He was with USAID or somebody and he did something with refugees. He should live in one of these hooches." They turned the corner and went into a little building.

It was a small office. There were maps on the wall and charts all over. An attractive Vietnamese girl sat in one corner at a typewriter. At the desk was a young man, not any more than twenty-four or twenty-five. By Marine standards, his hair was long. His clothes were an odd mixture of American and Vietnamese; simple, green, and evidently military of some sort, they were devoid of rank or insignia. They were similar to what thousands of Vietnamese men wore as everyday clothes.

"Hello, Mel. Glad to see you're still around."

"Jim Ragland. Glad to see you." They shook hands. "What are you doing here?"

"Investigation."

"One of those, eh? When's your outfit going to run another County Fair out here?"

"I don't know, Mel, I'm pretty busy with PSYOPS and CAP units these days. Besides, I hope to get a company before long anyway."

"I thought you liked civil affairs?"

"I do, but I also want to do my share in the bush."

"Do my share—O horseshit!" Mel laughed, "All you military career-types are the same. Got to have some command time for the old record books."

"Hey, Mel, say hello to Chris Hawkins. He's got one of the platoons guarding your place tonight. Chris, meet Mel Northcutt."

"Howdy," Hawkins said tersely and managed a smile. Hawkins was conscious of shaking hands for the first time since coming to the bush.

"Say, how about a drink?" Ragland said. Northcutt glanced at his watch. "Five forty-five. Okay. Only fifteen minutes until the Vietnamese staff knocks off anyway. Co Lin, you might as well go home early."

"Thank you, sir." The delicate little female carefully locked the drawer in her desk and, rising, tripped gently out the door, her heeled sandals tapping daintily.

"Where does she live?"

"Oh, down in the vill."

"You getting it?"

"No, damn it. She's pretty friendly in the office, but if I see her on the road, she won't even turn her head."

Hawkins said nothing.

"Come on, let's go get that drink."

Ragland gave Hawkins a triumphant didn't-I-tell-you-so glance.

They filed out just as a green Ford Bronco drew up and stopped at the main headquarters. It was driven by an Oriental in green fatigues. But somehow he didn't look like a Vietnamese. The American beside him was dressed in slacks, a sport shirt, a wide-brimmed Stetson, and regulation jungle combat boots. On his hip was a .38 revolver, hung low—cowboy style. But most unusual of all was the weapon he carried over his shoulder. It was short with a ventilated barrel, folding stock, and a long straight magazine. Hawkins couldn't keep from staring at the weapon. After the man waved and went into the building, Hawkins called to Northcutt. "Hey, what was that weapon?"

Northcutt turned back and paused. "That's a Swedish
K. All the spooks got 'em."

"Spooks?" Hawkins' expression was plainly puzzled.

The other two men both laughed. "You *have* been in
the bush," Ragland said.

"Yeah, spooks. You know. CIA. They all run around
like that. Only over here they have to be mysterious and
call themselves 'The Company.' "

"Well, why does he try to look so ah . . . so different?"

Again they both laughed. Hawkins began to get a little
annoyed.

"I'm sorry, Chris. We're not laughing at you." Mel had
seen his expression. "It's just that you're so right. Christ, I
wish he'd heard you say that." He stopped laughing and
explained. "You're absolutely right and those people are
ridiculous. They all drive those green Broncos and carry
those Swedish K's. All the spooks from here to Saigon
have them, and they're the *only* ones who do. It makes
them stick out like sore thumbs. Civilian clothes would be
all right around Saigon, but up here everybody's in the
military, so civvies are more of a sign than a disguise."

"Come on you two, fuck the spooks. Let's go have a
drink," Ragland said.

They went down a row of sandbag hooches until they
came to a prefabricated trailer. Like the others, it was
sandbagged. As Hawkins walked by, something dripped
on his arm. He looked up and his jaw dropped. "Jesus."
Sticking out through the sandbags were the ventilated lou-
vers of a Chrysler Air-Temp air-conditioner. As he stepped
inside, the cool air flowed over him like a wave. He couldn't
remember ever feeling anything so good.

The first thing that struck him was the sofa. An inex-
pensive leatherette type, but a real American sofa. There
were matching armchairs and a table. Northcutt went to
the corner where there was a bar which was made of
bamboo. It was handmade but very nice. Behind that
there was a full-sized GE refrigerator. Hawkins stood in
the center of the room, staring even while trying to act
nonchalant. His eyes roved the walls, and he eagerly
drank in the mixture of homey comfort and military hard-
ware.

It felt so damn good, just being in a real house with
furniture and air-conditioning. Mounted on the wall were

an AK-47 and a Russian SKS, the older semiautomatic rifle that some of the VC carried. Hawkins chuckled to himself at the sight of those two familiar objects. Then his eyes fell on a gun rack near the door. There were at least a half a dozen different weapons there.

Northcutt and Ragland were gabbing on about some past experience, and Hawkins took a bourbon and soda, consciously acting casual. He ambled over to the gun rack and eagerly examined the assortment, looking at each one in detail. He noticed an M-79 grenade launcher in brand-new condition. Jesus, he thought, we're the ones who need that and all we got is old battered-up ones. Still suppressing his excitement, he examined each weapon. There were an M-16 and one of the new M-17's with the short barrel and stock, an AK-47 with a folding stock, an Italian Beretta machine pistol, and a Browning 9-mm pistol. The Browning pistol was beautiful. He hefted it in his hand, light and sure. More accurate than our .45, he thought. Holds more rounds, too. Longingly, he put it back. Then he spotted the Swedish K. It was identical with the one he had just seen outside.

Immediately he glanced at the other two men. Northcutt had said *all the spooks* had these weapons. Did that mean? Was *he?* Hawkins' interest rose in spite of his effort to stay cool. Was this guy part of the CIA? Cautiously he drifted to the couch and waited for a break in the conversation.

"Say, Mel, who do you work for?"

"Oh, I'm in the Foreign Service" came the easy answer. "Started out with refugee work, but now I'm the assistant DSA."

"DSA?"

"District Senior Adviser. We work with the local Vietnamese government, which is, of course, military and appointed."

"Oh, I see. Well, uh . . . reason I asked is . . . that I saw that Swedish K over there and I wondered. . . ." He stopped and pointed to the gun rack, hoping not to be obvious.

Northcutt glanced at the gun then back at Hawkins. "Oh, I see." He laughed. "I told you all the spooks had them and you thought——" He laughed again. "No, that's a hot one. I traded an SKS and two pieces of ass for that."

The intrigue vanished. Weapons not registered on books—and trading. He understood that everyone traded in Vietnam. But Northcutt had said something else. *Ass.* Ass okay. But how does he have it to *trade?*

Still trying hard to act casual, as if he knew all about it, Hawkins gave a good-natured chuckle. "Sounds as if you've got a good source. That easy to acquire around here?"

For the first time Northcutt seemed to hesitate. "Oh, when you work for the Vietnamese, it's always around," he parried.

"Yeah, but can you just dish it up like that?" Hawkins tried hard not to sound eager.

The man looked away. His manner cooled a little bit. Then he added with a wink, "Well, I don't have my own private whorehouse, but it's—well, *available.*"

He sat in the back of the jeep and the soft night air brushed over his face. He gripped his pistol—scared shitless. He'd never gone anywhere without the platoon and certainly not at night, and yet here were three men whipping through the dark alone. He had to be crazy to have come along for this, but he felt the tingle of excitement that always goes with doing something forbidden. Of course, when they asked him if he wanted to go see a couple of girls, he pretended to keep cool with a "yeah-I-do-this-everyday" front; then he ran like mad to tell the Chief to cover for him. He leaned forward and said through clenched teeth, "Is it safe to go out at night like this?" After all, what was the company doing in the compound?

"Oh, no sweat, as long as we stay right here in town," Northcutt said calmly over his shoulder. "There's all kinds of friendly patrols. Just don't go outside into the country."

Hawkins wasn't convinced but reminded himself that this guy lived here and seemed to know what he was doing. He expected a shot to crash out any minute.

The jeep turned into an open lot behind a couple of gas pumps, and they pulled up beside some junky old trucks. They went single-file down the dingiest alley Hawkins had ever seen. Hawkins walked tensely at the end of the three-man column as they stepped around little puddles of oil and water. Human feces lay along the way. He saw into an open-sided house, and a whole family calmly watched him go by. He felt ridiculously on display. The family must know. The path led between a dinky tumble-down shack and a two-story house. He had to duck under some clotheslines and overhanging roofs. The ground was littered with discarded boards and papers. He picked his way carefully. Mel seemed to be on a Sunday stroll. Suddenly there was a snuffle and a grunt. Hawkins flinched at the sound, his hand halfway drawing the pistol. Then he was relieved and yet disgusted. A pig. They came to a shack and ducked under the corrugated tin slabs that formed a porch. There was no door, just a row of colored plastic streamers hanging in the doorframe. Inside, a single overhead lamp glowed.

Mel flopped easily and casually in one of the low chairs, and Ragland sat in a straight chair, considerably more ill at ease than before. Hawkins stood in the door and fidgeted. He felt his stomach trembling slightly. Damn, calm down. You're acting like you're only fifteen. His eyes scanned the room. There were two large, smooth round posts in the center which seemed to hold up the whole house. The walls were partly corrugated sheet tin and partly wood. One part of the wall said MORTARS: 81 MILLIMETERS.

Ammo boxes; he grinned. In the center of the room extending back to the far wall was a sort of big wooden chest. On it were a long picture of Buddha and a lot of red-looking frills. In front of the Buddha, an incense stick burned, sending a sandalwood sweetness through the room. Hawkins sniffed; it smelled better than the path he had just walked up. Except for two of the low easychairs and a table with straight chairs, the room was filled with what appeared to be beds—at least each had a mosquito net over it. Actually they were only bedframes with flat boards across. Each one had a woven plastic mat across it and a Marine poncho-liner. The floor was hard trampled dirt.

Mel was calmly talking in pidgin Vietnamese-English to an old crone he called Mama-san. Nervously Hawkins sat on the edge of a chair and looked around. With a shock he realized they were not alone. The doorway seemed to be full of kids. He began to sweat uncomfortably. Through another door he could see more kids. Christ, do

they just let the kids run all over a whorehouse, he wondered. Presently two kids came in and looked him up and
down; Mama-san said something and the kids got in one
of the beds.

Soon the room was filled with people of all kinds—old,
young, kids of all types, but no men. There was an an-
cient woman who sat cross-legged on one of the beds in
faded baggy pajamas, rocking a baby. Her hair was about
one-quarter of an inch long all over her head. Her eyes
were puffed almost shut. Her skin looked like rumpled
corduroy. She had come down the path wearing faded
baggy pajamas and had crawled right onto the bed with
them on. Hawkins wondered if she ever changed them.

Mel gabbed on, and Hawkins began to doubt that they
were ever going to get any whores. The fear had left him,
but he got a little edgy. Damn, he muttered silently. How
did I ever get into this? The kids would stare at him a
while and then run on. About half the beds were now
filled, mostly with kids. The ancient one grunted and puffed
as she rocked. What a zoo, he thought, an unbelievable
zoo, and Mel doesn't seem to care at all. Hawkins began
to wonder if this clown was going to sit there and just talk
to that old crone. Then he saw a large man in a green
uniform go past the side of the house and down the path
they had come up. He blinked in surprise. The man was
obviously an American. He started to ask Mel, but just
then two girls came out of a low door in the back. They
wore what looked like faded pajamas.

As Vietnamese go, one was a "C minus." The other was
about a "B." Hawkins got the "C minus."

She led him back through the door in the rear. God,
that had been embarrassing, he thought. Ragland had
taken the other one right away, and he had stood there
not knowing what to do. The Mama-san had asked him if
he wanted this one. Jesus Christ. What could he say? No
thanks, he didn't want her? There must have been ten
people in the room, and Hawkins was sure they all had
been laughing. He had just wanted to get away, so he
muttered something and nodded. He'd never felt so on
display in his life. Didn't these damn people have any
modesty?

As he stepped into the back room, the crone caught his
arm. "You pay Mama-san first."

"Uh, how much?" he squeaked meekly. His ears were burning red.

"Seven dolla for short time." Her hand was out.

"*Five* dollars, Mama-san! I told you, he's my friend." Mel's voice cracked through from the other room. Mama-san scowled, and Hawkins felt a wave of embarrassment but also sudden relief. He handed her five and she nodded like a gatekeeper accepting the toll.

It was dark and he had to stoop. As his eyes became accustomed to the gloom, he felt a wave of revulsion. There was an old smoke-blackened stove and little bits of wood lying around it. Behind the stove was a sandbag bunker, very neatly stacked but covered with layers of dust and dirt. What the hell, a bunker inside. The girl beckoned to him, and he went over to her and crossed around the bunker. A powerful odor hit his nose and at the same time he heard a deep grunt. He looked around the filth but could see nothing. "What's that?"

"*Con heo,*" she said. "Pig."

He wasn't sure he could go through with this, but if he came out now they would surely all make fun of him. What would the girl say? He gritted his teeth and ducked under the flap she was holding. There it was, just a little cubicle bounded on three sides by corrugated tin. The fourth side consisted of one wall of the bunker and the flap. There was just room to stand beside the bed, which was an old military cot with a single dirty mattress on it, the kind that has three inches of stuffed cotton.

Hawkins had the same feeling he got in the restroom of a dirty country gas station. The cubicle was so filthy it made his skin crawl. Above all, he didn't want to touch anything.

Gingerly he sat down on the edge of the bed, and at once he could hear the people talking in the other room. He realized that they were only a few feet from him and separated by just a single sheet of corrugated tin. He wondered how he was ever going to go through with this. Actually he had only had one other whore in his life and that was in Spain, which didn't really count because they were friendly and clean. And he had talked to her for two days before he had got up the nerve to take her to bed. She had done everything and, besides, he had been drunk.

This girl's face was a stone mask of boredom. She took

off her pajama top mechanically. Hawkins saw the black bra. He couldn't move and couldn't decide what to do with his clothes. Should he strip? Oh, Jesus. "Mumble-buzz"—he heard the voices from the other room. Suddenly the girl turned and smiled at him. "Hey, GI, you no like *Co* Hue?"

That broke the ice. There was something in her manner that appealed to him, and he grinned, reaching for her. "Yes, I like you." Her bored look fell away and she giggled and jumped onto his lap.

"What your name, GI?"

"Chris." He felt her sides and hips. Boy, she really is small.

"My name Hue."

His starved hands were going all over her and she leaned forward and reached under her thighs.

"Hey, Chris, you boo-coo horny." He flushed but managed to laugh. His throat was getting thick. He *was* horny. He reached for her bra and she gently pushed him back and stood up. Without a shred of shyness, she undid the bra and dropped it on the bedpost.

Hawkins was amazed. Her breasts were really large. He had always thought the Vietnamese had no breasts, judging from the ones that he had seen walking on the roads. He continued to stare as she peeled off her bottoms. Her panties, like the bra, were black, and without batting an eye she tossed them on the post and calmly lay down.

Hawkins gulped, his eyes running over every inch of her. Her stomach was large and it protruded slightly with sagging flesh. Her skin was all firm except for the stomach, which hung down in wrinkled folds. It appeared odd and old compared to the rest of her. She seemed strong, but her legs were just like matchsticks. She looked like a pear on a couple of stilts, except for the big tits. He stared at the stomach with the wrinkled, dry, loose skin. There were deep stretchmarks on the sides.

She lay completely relaxed under his gaze. "Hey, Chris, you want look or you want boom-boom?"

Immediately Hawkins flushed and tensed in shyness. He fumbled with his clothes, feeling himself getting excited. Savagely he tore off his boots and dropped his trousers in a pile. Naked, he stretched out, shut his eyes tight, rolled over and lay against her. "Oooohhhh." Does that ever feel good. Eyes still shut, he held her and for a long moment just felt the feminine smoothness of her next to him.

For that moment he forgot all about the filth in the room and the war and death, the heat, the months since he'd had another girl, the manginess of this girl, everything except that she was in his arms, warm and smooth and cool and willing all at the same time. Except, of course, for her wrinkly belly. For that moment she wasn't even a whore.

"Hey, Chris, what matter? You want sucky-fucky?" The moment ended sharply.

Well, he might as well get on with it. He grinned down at her weakly and put his mouth on hers. It really wasn't a kiss, more like just pressing mouth holes. His hands swarmed over her and the lust ran up in him. His mouth slipped down to her breast and his lips clamped over the bulbous nipple. Ah, that's good, he thought, feeling the passion jump up in him, and he sucked down hard. Instantly his head popped up. What the hell, he almost said aloud. He put his mouth down again and tasted the warm syrupy sweet milk.

This girl's got milk! No wonder her tits are so big. She must have just had a kid. And that must be why her stomach is all stretched. *Ugh.* He stopped sucking.

Out of the corner of his eye he looked down at her stomach. He put his hand on it and gently caressed the wrinkles. He picked up a fold of skin, fondled it and rolled it between his fingers like putty. His hand slid on down. Jesus, she hardly has any hair at all, he thought. He lifted his head and stole a glance. Was it really sideways? There was just a little tuft of straight black hair. How funny it looked. But he quickly lowered his head back to the boob, not wanting to stare and certainly not wanting to look into the eyes. She was just a body. He slid his leg up and down along her body and felt the sensuousness. Ooh, ohh, that's good, that's good, he thought. When he did this, she reached down and found him with her hands.

"Goddamn, Chris, you got boo-coo big dick." It was just as if somebody had slapped him. He jerked up and looked at her face, shocked to the core. There was only a smile and a girl. But the *language*. Sure he'd heard it thousands of times from the Marines but never from a girl.

It was said simply, not as if it were a curse. Just as if they were normal words. And then he knew she was only repeating English which she must have heard from hundreds and hundreds of GI's. She probably didn't even know the meaning of the words. At once he was shy again and felt ill at ease. He heard the voices from the other room, but her hands were doing things and his passion brought him up short.

Quickly and purposely now, just wanting to get it over with, he slid one leg between hers and rolled over on top of her. Her thighs opened automatically like the exit doors of a supermarket. His blood was going crazy. He pushed down.

Oh, she's dry, he thought. She's dry as a bone. God, I can't even get it in. Course that means she feels nothing. Well, what do you expect? Just fuck it and enjoy it and forget it. Her hand guided him in, dry and all. It was over in about two seconds.

He lay flat on his back, feeling greatly relieved but oddly unsatisfied. She got up and fumbled for her clothes.

You know, that's what I like about whores, he thought, forgetting this was his second. You can bang 'em, pop, and roll right off. It's much better to lie alone flat on your back and catch your breath than to have to rest on your elbows. Now if I were going with a girl, I'd have to stay on top of her and hold her tightly and pretend like I wanted to keep her close to me.

Hawkins closed his eyes and relaxed. He didn't even hear the voices in the next room. Yes, sir. Nothing like a whore for rolling right off and relaxing. She touched him on the shoulder and his eyes opened.

"*Ich.*" He felt the gooey stickiness and the gritty mattress, but to his surprise the girl was holding a pan of water.

"Wash, Chris?"

"Yeah." He swung up and sat on the edge of the bed, but as he faced her, his shyness came back. She put the pan up to him and in great embarrassment he put himself into it.

"Yeow, that's hot."

"Yes, hot, good." She laughed. Some of the embarrassment slipped away, and she calmly pushed his hand away and began to wash him off. Quickly he flipped himself dry and began stuffing his legs and arms into his clothes, which were all balled up. Just as he got his clothes on, she moved to the corner and squatted down, holding the pan under her bottom. Calmly she reached between her legs and began to douche herself. With his pants on, he grasped for his boots, trying to keep his bare feet off the dirt floor. He began to feel a little more detached and watched the girl as if she were something in a sideshow. How crude that looked. I wonder if that's the difference in Oriental women or just the difference in class. Somehow it would be impossible to picture a cultured girl back home doing something like that. The incongruity of the two images made him laugh. It would be absurd to even think of Poo doing a thing like—as if a hammer had hit him, he wished he had never had that thought. He couldn't help it; it had just popped out. Shame, revulsion, and finally a terrible sadness crept up in him at the thought of the only girl he had ever loved.

He jammed his boots on angrily.

"Hey, Chris, you souvenir me two dollar?"

"What?" He spat the word through his teeth as he grabbed for his shirt.

"Five dolla for Mama-san. You souvenir Hue now."

Oh, the bite. He should have known. He knew perfectly well, because Chief had told him, that the girls kept fifty percent and Mama-san got fifty percent, and that this was just a trick to get him to pay more. "No." He flung down the word, stooped over, and started out of the little enclosure.

"Cheap Charlie!" The words bit into him. They were mean and hard, a total switch from what the girl had been.

Then he thought of the room full of people and that wise-ass Ragland. What if she got out there and said something. They'd surely all laugh. Maybe the other Vietnamese would make a fuss. What should he do? More angry than ever, he ripped out his wallet and took out two dollars, threw them down on the bed and turned to go. Just as instantly as her mood had swung hard, it now swung back.

"Chris, you numba one," she cooed. "Come see Hue boo-coo times. No butterfly." He felt like throwing a grenade, but he set his face in a blank mask and walked back to the room.

They rode home in silence. In the night air his anger washed away. He felt dirty and wanted a shower, but the air was refreshing. God, what a guy wouldn't do to get laid. But once he'd popped, forget it. Then only the sadness of Poo lingered with him. He blinked his eyes at her image and tried to think about Vietnam.

The Platoon—Indian Song

The last trip to Quang Tri was a riot. The two weeks of convoy security duty were over and the company was sent to the rear for a couple of days of rehabilitation. Showers, clean clothes, hot chow, beer. The men were yelling and laughing, dancing in the truck; they hollered at everyone on the road and wrestled in the dirt.

The Lieutenant herded them into the sheep-dip, a row of outdoor showers. They stripped and threw their old clothes in a box at one end. When the men got through washing, they came out of the showers at the other end, and there were a couple of guys from supply who were waiting for them with a line of big boxes. New clothes. They got everything new. Sometimes the new clothes even fit.

The mess hall was open explicitly for them and they were supposed to get steaks. Well, what they were served was steak, if you hadn't had steak in a long time. Finally the officers turned them loose, and Hawkins watched the Chief lead the platoon off in a mob—to the PX.

Oh yes. It was the Chief. Leading them away from the officers, from the war, from the Corps; leading them to the PX. And as the war and the Corps and the officers fell behind, the hardeyed Indian—Corporal Eagle—the cold killer was cast aside and a new man burst forth—Screaming Sky Eagle—the Crazy Californian—the Malibu Kid. Leading them to the great PX to get—yes, yes—deodorant, comic books, candy, cameras, stereos, shoe polish. Leading them to the PX for everything—for God, country, mom, apple pie, and red-hot-snapper-pussy. And most of all he was leading them for *Magic Markers*.

Helmet graffiti—the new American art form—Vietnam inspired. Groovy. Here's how ya do it: Go over to the shiny-bright, sun-reflected, aluminum-sided, hot-ass dusty *PX*. Pass up all the Trojans and Shieks and Peacocks cause you not gonna be gettin' any for a long time, don't even know why they stock'em, maybe the brass is screwin' each other. Anyway, go over on the far side where all the *Superman* comics are—save your scratch I'll loan ya my copy, got the latest one—and you pick up one forty-cent black-felt Magic Marker and walk directly to the checkout line scoping out the gook chicks in Hong Kong bras. Look, but don't touch, you don't remember how anyway, been so long. And you pay Miss Hong Kong Bra with funny money Mickey Mouse money MPC Military Payment Script or somethin' stupid like that, a red twenty-five-cent bill, a green ten-cent one, and a blue five-cent one with the broads' pictures on 'em (It's Lana Turner, I tell ya; no, it's Marilyn Monroe; no, ya dumb asses it's Jackie Kennedy; no, it's nobody, just pitchers, stupid shits, or maybe your ol' lady when she worked in Suckahachi Alley). Anyway you pay quick and get out before you cream your jeans lookin' at Miss Hong Kong Bra cashier girl cause even if she ain't too sharp and don't smell too good she is a girl and come ta think of it you don't smell too good either. Anyway you get out with your artistic senses un-*co*-rapeted by thoughts of chicks you can't have and you go back to your hooch at Quang Tri where your company is restin' up and gettin' replacements. Cause as everybody knows (read it in *Stars and Stripes*, motherfucker) Bad-Ass Delta Two-Seven done kicked Charlie's ass, though in the process also getting own ass booted slightly, which is why we're now sittin' round our hooches feelin' salty as mean-vet motherfuckers compared to snotgreen replacements, so we can now take our new Magic Markers and write all kinds a good shit on our been-through-fuckin'-hell-an'-back-green-an'-brown-splotchy-camouflage helmet covers.

DO NOT REMOVE—HEAD ATTACHED
VICTOR CHARLIE EATS SHIT

SNOOPY IS A SON OF A BITCH

"Hey, Chief, I hear you're up for sergeant, man."
"Yeah, and the Captain put himself in for a Navy Cross."

BORN RAISING HELL—ASK MA
MAN LIVES NOT BY C-RATIONS ALONE
BUT BY SUDS AND POONTANG
WAR SUCKS

"Who knows what'll happen next—maybe Red'll even make PFC."
Never happen—the only thing he'll make is his fist."

FRAGILE—HANDLE WITH EXTREME CARE
THE RED BARON EATS KRAUT
THE COLONEL SMOKES POT

"All you guys makin' out, huh? I always said it's not what ya know or who ya know but who ya blow."
"Nah, man—that's *out*. These days there's so much competition it's not who ya know or who ya blow, but *how well* ya blow who ya know."

DON'T SOCK IT TO ME!
LOVE IS STONED
KADER IS ALIVE AND WELL AND LIVING UNDER THIS HELMET

"Keep talkin', Wilson—you know how we handle dark dudes like you back home? We cross'em with Chinese, call 'em Chiggers and spray DDT on 'em."
"Yeah, man? Well, Chief, you can cross *me* with a chink chick anytime, baby, and spray away! I'll just keep on a-crossin' and a-sniffin' and a-crossin' at the same time. Yeah!"
"Where you goin', Little Doc?"
"Hit the rack, man. I'm beat."
"Little Doc, you squids get more zulus than anybody I ever saw, man. How can you sleep so much?"
"Every minute I sleep 'sa minute I'm away from Nam, man, so fuck off. I'm fleein' the scene right *now!*"
"Get some grass for me too, Little Doc."

"Hey men, dig Sail—he's got Mary Lou's picture out again, slobberin' on it."

"Hey, Sail—no shit paper in the head, man. Lemme have Mary Lou's pitcher so's I can wipe my ass on it!"

"Yeah, Sail, me, too!"

"Ahh, eat it, motherhumpers."

"How 'bout a *song,* men:

I *won*-der who's fuc-king her now,
I *won*-der who's tee-ching her how,
I *won*-der if she'll eh-ver fuh-uhk me, too,
I *won*-der who's fucking her now."

"At least Mary Lou ain't been beat half to death with no ugly stick like your broads. They all look like their face was on fire and somebody put it out with an ice pick. You dippy dudes ain't even smart enough to piss holes in the snow, so fuck ya all!"

Hawkins

Hawkins sat in the officers' hooch. He had been to the Staff and Officers Club to get a drink, but having no real friends in Quang Tri, he had come back to read. It was satisfying to read again. It had been too long. He had bought *Time* and an old edition of the *National Reporter* at the PX. The rest of the magazines seemed to be all cars, musclemen, detective, real man, how-to-do-it, Westerns, flying, jokes, and sex—not pornography, of course, but *Gent, Playboy, Nugget, and Cavalier.* Hawkins asked the guy in charge if they ever got the Sunday New York *Times* but the guy was from Texas and had never heard of it.

However, it was nice to just read. Sometimes a couple of *Reader's Digests* came in the mailbags, but nobody except Joseley ever read those. Most guys used them to write on; they made a flat surface for letters.

There was a doctor in the hooch, too, not a corpsman-type doc but a real MD. He was a Navy lieutenant and served as battalion surgeon since the Navy provided all the medical and religious personnel for the Marines. They were the only officers in the hooch—the rest all off drinking. Hawkins and the doctor talked for a while, but then they both turned to their reading.

Soon, however, Hawkins began to think about the men. He wished he were with them, talking, laughing, drinking. He knew some would be smoking. He longed to talk, to be their buddy. Yet he couldn't; no matter how close they were, they were still different.

He went out on the steps to sit down, and in a few minutes he saw several figures approaching. They came up cautiously, stopping to look in the hooches. Hawkins sat still. They were obviously looking for something. When the figures saw him, they stopped.

"Lieutenant Hawkins?"

"Yes. Who's that?"

"Sail."

Hawkins heard them exclaim and they came forward shyly. It was Sail, Red, and Christian. They had been looking for him. He felt a rush of pleasure and affection.

"Sir, we were wondering if you could . . . ah . . . aah . . . get us some liquor—stateside-type."

"Liquor?"

"Yes, sir, you know, we can't get it and thought you might buy us some. We'll give you the money, sir."

Hawkins remembered that enlisted men were not allowed to buy hard liquor anywhere in Vietnam. "Sure, I'll buy it for you, but I don't know where to get a bottle now."

They glanced at each other and Sail stepped forward and peered into the hooch. The doctor had gone to sleep.

"Sir, you can buy it at the Staff and Officers Club."

"By the bottle? They only have it by the drink there."

Again they glanced at one another, but the Lieutenant's tone wasn't condemnatory. "Well, you have to see the Top or the sergeant major because they run the club; but they'll sell it to you, sir."

The sergeant major. Hawkins frowned—the highest enlisted rank. "Well, okay."

The men smiled eagerly and turned to pool their money. Sail counted and gave the money to Hawkins. "That's eighteen dollars and fifty cents, sir, that's all we got. If you could get two bottles, that'd really be great."

"Eighteen fifty!" Hawkins exclaimed. "Hell, that ought to be enough to buy three or four bottles at military prices."

Sail frowned, "Well, get as much as you can for that, sir. If it's just two bottles, we will be glad to pay it. It will be worth it."

"All right, what do you want?"

"Scotch," they said in unison.

The club was in the same hooch as the Officers' mess hall; the bar had been built into one corner. Hawkins found Top Goresuch and, after some hedging around, managed to get the man off by himself. Top was the nickname commonly given to all first sergeants. Top Goresuch was a big, hammy man. His beefy shoulders, once broad and hard, had long since been covered with layers of fat; his belly protruded over his belt, pushed out from years of beer drinking; but it was hard fat, unlike the soft flab of a civilian. Of course, he had the skinned sides and burr top of the career NCO. Hawkins felt uncomfortable around the man, yet he was determined to get the liquor. The first sergeant seemed annoyed but, condescendingly, put on a polite tone.

"Er, Top, I understand that I can buy liquor at the club here."

The hard pig-eyes flicked quickly around the tables and the face lost its polite look. "Well, now, Lieutenant, I don't really know. Sometimes, but ah—you have to ask the sergeant major. He's the one in charge of the club."

"Is it for sale or not?"

"I myself can't really say." His voice lowered confidentially, and he leaned toward the Lieutenant, pushing his drink forward with his belly. "See, we ain't really s'pose to sell it that way, but seeing as how you're an officer and just out of the bush, we might fix you up—but you'll have to ask the sergeant major."

"All right, let's ask him."

Hawkins straightened to go, but the Top put his hand on Hawkins' forearm. "You know, Lieutenant"—his face was sorrowful, almost apologetic—"that we have to sell it at bar prices; that's the rule."

"What's the price?"

"Oh, I don't know, that depends on what you get. You better ask the sergeant major. He'll tell you."

That seems reasonable, Hawkins thought. If it's a club, they have to show the profit, I guess.

They went over to the bar where a large man of about

forty-four or so was arguing loudly. His face was gnarled and lined, and he had that permanently weather-beaten look. Like Top Goresuch, he was beefy, with a big gut, but it was beef that covered big muscles. He reminded Hawkins of a professional wrestler just a little past his prime. He was also half drunk.

Top Goresuch pulled on his arm and succeeded in getting his attention after about two minutes.

"Sergeant Major, Sergeant Major."

"Yeah."

"Sergeant Major, this here lieutenant wants to buy a bottle."

"Oh he does, eh?" The sergeant major looked dumbly at Top Goresuch for a moment, then examined Hawkins with a runny stare. His eyes wobbled, then narrowed. "Whaddya want, Lieutenant?"

"I'd like two bottles of ordinary Scotch."

The runny eyes flushed just a hint of surprise, then narrowed tightly. "Now, Lieutenant, if I sell you these, it's got to be at bar prices, you know."

"What's the price?"

The man leaned back and examined Hawkins silently before speaking, then the runny eyes shifted for a second to Top Goresuch. "Well, now, Lieutenant, I don't know just what I got in stock; we'll have to go see. It's gotta be the bar price though."

Hawkins thought he had never heard a man say "lieutenant" more contemptuously. "Okay, tell me approximately what the price is."

"About nine or ten dollars."

Hawkins' jaw tightened. He remembered what Sail had said, "All right, let's get it."

The sergeant major looked at Top Goresuch and abruptly jerked his head. "You wait here, Lieutenant, Top Goresuch'll go get it." He leaned back over his drink, then turned just his head back over his shoulder, his lips curled in a half-sneer. "You got the money?"

"Yeah, I got the money," Hawkins said sharply. He was becoming angry at the way the sergeant was treating him. He couldn't remember once that the man had said "sir."

In about ten minutes Top Goresuch came back with two bottles of Johnny Walker Red. They were wrapped in a sack and Goresuch flashed them to the sergeant major.

Hawkins took out the money. "Those are fine—how much?"

The sergeant major seemed friendly for the first time. "Those are eleven dollars each."

Hawkins stopped and folded the money back. His face went sour. He knew they were trying to gouge him for the extra dollar. "Now, wait a minute"—his voice was even, and he put the hand with the money back in his pocket—"you said nine or ten dollars."

"Yeah, but these are *quarts,* Lieutenant—not fifths—they cost more."

"Oh." Hawkins had a flash of embarrassment. He looked down at the eighteen fifty. "I see—that's okay, but I'm not sure I have that much."

"I'll tell you what, Lieutenant, I'll take fifty cents off each bottle—I'm not supposed to, but seeing as how you're just outta the bush, I'll do it."

Hawkins bit his tongue and breathed out sharply. He knew the men would be glad to get the extra amount in the quarts. He remembered them saying they didn't care what it cost. Hell, they deserved it. "Okay," he said, taking the extra money from his own wallet. "It's a deal. Twenty-one dollars."

Abruptly the sergeant major turned away. "Give it to Top Goresuch." He flung the words over his shoulder as he lurched back to the bar.

Hawkins was startled by the abrupt change but shrugged and went to get the bottles. As he was leaving, he stopped and watched the large man. They were rolling dice and he was arguing again. Then the sergeant major looked up and saw Hawkins watching him.

"Gwan, ya got it, didn't ya—get outta here."

Hawkins stiffened, the veneer of his combat toughness and bravado sought to assert itself, then the old reason-ableness took over. He spun around and walked out.

The man is drunk. Forget it, what do you care, he told himself. And as he walked, he cooled off. Then he grinned bitterly as he visualized a second lieutenant and a sergeant major explaining their story to the colonel. Better forget it.

Anyway he had the liquor; that's what counted. He peeked down at the bottles. They had a good, cheery feeling under his arm, and he stepped along gaily.

And not a bad price, too. He wondered whether they really had to sell it at bar prices. Oh, well, he had no way to find out. The men would be happy so it didn't really matter. It is reasonable that they have to get what they could have made if they sold it over the bar. Let's see what would that be? One drink is twenty-five cents. One drink is usually a jigger and that is one ounce. So it's thirty-two drinks in one quart. So that's twenty-five cents times thirty-two. Hmmm, that's . . . oh shit. I can't do it in my head. Sounds about right though.

3

Wilson

Wilson looked down at the cigarette, aware that he was holding it awkwardly. Chief and Big John peered through the gloom of the bunker and watched him intently. Forcing himself to be casual, Wilson took it out of the plastic bag and nervously twisted the little tit tighter. It was made of thin brownish paper and looked like a tiny hand-made cigar. He put it to his nose and sniffed cautiously. The pencil mustache twitched and his nose crinkled as if the smell were foul. Wilson frowned and pushed it toward Big John. "Don't smell too good to me; think I'll stick to the Scotch."

"Come on, nigger, wha'sa matta wit' you?" Big John said.

Wilson looked nervously around the bunker and went over to the opening. He looked out into the night but saw nothing. They were supposed to be on guard duty, but they were at Quang Tri. Wilson frowned unconsciously, turned back into the bunker, and sat back down.

"Nothin', but you never can tell when we're gonna get hit. That's all, I just don't like to smoke when there's a chance."

"Bullshit!" Chief snorted and snatched the cigarette from Wilson. "Wilson, sometimes you are a funny dude. Here we are back in the rear with a thousand Marines around us and you get worried. Jesus Christ, man, the time to worry was when we were out there on the 'Z' sitting on some lonely hill with just one company. Now *that's* when I worry. You won't catch me smoking or drinking out there when we *really* might catch some shit."

Chief fired his lighter, inhaled deeply, and passed the cigarette to Big John. The pungent bittersweet odor of marijuana crept through the bunker.

Big John took the little cigarette and held it delicately between his thumb and forefinger. It was dwarfed by the thick thumb. He put it in the middle of his mouth and sucked slowly, taking little puffs at a time until his lungs were full. The massive head rolled back, with his eyes scrunched shut as if in pain, and his arm extended the cigarette toward Wilson blindly. After a full minute he began to let the smoke eke out with a deep rumbling sigh.

When he opened his eyes, Wilson was still holding the cigarette.

"Well, Sonny, you gonna join in or you gonna worry 'bout all them gooks massin' fo' a'tack?"

Abruptly Wilson's eyes flashed and he put the cigarette to his mouth quickly and inhaled, but he held most of the smoke in his mouth. "Okay, I was just worried about somebody checking the lines."

"Who?" Big John asked.

"Only person that would be checking the lines would be Hawkins, and I'll bet he wouldn't say a damn thing even if he caught us," Chief said assuredly.

Big John and Wilson looked with curiosity at Chief.

"Maybe some beast, come along," Wilson said.

"Naw, Wilson," Big John said. "No beast here—beasts all off worrying about Carlysle." He poured a drink in a B-2 can and swirled the liquid.

As the name was mentioned, Wilson visibly jumped, dropping the cigarette.

Hawkins

About midnight the clouds rolled across the moon and a dark figure slipped somewhat tipsily along the trench line. It came to the bunker, went around back, and raised the flap. As the soft candlelight flowed out, the figure dropped into the hole and lowered the flap.

"Lieutenant!" Wilson gasped and stood frozen.

"Oh, Lawdy."

Suddenly, Chief's eyes went wide and he grabbed his hat and jammed it on quickly. "Howdy, Lieutenant," he said, trying to appear casual.

Hawkins nodded, his squinted eyes looking in amazement at the beer and whiskey bottles. "Better cover these up, no telling when some officer will come in here." His voice was heavy and somber. Then he hiccuped.

"Yes, sir." Wilson hopped up, chuckling in relief and threw a poncho over the cases.

"Have a drink, sir." The Chief jumped off the lone box and quickly dumped some whiskey in a can and offered both the drink and the box to the Lieutenant. He was still shaking from his close call. Getting caught with his hair down was the only thing that would bother Chief.

Hawkins took the can, sat down a little too fast, and grinned crookedly. "Hi."

The men looked closely at the Lieutenant, then glanced at each other with knowing grins and relaxed, reaching again for their drinks. But the Chief stood behind the Lieutenant and held open the flap, madly fanning the air.

Big John grinned. This dude's going to drink with us— man, he'd never had a drink with an officer before. Good thing they finished smoking the shit.

They stared at one another in silence for a while, a little self-conscious.

"How's this bunker?" Hawkins asked gamely, unable to think of anything better to say yet wanting to talk.

"It's okay, sir," Wilson said, nervously watching the Chief fan the air behind the Lieutenant's back, and Big John, who was lying against the wall, conspicuously relaxed.

"Got any rats?"

"Oh, yeah, always got rats, but these bunkers are a lot cleaner than the ones at Khe Sanh."

"These probably ain't been *pissed in* as much," Hawkins said, giggling, and took a long drink from the can. "*Oouagh!* What's that?" He grimaced and put the can about one inch from his eye, then commenced to peer intently into the liquid.

"Colt Forty-five, sir," Chief said, trying not to laugh.

"Gook whiskey," Wilson said, grinning broadly.

"Tha' ain' whiskey," Big John sang out suddenly, "it's waterboo piss. Zips mix it with rice-paddy water and bottle it."

"The who?" Hawkins lurched around.

"Who? Waterbooo. Tha's whooo!!" Big John lay on the floor, leering insanely.

"The zips." Wilson cut in quickly and shot a dark look at Big John. "Zipper heads, the gooks, sloops, dinks."

"Oh." Hawkins contemplated this and frowned deeply. "I thought only the enemy gooks were gooks."

"Them is the bad gooks, but these gooks aroun' heahr is gooks, too, only de'da good gooks," Big John said positively.

"Sir, it used to be that just NVA and VC were called gooks, but now they're beginning to call any Vietnamese gooks," Chief explained soberly.

"Oh, I see. Yes, I see. Well, gimme 'nother shot of that gook piss—whatever it is," Hawkins said thickly, waving the can at Chief.

Chief poured immediately. Hawkins sat back and swirled the cup. He took a little drink and realized they were all watching him. He looked around the bunker and fidgeted, not wanting to go back by himself. "Hey, guess what?" He brightened and leaned forward. "We're going to get some more men."

"That right, sir? How many?" Chief asked quickly.

" 'Bout three or four, I think. Yeah, I even got their names here somewhere." He fished in his pockets. "Gunny gave me a list this afternoon." He set the drink down and half stood to reach in his pants' pocket.

"When do we get them, sir?" Chief asked.

"Oh, I dunno that yet." Hawkins pulled out a scrap of paper and sat back down, holding the paper close to his eyes, squinting.

"Supposed to get two old men that's been wounded or something. I don't know when they'll come."

"Who are they, sir?" All of them leaned forward anxiously, wondering who was returning to the bush.

"Ah, lessee here." Hawkins studied the paper in the dim light, pointing with his fingers. "The old ones are Wyman and Carlysle. Know them?" he asked groggily.

"Carlysle!" Wilson hissed in a low voice.

Big John sat bolt upright as if someone had kicked him.

Wilson's eyes bugged wide, and he looked quickly over to Big John. Hawkins, unmindful of the violent reaction, lazily reached down, picked up his can and took a drink. The three sat stone still.

"Ah . . . could I see that list, please, sir?" Wilson forced his voice to be casual.

"Sure. Friends of yours?" Hawkins asked, waving the paper over.

Wilson took the paper as Big John and Chief moved to peer over his shoulder. Wilson looked once and said nothing.

Hawkins babbled on, not waiting for an answer, "Does a man good to drink a little now and then. Right, Chief?"

"Right, sir," Chief said quickly, glancing at the other two.

"Course we'd never do it out in the bush, but shit this ain't the bush." Hawkins began to slur his words markedly. "Not fer this p'toon, it ain't. Right, Chief?"

"Right, sir."

"No fucking gooks around here to make us worry. Right, Chief?"

"Right, sir."

Lieutenant Hawkins talked gaily, happy to be doing drunk what he could not do sober. But like a spring winding down, he talked slower and slower until he finally stopped. Then he got up and left, without another word. As he went through the flap, the little scrap of paper fluttered to the floor.

Wilson

The three sat silently, listening a moment to the footsteps fade, then turned eagerly to one another.

"Carlysle," they breathed in unison.

"You think he come t' d'bush?" Big John asked.

"I don't know, John, maybe, but I don't think so. They got him up for a Summary Court."

"But tha' paper, you seen it."

"Yeah, but he ain't here yet. Way he feels now, they'd have to tie him up to get him out here."

"If he do come, how you reckon he get on with 'tenant?"

Wilson frowned intently at the thought, then his voice

rasped wearily, "Carlysle is in the brig again."

"Wha' fo' now?" Big John frowned.

"Beating some Chuck."

Chief said nothing but sat immobile watching Big John and Wilson curiously. Chief had transferred from another unit and had met Carlysle only once or twice in the rear, but the reaction of Big John and Wilson fascinated him. He had known blacks like Carlysle back at Berkeley, and Wilson's sudden passion stirred old memories. "Wilson"— Chief spoke casually and his voice was innocent—"what makes Carlysle that way?"

Wilson looked over at Big John furtively, then stared away from Chief.

"Tell 'em, Sonny. Chief's no beast; he's a red man."

Chief felt the pain of the unintentional irony but kept his face set in the mask.

Wilson poured another drink and stared into the amber liquid; finally he spoke. "Carlysle wasn't always the way he is now. He used to be the best squad leader we had. Aw, I don't mean he had any great love for the Chucks, but he didn't out and out *hate* 'em like he does now. Lemme see, it was back when I first came incountry that Carlysle was my squad leader. Christ, he was good! He had only been there about two months when he made squad leader. They almost *had* to put him there because everybody would do what he said. He was from Washington, D.C., you know, and he was a wild, mean motherfucker; but, Jesus, was he a fighter and nobody would cross him. During Operation Auburn when so many got dinged, they made him platoon sergeant."

"As a lance corporal?" Chief's voice was skeptical.

"Most affirm. The lieutenant was dead. Sergeant Hickland got wounded. Of course, there were others, even a corporal, I think, but they gave it to Carlysle because he was so good—at least until the Op was over; then he went back to being snuffy. But that was all before I came. When I first met him, he was squad leader and at that time he had a buddy named Carlos. Carlos was a Cuban mulatto and he carried the radio for Carlysle, but they were tight.

"We were out on this patrol, see—really just a little walk. Well, all of a sudden, there is a single shot and it hits Carlos right in the head. Sniper. Now what happened in the rear, I only heard about, but I saw Carlysle in the field that day and I can believe what happened later."

"What happened?" Chief asked intently.

"This one shot goes, see, and the next thing I know Carlysle's blazing back at the hill and then he's down holding Carlos' head, crying. The captain fanned the troops out and the corpsman ran up, but it was too late. They tried to pull Carlysle away, but as soon as they saw Carlos' head they knew, and they just left him.

"Knew what?" Chief cut in.

"Oh, man, it was a mess. Perfect shot. Caught him right through the base of the skull, just under the helmet. Carlysle had blood all over him, but he just kept holding Carlos' head, touching his face. He kept saying over and over, 'The radio. The radio. He carried the radio for me, and they shot for the radio.'

"Well, the captain puts arty out and then calls for the medevac chopper, but Carlysle was still kneeling by Carlos' body. Two new dudes came over—brothers—and they didn't quite figure Carlysle crying. I don't know why, maybe 'cause Carlos was Cuban or something, and one says, 'Hey man, why you crying over that dude?'

"Carlysle looked up slow like and I could see the tears on his face and he says. 'He was my brother.' Nothing else, just a long sad look, and the other dude sort of sneered. Then BAM—Carlysle glares over at them like ice and he said, 'If any of yu'awl don't like what I'm crying about, then slide. Just slide on off, but don't say nothin' to me cause I just don't want to hear about it.' "

"Point man or radioman, they'us always the fust uns t'gettit," Big John added.

"You'd think they know that, but, man, they must not have believed that in the rear."

"Why's zat?" Chief cocked his eyebrow.

" 'Cause next thing we hear there's gonna be a big investigation. Something to do with there only being one shot. Well, I don't know what they thought back in the rear, but I know it was a sniper. It came from a little hill and had that special sound only gook rifles make. But, anyway, they send for somebody to give a statement and identify the body and all that shit. Well, the captain sends Carlysle to make the statement. Now, like I said, I wasn't back in the rear and this is only what I heard tell."

"All right man. Tell it anyway."

"Carlysle gets back there to Quang Tri and goes straightaway to the company hooch. Sergeant Smiles, the head clerk, sort of looks him over and seems surprised that they'd sent Carlysle. But Carlysle just stands there and tells what he's supposed to."

"So?"

"So I'm getting there," Wilson said deliberately and poured another dose of the warm liquor in his can. "Top Goresuch is back in his little cubbyhole and Carlysle couldn't see him; but Gunny Culls, that fat bastard from supply, was there talking to Goresuch sitting in the back behind a little desk, where he could see the whole hooch. Carlysle, as usual, ignores 'em all. Well, Culls gets a hair up his ass and starts in on Carlysle. He says, 'Hey, boy, I'll betcha it was one of your *brothers* that killed him. Little feud amongst the plotters, eh?' "

Big John shook his head slowly and the Chief's eyes narrowed slightly. "What'd Carlysle do then?"

"Some say different, but I heard Carlysle just went right after Culls on the spot. Leaped over the desk, busted him in the face, and grabbed him by the throat. Course all the clerks and everybody jumped up and grabbed him off, but he'd already ripped Culls' cheek open."

"Musta scared the shit outta him, too." Chief grinned.

"Yeah, I s'pose, but while they struggled to hold him, Top Goresuch roared, 'What in hell are you doing, shit maggot?' They're holding him by the arms, but Carlysle's so pissed he still tried to kick Culls with his feet."

"O Jesus."

"Well, that was all Goresuch needed. He slammed Carlysle in the stomach, chopped him in the kidneys, cuffed him with his palms on the ear—you know—all the stuff that hurts like hell but never leaves a mark."

"Yeah, that figures, Goresuch used to be a DI," Chief said.

"Then while Carlysle's about to puke and the clerks are holding him up, both Goresuch and Culls start yelling at him: 'Lock them heels.' 'Why'd you hit Gunny Culls?' 'I'm gonna throw the book at you—assaulting an NCO.' "

"What'd Carlysle say?"

"By then he got hold of himself and played it just like you do when you're in boot camp. He just stood at attention as best he could, staring straight ahead and said, 'Yes, sir—no, sir.' He had a sort of bush Afro and they started on him about his hair—about being a racist troublemaker."

"What finally happened?"

"Well, that's when the harassment really began. They never pressed the charge about hitting Culls, but they tried to get him on everything else—marijuana, insolence, what all."

Chief stroked his hairless chin and stared intently at Wilson, then he turned deliberately to Big John. "Well, Big John, all that shit with Carlysle; you ain't prejudiced like that, are you?"

"Shee-it." Big John spat.

"What's this? You haven't got the fire like Carlysle. I didn't think you cared about color." Chief spoke to Big John but was expecting Wilson to react. To his surprise it was the big man, usually so mild, who spoke out.

Big John

"Lemme tay you somethin', Chief!"

Chief was startled at the sudden intense outburst and lapsed into the mask.

"Sonny, gimme 'nother drink."

As Wilson handed Big John the whiskey, their eyes locked for an instant. Big John's eyebrow lifted just a shade in question, and Wilson gave a barely perceptible nod in answer. Even the Chief missed the little communication.

Big John took a long swallow, grimaced at the bite of the harsh liquor and leaned back. "Chief"—Big John began slowly, straining at unaccustomed words—"eva'y black man be concerned 'bout hisself an' his color today. Ih doan care wha' he say or how he act, eva'y young black man, at least, knows weahr gettin' fucked ohvur. An' they goin' t'do somethin' about it. Some of 'em doan say it, and eva'y one got a diff-runt way, but they all feels it. Tha's why Ih'm gonna play pro ball." The candle flickered on his face dully and made a weaving shadow on the crude timbers and sandbags.

"Chief, eva' time the lifa's see two brothers gettin' tugethur, they think weahr plottin'. Plottin' t'do somethin'. But when they see two Chucks tugethur or a whole bunch of Chucks tugethur or hell . . . twenny or thurty of 'em tugethur—aw, nothin' wrong with that. But three or four brothers get tugethur . . . they plottin' somethin'. And the lifa's gonna break it up. They doan even want us to talk tugethur 'cause they figger we stahrtin' to plot somethin'. Well, when we get tugethur, we gettin' tugethur fo' a *cause*. Because we wanna be happy. We wanna pahrty tugethur."

"Everybody ain't fucking you over," Chief said flatly.

"No, tha's right. Theahr three kind o' people. The black people, the white people, and the beas's. An' when the black people and the white people get tugethur, we call those white people blue-eyed soul brothers, because they doan care about the beas's. They can see d'problem's like we see 'em. But d'problem's the beas' is outta get ya. He's tryin' to *do* eva'body out of eva'thing they got."

"To make it simple—a beast is someone who's prejudiced," Wilson added.

"Is a beast always white?" Chief asked.

Big John stopped, the question unsettling him.

Wilson cut in. "Yes, we got black beasts."

"Yes, goodness! We got black beas'," Big John added strongly as if suddenly remembering. "But, Chief, sometimes all the white man make us feel second-class citizen. Eva'body feel it. Even in d'Nam weahr second-class citizens. An' a man wants t'do somethin' a-bout it."

"Well, when you're fighting in the bush, it doesn't make any difference," Chief said with conviction. Then his voice dropped. "It's when you get to the rear that you find the tension."

"That's right! That's right!" Wilson said excitedly.

"The reahr. Tha's wheah it all stahrts. In the reahr. Tha's right, Chief, you doan fin' it in da bush. People ha' t'be ohvur heahr in Vee-et Nam before dey could see wha' life is really like. An' they got t'come ta d'bush before they can see how it *should* be. Jus' like playin' ball. Yo'all a *team*. T'aint you'hr *color*, it's you'hr *ability*." Big John jumped up and his shadow careened ominously on the sandbags.

"Out in da'fiel' nine times out of ten a black dood an' a white dood gonna be in a hole tugethur. An' if you wanna get at leas' a couple hours' sleep you gotta be able to really trus' this person and to know he gonna look ohvur you while you sleep. If you get a new dood you know is prejudis, then you ain' gonna sleep that night 'cause you gonna wonder what he gonna do. Is he gonna kill me? Is he gonna let somebody come up on me?"

Wilson nodded. "That's right, Chief, you know that yourself."

The Indian said nothing.

"But afta' two doods been in d'bush a while they tugethur. They jus' like brothers; they *know* one's goin' ta protect the ohthur. An' it doan make no diffronce wha' color they ahr. One gives the ohthur a drink of his water. They drink outta the same canteen. They eat with the same spoon. They sleep unna the same poncho-linna. They doan cahre. The'ahr tugethur. The'ahr brothers."

"I know that's the way it is in the bush"—Chief cut in and his voice was hushed—"but there's some in the rear . . . like Carlysle."

Wilson shot a quick warning glance, but Big John's words were gushing.

"Back in d'reahr there's them like Carlysle what got the fire in 'em. But mos' in d'reahr jus' doan know. They jus' gotta put on a big ole *show*. These people back in the reahr, they got theah own rack; they doan ha'ta worry 'bout nobody comin' up on 'em in the night. So they doan know how it really is. But inna bush weahr tugethur." He stopped abruptly and fumbled in his pack. "Look heahr. This is one of my white pahrtners in da bush, rotated now, but Ih got this pitchur of him. Five brothers and one Chuck dood tugethur."

"Yeah, John, but the brothers in the rear . . ." Wilson hesitated. "Tell him."

Big John frowned deeply and sat down. "Sometimes the brothers doan want to take a pitchur tha' way," he said wistfully. "One time when me and Red was at Dong Ha, we was gonna take a pitchur, an' this brother said to Red, 'You got to move ohvur theah,' and I said, 'Naw, if he moves, Ih moves.' Ih say, 'He's with me, theah ain' no need for him to go to the sideline jus' cause weahr all black and he white. Weahr gonna take this pitchur tugethur. I mean he's my pahrtner, too. How come he can't git inna pitchur? If he can't get inna pitchur, Ih'm not gonna get inna pitchur.' "

Wilson listened in silence; he had heard this before and

seen similar incidents. He stared down at his long slim fingers and wrapped each one tightly around the can. He wished he had Big John's courage. Simple courage to do what he wanted.

Big John lit a PX cigarette and took a drink to fortify himself after such a long and unaccustomed talk. But he was caught in the sweep of his expression and plunged on. "Ih like it tha' way. T'see a white dood and a black dood tugethur—talkin', walkin' down the street tugethur—jus' havin' a good time." He looked down and slowly shook his head. "If . . . if just eva'one could see that—could see like it is in d'Nam—in *d'bush.*

"After Vee-et Nam. Ih be stationed at Quantico because Ih'm gonna play football. Ih hope li'l Red'll be theahr, too. An' we'll get back theahr an' weahr all gonna be tugethur, jus' like it was ohvur heahr. Because the way he see it and the way Ih see it when we get back to d'wourld, *nothin'* gonna change. Nothin' at all! Even tho we not in a fightin' zone, weahr still gonna be tugethur. We'll still be inna same uniform—an' even if we wasn't we'd still be tugethur, because he's an uptight fella."

"It isn't going to be that way, Big John," Chief said flatly. "Your own black people are going to pull you apart just as much as the whites."

Wilson looked sharply at Chief, but the Indian returned his gaze without expression.

Big John drooped his head and stared at his boots. He knew it would not be the way he wanted back in the world, but he was afraid to admit it to himself. He struggled with Chief's plain assertion but could not bring himself to face it.

"What makes you think it's going to be that way back in the world, Big John? What are you going to do to change people's feelings?" Chief's words came softly but firm.

Big John scowled deeper. The Chief had read his mind, but he was unwilling to give in. He felt the urge to tell Chief . . . to make him know what *could* happen. "Ih figgur when Ih get back to d'wourld an' Ih go see one of my white pahrtners like Red—an' Ih'm gonna see boo-coo of my white pahrtners—Ih figgur if Ih go to Red's home an' his family act like they doan like me, then Ih figgur that he's gonna tell 'em. He's gonna set 'em straight. Ih figgur he's gonna tell 'em: 'Look, Mom, look, Pop, John is like a brother to me; he's like pahrt of my family because he saved my life an' Ih saved his life.'

"Ih figgur that he'll jus' sit down and get his parents straight. An' after tha' eva'thing will be all right because he will try t'explain to them what life is like ohvur heahr; to get 'em to understan' tha' we'ah been tugethur a long time. We'ah protected each other; an' because of him Ih'm back in d'wourld an' because of me he's back in d'wourld. Tha' the way it is. An' weahr tugethur and weahr not worried about—*'Aw he's black, he might contaminate me.'*" He stopped and his eyes darted pleadingly back and forth from Wilson to Chief. Then he frowned. " 'Course Red ain' got no Pop; but same with his Momma."

Wilson slowly shook his head. "That'd be great John, but you know it's not going to be that way. Not for a long time; because of the beasts and because of our own."

Big John jumped up, shouting, his voice almost trembling, "Well, it can be! Ih doan care what Carlysle says to me. People like Carlysle doan rule me. The beas' doan rule me. Ih'm my own man. If they doan like it— fuck 'em!"

V
Da Nang

1

Doc Smitty

"Smitty! Smitty!" Red came flying toward the platoon CP. The Lieutenant, Joseley, Chief, and Doc Smitty were frying dehydrated steaks on the can lid using C-4 type dynamite for fuel. Unless a blasting cap is used it burns not explodes.

"Doc, come quick. Wilson's sick."

"What's the matter with him?" Smitty's slow Southern drawl flowed out, confident and unhurried.

"He's got the fever, Doc. He's burning up."

"Well, for Chrissake. Just all of a sudden like," he grumbled, reluctantly putting down his little square of meat. Smitty picked up his medical bag and followed Red, grunting as he went.

"I swear. Marines just can't hack it. Afternoon gets a little bit warm and yaw'l start passing out all over."

The Navy corpsman who derided the Marines so often was a tall, well-built young man with blond hair and a thin blond mustache. He was from South Carolina, and after having been bounced from a succession of Southern institutions of higher learning, he joined the Navy—primarily because his father had cut off the funds which paid for tuition, liquor, Southern belles, and gas for an Austin-Healey. Very few people knew his name. He was always called Smitty. Actually his name was Beauregard Cornelius McCaulley II, which he thought was sufficient reason to be called Smitty. Corpsmen were considered non-combatants and weren't supposed to carry weapons. Smitty carried two. An M-16 and a .45 in a shoulder holster.

Doc Smitty bent over Wilson's curled form and felt his forehead. He immediately put a thermometer in his mouth.

"Have you got stomach pains?"

"Uhmm." Wilson nodded affirmative.

"Had the shits?"

The head moved again and pain flashed across the face.

"Christ, yes, Doc, he's been on the shitter every fifteen minutes," Red interjected.

"Got a headache?"

The head nodded slowly, affirmative.

Smitty ceased questioning and pondered the body, waiting for the thermometer. Wilson was obviously in pain. He lay holding his middle and his eyes squinted. Smitty reached for the thermometer and read it carefully. A hundred and three! "Go find the Gunny or the Lieutenant. See if they can get a jeep or a truck. I'm taking Wilson to Delta Med."

"Okay, Doc." Red ran off.

"Do you feel hot, Wilson?"

"Yes." The reply was weak and said almost without breath.

"Have you had any bad chills?"

"Yeah, I think so. Mostly I just feel weak."

"Okay, I'm going to take you down to the Delta Med. You're lucky we're in Quang Tri or we'd have to call a medevac chopper."

"What have I got, Doc?" the words were whispered. His head rested oddly on the ground. He made no motion to lift it. Even his eyes seemed to droop with weakness.

"I don't know for sure. That's why I'm sending you to see the doctor."

"What do you think?" came the whisper.

"Since you ask, I'll tell you. I think you got malaria. But I don't know for sure. We'll take you down there, and they can make tests and tell for positive."

"Oh, no. I don't want malaria, Doc. Don't send me."

"Just take it easy. They have racks there. You can sleep good."

Wilson thought about the beds, and his mind swam off into a sea of longing for sleep. His body began to shake. Smitty covered him with a poncho-liner.

Smitty half-walked, half-carried Wilson into the triage room. The real doctor rapidly asked Smitty the symptoms, took Wilson's temperature, and tagged him for the ship.

"Smitty, what they going to do with me?"

"They're going to send you to the hospital ship, the *Sanctuary*. Out there they're going to give you all the tests. Have you got anything in your pack that you care about? They'll take your gear."

"Keep my M-14. There's only two in the platoon now."

They hobbled on the chopper and Smitty took the big rifle. It was immaculately clean and oiled for a bush weapon.

"Smitty?" Wilson's voice said weakly.

"Yeah?"

"Keep my helmet cover, too, willya? It's got my calendar on it."

"No sweat man." Smitty took the battered helmet with the intricately designed calendar.

"I'll be back," Wilson whispered grimly. "I promise."

Marines—Smitty grimaced and shook his head wanly, then the engines started and he ran off.

Wilson

The ramp closed and the roar came on. The chopper shuddered and seemed to shake Wilson's every bone. He huddled against the wind and he tried to crawl to a sheltered spot, but the floor was lined with litters. Weakness flooded over him and his head rolled down on the steel floor; he was too weak to lift it. He only wanted to sleep. The wind came stronger and he curled into a shivering ball. The gunner's foot was right in front of his face.

Wilson lay for a long time in the half-zone of feverish sleep. The wind and the vibration plagued him, keeping him awake. His weakened body sucked him down. Then he heard the shrieking, droning whine, and he was sweating. The chopper was hit and they were burning.

The crewmen smoked on nonchalantly.

Suddenly voices were yelling and people were moving.

He staggered weakly to his feet. It's a hot LZ! Get off the chopper, run, run. "Oh, my God," he yelled. The fantail seemed to end right before him. The water was coming up. He swayed over and then strong hands were guiding him toward the door. A sailor stopped him.

"Got any ammo, knives?"

He thought of the treasured K-bar buried in his pack. "No," he said weakly. His whole strength seemed to be clutching that pack. Hands went over his pockets, patting, and then he was stumbling on.

He heard a voice behind him, "That one's not hit, but

he looks like a walking zombie."

Somebody propelled him toward a desk. Others were in front of him. Oh, let me sleep, he thought. Oblivious of all Wilson lay down on the floor clutching his pack. Man, it's hot in here. Turn off the heat. Oh Sylvia, so hot.

"Hey, you, let me see those papers." The voice cut into Wilson's consciousness. Hands helped him up. The man took the papers and wrote something on them and handed a few back. "Corporal Wilson, okay. Follow that man."

Again he had to wait in the corridor. "Oh, fuck it, I don't care what they say." He murmured and lay down in the corridor. His head rested on the floor and he felt the ship's engine throbbing.

A ship. I'm on the hospital ship, Wilson thought dimly. How did I get here? Am I wounded? Presently the door opened. Shoes came out, shiny black shoes. Wilson frowned at the shoes. I must be dirty. Oh, I don't care, just let me rest.

"Get this guy in to the doctor. He looks bad." Again hands, helping hands, kind hands lifted him and he groped on.

This is a hospital, he thought. It smells like a hospital. He had glimpses of men in blue gowns and others in green gowns.

Beds, tables, machines.

A door opened. He staggered in. Three figures recoiled. Wilson's eyes went wide—a white girl, a round-eyed white American girl—and he saw the bars on her shoulder.

"Ohh," he gasped and slumped into a chair. I don't care, just let me sleep.

The three stared. The girl's mouth hung open. The doctors recovered, but the girl continued to stare. She had seen the door burst open and a tall black man in incredibly filthy clothes virtually fall into the room. For a second his eyes were wide as if in horror. His grimy face had a scraggly beard. He clutched a bundle firmly in his hands. Suddenly his eyes seemed to bug out and he dropped into a chair as if he were dead. The powerful stench of a long-unwashed body filled the room.

"My God"—she finally broke from her trance—"he looks awful." The doctors flashed her a warning look. "Just get a blood sample." The doctor took the papers and began asking questions.

"I'm tired, doctor. I want to sleep. But . . . ohhh." He grimaced as a spasm of pain worked its way down his stomach; he looked around the room wildly. "Have you got a . . ."

"Yes, right there. In through there—quickly!"

Wilson ran into the bathroom and barely got his pants down, oblivious of the fact that he was sitting on a flush toilet for the first time in seven months.

After the tests the nurse led him to a bed.

Clean white sheets, a real mattress. His mouth worked soundlessly and his hands moved to his shirt.

"Don't you want to take a shower first?"

"Huh? Oh." Wilson's brain pondered the question dimly. "No. Sleep."

"You can have a hot shower now if you like." The girl held his arm, firmly urging him.

"*Hot* shower?" Christ, he hadn't had a hot shower since . . . but he wanted to sleep, so tired. But a hot shower. No, he had to sleep.

"Come on, it'll feel good," the honeyed voice purred on. Yet it was insistent; her words were firm.

"Okay," he said weakly. He stripped and dropped the clothes into the locker. He took the towel and groggily followed the nurse to the shower, oblivious even of the fact that he'd been naked next to a white girl. His only thought was of the shower and of sleep. He swam on through the fog.

He groaned aloud in both pleasure and pain, leaning weakly against the side of the shower and letting the warm water flow down over him. The water in the drain turned brown; the suds were brown, and the dirt streamed off in muddy rivulets.

He lifted the sheets and crawled in, feeling himself sinking. He'd never wanted to sleep so badly. He was asleep before his head hit the pillow.

Four days later he was up running all over the decks, playing ping-pong, ogling the nurses.

It wasn't malaria. Only Ho Chi Minh's revenge in triplicate, maybe dysentery. Something like that, the Doc had said. Wilson did know, however, that on the second day he'd gone to the head eighteen times. He held himself gingerly. Have to requisition a new asshole, he thought; though the cramps and the pain had been worse. He couldn't get over the ship. White sheets, mattresses, flush toilets, air-conditioning, cold-water fountains, round-eyed nurses, silver tableware, TV, ice cream, white round-eyed nurses.

Hot showers! It took three days and five separate showers before all the dirt finally came off. On the third day he opened the locker for his clothes.

"Jesus Christ, what a stench," he exclaimed aloud and recoiled. Had *he* smelled like that? No wonder they had wanted him to take a bath. But considering that he had worn the same clothes for twenty-one days straight, he guessed that it wasn't surprising.

Wilson felt wonderful, but when the doctor came, he regularly complained of a terrible pain. There were many others like him. It might have gone on for some time— had he not bought the whiskey from the sailor.

He and about four others who were faking their sicknesses lay in their racks guzzling steadily. Some other stuff was provided and consumed. They were feeling quite fine, for sick men, and they trooped off to chow.

"Chow call, grease call, garbage call." They ducked into an open hatch and clattered down the steel stairs toward the mess deck.

"Chow call, grease call, garbage call," they chanted in unison.

"Chow call, grease call, garbage call." People began to look.

The enlisted men's mess aboard the ship was designed for speed and not for comfort. The men took aluminum trays as they entered and passed through a serving line where they held out the trays. Sullen sailors in skivvies dropped globs of food in flowing, melting, mixing, streaming, dripping mounds. The Marines then carried their blob-filled trays to chest-high aluminum tables where they ate standing up—those who weren't too sick, that is. Minions of the master-at-arms moved through the mess hall urging them to "Chow down and move on."

"Mashed 'taters and gravy. Slop it on there, sailor, that's it, right on top of my salad. Well done, lad, well done."

"Fried chicken. Just like Mom used to make. She always burned it, too."

"How 'bout some more ice cream, sailor?"

"Thanks a fuckin' lot. Right on top of my mashed potatoes. Jesus Fuckin' Christ."

The drunken force swayed on down the lines.

"Goddamn, swabbie, don't you wash your hands before you serve our chow? Give me another drumstick, will ya?"

"Watch Wilson. He thinks he's a fuckin' animal or something."

"Hey, bread on the line over here."

The five of them carried their trays over to a nearby table and started eating. As other Marines passed by from the line nearby, Wilson reached out and stole the chicken from their trays. He soon had a large pile of legs, thighs, and wings.

"Milk, *mmmm* good," Wilson grunted. He picked up the cardboard container and carefully tore off one corner. He looked across at his buddy on the other side of the table.

"How you doin' there, Wilson, uh, Wilson man?" his buddy asked. Wilson squeezed the container and a stream of milk shot across the table into his buddy's face.

"Why you maggot." The buddy laughed. He aimed his container and splattered Wilson's face. The second one tore open his container and sprayed the third one's neck. The third one shot a stream into the first one's chest. Others at the long table began tearing, aiming, squeezing, cursing, laughing. Wilson picked up a handful of mashed potatoes and gravy and lobbed it at a PFC. The PFC ducked and it hit a corporal behind him in the ear. The corporal seized his drumstick and fired it at Wilson. Wilson shot his ice cream potato mix at a lance corporal at the next table. The lance corporal fired back a wing. Soon the sky was filled with missiles flying back and forth. Legs raining down, mixed salads bursting into a thousand fragments, mashed potatoes exploding.

"Corpsman, corpsman, corpsman, I'm hit!" someone shouted.

When trays were emptied, knives, forks, and spoons began zinging across the room.

"Corpsman, corpsman, I'm hit!"

"*Agghh,* they got me."

"You'll never take me alive, Charlie."

"Chew on this, mother-fucker."

Trays began sailing through the air.

"Heavy artillery—hit the deck!"

Men were under the tables, crawling on the floor, looking for more ammo.

"Watch it, ground attack coming."

The master-at-arms and several of his men burst into the room blowing whistles. A heavy barrage of slop drove them out again. Then the sailors on the serving line came under fire. They retaliated with fresh ammo from their pots.

The master-at-arms ran back in. Another bombardment drove him out.

Over the PA system a voice was blaring, "Now hear this. Now hear this."

The battle stations.

Wilson went back to the company the next day.

Wilson climbed down the ship's ladder still laughing over the food fight. He leaned back against the rail of the little boat as it started toward Da Nang. The fresh salt air brushed softly against his cheek; without it the afternoon would be unbearably hot. Once he looked back and saw the big white ship with the giant red-colored cross on it. These two ships, the *Sanctuary* and the *Repose*, are about the only good things the Marines got, he thought. I s'pose that's because they're provided by the Navy.

As they rode across the bay, all Da Nang seemed to be one-storied tin-roofed shanties. Here and there a tall building rose up. Except for the hustling coming and going of the Navy yard, it seemed very still. He glanced at his watch and remembered that the Vietnamese took a long lunch hour and everything stopped. But the Navy kept on going, endlessly unloading cartons, boxes, military supplies.

Da Nang. Headquarters of the Third Marine Amphibious Force, III MAF, and the First Marine Division. Second largest city in South Vietnam. Supply point for all of I Corps, the northernmost five provinces of South Vietnam.

The bus from the dock to the transient center turned out to be an open truck. As it jounced along, Wilson wished he could stay there a day or two and see what the place was like.

The squalid buildings with tin roofs went by. At least they have a few paved streets, Wilson thought. That's better than anywhere else he'd seen in Vietnam. They bounced on through streets teeming with Vietnamese. Wilson had never seen so many Vietnamese. Babies played in the dirt and wore no clothing except a shirtwaist which came to the middle of a protruding belly. Children only a few years older carried babies sidestraddle on their hips. Bicycles and Hondas in a never-ending mass streamed around the truck. Old women carrying bundles. Men sitting on the sidewalks. In the jungle mountains along the DMZ the Montagnard natives had been evacuated and the only Vietnamese Wilson had seen were enemy. But here they milled in all directions. Little girls in nondescript baggy clothes came up to the truck selling soda pop and beer.

"You buy? You buy?" They wore loose black silky-looking pants and usually a faded pastel shirt squared at the bottom and worn outside the trousers. Wilson noticed immediately that they were all flat as a board. There was not a bra or a tit on one of them. And always the women wore the large conical fiber hat with a ribbon under the chin, the men a pith helmet or a military cap, the boys a Marine soft cover.

The women carried immense loads over their shoulders on their "chogie sticks." The shoulder was at the balance midpoint of the stick; on each end, suspended by wires or straps, were two large baskets containing all manner of things. Sometimes the baskets were replaced by two large cans filled with water. Little girls carried them. Wilson eyed the size of the water cans and wondered if he could lift them himself.

The truck went through a downtown area and the houses changed to one- or two-story affairs. Faded yellow bricks or plaster with slate roofs. Must have been built by the French, he thought.

There were shops and stalls everywhere. Every kind of food seemed to be piled on the sidewalks for sale. Chickens, ducks, pigs, oranges, melons, greens, mysterious vegetables. Other sidewalk shops had pots, pans, clothes, hats, junk of all types.

The truck stopped at an intersection. Wilson was enthralled by the panorama of things for sale on the sidewalks—the multiple colors. Suddenly an object with English lettering caught his eye. He looked closer and burst out laughing. There were row after row of cans, each one neatly labeled:

VEGETABLE OIL (COOKING)
MADE IN USA
FOR DISTRIBUTION TO THE PEOPLE OF VIETNAM
NOT FOR SALE

Beyond that he saw large bags of rice, similarly marked:

LONG GRAIN RICE
PRODUCT OF USA
NOT FOR SALE

He'd heard of the black market but always supposed it would be something sinister, a transaction hidden in a dark corner. Here they were selling stuff right out in the open.

The truck rolled on and now Wilson saw women dressed very differently from the sellers of pop and carriers of bundles. Here they were much more respectable. Some of the women walked, some rode bicycles, others were in cyclos—the bicycle-pushed rickshaw. A few even rode in jeeps.

They wore the *ao dai*, the national Vietnamese dress. It was a single thin garment with long sleeves and a tightly fitted bodice and waist. The bottom part was split to the waist along both sides, but the two halves of the skirt hung to the ankles. Under that was worn black or white pants—loose by American standards. The *ao dai*'s were many colors but purple or white seemed to be the most popular. He noticed that those in solid white seemed to be schoolgirls with books.

The women were tiny and delicate. The young ones wore their hair long and straight, often hanging to the waist in back. The older ones all wore it done up in a ball at the back of their necks. Both wore the open-flap-type sandals; whereas the peasant women all had been barefoot. It seemed to Wilson that there was something else different about these downtown women, but he couldn't put his finger on it.

A pair of pretty young girls rode by on bicycles right next to the truck. Wilson could see the hem outline of their panties through the thin white cloth. Their bras showed plainly in the back. *Bras!* That's it. Tits, he realized in a flash. The fancier women got tits. Wait a minute, he thought. Looking closely he saw that the bras all poked straight out, just two lines coming to a point. They didn't bounce. They weren't round. "Wow," he murmured. Falsies. He quickly looked at the other women—they were all the same, either flat or with no variation in size. I'll be damned—Hong Kong bras on all of them.

The paved road ended and the houses became more scraggly. Now they were made of old pieces of wood, mostly discarded ammo boxes. The roofs were a mixture of tin sheets held on with sandbag weights and grass thatch. Sometimes they were just canvas pieces. Hanging canvas and ponchos served as doors on sidewalks. The poorest had sides only of cardboard C-ration boxes. He wondered how these people had lived before the Marines had come to Vietnam.

As the truck bumped along, the kids all seemed to wave or give the thumbs-up sign. Others just stuck out their hands in the universal begging gesture. Another Marine on the truck took out some gum and flipped it at the line of kids along the street. Suddenly it was as if the truck had become the Pied Piper. Dirty kids of all sizes swooped down on the gum, and hordes more ran after the truck.

"Chop, chop."

"Gimme chop-chop."

"Gimme candy."

"Okay—Salem."

"You, you, you."

There were little ones in shirtwaists, babies in nothing but pokey bellies and rounded bottoms; middle-sized ones in shorts; but they were all yelling and begging.

The Marine then took out a package of cigarettes, carefully removed the last one, and tossed the empty box to the trailing mob. There was another mad scramble, but this time the faces came up scowling.

"Fuck you" was yelled in clear English. Another one shot the truck a bird.

The Marine laughed. "Little bastards will run after anything."

Wilson didn't laugh.

As they neared the base, crude signs began to appear:

WASH HERE
WE FIX FLAT

He saw Marines standing about in little shacks while Vietnamese eagerly washed trucks and vehicles. A girl near the door looked him squarely in the eye, lifted her clenched fist and shook it in the air. She smiled broadly. Wilson was so surprised he only gaped. The other black man on the truck grinned and returned the black power salute, then looked cooly at Wilson. Wilson flushed but said nothing. He'd never seen a Vietnamese girl throw power before.

But his mind went back to the truck wash. There was something odd that stuck in his brain and he couldn't place it. He looked ahead watching for another. They rolled past a large one, and there were at least five or six vehicles with about fifteen brothers standing around. He saw a few kids washing the vehicles, but the brothers didn't seem to be interested in that. Intrigued, he looked closely. There were no Chucks. This was an *all-black* truck wash. Then he saw the sign: LINDA AND SALLY'S TRUCK WASH.

Linda and Sally? That's no Vietnamese name. Then he saw a girl come out of one of the shacks and he understood immediately. She was Vietnamese but didn't look like one. She wore tight American-style pants and her shirt was open wide at the throat and tucked in at the waist. Her face was pretty but hard with heavy makeup. Red lips, black eyeliner, even blue eyeshadow. Wilson quickly raised his fist, and from the ground 15 proud fists answered in unison. He felt vindicated and glanced over at the other man. The brown eyes flashed back and smiled.

"Got some good laig there."

"What they cost?" Wilson asked.

"Five bucks for a short-time."

Wilson worked with the phone for more than half an hour before he got his cousin. He'd been amazed that phones were available but had about decided they were useless anyway. It had taken him fifteen minutes of asking and questioning to find out how to call and another twenty to get through.

His cousin was a Navy officer, a lieutenant jg, and Wilson was hesitant to call. But they had been good friends a few years ago and Wilson's father had helped Clem through school. Now he was glad he'd called; Clem had been real friendly and had told Wilson that he would pick him up after work that afternoon.

"How are you going to get me?"

"In my jeep, how else?"

"You got your own jeep?"

"Sure. We'll have drinks and dinner. I've got a lot of things to show you. It'll be a ball. See you about four thirty."

Four thirty! Regular working hours? A jeep! Drinks and dinner! Wilson couldn't get over it all. For months he'd had no concept of time or days other than time marked by the appearance of the sun and the taking of a malaria pill on Sunday. There were no hours. They worked all hours. Day in and day out. Except twice, in the rear at Quang Tri when they were allowed to drink and loaf for two days. Happiness was not being attacked in the night or keeping the same position for an extra day without patrolling. A crate of apples with the C-rats was a grand occasion. A can of dehydrated steaks and enough time to soak and cook them was a party.

Wilson had no sooner walked in the door of the transient center than someone threw him a salute. They gave power and Wilson noticed the technique was a little different in Da Nang. They didn't blow in their fists. The brother told him about the China Beach R 'n' R center and they took the bus together.

"Who're you with?" Wilson asked his new friend as they slid into the seat.

"One-Nine."

"One-Nine, but they're up north. How come you're here?" The other grinned. "You haven't been out of the bush much, have you?"

"Well, no, but . . ."

"Look man, ain't no point bein' in the bush if you don't have to. I been eight months in the bush and I got one Heart. That's enough. I figure I done my time. Gonna stay in the rear from now on. I got forty-six days left and I ain't about to go back and get my ass blown away now."

"But how do you stay down here?"

"Simple. I told the doc my knee was hurting me, hurting me bad. I got shrapnel here in the knee, you know, so it sounds legit. Doc ain't got no way of telling about my knee. Maybe still some shrapnel. Maybe something's fucked up; so I come in every day and say, 'Hurts bad, Doc.' Well, he sends me down to NSA hospital here in Da Nang. So I takes a few days to get there, and 'course I ain't never in a hurry to get ahead of the other dudes in the line. And so it takes a couple of days for the doc to get round to see me. Then they takes all kinds of tests, X rays and shit like that, and they can't find nothin' wrong and so they send me back. That, right there, is good for a couple of weeks. Now they's supposed to send a notice to your unit, but I know lots of time they don't. Or else the notice gets lost." He grinned.

He lit a cigarette and thought for a minute. "There's lots of ways, man. Me, what I done is simple. I see this brother at the desk and I says, 'I got to see another doc; don't put no release date on my papers.' Well, he's up-tight, see, and he grins and just signs away but leaves the date blank. Now if I get picked up by the MP's, I just fill in the date and say I'm on my way."

"Pretty slick." Wilson's mind was spinning with the possibility. Then he thought of his squad. Something pulled inside him. No. He'd be letting them down.

"Man, there's lots of ways. That one's just mine. I'll go back in a day or two so it don't look too suspicious. Long as I can stay away from the top, I'm okay."

"Yeah, I know about that."

"If this is your first time here, you won't believe some of the shit that goes on."

"Like what?" Wilson asked, letting the men back in the squad slip from his mind.

"Like the number of brothers what gone UA or AWOL and live with the gooks."

"With the *gooks?*"

"Yeah man. The women will keep 'em. . . ."

The bus had been rolling for nearly an hour when it crossed a long bridge and stopped at a large complex of buildings. A big sign read CHINA BEACH EXCHANGE.

Wilson saw men in Air Force, Army, and civilian clothes.

Just then two men with blond hair got on and Wilson's eyes practically fell out of his head. They were wearing Bermuda shorts and sport shirts and had open beer cans in their hands.

The brother saw Wilson's amazement and laughed. "Probably on incountry R 'n' R. They stay down at the beach center and they're allowed to come up to the PX like that. Or they could be Air Force. Air Force's allowed to wear civilian clothes off duty. Also got a lot of civilians working here, but I don't think they're civilians—hair's too short."

"Civilians?"

"Yeah. Private contractors, USAID, CIA, and all kinds. Most got long hair though."

The bus stopped and Wilson's friend led the way down through a grove of swaying pine trees which opened out onto a great expanse of golden sandy beach. A bright blue sea lapped up on the shore, and the sharp furl of a sail cut the water in a white foamy trough.

"Jesus Christ."

Wilson stood absolutely dumbfounded. Men were lying about, sunbathing, swimming, drinking, a couple were tossing a football. They walked toward the beach and Wilson could already feel the warm sand between his toes and fresh salt air on his face. The friend went in a log-cabin-like building and came out with some beers. He sat down at the water's edge and the sun was warm on his back. The friend handed him an icy beer.

"I just can't believe it. Man, I *just can't believe it*. This can't be Vietnam."

"Who wants war, man? This is livin'."

"Just a few days ago, I was up in the hills—dirty, smelly, getting shot at. Wow. Look at me now. Do they ever get hit down here?" Wilson looked around suddenly, conscious of security.

"Are you shitting me? Get a couple rockets now and then, but there's no sweat. The local dudes get all bent out of shape, but there's no sweat. Particularly for a man that's been up north by the Z."

Wilson took a long drink and lay back. Maybe he'd just stay here a while, too. Why should he go back?

"I'll tell you who's really got a skatin' job. Skatin' the whole of d'Nam."

"Who?"

"See them two Chucks running that water-ski boat?"

Wilson saw two deeply tanned men in bright swimming trunks. Their hair was bleached straw-colored, and they had that heavy muscled look, with the big veins and sharp definition that comes only from extensive weight lifting.

"Yeah, I see them. What do they do?"

"They're assigned here to the beach R 'n' R Center. All they do is run the boat, check out sporting gear and shit like that. Just a Goddamn beach boy."

"Is that all they do for the whole tour?" Wilson asked incredulously.

"That's it, man. Thirteen months in d'Nam, surfin' and swimmin'. Never hear a shot fired."

"Damn!"

"Don't see no brothers with a job like that, do you?"

Wilson didn't answer but scowled and quaffed his beer. "Fuck it, man. Let's have some more beer."

The jeep screeched to a stop at four thirty-five. A tall good-looking man got out. He had square shoulders and a smooth even-featured face. He was darker than Wilson, but his features were thinner and more delicate. It was his manner, however, that people noticed. He appeared animated, as if he were always swimming with swift clean strokes. His personality matched, being direct and open. He had that ability to speak directly to a man and establish instant communication.

"Bob, how are you? You're looking swell."

Wilson had been waiting on the steps. He sprang up and shook hands, conventional-style. "Okay, Clem."

He was glad to see his cousin and Clem greeted him warmly, but he felt a sudden embarrassment or uneasiness at being with an officer. Though they had played together often when they were younger, Wilson now felt the weight of the rank. Clem seemed breezy and unperturbed.

They left the Marine area and presently pulled up to a long wooden building which, in contrast to the ramshackle condition of the Marine transient area, wasn't new but was clean and well cared for. Inside, Clem had a room which, evidently, was shared with one other man. There was a bench and Wilson noticed the white sheets. There were bunks, wall lockers, bureaus, and small tables that doubled as desks. Along the wall there was an AKAI M-9 tape deck with Cross Field heads and Sansui 320 speakers. Two lawn chairs faced an eighteen-inch portable Panasonic TV.

The usual *Playboy* pictures were on the wall. Wilson glanced at them briefly. He'd seen them all a million times. His eyes suddenly riveted on a giant photograph which was as large as the *Playboy* pictures. It was in black and white but stood out sharply from the peachy, powdered perfection of the *Playboy* manikins. This was a real girl and she looked very warm and human. It was a full-length picture of a completely nude Vietnamese. She was turned slightly, and the position highlighted her slender curves; her whole manner spoke demureness and modesty. Yet it was strangely and strongly appealing.

"Where did you get that?" Wilson asked, pointing to the photograph.

Clem looked up from changing and said casually, "Oh, that's Kim Lan."

"Ah, well, uhh, how did you . . ."

Clem straightened, delighting in the obvious awe and puzzlement on Wilson's face. "*Co* Kim Lan. She's my girlfriend. I took the picture myself, right over there against the wall," he said proudly, pleased with the reaction it had on Wilson.

"Wow, that's all right. She go with you regular?"

"Anytime I'm ready."

"Can you bring her here?"

"Better believe it. Carl, that's my roommate, we switch nights using the room. He's got a girl, too. Sometimes we bring them both here for a party, but they're pretty nice girls and they get shy around each other."

"Man, a steady piece of ass in d'Nam."

"It's Carl's turn tonight. That's why we're going to the Stone Elephant."

"Stone Elephant? What's that?"

"Let's see"—Clem ignored the question and was looking Wilson up and down—"your utes are clean because you just got off the ship. But that jungle hat will never do. Look, sit here a minute and throw some polish on those boots. I'll go over and get you a regular Marine cover and some bars."

"*Some bars?!* Wait a minute. What's going on?"

"*Ba* Tuy, my Momma-san does mine. I think she keeps the polish in the drawer."

"Hey, what is all this? Who's *Ba* Tuy?"

Clem laughed. "She's our maid. Cleans, washes clothes, shines shoes every day. But she's not here now, and those decrepit things of yours will stand out like a sore thumb without some polish."

Wilson looked down at his jungle boots. They were worn, almost tan-white. "All right, I'll polish them. Just tell me what's going on."

Clem darted out and returned in a minute with a Marine cover and a pair of gold bars—Marine second lieutenant's insignia. "Now listen, put these on and I'm going to take you to the best place in Da Nang. It's probably one of the nicest spots in Vietnam. It's the Navy Officers Club and it's called the Stone Elephant."

Wilson's eyes got big. "Waait . . ."

"There's no sweat. Just put on these bars and we'll walk in together and nobody will ask you a thing. Just do what I do."

"But what if they ask for my ID?"

"Look, don't sweat it. They know me, and besides if you're in uniform, they never ask for an ID. Once inside, just drink and enjoy yourself. I'll introduce you as my cousin, and we'll say you just got off the *Sanctuary;* which is all true. Nobody will suspect a thing."

"Okay, man, if you say so. After all—what the hell can they do? Send me to Vietnam?"

They rode through the twilight and bounced over the patched and torn streets. Wilson had thought that the whole Vietnamese part of the town was as junky as the section he had seen from the truck, but now he saw that there were one or two areas with big estate-type houses. These all had a wall around them with a guard and a sandbag bunker at the gate.

Clem pulled up to a low nondescript building and parked in the street.

"It's over there." He pointed down toward a lighted gate with a sentry before it. "Now, don't forget to salute the sentry."

Wilson's throat went dry for a second, but inwardly he was pleased at the thought of the man saluting him.

Wilson followed Clem across the street. He could see the sentry. His plastic helmet had a white NSA on the side. Wilson was trembling inside, but he forced himself to be calm. He pressed close behind Clem as if for protection. It seemed to take forever to cross the street. It was as if they were standing still and the sentry was coming closer. Act calm, act calm, he told himself.

They drew closer and Wilson forced his eyes to look straight ahead. Out of the corner of his eye he saw the sentry's hand go up. It seemed to be reaching out for him. But Clem was saluting. Clem's hand casually waved up near his forehead and flipped outward, more like "Howdy" than a salute.

Salute, damn it, salute, he said to himself. He felt frozen. Conscious of every muscle moving, he brought his arm up and touched his hat-bill precisely. His arm snapped down in a perfect textbook salute. Wilson hadn't saluted like that since boot camp. They breezed on in and the sentry never even looked at them. They went in the door and no one stopped them; Wilson felt his chest easing, but he stuck to Clem like glue. Clem checked his .45 and hung his hat on a rack.

They were in!

The place hit Wilson like a bomb blast. He was conscious of cool air meeting him. Air-conditioning. *Ahhhh.* He was covered with sweat from the sultry temperature as well as from his own tenseness. There was a stone wall to his right with elaborately sculptured holes, and through them he saw bars, tables, colored lights. They rounded the wall and the cool air flowed over him. Wilson blindly followed Clem, but his senses were lost in a panorama of pleasure. The beach had amazed him, but this was beyond all comprehension. The bar ran the length of the room. It was glassy black formica with a heavy leather-covered elbow rest. There were high barstools with curved wooden backrests in captain's-chair form, and they had tufted upholstery of deep-red naugahyde. Wilson sat gingerly in a huge chair which was shaped like a sculptured eggshell. The chair seemed to come up around him, and he sank down into the plush softness of it, sensuously enjoying the smooth black leather.

"My God, what chairs these are," he said aloud.

The tables were finished in a highly polished wood, set at a perfect height for glasses. He looked around the room and was thunderstruck. The room was plush. Soft indirect lighting glowed. Bottles gleamed. Chromium fixtures glistened. In the light, polished wood reflected a mute luster. Soft music came from somewhere. Yet the room was filled with men in utilities and dungarees. Heavy jungle boots were propped on the brass bar rail. The .45's and .38's hung in the hall.

Clem's voice cut through Wilson's awestruck staring. "What'll you have?"

"Ahh, what're you having?"

"A vodka gimlet on the rocks."

"Oh, I'll just have a beer." He became conscious that two others were at the table and that Clem had greeted them with great gusto and funny sayings like "Hello, you old Marine bastard." Wilson suddenly froze. These were white officers and one was a Marine Corps captain! Wilson nearly fainted.

"Ray, this is my cousin Bob, Bob Wilson. Say hello to Ray Carter and Al Jacobs."

Wilson saw the hands coming at him and he heard the voices booming out cheerfully. "Bob, how are you doing? Good to see you." The hands and voices were as if in a dream. He clicked back in and shook the hands, nodded, smiled, and uttered a weak hello.

"What outfit were you with?" The Marine captain asked.

"He's from up north—Third Marines." Clem cut in smoothly. "Just got off the *Sanctuary* from a case of dysentery."

Good old Clem, Wilson thought.

The Marine started to say something, but just then a Vietnamese waitress in a short American-style miniskirt came up and leaned on Clem's chair. They all seemed to know her and immediately started chattering; she flirted gaily. They joked with her and offered to take her out for the night. She fielded their swaggering offers easily, laughing and avoiding their wandering hands. Finally she went off after the drinks. Wilson noticed that some of the other waitresses wore the Vietnamese *ao dai* and seemed more demure.

The drinks came and Wilson began to relax. He tilted back and sipped the beer. Never in a million years would he have guessed that this place was here.

Presently they went into another room for dinner. Clem bought them both a steak and got a bottle of red wine. The steaks were thick and juicy, obviously fresh or frozen. He couldn't help but laugh as he remembered his C-rations and the fried waterboo shit at the Rockpile.

After dinner they went back to the cocktail lounge. A band was warming up and Wilson felt a surge of memories come to him. He felt the urge to be going up there, taking the microphone and singing.

Slowly the shock of the surroundings began to wear off, but a new uneasiness crept into Wilson's mind. He'd already passed the entrance test and nobody had asked him for an ID, but now he became aware that they were the only two black men in the place. For a while he watched Clem; how free and smooth he was. Everybody seemed to know him. Wilson realized he was envious. My God, Clem was laughing and joking with all those Chuck officers. They actually seemed to seek him out, as if he really was somebody they wanted to be with.

The band started up and the sound filled the room. Not quite the stuff he would have liked, but it didn't matter. Then a door opened and the girl came out. Everyone hooted and shrilled. Wilson's eyes became glued to her breasts. She was tall and curved just right. Long blond hair hung down below her shoulders. Heavy eyelashes fluttered over pale-blue eyes. Australian. She began to dance to the music and the long diaphanous wrap swayed. Wilson forgot himself, forgot Vietnam, forgot the bush, forgot he didn't belong. The girl dropped the veil and gyrated in only a tiny French bikini. The room went wild.

Clem leaned over. "How 'bout that?"

"That's all right," Wilson's voice was a little thick.

"Her nose is a little long, but I'd still screw her." Clem laughed lewdly and took another drink.

Her nose! Wilson hadn't even noticed her *nose!* Suddenly he realized what Clem had said and all his doubts came flooding back. What did he want? Did he want to be like Clem—accepted, looked up to, sought after, part of the Man's world? It was a question he'd fought with himself about a thousand times, yet there was never any answer. He slumped back, sweating in spite of the air-conditioning, and an image of Sylvia's Afro hairdo floated before him.

He became aware of two Vietnamese waitresses looking curiously at him. They were whispering. Did they know? Wilson was sure they were looking right at the bars. My God. Somehow they knew he wasn't an officer, that he didn't *belong* here. It was only a matter of time before they'd tell. Then someone would check. He'd be thrown out. He didn't think of the legal consequences; he only thought of the shame and humiliation of being thrown out. He was masquerading. He didn't belong here. He wasn't good enough. He was second-class. He'd always been second-class. They knew and they were looking at him. Their eyes seemed to say second-class black.

Suddenly the music stopped, the girl ran off the floor, and everybody was clapping. The Vietnamese girls were serving drinks again. He gulped down his beer and shook his head to push the thought away. Clem and a Marine lieutenant were busy talking, but the lieutenant noticed Wilson and politely started to bring him into the conversation. "What basic school class were you in?"

For a moment Wilson sat stone-still, the question ringing numbly in his ears. Then red-hot panic charged through his whole body.

"What?" He stammered.

"We must have gone through training about the same time. What was your basic school class?" the lieutenant asked again.

"I . . . I uhhh, excuse me, I got to go to the head." He jumped up, knocking over the egg chair and tore from the room.

Clem stared for a minute and then laughed. "He's still got the runs from the dysentery."

After the Stone Elephant closed, Clem had wanted Wilson to go on to the MAC V Club, but Wilson had had enough. Clem called a Navy taxi for him. It was a large pickup truck, the driver up front with a shotgun rider. The back had two parallel benches for seats, and the truck was covered with a wire mesh to keep hand grenades from getting into the bed. Wilson settled back and the truck sped through the darkened streets. The warm night air soothed him and washed away the tensions of the Officers Club. He was Lance Corporal Wilson again. The air was soft and so dense it almost had texture—like a large breast.

Da Nang changed completely at night. Gone were the floods of people, the herds of Hondas and bicycles, and the women with the bundles on their shoulders. The sidewalks were bare, doors closed, windows barred. Night time in a city at war.

Here and there down an alley Wilson caught a glimpse of children or women squatting around a few bowls, a tiny light glowing. No one walked the streets, apart from the Vietnamese patrols. Darkness had turned the city into a maze of security checkpoints, flood-lit machine-gun towers, fleeting shadows.

The truck sped on, roaring from one sentry post to another. In his pool of light the sentry leans forward, peering intently for a moment, then slouches back and waves them on. Headlights leap up again and bore through the night. The shadows flashed by, carrying the real or imagined threat of VC, a grenade, a shot in the dark. Wilson's senses went back to the jungle. Who was in those shadows? What was lurking in those narrow alleys? But it's like a dream and the night whispers by.

VI
The Road to Laos

Colonel Gaither

"Colonel Gaither?"

The young officer knocked again on the door. The banging carried clearly through the early dawn.

"Yes, yes, what is it?" The Colonel's voice was thick with sleep. Then it became anxious and demanding.

"Recon patrol in heavy combat, sir. Do you want to monitor?"

"Yes, yes, I'll be right there."

The watch officer waited a moment to be sure the Colonel was awake, then returned through the darkness to the command bunker.

Colonel Gaither, regimental commanding officer of the Seventh Marine, dressed hurriedly. He was a tough man. His every move spoke of command. His gray-speckled hair was cut short, though still full. Although his manner with subordinates had mellowed with the rank, his eyes had not.

As he dressed, the slight cool of the early morning reminded him of Korea, where as a young lieutenant he'd walked out of the Frozen Chosen with Chesty Puller. Toward the bitter end he had taken over command of his battalion. They made it out with barely a hundred men.

As he opened the door, there was a tremendous boom. The whole hooch shook and something fell off the wall. "175's again," he muttered to himself. "Must be something big this time." The long Toms of the Army's heavy artillery began firing in volleys. The ground trembled.

He hurried along the path to the command bunker. A little pinkness was showing on the eastern horizon. Down the steps of the tunnel he could see the light at the bottom. When he reached the underground room, his eyes blinked at the fluorescent lights. A Pfc brought him a cup of coffee. The contrast between the squalor of the camp and this room never ceased to amaze him. Camp Carroll above was just dilapidated bunkers in dingy disarray; a few hooches had lightbulbs. But here bright lights burned twenty-four hours a day. The smooth plank floor was swept clean. Along the wall was a huge map of the entire area along the DMZ. It stretched from the ocean into Laos. Clear-plastic acetate was stretched tight across the map, and every allied unit was marked in black with a grease pencil. Around and north of the Ben Hai River he saw the same symbols for companies and battalions; only these were in red—the last known positions of the NVA.

To his left sat a gunnery sergeant and the lieutenant who had awakened him. In front of them was a bank of field telephones—lines to all the battalion and regimental headquarters. There was a special hotline to division headquarters.

The lieutenant gave the gunny a paper, and the gunny stepped to the map, erased one of the marks and redrew it a slight distance away. Directly behind the lieutenant was an alcove of radio equipment and three operators. One of them worked the switchboard. The other two, both skilled technicians with headsets on, kept open a network with the battalions, the other regiments, the artillery batteries, the air control, even the ARVN units. Near the wall was a special radio, used only with earphones, called a KY-A. It was the Marines' latest thing for absolute security. The voice signal was scrambled so that anyone interrupting would hear only a garbled gibberish. Even if the enemy had a duplicate machine, they couldn't intercept because the scrambling was mechanically adjustable. The mechanical adjustment was changed secretly every day at both ends. Glancing at the machine, Colonel Gaither wondered what fantastic things the Army and the Air Force must have—if the Marines had this.

The coffee was bad but hot. It went down, pulled on his insides, clearing away the mist. He felt as if his blood had been too thick and now had begun to flow again.

"Okay, John, what's up?"

The lieutenant stepped to the map and pointed to the Laotian border. There was a little triangular mark beside the words "Shooting Star." It was not near any other black mark, and it seemed as if someone had stuck it out there by itself. It marked the position of a special reconnaissance team, used as intelligence gatherers and more

lately as hunter-killers. Such units were called inserts because they were inserted by helicopter into enemy country. To the snuffies they were "supergrunts."

"As you know, sir, Shooting Star ran across a graded
road at this location yesterday, just before dark. They set
in for the night, but about two in the morning the moon
came up and evidently the patrol leader decided to move
them out. From the reports we have so far, it appears that
they came across some large weapon caches. As they
moved away, they must have been discovered because
they're now being chased. We don't know how many."

The room shook again with the huge booms from the
175's.

"Are they making an extraction now?"

"Yes, they're going to try to take them out on this hill.
The 175's are firing cover now, and the helicopter will go
after them at first light."

But the Colonel's mind was already turning. He mumbled half to himself, half to the lieutenant, "That means
we'll probably have an operation in there. If they've stumbled on something big, we'll probably send out at least a
battalion. Have to use Two-Seven. Have you notified Division?"

"Yes, sir." The lieutenant appeared miffed that he
should be asked, but the Colonel ignored him.

"Make sure this gets spotted on the general's briefing
map. The general will be here this morning, probably before noon. I suspect he'll have visited Colonel Richards
and have a plan of action all ready. Have one company
from Two-Seven standing by. I want to be prepared."

"Do you think we'll have a battalion op, sir?"

"Could very well be."

The lieutenant grumbled to himself, but the Colonel
caught the look and grinned. "Come now, John, you'll enjoy the paper work."

"That's what I'm afraid of, sir. Once it's going, the operation is okay, but it's the paper work in preparation that
bothers me."

"Well, the new Three officer, Major Tolson, does most
of it."

The Colonel went back to his hooch-office, sat down, lit
his first Salem of the day, and sucked in the menthol
sweetness. He exhaled sharply when he picked up one of

the many papers on his desk. Damn it all, he thought. How did that get started? There have always been racial problems; they just didn't get the publicity they do now. Trouble is if anything happens they're sure to come right to the CO.

He looked at the investigation. Carlysle the name was. No doubt about it, this one was an outright militant, but they really didn't have a good case on him; insubordination, fist fighting under "Conduct unbecoming military personnel," marijuana. The marijuana charge was the one, he thought, but *any* lawyer could throw that evidence out. If we'd court-martialed this one, he was just the type to raise a really big stink and get some reporter up here accusing us of racism. No, he thought closing the record, the right thing had been done. Orders were being cut to send him to the bush with an infantry company and keep him out of trouble.

At precisely eleven thirty the Army Huey helicopter with "U.S. Marines" painted on the side flew into Camp Carroll. It descended, and Major General Davis and his staff walked to the waiting jeeps. They went straight to the command bunker. Underneath, the light still burned and the coffee was still bad and hot. Only the lieutenant, the gunny, and the radiomen had been changed, replaced by identicals.

The General and Colonel Gaither went into a smaller, separate room. There were two canvas chairs. The back of one was marked with two stars. Here another map, but of lesser size, was covered with plexiglass and set in a small, windowsill-like frame. At the top there was a fluorescent tube. The units were painstakingly drawn on the plexiglass in various colors; and the crayon picked up the light from the plexiglass and glowed brightly. When the room was darkened, it was almost like a toy war game, right out of the Staff and Command College.

"The report from recon said the cache was quite large. They were able to retrieve several of the weapons. Did you get the read-out on the debriefing?"

"Not yet, General."

"I saw the weapons myself. One was a light machine gun, an RPD, brand new, still in the cosmoline and the factory wrapper. Czechoslovakian-made, not Chinese."

"Did they get a count?"

"No, they were discovered before they could take an accurate inventory. But the patrol leader estimated there were at least twenty-five to fifty cases, and he felt this was only one of several caches."

The Colonel's eyes narrowed and he gave a low whistle.

"It's just on our side of the border. I want to send an operation in there and destroy those caches and search the area. But there's a road in there which really interests me. Now where are your battalions? We can only spare one."

Colonel Gaither smiled to himself. "We can send Two-Seven, sir. I've already notified Jack to stand by. His lead company, Delta, is waiting now."

"Black Jack Ryan. Good." The General glanced at Colonel Gaither with pleased respect, then moved to the map and began pointing. "We'll heli-lift a battery into Fire Base Pete; that will provide good arty support, and after heavy air we'll move in at first light. Then we'll move south paralleling the border. Mission is to look for caches and any other signs of enemy buildup and destroy anything they find." The General paused and stroked his chin in a characteristic manner. "You know, Colonel . . . a road. We just might run into something big."

Hawkins

Hawkins hit the ground running, frantically leaped through the blast-tangled vegetation, and dove into the jungle. He lay on the ground listening for the mortar tube, but only his pulse pumped in his ears. Quickly he fanned the platoon in a circle to secure the LZ. The whole battalion was to follow.

He wriggled up by a torn tree and stared back at the LZ in amazement. Every tree, every bush, everything, was flattened for an area twenty-five yards wide. Limbs, trunks, vines, dirt, leaves, were blown out from the center and flung into the surrounding woods. He couldn't believe his eyes. "Wow," he breathed. They had dropped one of the new experimental "blast" bombs from a chopper to clear the jungle for an LZ. It worked.

He worked his way through the wreckage so he could see down into the valley and pulled the new map from his big thigh pocket. It had just been issued, so he folded it carefully to the right spot and put it in one of the clear-plastic bags that the radio batteries came in.

He looked over to the next ridge, less than a mile away, and gulped dryly. Laos. They were practically within the gooks' 82-mm mortar range of the Ho Chi Minh trail. He wished he knew where they were going.

"Joseley"—he spoke more to himself than aloud—"I have a feeling about this operation. I think we're gonna see a little bit of Mr. Charles."

They moved in a single-file column along a tiny trail cut through a solid mass of jungle. Except for the point squad no one could do anything but follow the man in front like ants. The jungle canopy went up and closed overhead, the leaves almost cutting out the sky. It was distinctly different from the Khe Sanh area where everything had been defoliated; here there were no huge craters in the earth from the B-52 bombs, which made a big hole but did nothing to the surrounding trees and jungle. Exactly the opposite of the blast bomb. He decided the B-52 types must be for buildings rather than open ground.

The company set in early because Echo, Fox, and Hotel companies, and the battalion CP with their own 81-mm mortars all had to follow. Each company would man an adjacent hill. The jungle came in very close, and Hawkins had to bear down to get the men to cut a fire zone. Then he and the Chief studied the terrain over and over before finally being satisfied with the machine-gun positions.

"We're gonna need some LAAW's, Lieutenant," Chief said.

"Hell, we need to replace the ones we got," Hawkins answered dryly.

Chief glanced at Hawkins with mounting respect. "Why . . . that's true sir. We *have* carried them too long; they might not fire."

"I know it, but the Captain won't order any more. I asked him twice." Hawkins didn't know it, but he felt salty guessing right. In fact, he'd never fired a LAAW before, but he had been told in training that they had to be changed often. Indeed, Hawkins was constantly surprised at how much he knew from training.

Confronted with the real-life problem, Hawkins remembered the class. The instructor's voice was clear in his mind's ear: "A LAAW is the modern descendant of the bazooka. Basically a rocket, the shell is designed to penetrate a tank, although in Vietnam it is used against bunkers and people. It looks like a green fiberglass tube, about two feet long and four inches in diameter, with a carrying strap and a firing mechanism mounted on the side. To use it the end flaps are unlatched and an inner section telescopes out, doubling the length; the shell is ready-packed within. A sight flips up and the tubular case becomes a launcher, which is placed over the shoulder and fired by one man. After firing, the empty casing launcher is discarded. It is light, easy to carry, and highly effective—modern disposable, throw-away weaponry at its best." Hawkins smiled at the memory. The one fault is that it often fails to fire after being carried around in the bush for a few weeks. They had stressed that.

"We need 'em, sir." Chief repeated himself solemnly, gazing out over the valley to Laos.

"Well, I'm not the company commander," Hawkins cracked.

"Not yet, eh sir?"

Hawkins jerked his head, but the Indian gave no clue.

"You're acting kinda strange, Chief. I've never seen you look this way. You look kinda worried."

"Well, sir, we can't get much closer to Laos. Everybody knows the NVA have a lot of troops over there. They surely saw the choppers come in, and they've been in the war long enough to know how many Marines go in on a chopper. And I'm sure they can count, so they must know our exact strength. And since we always set up on a hilltop, they must know our position."

"So it's always dangerous."

"No, sir, not like this. Wouldn't be anything for them to make a dash across the border, wax us, and then run back." The Chief tugged unconsciously at his hat brim. "The Captain tell you where we're going, sir?"

Hawkins pushed out a laugh. "No, I don't think he knows."

"That's normal; they never tell us."

"Captain wants to see you, sir." Joseley had come up quietly.

"What now?" Hawkins sighed and turned automatically. Joseley just shrugged.

A shout floated up from the jungle down the side of the

hill. Instantly Hawkins ran over to the perimeter and looked down the gully. Captain Calahan had told them that an unknown group would join them to rest and be re-supplied. But battalion had sent strict orders that there was to be no talk, no communication of any kind with the group. As Hawkins peered down, a man slowly emerged from the jungle. It was an American! Hawkins waved wildly, but the man merely turned and made a motion behind him. Then, without looking again toward the top, he came up the gully, hugging the bottom of the crevasse until he hit the cleared area.

Then others appeared. They circled the perimeter, keeping always in the jungle, and came from the eastern side. Hawkins stood in utter amazement as they filed in. They darted through the trees and ran into the camp one at a time. Immediately they spread out and sat down or lay down, all in dead silence.

Despite the orders not to communicate, everyone openly gawked. There were twelve men—two Americans and ten Orientals. But they didn't look like Vietnamese, Hawkins thought. They wore various clothing, some camouflage, some regular greens. Many of them had bracelets, and two had small gold rings in their right ears. Most of their gear was NVA. They had AK-47's and a few RPG rockets. Their radio looked like an American PRC-25, but it was a lighter green and had Chinese markings. The only piece of American equipment was an M-79 grenade launcher.

But it was the Americans that Hawkins couldn't believe. The first one had on blue jeans! *Faded old blue jeans* with a khaki shirt and a brown nylon windbreaker. His weapon looked familiar, but Hawkins couldn't remember where he had seen one. Then it hit him—it was the same as the one that guy in the Foreign Service at Cam Lo had—a Swedish K; that's what it was. Hawkins let out a silent whistle and felt his curiosity going wild. Northcutt had said that all the spooks—the CIA—carried Swedish K's. What were these guys? Mercenaries? Irregulars? What were they doing? Damn, he wanted to talk to them. But they didn't say a word. Two of them had fresh wounds, which Doc Smitty bound; then all of the Orientals ate and went right to sleep. They never once stood up.

The American in blue jeans asked to borrow a helmet and a flak jacket. Still sitting, he put them on; then he went over to the perimeter and began looking toward Laos with a pair of binoculars. After a while the man saw Hawkins staring and offered the binoculars. They were twelve-power Nikon but only about the size of a thick paperback. Hawkins tried them and marveled at the clarity. Abruptly the man gave back the helmet and flak jacket and went to sleep. For another half an hour Hawkins stood around looking at the equipment, trying to figure who they were. He noticed all twelve wore the NVA black tennis shoe, the ones with the distinctive circular tread on the bottom. There was only one other piece of U.S. gear; each American carried one thermite grenade, the kind that can melt steel. Shaking his head, he turned away and went to sit with Joseley.

Hawkins and the CO group were lying around talking about the strangers when the chopper started to come in. Slowly the bird circled and touched down on the little crest. Immediately the crewmen were throwing off bright-red nylon sacks. The men saw the bags. A cheer went up around the lines.

"Mail, Mail!" They began to count in unison.

"One—two—three—four. . . ."

"I'd better get some mail."

"Man, I ain't had no mail in a week. I'm due."

Another chopper hovered and dropped.

"Five—six—seven—eight."

"*Yaahoo.* There must be boo-coo packages. Allll right."

"Boy, I shore would like a dope," Sail said.

"Dope?" Joseley snorted.

"Co'Cola to you, Yankee Boy," Sail drawled back.

As always the Captain had ordered an LZ cut within the perimeter. In an emergency a bird could always come in with new supplies and reinforcements; even if it was shot down in the process, the company still got the gear. Hawkins watched the endless buzzing to the area, like bees to a hive. It occurred to him it would be better to avoid resupplying troops which were on a special operation. They were well within gook artillery range and the choppers could only pinpoint their position. But the sup-

ply people in the rear didn't think that way. Anybody on
a special Op got priority. So what did they do? They sent
out all the mail—packages and stuff like that that had
been sitting around for days while the choppers were
doing more important things elsewhere.

The platoon commander is always given his mail first.

"Wow, get a load of those packages for the
Lieutenant."

"Hey, Lieutenant, your birthday or something?"

Hawkins grinned and looked at the packages. One was
very large and heavy. "Well, matter of fact, I guess it is
or will be in another few days or so. I'll be damned." His
mind went back to his last birthday. Poo had a party, almost a surprise party. It had been a big spaghetti dinner.
Only, her package had been small. The Omega.

Eagerly he tore the wrapping off a package from his
mother. Inside a cardboard box there was more wrapping,
but like all packages in Vietnam it was bashed and
crushed from traveling in planes, trucks, and choppers,
from being sat on, thrown, shaken, dropped, and used for
a mattress. But it had arrived. Hawkins threw out the paper packing. "Holy smokes." Everything was perfectly
wrapped. A huge pound cake. A big, red, round Edam
cheese. Boxes of crackers, Ritz, Wheat Thins, and Tris-
cuits. There were cans of everything and a huge roll of
salami.

"Salami and cheese on crackers. Hot Damn!"

He found two big cans of black caviar. "Ah, you beautiful babies." And a can of black olives.

Chief and Joseley were looking over his shoulder fascinated. "What's that?" Joseley took the can of caviar. He
read slowly, "Ca-vi-ar. Jesus Christ, Lieutenant. What are
you, some kind of aristocrat?" he asked, laughing.

And last and best, there were two wonderful bottles,
very carefully wrapped. A Beefeater's gin and a Jack Daniels Black Label bourbon.

Hawkins ripped open the crackers and split the Edam
cheese with a machete and soon the CP group were stuffing themselves. He opened the gin and mixed it with Kool-
Aid.

"Kool-Aid and Beefeater's!" Hawkins twirled the scraggly whiskers on his upper lip and strutted about.

"Lieutenant, you'll never hump all this extra gear tomorrow. I saw you pick up an extra poncho at LZ Stud, too," the Chief said.

"Hell, you say. I can carry a mountain."

"Oh, yes, Chief, Lieutenant Hawkins can carry anything in his Norwegian rucksack from Abercrombie and Fitch," Joseley said solemnly.

"Ha Ha Ha." Chief threw back his head and laughed.

Hawkins' mouth dropped open and he froze, feeling the embarrassment flowing up in his neck. Doc Smitty and Chief were howling. Slowly the Lieutenant turned to Joseley, but the radioman was calmly reading a *Reader's Digest* that had come in the mail pouch.

"Joseley?" Hawkins said tentatively.

"Sir?" Joseley looked up, his eyes blank.

Hawkins decided against it. He never could be sure if Joseley was joking or not. After all, the rucksack *was* different, but you could carry a lot in it. His mother had sent it after he had tried the little 1930-vintage Marine haversack. "Lemme borrow your opener, you battery-operated funnyman."

Joseley tossed it without a word, and Hawkins ripped into the caviar. He wiped his fingers on his pants and scooped the little black speckles onto a Ritz cracker. Using a K-bar he whacked into the salami roll. Sitting cross-legged in the dirt, he stuffed it all into his mouth, then washed it down with Beefeater's and Kool-Aid. "Mmm—Good." Hawkins leaned over and began jamming the goodies in his mouth till his cheeks bulged. Then he sat up and his face split in a huge silly grin. Some caviar and green Kool-Aid ran down the whiskers of his chin as he waved the bottle. "Here's to Laos," he yelled.

"Hey, here comes another chopper."

"Here's to more mail," Joseley sang out.

"Here's to pussy," Doc Smitty drawled.

The chopper descended and a lone bag of mail came out.

"*Nine.*" The word thundered up in unison from three platoons.

"Look. People, too."

"Hey, there's Wilson. Wilson's back!"

"*Yooo*, Wilson!"

Wilson heard the hollering and waved wildly, his face beaming.

"New dudes."

"Hey, Indian," Hawkins said, spraying caviar, "go see if we get any of the new men."

Later, about dusk, Hawkins, Chief, Sail, and Wilson were walking the lines. Wilson was finishing telling them how he had finally got his allotment squared away just as they were passing by a hole with two of the new men. Hawkins held up his hand. He heard angry words and voices full of bitterness and resentment.

"The one talking now's named DeVecio," Wilson whispered.

"You heard we're supposed to be sending home troops, ain't you?" DeVecio's voice came through.

"Yeah, I heard," Holton said.

"Well, our unit was one," DeVecio said. "They're making a big deal of it in the States. Vice President even gives a speech how glad he is, and that this is the beginning of the end of the war. Big publicity. Well, it's all a lot of horseshit. The number of troops here ain't going down one fucking man. It's just a hoax on the public to make them think the war's about over or that we're pulling out of it."

"That don't make sense."

"Look, stupid, they do it like this. There are over half a million troops in Vietnam. And they all serve here just one year—'cept the Marines, of course, who serve thirteen months—well, a little arithmetic will show you that with 365 days in a year, somewhere around 1,500 men must go home and come over here every single day." He paused and took a drag on a cigarette.

"Here's how the shit works. The brass takes everybody in Three Twenty-six who's got eight months or more to go on his tour in Vietnam and transfers them out to other units. Witness we're here. Others went elsewhere. They spread us all around where we're needed. Then they take all the guys from the other units who've just got one month to do in Vietnam and they transfer them into Three Twenty-six. Matter of fact, if you go to your office, you'll find out that two of your dudes who had three weeks left in the country were sent to Three Twenty-six."

Wilson began to comprehend and he felt sick.

"Okay, so the whole regiment's going back and all the papers and politicians make a big deal. Troops coming home, war is over, not going to do any more fighting, combat level is going down." He stopped for effect. "Shit, everybody who's going home in that unit would have been home in one month anyway."

Wilson looked down sadly.

"That's phony," Chief said ominously.

Quietly they moved back to the CP and sat down.

"You think they know the truth back in the States about the way they're sending that unit home?" Wilson asked.

"I don't know—they're doing it pretty quiet," Hawkins said.

"Naw, they don't know," Chief said softly. "After my first tour I went home and people didn't understand about Vietnam. I couldn't talk to them. It was as if they didn't want to know what was going on. There are two kinds of people. Either they are dead-set against the war or they thought we should see it through. But the thing is, no one really cares. They seem to think if they go on about their business that they can forget the war. Unless they got somebody over here, the whole thing is unreal to them. But none of them really knows what's going on."

Wilson cut in. "I had a friend who'd been to Nam and he told me when he came home that people acted like . . . like while he was away he'd been sick. When he got back home, he was okay again. Their attitude was: Aw, just forget about that nasty illness you had. You were sick but you're okay now, so let's go do something. But don't talk about your illness. Like you say, the people at home don't know what's going on, so they don't bug me. The only thing gets me is when they start waving the VC flag. Uh-unh. Too many of my friends have died for me to go that route," Wilson said bitterly.

"I don't know about you," Sail said. "But I'd take all those Goddamn hippies, put 'em in a barrel, and machine gun 'em."

"Naw, that ain't the way," Chief said, looking away; and Hawkins saw a look he'd never before seen on Chief's face. The Indian gave a little ironic chuckle without any mirth. "Hippies," he said absently, "what's a hippie? Somebody different than you are? Somebody who wears their hair long, pulls it back with a leather thong, and tries to be something they're not? Or somebody who just

thinks different and wants the right to think that way?"
Chief shook his head and realized he had come close to
that indefinable something that goaded him on. "Look."
He stood up quickly and pointed.

The dark had settled and the strangers were moving
silently down the gully toward the west. The four watched
them go till the jungle had swallowed the last one.

"Wow," Wilson whispered, and he shuddered slightly.

For a long while the Chief stood in the dark staring
toward the mountains in Laos. There was a red glow outlining the peaks. Americans in Laos. He wondered if there
wasn't something phony in that, too.

Joseley

Joseley lay on his poncho-liner in the open because the
sky was clear. The night air was cool and delicious after
the heat of the day. It was the kind of night in which every star was twinkling until the sky was flooded with little
pinpricks of light. Joseley folded his hands behind his
head and luxuriated.

Hhmmmmmm.

Mosquitoes! One whirred around his ear and he slapped
in reaction. They were much worse here than they had
been around Khe Sanh. Annoyed, he sat up and reached
for his pack, fumbling in one of the big outer pockets until he found the plastic bottle of insect repellent. His fingers felt the greasiness around the top as he patted it on
his ear and neck. That ought to keep 'em away, he thought
smugly. He started to put the bottle away when he felt the
itchiness in his scalp again. Violently he scratched with his
fingernails, but the itch seemed to move around. I must
have fleas or crabs, he thought. He had had the same
itchiness several times lately. Thinking about fleas sent the
itch down his neck and around his ears, "*Aaagh.*" He had
a frenzy of scratching with both hands till his hair went in
all directions. Lightly, with his palm, he tapped the hair
tips and chuckled at what he must look like. He fished for
his comb and wondered when he'd see hair oil again. Suddenly he sat upright. *Hair oil?* Of course, the bug juice.
He could use bug juice like hair oil. For a moment he was
repulsed. Then he thought of the bugs. Why not? Almost
excitedly he poured about half of the bottle of insect re-

pellent in his hair, then began to work it in, as on the Greasy-Kid-Stuff ads on TV. Finally he ran the comb through his hair and parted it neatly. Then he just sat straining his neck, trying to feel his scalp. There was nothing. Hey, that's great. It worked. I'll have to write that in to the *Reader's Digest*.

He lay down again, feeling delicious under the stars and in the night air. He pulled the grubby poncho-liner up and chuckled to himself. The poncho-liner seemed almost a part of him, like a Linus security blanket.

As he drifted, he reached out and touched his radio. They were on a far-flung outpost, the fringe of the world, but the radio was their link. As the radio murmured softly, it was like a mother singing. He looked over at the Lieutenant sleeping. It was as if the radio were watching over them.

—Click. Click.—

Joseley heard the handset being keyed and his ears went up automatically. He waited. Nothing. Then the sound came again. Then a third time and he bolted upright. Immediately he reached out and shook the Lieutenant's shoulder.

"Sir! LP's got movement!" His voice was low but urgent. Joseley saw Hawkins blink. Then, as the tone rather than the words reached his brain, he sprang awake.

"Sir, LP's got movement!"

The Lieutenant rolled over, sat up and took the handset. "What's their call sign tonight?"

"Big Ears."

The Lieutenant glanced at the Omega. The luminous hands glowed eleven thirty. "Damn, they're early."

Joseley knew Hawkins was worried about the time the gooks started to probe. Near morning was better because they couldn't attack for long. Gooks always retreated come daylight because air strikes and helicopters could come in then. But if an attack were to start at nine or ten—they had all night to work.

—"Big Ears. Big Ears. This is Two Actual—have you got movement? Over."—

No sound came from the radio.

"Got to use clicks, sir; they're too close," Joseley whispered.

"What?"

"They can't talk, sir. Let me do it." Swiftly and smoothly Joseley took the handset and spoke low and direct.

—"Big Ears. Big Ears. If they are too close to talk, answer my questions by keying your handset. Two for affirmative, three for negative. Break . . . Have you got movement? Over."—

—Click. Click.—

He heard the sound of the break in the transmission as the man at the LP depressed the transmit button on the handset. It sounded just like someone pushing the receiver buttons on a telephone.

—"Big Ears—is the movement within twenty yards of you? Over."—

—Click. Click.—

—"Is it within ten yards of you? Over."—

—Click. Click. Click.—

—"Okay, I understand that they are between ten and twenty yards. Over."—

—Click. Click.—

—"Give me one click for every man you think is there. Over."—

—Click. Click.—

Two men, he thought.—"Okay, put yourself at the center of the clock. Our lines are at six o'clock. Give me the number of clicks for the hours which represent their position. Over."—

—Click. Click. Click.—

—"I understand you have two men, approximately ten to twenty-five yards at three o'clock from your position. Over."—

—Click. Click.—

—"Are these men moving now? Over."—

—Click. Click.—

—"Are they moving toward our lines?"—

—Click. Click.—

—"Can you see them? Over."—

—Click. Click. Click.

—"Are you sure it's men? Over."—

—Click. Click.—

Joseley felt the Lieutenant's hand on his arm.

—"Standby One."—

"Doc, go down by Wilson's squad and make sure

they're awake. Tell them that the LP has heard movement coming toward the lines."

"Okay."

"Go ahead, Joseley."

—"Big Ears. Big Ears—do you still have movement? Over."—

A low whispery voice jumped out at him.—"No. It's stopped now. Over."—

Joseley started. A whisper on a radio always sounded very real and close by. —"Big Ears, how could you tell if it was a gook? Over."—

—"I could smell them. Over."—The reply was excited and wary.

—"Are your other men awake? Over."—

—"They sure are. Over."—

—"Is this the first movement?"—

—"No, we've heard scattered movement all around us."—A little fear began to creep into the voice. —"Can we come in now?"—

Instantly, Joseley handed the mike to the Lieutenant. He felt relieved that he didn't have to give the answer. If the LP came in, there would be no one to give warning and the company could get hit with a sudden wave attack. But, on the other hand, if the enemy really is there, the LP must come in for its own protection. Bring them in too early and the lives of the whole company are in danger; too late and the LP may be dead.

Joseley reached for his M-16 and tested the magazine to be sure of eighteen rounds. He heard the Lieutenant trying to both comfort and advise the LP. He shuddered and remembered when he used to go on LP's; so many times they just heard noises and panicked. The night is full of noises and the imagination runs wild. Is it an animal, just a little probe, or the preparation for a full-scale attack? If the Lieutenant didn't calm them down, he would have to bring them in every night.

—"Big Ears, this is Two Actual. Stay out there for now. If you hear anything more, call me quick. Over."—

—"Roger."—The voice was shaky.

The Lieutenant sighed and handed Joseley the mike. As he took it, it seemed the burden shifted back.

"Did you alert the lines, Doc?"

"Yes, sir."

"Have they heard anything?"

"Not yet."

The Lieutenant took a deep breath and sighed. "It's going to be a long night."

Joseley lay back and waited.

Hawkins

WHAAMP.

"Grenade! Grenade!"

There was an immediate yelling and jumping, grabbing for helmets and rifles. Hawkins came awake in an instant, throwing off the poncho-liner and shoving his feet into the boots. Fumbling frantically with the laces, he remembered acutely that Chief never took his off at night.

"Which hole?"

"Wilson's second," Chief answered quickly.

Hawkins realized a couple of hours had passed because Chief was on radio watch.

It was Red and a new man, Baraby, a farm boy from Kentucky. Hawkins eased down and dropped into the hole. Baraby was shaking, but Red seemed calm. Actually Red was scared, but he felt protective to have a man newer than he was.

"What happened?" The new man could scarcely stand still.

"T—there's a gook right down there and I threw a grenade at him."

"Did you see him?"

"I . . . I . . . I heard him move." The man was shaking.

"Take it easy." Hawkins put both hands on Baraby. "Easy, man." He thumped his back and felt the damp sweat. "Where'd you hear it?"

"Right there, sir." Red pointed.

Hawkins stood in the hole and cupped his ears. Slowly he began to swing his head from side to side. "I don't hear anything."

"It's there, sir—we both heard it."

"What's it sound like?"

"Like somebody's sliding along through the bushes."

Again he listened, but there was nothing except night sounds—little rustlings in the grass—the wind and little animals. He heard the nervous breathing of both men.

"Lieutenant, I know they're out there. I heard them." Red's voice was shaky but growing determined. "Damn, it's spooky. I hate these black nights."

They strained their eyes into the black void, but it was useless. Only the night noises came.

"Can I shoot a pop-up, Lieutenant?"

"No! A pop-up flare would expose us. Use your head, man. We've only been here one night. They're trying to find out our positions. If there really is somebody out there, they're more than likely just probing, trying to find out where we are. It's jungle out there and we're in the open. If you shoot a pop-up, all it's going to do is pinpoint our position."

The Chief slithered down to the hole carrying the radio; he squatted lightly and handed Hawkins the receiver. "Captain's calling."

"Yeah, I figured." He pressed the transmit button.

—"Delta Six. This is Delta Two."—

—"What's going on, Two? That incoming or outgoing? Over."—

—"Outgoing. Over."—

—"Did they have a positive target? Over."—

—"Man says he heard a gook. Over."—

—"Well, you listen to me, Two. Ah'm not going to have them jumping up and down and throwing frags all night at shadows. From now on you get permission from me before you throw a grenade. Do you roger that clear?"—

—"I roger your last. Over."—

—"If there are any gooks, that's just what they want. For us to get jumpy and give away our position. Over."—

—"Roger."—

—"Now you go down there and kick some sense into that man's head. Six out."—

Slowly Hawkins pushed the receiver and his eyes met Chief's in silence. Chief merely shrugged and slithered back to the CP. Hawkins turned wearily to Red and Baraby.

"Now listen to me. Don't throw another grenade unless you see a man or unless he's really running right at you." He stopped and caught his breath. "You heard. I have to clear it with the Captain."

Baraby shook his head in obvious disbelief.

Hawkins stared out above the hole, avoiding his eyes.

"Lieutenant." Red's voice wavered.

"Yeah."

"Will you stay a minute? We did hear noises. Honest."

"Sure, Red." Hawkins felt a pressure behind his eyeballs and reached out, holding both men by the shoulders. "Sure I will."

But it was quiet, and after a while he lay down right behind their hole and dozed off.

"Lieutenant"—a hand tugged at his sleeve—"there it is."

Hawkins bolted up and listened tensely. The night sounds cheeped, ticked, and whispered. Wait. He did hear it. Cupping his ears, he began to swing his head back and forth. Then it locked in the direction of the sound. A big fist began to squeeze his chest. The adrenaline pumped into his body and his heart ran wild. It was the sound of cloth sliding against bushes.

"Get your guns ready, but don't fire unless I say to." His voice was a whisper. He patted his hand over the loose dirt until he found a large clod of dirt. Then carefully he lobbed one out toward the sound. As it hit, there was a little thud and the bushes plainly rustled.

The men had heard it too and they were straining to fire.

"No, no, don't fire." He dropped into the hole, and fighting hard against his own trembling, he whispered rapidly. "Look. That's exactly what they want us to do because the muzzle flashes will give our position away. They can see them clearly, and the next thing you know there'd be an RPG coming in at us. Don't fire until you see them running. If you're sure one is out there, the thing to do is to throw a grenade because they can't hear where it came from. They can't pinpoint our position that way. We're sitting down here in the holes and we've got all the advantages. They're out there with no protection."

Voicing the logical drained Hawkins' own tension. He listened again. There was a little slithery sound, and he knew it was a rubber tennis shoe on a rock. A hand tightened in his guts and sweat poured down his back. He moved his eyes in darting little arcs. From training he knew one could see better at night by not looking straight at the object. It was better to look slightly to one side. He thought of the flare. No, save it for the assault.

The shuffling drew a little closer and the men moved to throw a grenade. Hawkins put one hand on each man and gripped both tightly. "No, let me do this. Hold your rifles ready." Carefully he pulled the pin on a grenade, and holding the spring-loaded spoon down firmly with his left hand, he picked up a clod of dirt with his right hand. Forcing his lungs to take in air, he took a good stance. Gingerly, as if he were tossing an egg, Hawkins threw the clod high into the air. Immediately, but very carefully, he transferred the grenade to his right hand and drew back, holding the spoon down with both hands. The clod landed. There was a scurry. Hawkins held the grenade with his right hand and released the spoon with his left hand. The spoon popped free and the grenade was *live!* He started a deliberate count.

"One.

"Two."

The men's eyes panicked and they turned to flee the grenade. Hawkins' arm was cocked back.

"Three."

He threw. "Four. Five. Six."

Thud. *WHUUUUMMPPFF.*

Silence. Nothing moved.

"Damn, I think I threw it too quick. Better to get an air burst. That one hit the ground. I must have missed the gook because he surely would have yelled."

There was no sound. Even the crawling and cheeping night noises stopped. Hawkins heard his heart pounding in his eardrums. For fifteen minutes they sat waiting. Nothing happened. Then slowly the jungle sounds came back. Their breathing returned to normal. There wasn't even a rustle. Only the jungle whispered.

Next morning he sent out a fire team to search the area thoroughly. No bodies, no blood, no nothing. Had there really been something there? Hawkins laughed. It never seemed the same in daylight. "Saddle up," he yelled.

But on a hill to the west a pair of binoculars was watching them closely. They were Zeiss binoculars, made in East Germany. The dark oval eyes saw the searching. The yellow mouth spread slowly in a grin.

The General

At the same hour that Joseley was fighting the mosquitoes and fleas with bug oil, the Commanding General of the Third Marine Division was sitting down to dinner. A huge stone fireplace stood in the middle of the room. Beyond that was a long table set with a white tablecloth, embroidered napkins, and candles. Most of the General's staff had already had a drink at the mahogany and leather bar on one side of the fireplace. Some sat with the General around a low mirror-covered coffee table which was set with flowers and nuts. The others watched the large TV over the bar. The atmosphere was conducive to relaxing. The room was clean and air-conditioned, and there were deep leather chairs on the tile floor.

At dinner two white-jacketed enlisted Marines served the meal from silver chafing dishes. There was red wine, which the General tasted and accepted before it was poured for the ten or twelve other officers. The china was green and white with a gold border; it had a seal and was the regulation set authorized for a general by Congress.

The meal was excellent. There was fresh salad, broiled steak, peas, fricasseed potatoes, and bite-sized oven-hot biscuits. Dessert was ice cream covered with creme de menthe. The waiters cleared the dishes and served coffee from a large silver pot.

The General's headquarters were at Dong Ha, where the ground was covered with a thick layer of fine-powdered dirt. Every step made a little flower-puff of dust; a truck turned the road into a tan tunnel, a convoy of tanks made the whole base a dustbowl. And the wind blew the dust into every crevice. It settled on guns, beds, food, tables, papers, and people. Everything became powdered with the brown film. The General's quarters and mess hall were set away from the roads.

Truck convoys had to move with their lights on. Those in the trucks became no longer white or black or yellow; they were all brown. When they moved, it was like shaking a full vacuum-cleaner bag. Over on the Army side, it was not so bad—they put oil on the roads over there.

The Commanding General of the Third Division was a medium-sized man with sandy brown hair. It was thin and receded at the temples, but he still looked youthful. His face was narrow, with a thin nose and hawklike eyes, but the countenance was pleasing. It didn't have the toughness of Colonel Gaither's nor the bulldog aggressiveness of some commanders', but it had depth and intelligence. The voice was normal and clear, not the foghorn of many Marines. The words were quick and always to the point. The General was a trifle thick in the middle, but his hands and moves were those of a younger man. Here was no grizzle, no bluff, no bark; here was an executive. He could be wearing a dark suit. It was said that he was sure to be the next commandant.

During the day the General was almost always in the field. He constantly checked not only his regimental commands but the battalions and sometimes even companies. He moved so many places so fast he had to use an Army Huey helicopter. The old Marine choppers from Korea were too slow. They said the General was a genius. He had to be. The Third Division was responsible for the DMZ. It had to defend miles of mountains and jungles uncluttered with roads, engaging the large NVA units out in the hinterland to keep the populated coastal plain safe.

Because the General was a Marine and had little equipment to work with, he borrowed ideas. Quicky fire bases from the First Air Cav, mobility from the enemy. He put together a system of artillery-support bases on the mountain tops. The infantry moved up and secured the hill. They were followed by the engineers with their dynamite and chain saws. An LZ was cut; pits were dug. Later the same morning the big C-53 choppers began bringing in the artillery pieces. They heli-lifted the guns right into the pits. Half an hour later the cannons were firing, and men were filling sandbags to protect them.

As quickly as a base was made, it could be abandoned and the process went on. Soon there was a network of artillery bases all along the border and the companies moved back and forth, up and down the hills, patrolling and patrolling, always within range of at least two fire bases. There were not enough artillery pieces to man all these bases, but they could come in an hour—*if* the Marines got the helicopters.

Yes, this general was very good, better than his predecessors, those in charge during the battle at Khe Sanh. But after Khe Sanh they sent a three-star Army general up to oversee the Marines in northern I Corps. Now the Marine general had to contend with the Army brass and his shadow, ARVN General Trung, old persimmon face.

After dinner the General went immediately to the command center. Here were officers, briefing rooms, communication areas, and the center command room itself, similar in operation and organization to Colonel Gaither's regimental command bunker at Camp Carroll but far more elaborate. At this time the General and his staff reviewed the activities of the day. Following that they went over the schedule for tomorrow. First thing in the morning the General would be briefed on the night's activities by the men who had been in continuous contact with the regiments and battalions. All the information was assimilated and plotted on the maps, then sent to Saigon, and within hours it was plotted again in a basement room of the Pentagon.

This evening as they were discussing the day, a tall neat captain with a trim mustache entered the room without knocking and approached the General. All talking suddenly stopped. The General was slightly annoyed until he saw the captain with the neat mustache, then without a word he rose and went with the captain to a secluded corner. The staff said nothing, for this is *the captain without a job*. He had almost no friends and never discussed his work. The people who knew him never asked what he did. He reported only to the General. Of course everyone knew what he did. He was in charge of the special unit which intercepted and monitored North Vietnam's communications network, both telephone and wireless. He controlled ELINT, the super-secret electronic spy device similar to the one on Commander Bucher's ship, the *Pueblo,* which the North Koreans captured.

The captain with no job spoke hurriedly. "Sir, we're picking up considerable traffic from northern Laos. It seems they are quite upset about our operation along the border."

"Get any specific plan?"

"Not yet, sir, but two regiments of the 304th NVA division are in the immediate vicinity."

"What's the source that identified the 304th?"

The captain smiled faintly. "That's almost a certainty, sir. It's got an A-2 rating. That means an *American* had visual contact with the group."

"Okay, Captain, what's your own guess of their plan at this time?"

The captain frowned. He liked to report what he heard; he did not like to make guesses about what might happen. "Sir, we know the road is there, but we don't know what they are protecting. The indications, however, are that they might try a dash across the border. Perhaps as a decoy they would inflict heavy casualties or annihilate one company and then run back."

"What is our closest company to the border?"

"Delta Two-Seven."

Big John

The road was graded. It had guardrails and posts along the sides with heavy bamboo poles strung in between. Big John and the Second Platoon were in the rear when the word came down the column. A gook road! He looked back and saw the Lieutenant on the radio, listening intently.

Big John wondered what it was. What did they say up front? Where did the road go? Didn't the Lieutenant know? How had the observation plane missed it?

"We're gonna get it today," Wilson said ominously.

"Ohhh, shit." Big John had that sickening "not-again" feeling. He heard something about tanks. "Wha' is it, Wilson?" he asked urgently.

"I don't know."

"They got tanks?"

"Christ, I don't know yet."

"Wha'd the radio say?" Big John demanded; but Wilson had moved on up and the jungle closed after him. "Oh, shit. Shit! Shee-it!" Big John mopped the sweat from his face with the green towel around his neck and plunged on. He moved through the jungle thickness following Red. It squeezed in from the sides, but at least it was easy walking in the rear of the column. He thought about the point man having to hack with a machete and shuddered inwardly, knowing he would be hacking if they were on point.

"Hey, there it is." Voices in front carried down the line. Then the foliage opened and Big John came on the road.

A shudder of awe went through his body. Immediately he saw why they couldn't see it from the air. The big jungle trees almost closed overhead and the road curved erratically; it was almost a tunnel.

"Move it out!" the Lieutenant yelled. "Make a double staggered column."

Big John moved on and crept to the side of the road. Red went on the opposite side and Wilson was ahead.

"Keep off the road!" the Lieutenant was yelling again. "Stay right in the bush. Spread it wide."

Then the Lieutenant was kneeling in the road.

"Wha's he see?"

"I don't know."

"Hey, Wilson. Wha' is it?"

"Wait one. He hadn't said yet." Wilson was walking and listening to the radio at the same time.

What the hell is it? Big John wondered. Then he saw Wilson leave the radio and call softly to Red.

"Tank tracks," Red whispered.

Big John became conscious of each step. The sweat poured off his thick neck in rivulets and he drained another canteen. He saw the Lieutenant dragging, and it frightened him somehow. Hawkins had too much gear. He got those big packages last night and he was trying to hump it all. Big John found himself wishing the Lieutenant would throw it away. He saw the Chief walking with his rifle held horizontally at the hip, two fingers on the cocking lever; immediately Big John did the same.

BNOWP—BNOWP—BNOWP.

"AK-47's."

Instantly Big John dropped. The lines popped and snicked, as cocking levers were pulled and the bolts snapped home slamming a round into the chamber.

TaTowTowTowTow. RAAP.

He heard the M-60 machine guns answering.

"Face outboard!" the Lieutenant yelled.

The firing was all up ahead. Big John could hear the M-16's and the M-60's, but the column didn't move. He lay still, holding his M-16 pointed to the side. The firing up ahead was intense for a few seconds, and then it slacked off and petered to a stop. The radio was crackling madly, but he couldn't make it out.

BNOWP—BNOWP—BNOWP. New firing on the left

about the middle of the column.

"What's happening, Wilson?" he yelled darkly.

Bloop. Big John heard the little noise of the M-79 grenade launcher. *BOOMZT.* Then more gunfire.

Determined to find out what it was, he hunched up on his elbows and crawled over to Wilson's squad radio. He heard LeBlanc.

—"Six, this is One. We saw some gooks run off to the left. Fired on them. Don't know if we got any or not. Over."—

—"How close were they? Over."—

—"I think they were pretty close. I think they might have been trying to ambush us and the point came on them before they could get set. Over."—

—"One, put a squad in that direction for flank security. Break—Three, Three, this is Six."—

—"Go, Six—Three here."—

—"Three—did you get any? Over."—

—"Can't tell yet. They fell into a hasty ambush. But they deeded when we got the gun up. Stand by, One.".

"Come on," Wilson yelled and moved up, taking Cater and the radio. Big John ran forward and dropped again. He wished he knew what was happening.

"Get off the road! Get off the road! Move to the left!" The Lieutenant's voice rang up from the rear.

"Move it back. Slow, slow. Sail, keep your gun to the rear."

They ran in rushes to the other side of the road.

"Sanders. Pull out as soon as Three gets by."

There was yelling all up and down the column as the company recoiled and moved into the trees.

Tanks? An image of great tanks rolling up the road flashed into Big John's mind and he fairly leaped to get away from the road and into the trees. He bent over like an old man and scurried toward the departing column, feeling the safety of the trees envelop him.

"Move into a column. We're taking point," Wilson ordered.

"Oh, *shit*."

"Look out for an ambush and move it out."

About half the platoon were in the trees when they heard the first tube . . . *Poop, poop, poop.* They all froze. The whole column stayed motionless as if a movie camera had suddenly stopped and held them suspended in mid-stride. Nobody moved a muscle for what seemed an age. Big John's mind had galvanized on the noise. Wild yelling broke the spell.

"Tube! Tube! Tube! Incoming!"

The cameras turned again, in high speed. They flung themselves to the ground. Bodies dove for cover. Those near the ditches wormed their way into the very bottom. The men were darting and diving like rabbits. Big John mashed himself to the ground and pushed his face into the dirt. His hands cupped over his head and neck and he held his elbows and forearms tight against his face for protection. How long does it take a mortar? His mind whirled. Twenty seconds? He cringed, awaiting the blast. It seem forever. He was praying it wouldn't land near him. *WHUUMPZT. WHUUMPZT. WHUUMPZT.* A muted, hollow, crunching sound—and it was close! Sweat poured into his eyes. Stinging. But nothing on earth could make him lift his face from the protective dirt. The last one fell and he didn't hear the tube again. He sprang up.

"Move it! Move it! Get away from the road before they adjust."

The men scrambled madly. Chief and the Lieutenant were yelling, almost pushing the company.

Poop. Poop. Poop.

Big John dived again. Oh, God, don't let them explode in the trees.

"Yyiiiiah!" A sudden violent stinging sensation burned into his left arm above the elbow. Then something thudded into his back knocking the breath out. He couldn't breathe. "Oh, my God. I've been hit in the back . . . Corpsman!" He rolled over, gasping for breath, and saw the blood streaming down his arm. Smitty came running up, plopped down beside him, ripped up his T-shirt sleeve and started tying on a battle dressing.

"My back, my back," he cried. "I've been hit in the back."

Smitty looked around quickly, then whistled in amazement. "Jesus. No you haven't, Big John. It just hit your pack. You're mighty Goddamn lucky." He jerked out a large piece of shrapnel and dropped it instantly. "Ooooh, fuck!" He shook his hand violently. "It's still hot. Look what hit you. Here. It went clean through your pack and poncho and stopped in the liner. You're okay."

Big John gaped at the shrapnel. He took off his pack and patted his back, then gingerly touched his arm.

"Doc, am Ih goin' be okay?"

"Sure, Johnnie. Hell, it's just a little thing."

"Ohhhhh." Big John felt the choking fear drain out of him and his body shuddered involuntarily with relief. He was going to be all right. He could . . . a sudden rush of anticipation welled up in him and he wanted to laugh. *He would be medevacked.* He was all right, but he'd have to go back to the hospital. The rear! Out of the bush! He laughed aloud.

"Smitty. Doc Smitty. Will Ih be medivacked? You call the choppa'?" His voice was shaking with elation.

"Who's hit? Who's hit?" A running figure came crashing out of the woods. "Oh, no! Not Big John." The Lieutenant gasped and dropped to his knees beside the two men.

Big John sat up and stared at the Lieutenant.

"Are you okay?" the Lieutenant's voice cried in anguish, and he reached out both arms. He grabbed the big shoulders and squeezed tight.

Big John looked down and saw the blood trickle over Hawkins' fingers. The face was next to his own. *Had the Lieutenant heard him laugh?*

"John. John. Are you all right? Big John, are you all right?" The voice and face implored and it was almost crying.

Big John sensed the face and the hand and the voice as one. He felt a glow, and a mounting compassion seeped into him. He wanted to cry.

The Lieutenant touched the bandage. "Is it okay, Smitty? Will he be all right?"

"Yeah, Ih'm okay, suh. Jus' a scratch."

"Uh huh. He's tough," Smitty said quietly.

"Oh, thank God. Good God." Hawkins' hands still held the arms and Big John gingerly took his wrist.

"Come on, suh. We got t' be movin'."

Chief

Meanwhile the column had broken near the front of the platoon. Chief had been pushing the men forward, listening for the tube, when another sound caught his ear. Instantly in one smooth catlike motion he brought his gun up, turned, and dropped to one knee. He was sure it was a moan. It sounded very close off the trail. He called softly to the man in front of him, "Pass the word to hold it up." But the man was one of the new men from Three Twenty-six and wasn't used to moving in a column with a company.

"Cover me," Chief ordered. "There's somebody in there. Stay on my left. We'll move in together."

The Chief crouched and slithered forward. The top of his head was about two and a half feet from the ground. He made no sound but moved silently, twisting through the brush. The other man moved forward and crashed and crackled. Chief cursed to himself and motioned to the man to stop.

The man looked at Chief and blinked. No single part of the lithe body seemed to move as he glided forward. It was as if a shadow were flitting across the bushes, and then he couldn't even see the shadow.

Chief heard the sound again and froze; his rifle inched up. It must be a wounded gook, he thought. One of those who ran off from the First Platoon. He eased forward, parting the bushes gently with his hand, his head hardly moving. Careful, he thought. Never know what they'll do. He's sure to be armed and may figure to take one more with him. The jungle was so thick he could see for only a few yards. Then the sound was directly ahead of him. Slowly he pushed the bushes and saw the figure. His body froze as his eyes swept over the man.

The Vietnamese was lying on his side, curled in a ball. His face was turned away, but Chief could see the leg was shattered. Chief's heart beat again.

The bastards left him to die, Chief thought. Couldn't walk and so they left him. He sensed the hate rising and felt a sudden compassion for the man. Jesus, they even took his weapon. Dirty bastards. Still Chief moved in a wide circle around the spot until he was certain there was no trick or ambush. Then he stood and, carefully taking

the slack out of the trigger, called to the man. The Vietnamese looked up. His eyes flickered with fear for just an
instant. Then, as if in resignation, he uttered a word.
Chief motioned Wilson's squad to come up and check
thoroughly for a weapon. The man moaned the word
again. It was thick with accent; but this time it was recognizable.

"Corpsman."

"Well, I'll be damned. Calling for *our* own corpsman."

The tension broke and the men pressed in to see.

"Move it out. Get moving. Move on back on the trail,"
Chief said sharply. "Wilson, pass the word for the Lieutenant to come up here."

The line moved on, and Chief looked down at the man.
He was motioning that he wanted water. Chief thought of
the gooks that had run off and left. "Dirty bastards," he
said softly, "what kind of people are they?"

He took out a canteen. The Vietnamese started to sit
up, but the motion sent waves of pain up his leg and he
lay back groaning. Chief saw the red wetness glistening
through the pants as the blood spread out. "Put your rifle
on him." He laid his own rifle down a few feet away and
held the canteen to the man's lips. The man sucked
greedily, a drop trickling down his smooth chin. Chief
stood back. "Okay, buddy, that'll keep you from dying till
they get you in the rear."

"They gonna take him out of here?" the new Marine
asked, peering over Chief's shoulder.

"You'd better believe it."

"How the hell we gonna get him out?" the other asked
incredulously.

"Shit, for a POW they'll send a chopper to Hanoi."
Chief laughed sardonically. "You wait and see. Wounded
Marine, let him wait. But a prisoner—first priority. We
might as well start cutting an LZ right now."

Just then the Lieutenant came up, looked briefly, and
reached for the radio. At that same moment, however Hotel Company came upon what subsequently turned out to
be the largest enemy rice cache ever found in the Vietnam
War. And the enemy, seeking to prevent battalion from
discovering the other caches, began to mortar at random.

WHUUMPZT. WHUUMPZT. WHUUMPZT.

The rounds were not close, but the men dug themselves

into the dirt. The Lieutenant eased the handset into the ground beside his face while his elbow still covered his head.

—"Two, this is Six. Go ahead."—The Captain's voice was agitated.

—"Six, we got a prisoner back here—wounded. Hit in the leg. Found him just off the trail. Over."—

There was a long pause. Hawkins frowned and just started to call again . . .

—"Can he walk?"—

—"Negative on your last. Leg's torn up pretty bad. Over."—

—"Will he last if you have to move him? Over."—

The Lieutenant looked down at the man. Doc Smitty was bandaging his leg, the man wincing and trembling at the pain, his face squinched up tight.

"How is he, Doc?"

"He'll be okay. Leg's probably gone, but we can move him." Doc looked at the Lieutenant and went on slowly, almost matter of factly, "If we can carry him on a stretcher."

The mortars were crashing again, and Chief buried his head in the dirt.

WHUUMPZT. WHUUMPZT. WHUUMPZT.

They finally stopped and for a long moment the silence seemed to echo in the wake of the crashes. At length all eyes turned to the microphone—waiting. Finally, the Lieutenant moved his thumb to the button, when it suddenly sounded in his hand.

—"Two, Six here. We've got to move fast. Impossible to bring him in. You know what to do. Six out."—

The Lieutenant shook the handset as if doing this would cause the Captain to say more.

Wilson let out a long whistle. "Man, he's trying to tell us something."

Chief watched the Lieutenant's face as it twitched and frowned. He guessed that Hawkins probably *didn't know* what to do. They'd never come on this situation since the Lieutenant had been in d'Nam. Chief studied the clean-cut features, the sandy hair—would he think of ethics? Court-martials? Geneva Conference? Atrocities? Their gaze met and locked. Had they taught the Lieutenant about this at Quantico? Had he studied it in graduate school? Chief wondered what Hawkins would say if he knew his "Indian" had been to Berkeley.

Abruptly the Lieutenant stood. "Wilson, take the people out on the trail. Move up a ways and wait for the Chief and me."

There was a deafening silence. No noise at all. Nobody spoke. Only the jungle moved.

"What are you going to do, sir?" Wilson's voice quavered slightly.

"Just move on up the trail." He pointed. "Move!" Wilson glanced at the others, shrugged, and they shoved off silently. They had felt the strength in his decision and were relieved.

"I'll do it, Lieutenant," Chief said flatly. Their faces swung up, the eyes locked, and for a fleeting second there passed between them that affection of men who fight together. It might even be considered effeminate in normal society.

The Lieutenant dropped his eyes. "No, Chief, I can't ask you to do that."

Chief put his hand on the Lieutenant and gently pushed him toward the trail. "Sir, you're an officer. Better me than you. Cover me down the trail—and don't look back."

"But . . ."

Numbly the Lieutenant let himself be guided. Chief knew a corner had been turned and his mind flashed to their talk after the Banks' Hill fight. His face grinned, but this time the eyes smiled. "No way, Skipper."

Seeing that Hawkins was not going to argue, Chief turned back abruptly. Chief had that ability to compartmentalize his mind; he did what must be done without thought. One moment he was all rational and cold; the next day he could go on R 'n' R and have a ball. He heard all that crap about becoming a killer, war-hardened, the killer instinct. Baloney. You did what you had to do in war and then you forgot about it. Sort of like taking a crap and eating. You do one, then forget about it and go do the other. You don't keep talking about shit at the dinner table. The same with war. You forget about it and go on. They couldn't bring the gook, and they couldn't leave him because he might be found and give them away. He stepped back a few yards away and shot the man at an angle through the chest. That way, were he ever found, it would be like a natural war death. Ones like this—you leave the papers and souvenirs. He turned and walked lightly back toward the trail.

Hawkins

Hawkins was staggering. His pack got heavier and heavier until he was sure it weighed a ton. For the umpteenth time he rebelled against throwing the stuff out; later tonight it would be so good. But at every rock or ledge he had to put both hands on his knees and push down to get himself up. His whole strength seemed necessary for every step.

The Captain kept calling to speed it up. Over and over Hawkins took out his compass and map. The ground and the map just didn't match. The problem was to get around the hill they were on and up the main peak of the mountain. They had to cross a little gully or ravine, but it wasn't that easy. At times he could see it, but then the jungle closed over. Hawkins wiped the sweat from his eyes and squinted through the trees. The map just didn't fit the ground. A green curtain closed over their heads and they were like ants crawling deep in the nap of a rug. Hawkins moved up until there was only a small fire team in front of him. He had to be there directing, guiding every step of the way. If the point man went in the wrong direction, they had to stop and turn back and get on the right path. Then all the men had to backtrack. It was impossible to rely on a squad leader, and the point man had all he could do just hacking a path without even thinking of gooks.

Joseley said nothing, but his face protested. Joseley would walk absolute point if the Lieutenant did, but he didn't like it. If they were ambushed or came upon a chance contact, there was less possibility of the Lieutenant's getting zapped if they weren't on point. Joseley believed in the theory that the Lieutenant must keep himself alive in order to lead and direct the platoon.

Fatigue numbed Hawkins' brain and the whole platoon seemed to flounder. He had to force himself to think. When he concentrated, the platoon moved. He could actually *feel* himself will the platoon to go—and when his will gave out, the platoon didn't move. He had to be on point.

He came to an opening and stopped, checking the map for the hundredth time. There was a slight trail leading around the hill to the left. But it might be more direct to cut straight across the hill or circle to the right. He opted for following the trail. It was a hundred thousand times easier than hacking their way through the bush with machetes. The pack dragged him back, sucked him down into the void of plodding along and following the man in front. No thoughts, no feelings, just rivet your eyes on the man's back and trudge along like a zombie.

The day became insufferably hot. Little aches and pains were magnified and tormented the individual. Gradually fatigue and heat overcame everything else, and they moved mechanically, grabbing at the elephant grass to pull themselves up.

"Six calling, sir." Joseley panted.

"Hold it up."

The men dropped like rocks, not bothering to move from the spot they were in, just letting go and rolling back on their packs. Hawkins held a tree for support.

—"Six, this is Two. Go ahead."—

—"Which way are you heading? Over."—

—"I'm going to the left of the hill in front of us, over and around it, and then down. There's a slight trail. Over."—

—"That's not direct route, is it? Over."—

Dammit, he knew Calahan didn't like trails, but couldn't the man see it was the quickest route. He pushed the transmit button.

—"That should put us going up the left ridge of the main slope as we face it. Over."—

—"Did you see the clearing with the finger ridge which leads to the main slope? Over."—

—"Uh . . . negative on that. Over."—

—"Come back here and look. Six out."—

Slowly Hawkins trudged back through the column, one hand on his shoulder easing the pack strap. Maybe the Captain would put somebody else on point, he thought. Anything. He just needed some relief from pushing the point. But surely the Captain *couldn't* have found a better way. The thought startled Hawkins; tired or not, he was too good for that.

Captain Calahan was right. Patiently, as if training a dog, the Captain pointed to an opening in the trees, guiding the Lieutenant by the sleeve. Hawkins followed the pointing arm. The bush cleared and a little ridge ran from the side of the hill they were on right up to the main one. It would be more level and easier going.

He'd missed it.

The instant Hawkins saw the good route he knew what he had to do. The anger pushed away the fatigue, and his only surprise was that Calahan had left him on point. He clenched his teeth. To hell with the gear—no captain would beat him again.

He called for the platoon to turn back, and he moved until he was out of sight of the Captain. Immediately he shrugged off the pack and pulled at the flap. He took out the extra poncho and dropped it in the weeds. Haven't even got time to rip it up so the gooks can't find it and use it, he thought.

Next went the big pound cake, the olives, and the rest of the cheese and crackers. He threw out the other cans, the sardines. Finally he took out the gin bottle; it was still half full.

"You want this?" he said, holding out the gin to Joseley.

Joseley liked gin, but the radio weighed twenty-five pounds. He shook his head sadly. Hawkins shrugged, poured the contents on the ground and flung the bottle into the weeds.

Last came the bourbon. Bourbon was Hawkins' favorite. He hadn't had any because he was saving it. He unscrewed the cap, thinking he might as well have one last drink. He gulped down a swallow. "Oh wow." He grimaced and shook his head. It was awful. Warm bourbon drunk on a hot day is not refreshing, but something in his mind made him think that it should be. How many times in the movies had he seen cowboys come in hot and dusty and down a straight shot of whiskey? They wipe their lips and say, "I got a powerful thirst." He tried again.

"Eughit." He spewed it out. It was like hot turpentine. "To hell with the cowboys." He raised his hand to throw the bottle. Wait a minute, it can be good for something. It's wet. He stopped and grinned, then deliberately took off his helmet and solemnly poured the bourbon over his

head. It washed down his nose and chin. He let it run over his back. His face was now a huge grin. It soaked his already soaked shirt. The alcohol dried quickly and had a cooling effect. With eyes closed, face tilted up, he tipped the last drops onto his forehead and luxuriated in the flowing bath. He opened his eyes and saw Joseley staring at him in astonishment. His tongue flicked out and tasted the drops which caught in his whiskers. He chuckled and flipped the empty bottle against a rock. It smashed to pieces.

"Yes, sir, Mr. Joseley. That's what a man needs every day. Nothing like a bath of Jack Daniels Bourbon." He grabbed up the now light pack and tested its weight. He debated a second, glanced to the peak, then took out the .45 and hooked it onto his cartridge belt. At last he thrust his arms vigorously into the straps. "Ummm. That *is* better." He flashed a grin at Joseley and rapidly stepped off after the departing squad. He felt like a ten-day laxative had just worked.

"Hey Jose"—he grinned over his shoulder—"just call me a Vietnamese highball. Bourbon and sweat."

The Lieutenant was refreshed but the men were not. They sagged and passed out like flies. Hawkins told Calahan and was ordered to keep on moving. There was no possible way to stop here. No chopper could land. The only thing to do was to get to the top. By four o'clock they were approaching the crest. He rotated points over and over. The density of the jungle cut off any breeze and the heat became insufferable. Water was becoming low and he fought to keep from drinking. He was wondering how the new boys were doing when he heard the cry.

"Corpsman up. Corpsman up."

From below Doc Smitty heard the cry and leaned into the hill. Smitty knew some of the men couldn't take much more. One look was enough. It was Sedgewick. He was pale and clammy. His pulse was weak and rapid. Heat exhaustion.

They laid him out flat on the dirt and pulled open his clothes. He was gasping. His chest heaved and his eyes rolled up in his head. Smitty pulled out one of the seven canteens he carried, wet a towel, and began sponging the man's face, but it didn't work. Sedgewick began to moan and cry.

"Got to cool him off somehow," Doc said, mentally counting his remaining canteens. "Take this towel and sponge him," he yelled at Wilson. He pulled out another canteen and carefully poured some into Sedgewick's hair.

Hawkins halted the column, dropped his pack, and moved down to the group. "How bad is he, Doc?"

Doc glanced up angrily and didn't answer.

"How long before you can move him?" Hawkins asked again.

"He's bad, Lieutenant, real bad."

"Well, we can't chopper him out. He's got to go on, get him going as quick as you can."

"Dammit, Lieutenant! You want this man to die? He's got to be taken out of here."

The men standing nearby shifted uneasily and looked quickly to the officer. Hawkins drew back at Doc's words and then reached for a cigarette.

"Take it easy, Doc." Hawkins struck a match heavily. "You know we can't get a chopper in here. I'll ask Captain for a break and you do what you can."

"Well, if he doesn't call a chopper soon, this man is going to die, sure as I'm standing here."

Sedgewick began to thrash as if in a fit. Two men held his arms and another sat on his legs. Doc ripped the shirt open and pulled it back to his arm. He opened Sedgewick's pants and pulled them down to his thighs; then he sprinkled water over the exposed skin.

"Get some shade. Hold up a poncho."

Two men moved around and held a poncho in a little square above the body. Frantically Smitty wet the body with a cloth and fanned him with his cover, trying to cool the temperature before it cooked the brain. But Sedgewick began to twitch, then buck. His eyes rolled. He screamed and cursed and fought wildly against the men holding him. Another one jumped on his legs. Doc cursed back at him and slapped him. Sedgewick convulsed and made a choking gurgle. Doc pried open his jaw and pulled at the tongue. Smitty knew he was losing the battle. It wouldn't be long before the man would go into shock and die. He felt him slipping.

"Get Little Doc," he yelled. There was only one thing left. Little Doc had a can of glucose. Smitty ripped open the container and prepared the needle. He didn't know why, but the glucose was supposed to bring down the temperature. He slammed Sedgewick's arm to the ground and kneeled heavily on the wrist. He gripped the arm tightly at the muscle, his fingers digging into the flesh. The vein popped up and darkened. Smitty pushed once with the needle. The vein rolled aside. "Damn." All the time Doc's mouth kept talking, urging, coaxing. The Southern drawl just kept on pouring out. He inched the needle in again. This time the blood ran up the tube. Quickly Smitty squeezed the bulb and started the flow in the other direction.

"Hold that," he said to one man. Tensely he sponged Sedgewick and watched the fluid. His eyes went to the black face, and then he saw the muscles sag. It was working! In a few minutes Sedgewick calmed; the peak was past.

They had to carry him up the hill. The drop in temperature at night was the only other treatment he would get. The others collected his gear.

Hawkins was about thirty yards from the top when the first man went over. About three men were already up when the AK fired.

BNOWP—BNOWP—BNOWP.

CRWACK—CRWACK—CRWACK. An M-16 answered. There was a sudden outpouring of fire.

"Get up that hill," Hawkins screamed and leaned forward, the adrenaline pumping in at the first shot.

"Sanders, what is it?"

"They opened fire on us just over the crest."

"How many?"

"I don't know. Just a couple fired."

"Set up a line."

The firing had stopped but they could see nothing.

He waved the men into a line across the hill.

"Hold that position. Shoot slowly. Keep up a base of fire, but hold your position. Move it on up." He had to get more men up here before he could do anything else. They couldn't move until they had enough force. The Captain had prepped the top with artillery so the gooks must be in bunkers. All down the column the men heaved and began to scramble with the speed of desperation.

Suddenly Hawkins caught the flash of a dark head mov-

ing toward them. They're attacking! The three men in
front of him panicked, jumped back, and started to run.

"NO," Hawkins screamed with all his might.

In a microsecond of thought Hawkins knew they had to
hold off the gooks until the others got up the hill. He
leaped from the hole and fired a shot, screaming. It had
been Baraby, the new boy, who had seen the gook and
panicked first, forgetting all except the terrible urge to
flee. The Lieutenant's voice caught him cold. The discipline of a thousand commands on the drill fields of Paris
Island came back to him. The unquestioning, unhesitating
obedience to command—pounded into him over and over
at the expense of all else—seized his mind and body. His
leader shouted. The command had him. He would stay.
The gook head moved again. He didn't think. His mind in
no way willed his body to act. It didn't need to. The reaction was automatic. Trained into him. Drilled into him.
Beaten into him. His rifle swung up smoothly. He aimed,
he squeezed. The gook staggered over dead. Baraby never
knew what happened.

The platoon got up and rushed the crest. There was
nothing. Whatever it was had fled.

The hill dropped away and for the first time that day
Hawkins could see the terrain clearly. The platoon ranged
across the crest, guns ready. They could see everything
perfectly, but there was no one in sight. They felt almost
cheated. Once again the gooks had run; the one they got
was probably wounded or left as a delay decoy. Once
again there was nothing.

"There they go!" One man was suddenly yelling and
opened fire. There was a movement on the ridge in front
of them. Three gooks were running across the low grass
toward the foliage. The platoon erupted. Every weapon
fired—M-16's, M-14's, M-79's. Some fool ran up with a
shotgun but it was too far away. The other platoons came
up and joined in. It became that plutoria of d'Nam—a
turkey shoot. Zwrowski stood up, held the machine gun at
his hip and fired. Ski's eyes were blazing. One foot was up
on a rock. The gun bucked and kicked; but he held it
firm, his body absorbing the shock. His helmet had
dropped and the golden hair fell down over one eye. He was
John Wayne. Standing on the crest, outlined against the
sky, the machine gun ramming and bucking against Ski's

body, Ski slammed into it like it was a jackhammer. Fire blast and red tracers poured out the muzzle. He kept on going, guiding the tracer streaks in and out, up and down the gullies. Man and machine gun.

Then the firing slowed and stopped. The gooks were gone. The adrenaline flowed out, and Ski toppled into the shade and passed out.

It had been the urge to fire, to release the pent-up tension of continuous alertness, of getting mortared, of noises in the night but never being able to fire back, never actually seeing the enemy.

Battalion wanted a body count.

"Only one, sir."

As Hawkins walked away to set up the platoon, a figure rushed at him, tugging his arm. The man had a child's face of wild, eager delight.

"Lootenant, Lootenant! Ah got one!"

"What?" It was Baraby.

"Ah kilt a gook, Mah first one."

Hawkins tried to hide his smile at the bubbling glee.

Baraby tugged on the Lieutenant's arm. "Come see, Lootenant. Ah got me a gook. Come *see* him, sir."

"Okay, okay, that's good." Hawkins almost had to laugh. "You did real fine."

"Come see him, Lootenant." He tugged insistently.

"Good boy. Look, I know. I'm damn glad you did." Hawkins extracted his arm.

"Right over yonder. Ah shot him, sir!"

"Did you get his belt?"

"Huh? . . . Uh! . . . No, no Ah didn't. Guess Ah didn't think 'bout it." Baraby was suddenly bewildered.

"You'd better run over there and get it before those dudes in mortars get it."

"Oh, yes, sir. Yes. Thanks. Ah'll do that. Thanks, Lootenant. Thanks a lot." He ran off toward the body.

Hawkins

Twilight was coming, but the Lieutenant lay flat on his back. The excitement and the fury of firing flowed off and deep fatigue crept in. He was conscious of only two thoughts: the exquisite relief of lying perfectly motionless and the urgent necessity to get up and set the troops in

position. The two forces fought in his mind and made a
growing pain until at last he willed himself to move.

"Where do you want Second Platoon lines?" Hawkins
asked.

The Captain looked up in silence. Almost as tired as
Hawkins, he had been on the radio to the battalion.

"Sir, we got to set in. There are a lot of gooks around
here. We got to get moving."

The Captain stared as if in a daze. Hawkins waited. By
habit the company had fallen into a loose perimeter
around the hill, one platoon picking up where the other
one stopped. After some minutes of staring, Calahan's
eyes blinked.

"Take that end of the hill. Tie in with First and Third."

Instantly Hawkins knew something was wrong. Calahan
always insisted on placing each squad personally. Hawkins, realizing he would get no further answers, turned to
go. Then he stopped and looked back hesitantly. Just
seeing a gook in daylight meant trouble, and he wanted all
the preparations and weapons he could get.

"Sir, did you order those LAAW's I asked for?"

The Captain glared at him. "Look, Lieutenant. There's
no point in ordering more till you've used the ones you
have."

"But, Captain, we can't shoot what we've got till we get
more, because the new ones might not come in and we
could run out."

Calahan smiled condescendingly. "I'll order what supplies are necessary. This isn't the Army."

"Dammit, Captain, you're afraid to requisition them.
You're afraid it will look like the company is losing too
many. You're afraid the Colonel will notice and ask you
what's going on."

The enlisted men fell silent and studiously pretended to
ignore the sudden outburst.

Calahan stood, his face flushed purple. "Who in hell do
you think you're talking to, Lieutenant? I run this company. And don't you forget it, because I won't tolerate insubordination from anyone!" His voice was bellowing and
his eyes glared hard.

Hawkins felt the fluttery panic run up his mind. Calahan's blast choked off his angry words. He looked down.

"I'm sorry, sir—it's just that—well, some of ours are sort of . . ."

"Shut up, Lieutenant."

Hawkins turned and strode off. He had groveled. As he walked back, his tiredness returned.

In a stupor he called the squad leaders to assign the holes. As the men drew around him, he sensed the pressure of the old question—three or four men to a hole. They seemed to get so much more sleep with four; and he wanted to give them all a break, but he couldn't cover the ground with only seven holes. He needed nine. It wasn't fair; he could hardly stand up himself.

He felt the indecision and weakness; then abruptly he clenched his jaw and decided. Nine. Immediately he felt a flow of relief.

"Wilson, you'll have three holes, the last one over there next to the Third Platoon." Wilson said nothing; his face just looked sour, his lips set in a straight hard line.

"With an LP, too?" Chief asked. Hawkins wavered.

"Lieutenant, I've only got nine men, including myself, and one of them passed out today and Big John was hit. Wouldn't two be okay, sir?" Wilson asked.

Hawkins felt their pressure. He looked away from their faces and his breath stuck.

"Well, I'll tell you what. We must cover this area." Instantly he hated himself. "You dig three holes and have two men sleep in each one. But you only need to keep watch on two of the holes. That way you'll all get more sleep and two men will be enough to listen. If we have to fight, everybody is up anyway."

"All right, sir."

Hawkins felt sticky and disgusted with himself. But he was too tired to care. He wondered why he hadn't yelled and become angry with them as Calahan had with him. He started back to his CP, then remembered the LP. "Chief, put out an LP." He flung the words over his shoulder and went over to his pack and sat down.

"Joseley, we got to dig us a hole. We'll both work."

"I know, sir."

Neither one of them moved. He lay for a long time, again unable to move, knowing he must dig, must eat, must check the lines, particularly the corner hole down by the Third Platoon. They would never do it right if he didn't go down and sit on their necks. His mind struggled to get up, but his body wouldn't move. The gooks wouldn't come tonight, and tomorrow they would stay here for sure. Tomorrow they would have time to dig good positions.

Hawkins' mind eased and he drifted toward sleep. Gradually he came to focus on the wounded gook. Why had he let Chief do it? He should have done it himself. It was his duty. He fought at the idea pushing at his mind. What was it he had felt? Hawkins, you didn't push against duty; you resisted a desire. You wanted to kill that gook. No. The pain in his forehead began to twitch and ache; suddenly he felt hot and itchy all over. He yelled aloud and sat bolt upright, then sank back and drifted into an uneasy sleep. His muscles were too tired to relax and he twitched and turned.

He dreamed. He dreamed he was lying there sleeping and he could see the men around him. He saw himself lying there dreaming, yet he went on. He was walking back to the Captain. Calahan was yelling at him: He had to have those LAAW's—my men need them—don't let him yell at you—show him—his hand tightened on the pistol. It lay beside his head—he raised the pistol. It was a shotgun, LeBlanc's shotgun. He looked again for Calahan. Calahan was yelling at him: Finish your school, son. Marines are animals—killers. There's a good job for you with the company—you can travel. *No,* I don't want it, I don't want your damn job. His father was angry and shouting—his father was a big man—his father was coming at him. He raised his gun—his father became a gook—he saw himself lying there. *It wasn't a dream.* The gooks were in the perimeter! They had broken through where he hadn't put the hole in properly. They're really coming! The gook was reaching for him; he saw the bayonet.

"*Yaaghi!*" He screamed and leaped up in the air, his fist jacking the receiver of the .45. He landed in a crouch, holding the cocked pistol. He saw the sleeping bodies and packs. Nothing moved.

The Listening Post

At dusk Big John led the other three—Red, Christian, and Gerwell—warily down the path. They were all dog-tired, but Chief had said there must be an LP at the end of the ridge.

Big John could still hear the bitching and the moaning when Chief called for the LP. They cursed the Chief, the Lieutenant, and the Captain. Why had *he* volunteered? Now he wished fervently that he hadn't. What a stupid thing to do. Why? Because somebody had to go. *Why me?* Because he was the most capable. Shee-it. You know the real reason you came. Because of that damn Lieutenant. Now he regretted it even more bitterly because the Lieutenant hadn't even seen them go. He was asleep. Fool. Never volunteer for anything. But he had. And there they were, going two or three hundred yards outside the lines on an LP, only pissing distance from Laos.

Actually Big John had volunteered because he was ashamed of wanting to be medivacked that afternoon when he'd been hit. The wound was nothing, but he had laughed thinking he was going to get out of the bush. Big John remembered distinctly the Lieutenant rushing back, acting as if he needed him and acting as if he really cared. He felt the Lieutenant's hands on his shoulder. Shee-it. The fucking Lieutenant was *asleep* and didn't even see him go out. Well, he'd make sure the Lieutenant knew when they came in tomorrow morning. Go right over and discuss the LP with him. Yeah, that's it. But as they came to the end of the ridge, something told him the Lieutenant would know about it before morning.

The four men eased their way out on the long finger ridge, narrow on top and sloping off sharply on both sides. It made a slight dogleg about halfway out, and at that point the trees were heaviest and came up quite close to the top. At the end they found a little depression and took it for their position. Here at the forwardmost point of the finger, the ground sloped off in three directions. In front of them another hill rose up from a gully. Only back toward the lines where the faint trail ran along the ridge crest, was the ground level. At the company lines, however, the finger spread and fanned into a larger hill.

The ridge was covered mostly with thick, waist-high

grass, with an occasional patch of elephant grass or a
clump of bushes. They tramped down the grass in a depression, and the surrounding grass stood erect on the
higher ground, making sort of a pocket. But they all knew
it was a long way from the safety of a real foxhole. By
squatting and raising his head, Red could see to the bottom of the gully. At least he could see now. In a few minutes it would be really dark. An overcast had come up
and not even a star showed through.

Quickly they set out trip flares and Claymore mines. As
soon as he went out just a few feet away from the others,
the aloneness and the fear nipped at him. It was getting
dark fast, and the grass was suddenly full of the enemy.
Slowly Red crept down the forward slope. He knew that
the farther out he set the trip flare, the better it was, but
already it seemed as if someone were watching him, cutting him off. Any farther and they'd get him. He had to
get back, back to the others and safety. His hand began
to shake. He hastily strung the little wire. He tied one end
to a clump of grass and ran it back to the flare. Then he
stuck the flare into the ground, and carefully he took the
slack out of the wire. His body was trembling as he posi-
tioned the pin so the slightest tug would set off the flare.
The sweat ran down his side and he started to scuttle
back.

"Get out of here," he yelled to himself involuntarily,
galloping fear grasping at him from behind. His skin
twitching, he felt that at any moment a knife or a bullet
would cut into his back. He fairly ran into the crater.
Strength and relief flowed into him from the mere
presence of the others. He whirled to face the pursuer,
finding it a thousand times better to face the enemy with
Marines at his side than to run along cringing from the
unknown death behind him.

"Red, we need the Claymores out," Big John said. It
was a pleading question. Sweating profusely, Red un-
wound the electrical cord from the mine and plugged the
end into the blasting cap. He readied the prong to stick in
the ground so he would have nothing to slow him down
out there. He crouched and slid out. He strained to move
slowly and quietly. An LP depends on silence for security,
he kept telling himself. It's not a fighting post; they must
try to remain undetected at all costs. Move feet: one step,

two, three, four. Sweat stung his eyes as he peered into the dark grass. Five steps, six, seven. He jabbed the Claymore into the ground and fled back to the hole.

They decided on the watches. One man awake—twenty-five percent. One hour awake, three asleep. If they heard any movement, they would go to fifty percent watches, two men awake, one hour up, and one hour down.

Big John took the first watch. The others curled up uncomfortably and tried to sleep, one hand on their rifles. They took off only their helmets. Exhaustion swept over them immediately, but aching, overstrained muscles refused to relax. Ears pricked at every sound, sending tense jolts through the body.

Big John got a radio check.

—"I read you, Lima Charlie. How me? Over."—

He sat back and almost immediately heard the brush rustle. They had just come out! If the gooks were this close already. . . . He broke out in a fine sweat. When he touched his arm, it began to pain him again. He listened as he gingerly massaged the pain where the shrapnel had gone into his shoulder. It was numb now. He listened again for a step, a rustle. He couldn't be sure. He heard nothing. He listened with every fiber for at least ten minutes. Nothing more stirred. But he had heard something at first. The thought suddenly came to him. Maybe they could see him and stopped moving when he pricked up. No, that's crazy. He turned the radio a bit lower and hooked the handset onto his collar. He sighed and looked down at a Claymore. They hadn't even gotten the last one in.

After an hour Big John nudged Christian. His eyes were closed, but he sat up at once. Christian's watch came and went. One hour. Nothing. Gerwell came on. He'd slept only fitfully. Another hour.

Red had the fourth watch. It was eleven twenty. He had been too tired and tense to get more than a doze. He made a radio check and braced himself to be alert. This was his watch, Red thought, he had to stay sharp; they depended on him.

Lying down before, he couldn't sleep, but now, sitting up, he could hardly keep his eyes open. His eyes closed and slowly his head sank, then bobbed up as the neck muscles relaxed. *Whoo.* He shook his head. Got to stay awake. The platoon is depending on me. Hell with the platoon—I'm depending on me.

Then his legs began to twitch. First the left calf. It was as if he were about to have a cramp but the cramp never came, just the twitchiness. His toes curled. He had to walk on them or, better yet, stretch out flat and sleep. His head wagged. Then both legs began to twitch. He asked Joseley for another time check.

—"Delta Two. This is Why Me. Time check. Over."—

—"Why Me, be advised the time is 2350. Over." — It was Doc Smitty.

Only half an hour gone by. His body seemed to ache and twitch at the same time. Red remembered feeling that way on a long busride when he'd been up for twenty-four hours. He'd been riding on the bus or waiting in the terminal for a day and a half and he could hardly keep still.

He massaged his calf to ease the twitching muscle, wishing he could stand up for a minute and stamp his feet. But the weariness flooded back into him as he thought of standing. Maybe he'd call in and tell them he was sick. Yeah, that's it. I'll get sick. They'll have to replace me. Idly he looked back toward the lines, thinking how he would go back. With a jolt he realized something had moved! One of the shadows back there had moved! There was a noise of cloth scraping against the bush. His blood pounded with a frenzy and rushed to his head. Sleep and fatigue went out of him in a flash.

He stared into the dark. What was that shadow? Then with a sickening panic he realized it was a *man.* Frantically he fumbled with the rifle. Then the words of Lieutenant, Chief, and LeBlanc somehow came through: *Don't shoot, throw grenades, don't give away your position.* He grabbed a grenade from his belt and grappled with the pin. It stuck. He yanked with his last ounce of strength and the pin straightened. He had no other thought, nothing but that he must kill that gook. Die! he screamed to himself and hurled the grenade. He heard the thud as it hit the ground. Then there was no other noise but the pounding of his heart. He waited; maybe it was a dud.

BRUUMP.

Big John, Christian, and Gerwell scrambled furiously. "What's that? What's that? What did you see? Was that incoming or outgoing?"

"T—There. . . . There. There's a gook right out there." He tried to speak, but no words came.

"Did you get him?"

"I . . . I d—don't know."

Then they heard a rustle of cloth down the gully in front of them. There was a step, many steps, and rustlings.

Big John grabbed the radio.

Big John whispered harshly into the radio. —"Delta Two, Delta Two, this is Why Me."—

Nothing answered.

Red listened to the sound below. It was plain now, and he could hear them crashing around. It sent a wild fear through him.

—"Delta Two. Delta Two. This is Why Me. Ovhur."—

Inside the Perimeter

"Lieutenant, wake up! Lieutenant Hawkins."

"Yeah, Doc." Smitty's hand was shaking his shoulder.

"LP wants you. They got movement. Did you hear the grenade?" He shoved the handset at the Lieutenant and kneeled back.

Hawkins' mind automatically registered that it must be near the middle of the night because it was Smitty's turn on radio. He glanced at the Omega. The hand glowed on the inside of his wrist. Twelve ten. Grenade? He listened. The night was quiet. Had there been a grenade?

Where was he? What hill? Suddenly it came back. He felt the ache and the tiredness. He started to call and remembered he didn't even know what their call sign was.

"Doc, what's the call sign?" he asked with embarrassment.

"Why Me."

"Why Me?"

"Yeah, that's it all right."

"That's a good one." Why me, too, he thought.

—"Why Me, Why Me, this is Two Actual."—

—"Delta Two Actshul. This's Why Me. Be advise' we ha' moo'ment down at d'foot of d'hill. Ovhur."—

Hawkins frowned slightly and glanced at the mike. That's Big John's voice. What the hell is he doing out there? He'd been hit today. Hawkins started to ask and then stopped, remembering he hadn't done anything but tell Chief to put out an LP. Still, it wasn't like Chief to send a wounded man out on LP.

—"Why Me, this is Delta Two Actual. How far out is the movement? Over."—

—" 'Bout fi'ty yahrds."—

—"How many?"—

—"Boo-coo. Ih doan know."—

Hawkins heard the jitter in the voice. —"Okay. I'll put some 81-mm mortars down there. Get down in your hole."—

Hawkins called the Six. Calahan grunted but called for the mortars. A few minutes later Hawkins heard the whistle.

WHUUMPZT. WHUUMPZT. WHUUMPZT.

As he ducked, it dawned on him that he was in a hole. With mounting shame, he realized Joseley must have dug it after he was asleep.

—"Why Me. How was that? Over."—

—"Delta Two Actual, they were too far. Over."— This time it was Red.

Hawkins heard the tension and fright in their voices. The gooks must really be probing. He took a long breath and by a deliberate act willed himself to relax. This had to be calm, smooth, and simple.

—"Why Me, look now, take it easy. Calm down. You got to give me the distance in meters, and whether they are to your right or left. You know as long as the mortars are falling, no one's going to be coming up after you. Now calm down and tell me right. Over."—

—"Okay. Uh, be advised the rounds are all the way down in the bottom of the gully, about fifty meters too far to the left of the movement. Over."—

—"Good, I can follow that. Now get down. Over."—

The second salvo went out.

—"Okay, how was that? Over."—

—"Good, good, right in there. Over."—

There was relief in the voices, but they were still scared. They must really have seen something.

—"Keep listening for sounds and we'll fire again."—

Again Hawkins called for the mortars and again they whistled and crashed.

—"Why Me, hear anything now? Over."—

—"No, it's all quiet. Over."—

Good, Hawkins thought, gripping the handset; now he had to cut 'em off and be smooth before they got jumpy and wanted to come in. —"Why Me, that's fine. Now when you hear something, anything, call me and I'll call for mortars right away. I'm right here by the radio. Understand? Over."—

—"Delta Two, we understand."—

"Okay, Smitty, here they are." He tossed the radio back to Smitty and lay down, but something bothered him. What was it? There's something wrong; he could feel it. Get up and check the lines. He should check the lines. No, it's your imagination; there's nothing wrong. Something about a hole, a position, what was it? Wilson's hole? Tiredness swept over him and he slept.

The Listening Post

After the first mortars they didn't hear movement, but neither did they go back to sleep. It became a hundred percent watch. Red watched the front, Big John to the left side, Christian to the right, and Gerwell to the rear. It began to drizzle and fog followed the drizzle. They pushed against one another in their straining. They kept hearing things, but they couldn't be sure. Red thought it was foggy, but it really was too dark to tell. Jeez, it was dark. The gooks could walk right up to the hole and he'd never even see them. Startled at the idea, Red realized he had never thought of it before, but now wondered how the gooks could possibly move on a night like this. If a Marine unit were to try to go out in the dark, it would be chaos. Even if they went in a column and held on to one another they would bang, clang, and stumble around. His hair prickled as he remembered how the gooks could come right up to their position. They must be able to see in the dark, he thought.

What Red didn't know was that the NVA couldn't see in the dark, but they were trained in the dark. Being inferior in arms support and sometimes numbers, they employed the night to their advantage. It was as if there were two Vietnams. In the daytime Vietnam belonged to the Americans. In daylight Americans moved, searched, attacked, resupplied. At night time they pulled into a defensive perimeter and waited. In daytime the NVA and VC hid from the roving, searching Marines and the observation planes crisscrossing the air. But at night the planes didn't search and the Marines didn't patrol. Then the NVA moved. Their supply lines, trucks, boats, men, came out of hiding and pushed onward. The trucks bumped over the rugged roads without lights. The men filed silently along the trails, bent over with their loads, led by the spirit of nationalism and the magnetism of Ho Chi Minh, ordered by the iron discipline of Communism, goaded by their hatred of the imperialist aggressor who burned their homes, bombed their farms, and killed their families. Their armies attacked at night to avoid the bombs from the air.

The North Vietnamese colonel had been following the Americans since he had first seen the helicopters and the cache had been discovered. He estimated where the companies would stop for the night. When they stopped, the probers and preparation teams who trailed the Marines by day were ordered to begin at once. Their work went on while the decision to attack was considered.

Nguyen Mai Hanh was a prober, part of the sapper units, the most skilled of NVA reconnaissance men. This night he had spent hours slowly feeling his way toward the Marine lines. He checked for flares and mines. He circled the perimeter and searched for machine guns and the LP's. He listened for voices and watched for cigarettes. If he couldn't see, he made noises or occasionally threw grenades to make Marines retaliate and give away their position. Finally, when he had learned the Marine position, he took pieces of cloth with luminous arrows and taped them to trees. The arrows pointed to the Marine holes, the luminescence away from the Marines. Then continuing to grope, he inched his way along seeking the best avenues of approach for the attack squads. Quietly he unpacked the rolls of wire and, securing one end, began to unravel it away from the Marines. Then, at a point far removed from the lines, usually in gullies or ravines where the artillery couldn't land, he marked the assembly points.

Later, the attack squads followed the wire by simply sliding their hands along. This way they could move quickly and directly to the jump-off points. There was no hesitation or groping in the dark. The wire usually ran to within twenty or thirty meters of the lines.

To insure that squads and platoons kept together, each man attached a small luminescent plaque to the back of his helmet. The plaque indicated his unit or leader. During the move their faces were always kept toward the Marines, units and leaders glowing distinctly to the rear. A trooper had only to follow the wire and drop off at his properly glowing attack or firing position.

Sapper teams prepared explosives and readied the instantaneous fuses. Their mission—rush the enemy lines during the first mortar shelling when the Marines were surprised and down hiding in their holes. Slip by lines and go directly to the inside. Fall upon the communications radios, the leaders, the mortars, and pull their fuses.

Nguyen Mai Hanh knew the Americans would put out an outpost somewhere, and he had to find it. He had to make them give their position away.

But Red didn't know all this. He just knew the gooks could come up in the night and suddenly they were there.

The rain slowed, but he thought the fog was getting worse. The minutes crept by. Then Red began to hear noises. At first it was almost nothing. "Movement again," Red whispered. The others strained their ears. Imagination? No, there were noises. Down in the gully. They seemed to be moving toward the left side. Their hearts pounded in their throats and temples, breathing stopped. There *was* movement now, a lot of movement.

—"Delta Two, Delta Two, this is Why Me."— Red whispered.

No answer.

The noise increased.

—"Delta Two, Delta Two Actual! This is Why Me! Do you read me?"— He whispered as loudly as he dared. Couldn't they hear him? He couldn't talk much louder. Fervently he clicked the handset.

—"Delta Two, this is Why Me."—

—"Delta Two, this is Why Me. Do you read me?"—

"Goddamn they don't answer. We got to have some mortars."

"Big John, can you toss a grenade that far?"

"Yeah, theahr in easy range."

What? Red thought. No, they're way down there. Did Big John hear something else? "How far are they?"

"Thirty or forty yards."

"They couldn't be. They sound at least sixty yards to me."

Big John threw. There was an ominous silence after the blast. They tried the radio again. No answer.

"We gotta get out of here," Red whispered. "We gotta get back in the lines." They darted glances at one another, gripped their rifles tensely, crouched, but nothing was said.

The noise got closer. Red straightened the pin on two grenades and laid them in front of him. The movement increased and it was coming up the hill. He signaled Big John and he threw another grenade. All noise stopped, but then within minutes it seemed to move over to the left.

Again Red tried the radio. Again there was no answer. "Where is that damn radio watch?" he whispered.

"Listen, Big John, we can't wait for that Lieutenant to tell us, we gotta go now!" Christian said.

Big John looked intently into each face. It was cold in the wetness but he was sweating. The heavy brow clouded. "No, not yet. 'Tenant needs us heahr t'd'rect mohrtars."

"Where *are* the mortars?" Red moaned. He knew they were needed to direct the fire, but he wished desperately they could go in. Twice he pressed the handset and called. Twice there was no answer.

Just at that moment he heard it. *BNOWP—BNOWP—BNOWP*. It was far off on the other side of the hill, but there was no way to mistake it. AK-47 firing! His stomach leaped into a knot. "Oh, my God"—he breathed aloud—"we're in for it now."

The firing increased. More grenades could be heard. The lines were answering. Immediately the radio crackled and Little Doc came on. Goddamn that squid, Red thought, that son of a bitch must have been asleep. — "Give me the Actual."— he half yelled.

But before he finished, the Lieutenant came on.—"Why

Me, Why Me, get in here on the double. Over."—

—"Coming."—

"We're gettin' out of here," he croaked to the others.

They grabbed their gear and looked around. They were afraid of the run back to the company. They would be up, moving, exposed. But they had to go. They would surely die if they stayed here. The lines meant safety. It was as if they had to run across a rickety, rotten log over a deep canyon. But if they stayed, they would surely die.

"Ready?"

"Ready."

"Le's go!"

They were up. Big John was out of the hole, moving. Gerwell stepped up. Suddenly there was a dull pop high above their heads and a hazy glow bathed the area. The artillery flare pushed back the night and they were exposed. Everything went bright. Big John whirled and pushed Gerwell back into the hole, stumbling back in himself.

"Theahrs mo'ment on the trail behin' us! We can't go now—weahr cut off!"

"How far?" Red gasped.

"Jus' a li'l ways."

They stared out, suddenly able to see. There were shadows moving back there. It had been close. Big John reached for the Claymore mine detonator. That would clear the path. His hand trembled with the safety.

"Get down," he whispered. "Heahr go." Fear and worry were traced in the massive face. He stared for a moment at the detonator in his hand and then jerked the huge brown fist together. His eyes squinched shut, his body set for the blast. He waited. Nothing. He squeezed again.

Nothing.

"Oh, shit. Shit! Shit! A dud." It couldn't be—Claymores always go off. Then the thought went through him as a dreadful shudder. Were they close enough to cut the wire?

—"Why Me, where are you? Why don't you come? Over."—

—"We can't. We're cut off. There's movement between us and the lines. Over."— Red whispered, his voice barely under control.

The radio didn't answer, and Red could almost feel the

Lieutenant thinking. Finally the voice came.—"Why Me. I'm going to put mortars out there to clear the way. A lot of mortars. I'll try to put them between you and the lines. Over."—

—"Roger."—

They huddled and waited, then they heard the first whistle and rooted into the ground. The whistle-crash resounded through the yellow mist.

—"Why Me, how was that? Over."—

Red couldn't speak. He opened his mouth but nothing came. The enemy seemed to be everywhere in this yellow hell, and if he spoke they'd know where he was. Finally he squeaked out: —"They were too far out."— Tension and fright were choking his voice.

The voice from the radio came again, calm, cool, but hard. —"Why Me. Now take it easy and calm down. Tell me in number of meters how far out and how far right or left from your position the rounds fell. Then tell me where the movement is. Over."—

Instantly he felt better. The Lieutenant was there; he would get them in. The radio was their link to safety.

—"Yes, sir."— Red's voice was much calmer. —"Be advised the rounds were off to the side and about fifty yards too far left from where we heard the movement. Over."—

—"Good. Good, Red. That's the boy."—

Red looked at the receiver and realized that the Lieutenant had said his first name. A heady rush of affection came over him. For the first time that night he smiled, grimly.

More mortars came in. They were close but at spaced intervals. "Get 'em! That must cut them up," he whispered harshly.

—"Why Me, this is Two. How was that? Over."—

—"Good, right on the money." — He felt a little elation.

—"Okay, keep down. We'll fire for effect a couple more times. And as soon as it stops, the lines will start a big cover fire with rifles on each side of the ridge. When you hear the firing, you come in running. Over."—

—"Right."—

—"Get ready," he whispered to the others.

Red shivered. He thought it was hot, but he had stopped sweating. Artillery had started on the far side and now flares were always in the air. There was a *lot* of fog and the light from the flares made the whole area glow. The trees swayed and the shadows flitted across the ground. The light glared. It seemed to focus on them, exposing them.

The yellow fog lurched and one flare went out just as another went up. He saw Big John peering back along the trail, looking for movement. Damn that flare. They couldn't see a thing, but he felt sure it was exposing them. They seemed to be right in the middle of the glare and they couldn't see anything. Red remembered his home in Minnesota, and driving in the winter with his mother. She had taught him to drive. And when there was fog or snow, you never drove with your high beams on because the glare would blind you. Low beams were better to see by. Now it was just like high beams in the fog; they were blinded. They couldn't see anything except themselves. Surely the gooks could see them.

The rounds were falling again. They crouched and got ready to run. The earth shook and the shrapnel zinged around them. Their own mortars were so close Red could feel the blast. They would be killed by their own mortars. The mortars stopped and immediately a tremendous volley of firing broke out along the line.

"The covering fire! Come on! They're shooting for us to come in. Run!"

They were all out and up running. *BNOWP—BNOWP—BNOWP*. An AK opened up and seemed to be firing right across the trail in front of them.

"No! No. We cain't go." Big John shoved them back in the hole.

"Oh, Christ, no."

They tumbled back and fell over each other in near panic.

"We're trapped; we're cut off. They're still there."

The fusillade of firing from the lines diminished and petered away.

The Lieutenant was calling again—furiously. —"Why Me. Where are you? Why didn't you come in? Over."—

—"We're cut off! Over."—

—"No you're not! That's just the rounds from the other side cracking over your head."—

Then the radio was silent. Red realized dimly that the Lieutenant hadn't even said over. "Oh, *do something, Lieutenant*," he whispered.

The movement was all around them now. They were close. The flares kept popping and Red threw another grenade. He looked up at the light and back to the gully. This can't be real, he breathed silently. I can't die. It must be a dream . . . or a movie. It *must* be unreal. He thought of his house in Minnesota and his mom. I'm going to die. I'm never going to see her again. *Stop,* he told himself, but his teeth were chattering as though he had a deep chill. He put his hand down in the hole, feeling for something to bite. He didn't care what—anything. His finger found something; he clamped his teeth on it. That was better.

Then he heard voices. Shouts. Terror rose up in him and threatened to strangle him.

The voice was right there! Right on the other side of that bush. Red thought if his arm was just a little longer he could reach out and touch whoever it was; but he *couldn't see* it. The shadowy bush swayed in the foggy mist light. There was a shadow moving. He *saw* it. Get it!

BrrapRapRapRapRapRapRap.

Red half stood and fired from the hip on full automatic. The M-16 roared fire from the muzzle. He sprayed a full magazine into the bush and down into the gully. He ripped the magazine out and jammed in another.

I must have got him, he thought. But I couldn't see him for sure. He could see me though. I'm sure he could see me in this damn yellow soup. Oh, for daylight. Shadows, shadows, they were fighting shadows.

They crouched and waited; holding their rifles and grenades instantly ready, straining every nerve and fiber to see into the yellow void, and knowing the gooks were *right there*. In a minute the satchel charge would come.

"Should we make a run for it?" they all whispered to each other.

"No," Big John said. "We got t' wait till thea'hs a break. Theahr on the trail now. They ain't got us yet, so we'll keep tight till we get a break."

The Lieutenant was calling for directions on the mortars again.

—"Delta Two, you can shot *anywhere* out here and

you'll hit somebody. Over."—Red whispered desperately.

—"Why Me, all right I'm going to put them all around you. They'll be close. You may even catch some shrapnel, but the gooks will get it. So stay flat. Over."—

—"Roger."—

—"Why Me, now listen. When the mortars come in the gooks have to get down. They're not on the trail. Then immediately we'll put out a big cover fire and I want you to come in. Run for it. This time! Do you understand? Over."—

Red heard the insistence in the voice. The Lieutenant was almost ordering them to come in—but not quite. No, they had to decide for themselves. Big John had the most time incountry and he was here. He had to decide.— "Why Me. Do you understand? You've got to get in here this time. When we fire cover, you blow your Claymores, throw a grenade, and run! Over."—

—"All right. Over."—

Red didn't tell him none of the Claymores had worked and no trip flares had gone off.

The voices came again. This was his last grenade. He couldn't see them. They were just shadows. We have to keep them away or they will put a grenade or satchel charge right in on us.

"*Look out,*" Big John screamed, his voice banged into yellow mist after their whispers.

Red's head whipped around, his eyes bugged out, and for the first time he saw a man. The man had a helmet and a rifle. The man was small. A square package fell from his hand. In that moment Red saw his face; the face was afraid.

Then everything moved again and the man was just a dark blur. Red spun to fire. Big John sprang. His body moved with that incredible speed. He scooped up the little package, his voice still screaming. "Satchel charge." The package left his hands and started to sail out.

BOOOM. There was a great dazzling flash. Red felt a tremendous pressure pushing him down, blasting him back. Big John seemed to rise up in the air silhouetted against the flash. Gerwell came hurling down on top of him. Red was going down—down. The yellow glare dimmed.

Inside the Perimeter

The instant Hawkins heard the incoming rifle fire, he tore out of the poncho-liner and leaped down into the fighting hole. He came crashing down on Joseley.

"That's AK's." Joseley's face was white as a sheet.

"We're in for it," he whispered hoarsely, struggling for his gear. When rifle fire came at night, it was the real thing. Nobody fired a rifle at night until they were really serious because the muzzle flare gave the position away. "Where's the radio? Give me the handset." He half stood up and screamed at the top of his lungs. "Get in your holes. Get in your holes." He grabbed the handset.

—"Why Me, Why Me. Get in here. Get in here."—

He couldn't understand why they weren't already in here. "Joseley, who the hell was on radio watch?"

"Little Doc, sir."

"Damn it all. I'll bet that little fucker was asleep. I should have been called before this. Did you just wake up?"

"I think they were trying to call, sir. When I woke, I heard them calling on the radio and I was just going to get you. Then I heard the rifles go off."

Hawkins waited. For some reason the LP didn't come in. Where the hell were they? They should've been in here by now. He called them again. They said they couldn't make it. They were cut off. Hawkins couldn't believe it, but he knew he had to get them in. For ten or fifteen minutes he worked with them, calling in mortar fire, but they kept saying there were gooks along the trail. His mind went crazy trying to think of a way to get them in.

"Sail, is there room in the hole?" Hawkins called down to the line.

"Come on." The voice was sure but with an edge in it.

"Sir, you can't get out of this hole!" Joseley seized Hawkins' arm. His voice was urgent.

"I've got to go. I'll keep low." He grabbed the radio and slithered over the top of the hole. Joseley was protesting like mad.

Crawling on his elbows and belly, Hawkins wormed down toward the line. He felt as exposed as if he were standing up, and that made him squirm all the faster. He came to the hole and just crawled in head first, lungs gasping and legs waving upright. They grabbed him and pulled him in. Their eyes darted back and forth with keyed-up tenseness as the Lieutenant righted himself.

He looked quickly over the rim. "Don't fire the machine guns, but get ready to set up a covering fire for the LP. Fire on both sides of the ridge crest. Pass it down. Fire when I give the word." He put his hand on Sail. "Don't fire that gun *at all* until I tell you to. We'll save this machine gun for only when we have to use it."

It was tight with four men in the hole; they could hardly move their elbows. Hawkins laid the radio flat on the ground above the hole. He called the LP and told them to stand by. They were ready. Hawkins glanced right and left, then swelled his lungs and rose up. *"LP coming in. Fire."* A hurricane of bullets raked out, but no one came. The men on the line slackened their fire. Sail and the others raised up, peering over the top of their guns.

—"Why Me, what's the matter? Over."—

—"Delta Two, we're surrounded. There is firing between us and the lines. We can't get in. Over."—

Hawkins didn't know if the firing was between them or not, but he knew it was creeping around the lines and becoming more intense all the time. If he didn't get them in soon, they were goners.

—"Are you in a hole? A crater or something?"—

—"Yes. A little crater."—

—"Okay, I'm going to put the .81's all round you to clear the way. You keep down or you'll get hit."—Again he called for the mortars. It was going to be damn close. In a few minutes they came whistling in. They seemed to be right on top of the LP.

Hawkins banged the handset in the dirt and held his face with the other hand. What could he do? How the hell could he get them in? Slowly he slumped to the bottom of the hole. There was nothing else to do.

"Keep talking. Keep talking to them, sir. Keep talking and there's still hope."

It was a strong voice speaking about four inches from his ear. Sail was the angry young cynic, yet now he was urging, sincere. Through the glaring gloom, Hawkins read the message in his voice. They were counting on him, looking for him to tell them—even Sail.

Hawkins recalled with knifelike sharpness the time at Banks' Hill, and in the rain, when they had looked to him. He heard Sail again; they had confidence in him now. He put his hand on Sail's shoulder and a new note crept into his voice. Slowly he raised the microphone.—"Why Me. There's one chance left. Lie down flat in your hole because I'm going to walk the mortars right over the top of your position. When it stops, then you come in. Regardless of anything. Over."—

—"Delta Two. They're all around us, sir. Oh, no. Oh, damn. All right, sir."—

Hawkins called for the mortars and started the order to bring them in right over the top of the position.

The Listening Post

Red was thrown back by the blast. His mind reeled as Big John fell on top of him. It felt as if he were in a balloon and somebody had pricked it. The air's pressing in. And then it stopped. He struggled out from under Big John. Big John had been thrown to the bottom of the hole and then actually bounced over Gerwell onto Red. Dazed, Red looked back for the gook he'd seen, but there was nothing.

And then Big John began to wake up. At first there were little moans, but they got louder. Red crouched trembling, not knowing what to do. The moans became unreal. Big John was trying to keep quiet, but the pain screamed in his body.

"*Ooohhh, ohhhhmmmh, hnnnnnhh.* My hands. My arms. Oh, wheahr are my hands? Ih cain't feel my ahrms. Red, can you see my hands? Ahr my hands and arms okay?"

Red looked down at the arms and his stomach turned over. On the right arm, all that was left was a wrist with a lot of bone and frayed flesh hanging from the end.

"Red, Ih cain't feel my ahrms or legs. Ohhhhhhh."

Red's mind froze.

"Reeeed, Red. Do somethin'. Help me!" he called out, unseeing, unknowing.

"Yes, John?" Red bent over Big John's face.

"Put me out. Please put me out."

Red looked up at the others, their faces wrenched in horror.

"No, Big John, we'll make it." Red's voice trembled violently. *What does he mean?* His mind gagged. *To knock him out or to kill him?*

"Pleeeease, Red. The pain. Oh, God, the pain in my ahrms. Ih cain't stan' it. *Put me out. Pu' me aooooooouuuuuut!*"

Red started to raise his rifle. "No, John, oh, I can't John, I want to but. . . ."

"Pleeeeeaaase. Pllleeaase."

The butt lifted higher.

"I can't. I can't, Big John." His hands dropped.

"Please, Red. Do it. Do it fo' me." Big John's eyes pleaded with Red. *"Do it fo' meeeee!"* His voice was soft and begging for a second. Then it shrieked and his eyes were wailing torture.

Something snapped. Three sets of eyes went up and locked with one another. Their reaction was simultaneous.

"Fuck it! We're going in. I don't care what happens, we're going in. We're not going to stay here. And we're going to take John with us."

"Come on."

"John." Red said, "we're going in and we're going to take you with us."

"No, you cain't take me. Jus' *do it!*"

"We're takin' you," Red growled through his teeth. Suddenly he didn't care. Mad. Fuck the mortars! Fuck the gooks! Nothing could stop him. They were going *in.*

They reached for the giant body, vaulting it easily onto their shoulders. They moved up. They were almost out of the hole when the second explosion blasted them to the ground. It went off right behind Red. His body pitched forward onto Big John. Gerwell and Christian were thrown down. Gerwell dug himself out from under Big John and Red. He grabbed the microphone.

—"Delta Two, we got two casualties."—

"Gerwell, we got to try it now," Christian yelled.

"What about them?" He pulled free of the bodies.

"They're dead. They must be dead. We can't take them anyway. We've got to get out of here." Gerwell yelled. Panic was seizing him, making him lose all reason. He felt slippery. Whose blood was that? Big John had bled on him. He felt his head. It was his own blood. He felt wet all over. Wild, unreasoning fear and panic gripped him; and he was out and running. Fleeing in panic. Ten yards, twenty yards, thirty yards, forty yards, Christian right behind. They rounded the dogleg. Suddenly Gerwell screamed. He was engulfed immediately. Christian saw and tried to stop, his legs churning backwards. He'd bolted uncontrollably, dug his feet into the ground, and tried to run off down the hill into the trees. But many arms seized him. There were hoards of them. More rushed out from the trees.

Inside the Perimeter

—"Delta Two, we've got two casualties."—

The radio crackled, then there was nothing. They waited.

—"Why Me, Why Me, this is Delta Two. Do you read me?"—

No answer. Then suddenly a long scream came floating over the night. "LP coming in!" The lines opened up with firing, and Hawkins put his hand on Sail's shoulder. "No. Hold it." He could feel the sweating need of the man under his hand, wanting to shoot. But nobody came.

—"Why Me, Why Me, this is Delta Two. Why Me, Why Me, this is Delta Two Actual. Do you read me?"—

No answer. Nothing.

The night went dead. The firing and the noise seemed to stop.

Reeek ejeek, reeek, ejeek—the squeaking of the flares as they swung on the hinges of their parachutes was the only noise. He peered out into the yellow fog. Then out of the void came a scream of pure terror. It was a piercing, wailing scream of horror, a sobbing pulse.

"Oh, God they got us! Help!"

It was a horrible wailing in the night, as if the soul had given up and the body was making one last cry. They crouched and waited and looked at each other, fearful, sweating, hunched over their guns, unable to move. Then there were two single shots.

Horror-struck eyes stared at Hawkins.

"I don't know," he whispered, "I just don't know." But

Hawkins did know and he felt the tears, yet there was nothing he could do. Slowly, and at first silently, the curses began to pour forth.

Finally Hawkins shook himself back to reality. "I'm returning to my hole. There's nothing more I can do here. . . . One thing"—he turned to Sail—"don't fire that machine gun until it's absolutely necessary. Don't fire it even if you can see them. Use your rifles. As soon as they find out the position of that machine gun, you're going to catch an RPG. . . ." He slid out of the hole and paused. "Don't fire that until *we are about to be overrun.*"

He slithered out and scurried back to the hole. Artillery was all over. The Captain was asking for everything he could get. It was pounding down on all sides of the perimeter, a hot steel wall of encirclement. The flares were two and three in the sky at one time now, lighting the place clearly despite the fog. They came slowly down, squeaking on their hinges, the magnesium cartridges swinging with a brilliant glow, the parachutes invisible in the brilliance of the light. The light was wonderful, but now it would be suicide to get out of the hole. The hole? Hawkins looked down and had to grin. Joseley was digging frantically.

They huddled deep. The hole seemed like the very essence of safety and protection itself. Then Hawkins' bowels began to hurt. The diarrhea started. Fight it, he told himself. Keep yourself tight. You can't go now. You can't get out of this hole. Joseley and he were jammed down, their knees buckled up around their chins, their legs pushed together—he couldn't even take off his pants.

"Joseley, I may have to shit." He said it as a matter of fact but apologetically. Joseley said nothing.

The firing seemed to die a little bit. Something was eerie. They hadn't come to fire just a few shots. There was going to be more. They sat and waited.

"What's happening, sir?"

A thousand things kept flying through Hawkins' mind. What would he do? What if they break through the lines? What if we get overrun? Should he take the men and try to get away? No. They should stay in their holes and shoot anything that moves on top. Then what? He stopped thinking. You call in mortars on your own position.

He prayed for morning and looked down at his watch.

It glowed four o'clock. If I'm going to die, he thought, I'll smash that first. No gook was going to wear that. He thought of the inscription on the back—*All my love forever. Poo.* Somehow he could feel her snuggle next to him right then, her whispery breath speaking into his neck. "Nite, Pooh Bear. Nite, Poo." Where was she now? Married? Well, so it hadn't been forever. Bitter? No, you know you still love her and you bet she still loves you. You can get married lots of times but really love only once.

Suddenly it started and there was no thought but to bury oneself into the ground.

WHUUMPZT. WHUUMPZT. WHUUMPZT.

The gook mortars were almost in the perimeter. They adjusted and then came right in on top of the company.

WHUUMPZT. WHUUMPZT. WHUUMPZT.

No training had ever prepared him for the impact of a real incoming mortar. He felt the shock wave more than he heard the explosion. The blast slammed him, and he could feel it shake the ground, jar his bones. At the same time the deadly shrapnel sliced overhead.

Hawkins and Joseley put their arms around each other and stuffed their heads into the dirt corners. The hole felt so good. A mortar could land barely feet away, but if you were down in your hole, you were safe. Hawkins began to love the hole as if it were a mother—warmth and protection all rolled into one. His mind kept thinking. Mortars come straight down. What if one should land right in the hole? What are the chances of a direct hit? Suddenly he wished with all his might that he had overhead cover. If one dropped straight in. . . .

But there was no overhead cover, just the hole. So he crouched and hoped. Now the radio was all-important. It was the link of communication. He tried to think. He couldn't just sit there.

—"Six, Six, this is Two."—

—"Yes, Two."—

—"Don't you think we could call for a Spooky or a flare ship? Over."—

—"Don't you think I've already called for that?"—he shouted. The voice was irritated, almost out of control.

—"Okay, how long will it be? Over."—

—"Maybe half an hour. Maybe more. Six out."—

Suddenly Joseley's ears pricked up. "What's that?"

Hawkins strained to hear. He heard voices. He listened carefully. Yes, he could hear them. Someone was shouting. He could catch just a few yells. It was all around, but it seemed to be down the ridge line toward the LP. They were even yelling. What does it mean? he wondered. Are they getting ready to attack? The mortars will have to stop before they attack.

He called around the line and told the men to get their heads up and be ready to fire as soon as the mortars stopped. That's when they would come.

"And pass it to the machine guns not to fire until the last minute." The machine guns were their ace in the hole and had to be hidden until the last minute.

Then Hawkins went sick.

"Joseley, give me your knife. Quick."

"What?"

"Just give it to me quick," Hawkins demanded.

Joseley looked puzzled and got out the knife.

"Hurry, hurry." Hawkins grabbed the knife and ripped out the seam in his pants just as his control gave way. There was nothing he could do. The diarrhea had been building up all night. He had to go. He couldn't get out of the hole. It was almost impossible to move. There was nothing else. It gushed out, splattering.

"I'm sorry, Jo," he said stiffly.

Joseley said nothing but looked kind of funny. Hawkins felt as if he were sitting in warm soup. But, ahhh, the relief that came to his stomach—he didn't care. Joseley would have to understand. The spasms relaxed. Who cares if you're dirty so long as you're alive.

Abruptly the mortars stopped. Then something different came. There was a crash which was preceded by a whistle and flash. An RPG! They were going to attack.

"Get ready," he yelled. Then there was madness. Bedlam. Yelling. Firing. Screaming. Confusion, utter confusion. Hawkins remembered only flashes, a long shrill whistle like a police whistle. He didn't know what it was. But then he heard the Chief yelling.

"Get up. Get ready. Attack." The Chief had heard the whistle before.

Something white like a ghost rose up out of the smoke and the yellow fog. It came toward the lines. It was moving. It floated. There seemed to be three little white things.

And then he saw the wave.

They came running low, firing wildly from the hip, a CHI-COM carried in one hand.

Terror. Hawkins froze. Fear ripped through him. He wanted to run. He wanted to bury himself in the hole. The flares lit the area like a dome of horror.

Act, act, act.

"Fire," he yelled, but his cry was lost. They were barely out of the bamboo and brush when the line opened up.

"Sail. Now!" he roared. "The machine gun!" Hawkins didn't know if Sail heard him or not, but he fired.

TaTowTowTowTowTowTowTow. A huge long burst. And suddenly the eerie night was cut with the bright-orange tracer sticks zipping into the human wall. Sail kept on firing—now in rapid controlled bursts. They were falling, staggering. The orange sticks hit into the men and ripped them back, flinging them sideways, knocking them down. They clutched their stomachs, chests, and fell, stumbled, and died.

WOOMPZT. BOOMMM. Grenades. Explosions, bursts of light.

They stopped. The wave staggered, fell, and died. One ran to the side. The machine gun tatted out again; the orange sticks ripped into his back, sending him sprawling forward as if some giant had clobbered him from behind. Then it stopped. Everything seemed to halt. The bodies lay just barely visible in the grass. A few of the men moaned. Firing went on, but it seemed a great lull after the awesomeness of the wave. They stared out.

He felt relief but nothing else. Just tense. After he had first yelled there was no feeling, no thought, only action. He didn't even think to be afraid.

"Get the LAAW's out. Open them. Get the grenades ready. Get the Bloop gun. They may come again." Hawkins was yelling like crazy.

"The LAAW didn't fire," someone yelled back.

"Dammit, that son of a bitch Calahan! Why didn't he listen to me?"

Wheeee. The whistle.

"Here they come again."

He couldn't believe it. A dark bobbing mob of evil bundles of death came running low at the lines.

Then there was the white figure again. Now Hawkins saw what it was. It was a man wearing a white T-shirt. And . . . yes, waving them in. He's guiding them like a traffic cop. The M-60 machine gun began to bark and chatter. The orange sticks ripped into his body and cut his top off from his legs. Hawkins saw a sizzle of white light, heard the whoosh. A LAAW. It worked! It blasted from the side. A single shell hit the line obliquely. There was a brilliant blinding flash and a thunderclap. Half the line disappeared. Just vanished. But the other half didn't keep coming. They dropped into the grass about fifteen or twenty yards out and kept firing.

"Oh, my God!"

Another wave came right over the top of the last one. The first ones were firing cover. Hands automatically reached for K-bars.

Then Hawkins felt the blast to his rear. His head snapped forward violently.

"Gooks in the perimeter!"

"They've broken in on Wilson's side."

In the microsecond that it took to think he knew what had happened. They had probed and found the weak spot, that space between the platoons. And then, with great clarity, he knew what he had done. It was the hole he hadn't checked. It must have been empty.

He came! A *sapper*. Suicide mission. Hawkins saw the TNT strapped to him. He was running low, darting back and forth. He was looking for the CP, but he didn't know where it was. His side was toward Hawkins' hole. He turned, saw Hawkins and Joseley, and sprinted straight toward the hole. He was incredibly fast.

It was automatic. He didn't even think. There was no hesitation, no moral thought, no wondering if he could do it. It was act or die. Lieutenant Christopher Hawkins leveled the .45 and shot him.

The bullet tore into his side and spun him back about five feet. Hawkins stared blankly, amazed at what he had done, when suddenly Joseley yanked his head and jammed it down into the bottom of the hole. One second later the man exploded.

Plug the hole, Hawkins thought again. They're coming from Wilson's side. Suddenly he whirled back. The wave was still coming on. He swung back to the front in just a fraction of a second and saw the second LAAW erupt. A blinding flash.

Bloop. Somehow he heard the little pop of the M-79 grenade launcher. *BLAMM.* Frozen in his mind was the image of that one particular grenade. It hit the gook square in the face. His head popped off like a champagne cork. They would find him the next day. All he had left was a chin. The wave died, but Hawkins had no feeling of relief. He only knew he must plug that hole. Rounds were coming from that direction. How? Who with? Who was he going to use to plug that hole? Aside from the Docs, Chief and Joseley were the only other men on the platoon behind the lines.

Hawkins looked at Joseley, his eyes asking, pleading, and telling in a single glance. "Jose."

Two more men came running up. Hawkins ducked and raised the pistol to fire.

"No"—Joseley grabbed his hand—"those are Marines."

One twisted and fell, moaning and holding his leg. The other darted back and forth, looking like the sapper did.

"Here," Hawkins called.

He ran over and jumped in the hole; his body wiggled and convulsed. He wrapped his arm around their knees and held on.

"Take it easy."

"Hey, what are you doing?" Joseley shouted.

The man turned his face up. It was not even a human face. It was the face of panic, the face of fear. Hawkins had seen faces like that once before—in an insane asylum. The horrible, blank, pleading look. The eyes. In a minute he might be going mad, totally mad. His whole body shook. He hugged their knees in a viselike clamp. He crushed them to him and sobbed. Tears rolled down his face.

"Stop it, man. Come out of it." Joseley tried to slap him and shake his head, but the hole was so small that he couldn't get at him properly.

"What happened? For Christ sake, man, tell me what happened." Hawkins finally got his hands on the man's head and shook him by the ears. It seemed to work. He stopped crying, but he continued to hold their knees, and his breath came in gasps. His eyes looked like shattered marbles. He whimpered.

"I was in the last hole. There was another hole on our right when it all started and I thought somebody was in it. Big John had started to dig it earlier." Hawkins glanced over at Joseley, but the radioman didn't notice. The man whimpered on. "I guess it was empty, because all of a sudden the gooks came running at us straight from that hole. They got Merlin and we jumped back and got in the old trash-pit hole and started shooting at the hole we'd been in. I think they were in it. Then something ran past me. I don't know what . . . then I felt them coming at me and I thought the whole line had given away. Oh, oh, help me, Lieutenant."

"Joseley, take this guy and see if you can plug up that hole. I don't think the gap is that big."

"No, no, I can't go back." He was shrieking. His mouth sobbed in blubbering cries. "I can't. I won't go back."

"You've got to go. We don't have anybody else." But he knew it was useless. The man was too far gone.

"Joseley, get Chief. Try to frag 'em out of the trash pit or wherever they are and move on down and plug that hole. I'll move over into the hole behind you."

Joseley nodded.

"Chief," Hawkins yelled, "Joseley's coming over. You got to plug up that gap beside Wilson."

The knowledge of the hole spurred Hawkins, and he jumped into Chief's hole to cover, then he heard the cry.

"Gas! Gas!"

Hawkins looked back to where the assault had come from. Creeping sickly, the substance oozed and drifted over the lines. Men were screaming. He knew it was all over. It closed about them like a smothering pillow of death. They had no gas masks. This was it. They had us.

"Run! Get away!"

Hawkins sniffed. Wait. It wasn't gas; it was smoke. Suddenly he was screaming. "It's smoke. SMOKE. SMOKE!" He yelled as loud as he could.

"Smoke. Stay where you are. It's only smoke. Stay where you are." The men stopped. The smoke rolled in like a thick pea soup. The flare was still lit, but now each man was locked in a vault, isolated from all others. The fog had been misty, but this was unbelievable. He couldn't see his hand in front of him.

Hawkins held his pistol up, cocked, ready. He had it about ten inches in front of his face. It moved with his eyes like a turret. But they didn't come. Suddenly he knew. He heard them moaning. They're getting their bodies. He considered shooting. They might attack again. Just hold positions and use artillery and mortars. Slowly the smoke began to clear, and there was a fleeting glimpse of shadows flitting into the bushes. and then there was nothing. The NVA always get their bodies. They never leave anything to count.

Would they attack again? He radioed Six.

—"Six, they must be falling back to attack again. They'll probably move down the gully. Can we put some arty in there? Over."—

In a few minutes the artillery was pouring in, round after round after round. It was a mass Fourth of July. They mixed the regular shells with Willy Peter (white phosphorus).

The white and the red-orange puffballs came first, followed by the crash and the shock. But the Willy Peter was the worst. From the blackness of night suddenly a big glowing white-hot ball erupts. Great streaks of brilliant sparklers shoot off in all directions, then arc and slowly settle to the ground as they die out.

But the firing kept up on all sides of the perimeter. They sat in their holes and waited. Mortars were coming again, and they stuck their faces into the bottom of the holes. He could only guess that Joseley and Chief had plugged the gap in the lines—the gap that he should have plugged to start with. Finally he saw it or, at first, heard it. It made a pass over the position and the sky became bright as day.

Puff! Puff the Magic Dragon. A plane like an old two-engine DC-3, but equipped to throw the big flares, called basketballs, and armed with new rotary machine guns that could shoot about seven thousand rounds a minute, enough lead to put a bullet in every square inch of a football field in the time it takes to fly over.

Relief flowed exquisitely. Oh, thank God. We're saved. We're saved! Now we'll make it. Somebody is coming to help us.

Hawkins told Sail to fire the machine-gun tracers out where he thought the gooks were. "Put them out there to show Puff where to shoot."

Raaaaaaaaaapp. A long straight snake of solid-red bullets zipped from the plane to the ground, stretching the whole distance. It was like a lightning bolt thrown from the sky. Later on, Puff came to be called Snoopy, but it was always Puff to Hawkins.

Round and round the plane flew, lighting the sky and razing the earth with fiery tongues. After twenty or thirty minutes the pilot left, having used up his ammunition. They still had the artillery flares though. He glanced down at Poo. Five thirty. Then he looked up at the eastern horizon. It was becoming just a little more definite than the western horizon, a tiny glow behind the mountain line.

Dawn.

Now the jets, the air cover, the helicopters, the reinforcments, and everything else in the whole Goddamn United States armory would come. It would be *daytime.* Peter had never felt greater on the first Easter morning.

As soon as it was light enough to see, the first jets roared over. The Captain fired a 60-mm mortar Willy Peter round in the direction of the gully to mark the spot where the gooks had been dragging off their dead. Then the great silver birds soared in. The bombs burst in big, brazen, orange puffballs.

There were tears in Hawkins' eyes, but he couldn't help it. As each plane came in on the bombing run, he screamed. The tears ran down his cheeks. All along the line there was cheering.

"Sock it to 'em."

"Get 'em."

"Let 'em have it."

"That-a-way!"

"Kill those baaastards!"

"KILLLL 'EM!"

As soon as the fog cleared, they organized and crept out in search of the LP. A few dead bodies lay close to the lines, but the main area of the assault wave was cleared. Tense and raw, the men picked their way along.

Crawk. Crawk.

They fired into the bodies, in no mood to take prisoners. Inch by inch, they wormed down the ridge crest. Then at the dogleg they found Christian and Gerwell. Hastily flung into the weeds, they obviously had been killed on the spot, each one shot in the back of the head. Chief rolled them over. The men standing around gave a sickened gasp. Some turned away and vomited. Hawkins could only stare. Their faces were blown out from the bullet coming through from the back. Where Christian's face had been was now just a big hole. One eye dangled from his cheek by a cord.

Chief covered them up quickly.

But where were the other two? Where were Big John and Red? Had they been captured? What had happened? The platoon almost ran down the trail, forgetting security, frantically looking for the LP position. Maybe they were still alive. They lowered their rifles and began calling and sifting through the thick grass. Then the point stopped, spotting the hole. Hawkins ran over and looked down. He couldn't understand what he saw. The two bodies lay close together, face down, side by side, as if they'd been laid out in some special manner. There were very few marks on the bodies except for one of Big John's hands. On that arm was a handkerchief in a tight tourniquet.

"Chief, what? What killed them?"

Silently Chief pointed to Big John's flayed hand. "Must have been a satchel charge, sir. The concussion is what killed them." He knelt and felt the bodies. He started to turn them over, then stiffened and rose abruptly.

"What? Chief, what?" Hawkins bent forward.

"Nothing, sir. Don't look at 'em! Red's still warm; he must have lived on a while." Chief tugged at the Lieutenant's sleeve.

"Oh." Hawkins dropped beside the figures. His eyes went down between the two bodies. "They're, they're holding hands."

"I know, sir," Chief pulled at the Lieutenant's shoulder. "Leave 'em alone! I'll get a poncho."

The two hands had been hidden from where Hawkins stood. Now he lifted Big John's arm and Red's moved with it.

"Lieutenant!" Chief said sharply.

But Hawkins was transfixed. He raised the arm and both arms moved as one, hands locked together. They had died as brothers, holding hands. Gently he shifted them. Red's head rolled over. His balls were in his mouth.

After wrapping the Marine bodies, the platoon went after the gook dead. But the only corpses found were those right next to the company lines. Evidently the gooks had succeeded in removing most of their dead under the cover of the smokescreen. Hawkins had a hunch they had dragged them down the trail and then off to the left at the dogleg and into the gully. If so, he thought the arty and air should have caught quite a few.

They moved down the trail. Although it had rained earlier, most of the ground was dry now. But the trail here was muddy. Hawkins frowned, seeing the mud oozy and tracked with deep footsteps. He heard the gasps of the men and then he knew. It wasn't mud from rain; it was blood mud.

They had dragged all the dead and the dying straight this way. Bits of cloth, gear, and flesh were strewn along the path. Little gooey dribs hung from the bushes; it was impossible to tell what they were. He stepped gingerly, but the mud oozed up over the sides of his boots, making sickening sucking sounds as he stepped along. His boot was red with the wet blood mud over it. In some places their feet sank almost two inches into the stuff.

There was a new trail. It led down from the dogleg into the gully, through the woods. They found a single strand of wire running alongside it; some signs and arrows. Hawkins was puzzled, but toward the bottom of the gully he finally began to find the bodies. He knew they had been dropped when the air support came in. Bodies lay everywhere. Arms, legs, and all kinds of guts were mixed in with the blown-apart jungle. The stink wafted up. "Let's get outta here."

The Second Platoon later buried forty-eight NVA dead. Hawkins knew. It was his job to count the bodies. The men would loop a rope over a foot and drag the corpse into a crater, cringing at the thought of even touching it. Going back over the events of the night, counting the squad waves, and including the air and artillery, Hawkins estimated that since forty-eight bodies were found, they might possibly have killed one hundred at most.

The platoon returned to the position and gradually the

shock of the battle wore off. Somehow they went on with
the process of evacuation and resupply. Slowly the grief
for the dead ones faded.

The bodies were wrapped in ponchos, and stiff, dry-
eyed men loaded them onto the choppers. One forgets.
One goes on.

Then, inexplicably to Hawkins, the spirits began to rise.
The wounded were bandaged and begged to return to
their buddies. They clustered in groups and excited talk
sprang up. They had defeated an NVA battalion! *Oh, we
killed those sorry bastards. Oh, we were tough. We were
hard! We won!*

"Did you see that one . . ."

"I'm tellin' you I shot . . ."

"I got that gook right in the fuckin' head . . ."

"See the gook that the bloop gun got: he only got a chin
left."

"Did you see the Lieutenant shoot that . . ."

"Goddamn, Hawkins really called it in . . ."

"Lieutenant . . . Lieutenant . . ."

Unbelievable! Hawkins walked in a happy daze, eagerly
drinking in the adulation he saw in their eyes. Slowly he
returned to normal and began to check the area. He
found the sapper he had shot. He looked down at him
with a loathing mixed with disgust at the torn flesh. Some
flies were crawling on the neck. The upper body was partially blown away. Hawkins forced his hand to check the
pockets for intelligence information. He had just one letter, his name was Nguyen Mai Hanh, there was no other
identification, but—then he saw it. Hawkins stared down
at it with a curious feeling of desire. A belt! A wide
leather belt with a heavy brass buckle. It even had the
deep engraved Red Star. It was just like Chief's. His hand
reached down and tugged, then jerked back involuntarily
as he felt the stiff weight of the dead body. The flies
buzzed. For an instant he was repelled, then his mind
flicked to the rear and how those belts were treasured.
Anybody who had a real gook belt must be a *bad ass*. He
had shot this gook. Chris Hawkins killed this one. He
would have that belt. That was *his* belt. Eagerly he
reached down and got it loose without having to touch
any of the flesh.

He yanked it free and held it up. It wasn't hurt at all. There was a dent and a scrape on the buckle, but that was okay, maybe even better.

Then he realized the Chief was watching. Some others were behind him. Caught, Hawkins stared uneasily, but Chief's face spread slowly in a tremendous grin. The others were all grinning and looking at the belt. Hawkins saw it hanging in his hand, and suddenly his face could not keep from smiling. He held it up for them to see. Their eyes sparkled.

"It's a good one."

"Put it on, sir."

Put it on? Wear it? Then his hands were fumbling with the adjuster. Fervently he tried it—too small. Finally the Chief had to help him. It was on. He looked down at it awkwardly, then his head came up and he felt himself laughing, his chest swelling. But the Chief frowned.

"Not right yet, sir."

"What? What's wrong?"

Chief reached to take it, and Hawkins saw the others smile mysteriously. His eyes followed Chief as he turned and kicked over the dead sapper. Casually, but as if in a ritual, Chief stooped and smeared the belt in the blood on the gook's chest. Slowly straightening, he held it high over his head until it was dry.

"Now, sir."

Hawkins took it and snapped it on. The buckle glistened in the sun. He looked down once more, then back to the grinning men, and something passed between them.

Then the Chief gave a silent nod and they snapped to attention. Their hands went up in unison. They saluted.

VII
Indian Song—Tokyo

Chief

> SAIGON (AP)—A single company of the Third
> Marine Division held off an estimated Battalion of
> NVA regulars in a predawn attack on the Marine
> position Thursday. The Marine Company, part of op-
> eration Dewey Canyon, was encamped on the North-
> western border of the Republic of Vietnam. Under
> cover of heavy mortar fire the enemy attacked the
> Marine lines in repeated wave assaults.
>
> Artillery and air support was called to aid the be-
> sieged Marines and is credited with inflicting heavy
> casualties. 239 enemy dead were reported and an un-
> recorded number of weapons. Early estimates place
> the kill ratio as one of the higher in the war.
>
> Military spokesmen stated the position was not
> critical and constituted only a nighttime position on a
> continuing search and destroy operation. The position
> was being abandoned to continue the operation.
>
> Marine casualties were termed light.
>
> New York *Times*

"Jesus! That's us," Wilson exclaimed, staring at the
newspaper in the Da Nang airport.

"What? Lemme see that." Chief's eyes scanned the paper rapidly, his eyebrows arching at the "239." "Maybe,"
he said slowly, staring at the date. "The paper's old
enough—over a month. Aahh . . . forget it." He
crumpled the paper, tossed it aside. "This is R 'n' R.
You're supposed to forget all that shit."

"Hey! don't do that." Wilson darted after the paper and
began to carefully smooth the wrinkles. "I'm going to save
this."

"Forget it, man, you only have to do one year in

d'Nam—course Marines do thirteen months—and the U.S. taxpayers are officially sending us to forget."

Wilson and Chief walked gingerly because for the first time in months they wore street shoes. "Ow! Man, my feet must have grown while I was wearing them boots."

"Forget it!" Chief snorted. "When we get there, we're not going to need shoes. I'm going to be nekked the whole time, just lay in bed, drink, and fuck. I'm so horny I'm growing antlers."

Wilson looked at Chief and grinned. There it was again—the flip side was out—whenever they got in the rear Chief's personality yo-yoed, even his talk changed. Wilson never got over being amazed at the difference. "Not me, man, I'm going to get some fancy threads and a nice hotel and. . . ."

They had come out on the flight line and their eyes leaped out as both faces broke into a wide grin.

"Pan American! Are you shittin' me? Look at that! A big ole blue and white Boeing 707 civilian-type plane with. . . . Look, in the doorway! Top o' the stairs! O my God! It is! It's the *Female of the Species!* One fine round-eyed, sweet-smelling American chick just waitin' for me to run up that ramp!"

An immaculate little staff sergeant in crisp, starched stateside utilities strutted up with a bullhorn. He began a bored monotone harangue punctuated by accents on the words *"you will"*: "Awright, knock off the grab-ass and listen up. All personnel listed on the 1400 Tokyo R 'n' R Flight will line up at the window where you see the sign '1400 Tokyo R 'n' R Flight.' That is the proper window. You will have your orders and your ID card ready, and you will present them to the sergeant at the window. He will then check your name on the flight manifest. If your name checks on the flight manifest, you will then go to change your money. You will do that at the other end of the terminal where you see the green sign 'Money Exchange.' You will change your money there. You will present your MPC with your orders and your ID card. The sergeant at the Money Exchange window will give you green dollars back for your MPC. You will not take any MPC out of Vietnam. You will change them back to dollars if you have any left. You will do this at the Tokyo

R 'n' R center. You will get instructions on how to do that at that time. After you change your money you will proceed to have your gear inspected. After your gear is inspected, you will board your flight through the gate marked 1400 Tokyo R 'n' R 'Flight.' That is the proper gate. You will now line up behind the window where it says 1400 Tokyo R 'n' R Flight. Line up!"

They lined up.

Bangkok, Sidney, Taipei, Singapore, Penang, Manila, Hong Kong, Tokyo, and Hawaii. Every American in Vietnam is entitled to go on one R 'n' R, Rest and Relaxation, sometime during his tour. Five days of play away from the war; the transportation is free. It doesn't count as leave time, and the government charters the airplanes, all free. Almost every married man goes to Hawaii—if he can get it. He can meet his wife there, who travels at a special reduced rate—provided she gets the necessary papers in time.

"Wilson, how come you didn't go to Hawaii?" Chief asked as they stood in line. A flicker of bitterness passed over Wilson's face, but he answered casually, "Oh, I put in for it, but I just couldn't get all the papers worked out in time."

"Didn't that shit Top Goresuch do anything for you?"

Wilson scowled. "Naw, that back-stabbing son of a bitch didn't help me at all." Chief dropped the subject; but as they watched the eager line, Wilson felt a melancholy loneliness.

He remembered quite well when the word came to the bush asking for R 'n' R choices; he had put Hawaii down first and he had made a special note asking for the papers to be sent to his wife. But weeks later when the R 'n' R list for the following month came to the field, he was scheduled for Tokyo. Furious and sick with the thought of not seeing his wife, he had fought and argued with the Gunny until the Gunny had sent him to the rear to check on it. He remembered every detail of that visit to Top Goresuch. He had started off politely.

"Top, can I see you a minute?"

"Wha'dya want?" the growly voice came out of the beefy man. The pig eyes glared at Wilson with quick contempt.

"It's about my R 'n' R, Top; I'd like to go to Hawaii so I could see my wife. I requested Hawaii but the list says Tokyo."

"Everybody wants to go to Hawaii but everybody can't go; we only got so many slots allowed each month."

"But, Top, I requested a long time ago and told the Gunny I'd wait till an opening came up."

"Gunny didn't say nothing to me."

Wilson felt the anger rising in him, but he held his tongue.

"Top, I don't want to go to Tokyo. I want to see my wife."

"You sure don't hafta go, that's your choice."

"Can I go to Hawaii another month?"

"Well, I don' know"—he looked at some papers—"lessee, next month's filled. Oh yeah, Goodman just got wounded; he was supposed to go this month, you can take his place. Tha'll be next week."

"Next week?"

"Yeah, the twelfth of the month."

"Will I have time to send my wife the papers for the airplane?"

"Oh, hell no, you shoulda requested those long ago."

"But I *did* request the forms be sent out. I sent a special note." Wilson felt the bile of frustration and the sickly sinking feeling of hopelessness.

"Never got it."

Desperately Wilson's voice pleaded. "What about the month after next; then I'd have plenty of time to get all the papers."

"Can't guarantee it, pretty risky that far ahead. 'Sides I 'spect the Captain will be wanting to go about then. I suggest you take what you got."

The Captain. Oh, yes, whatever the fucking *officers* want. "That ain't right, Top!"

"Don't get smart with me, boy." Top's voice roared out. "I'm giving you a good deal. I got you a chance for Hawaii, now take it or leave it. But don't be mouthing off at me."

Wilson glowered in hate. Fuck it all! It just wasn't fair. They were discriminating against him. Yeah, sure he could go to Hawaii, but on lance corporal's pay there was

no way in hell he could afford to fly Sylvia to Hawaii and
back, regular fare. He could barely afford the special rate;
if he waited two more months he might, just might, get it.
But shit, he was due to rotate the month after that. He
could be dead by then.

For a month he worried what he would tell Sylvia. Finally he gave up and wrote he couldn't get R 'n' R, that he
was only going on incountry R 'n' R.

Chief saw the sad look, "Come on, Wil. You and I will
stick together and have a ball."

Wilson felt the warmth from his friend and forced his
voice to be hearty. "Yeah, man, we'll have a party."

"Listen, man—first thing I do, I'm gonna get me five
broads—you heard me—five. One for each end and three
in-between. Then I'm gonna get the beh-yust hotel—I
don't care what it costs—the beh-yust ho-tel."

"How much you got?" Wilson asked.

"Four hundred skins."

"Wow. For five days?"

"I'm staying in the shower two hours. Then I'm
gonna—" Chief's eyes fell on the R 'n' R Center advertise-
ment in the literature in Wilson's hand. "What is that
you're readin' there?" He grabbed the folder. *"USO? Temples? Sightseeing? Swimming? Horseback Riding? Ping-
Pong!* Oh, you *gotta* be shittin' me!"

Wilson squirmed uncomfortably, then a slight grin
broke over his handsome features, "Well, you know . . .
I can't be ah. . . ."

"Aren't you even *curious* to find out if it really is sideways?"

Wilson laughed outright. "Okay, Chief, what the' hell?
How many did you say—five—shit. I'll get ten." For just
a moment there was a little pain of guilt.

The bullhorn cut back in: "It is illegal to take out of
Vietnam any of the following items: firearms, any ord-
nance or explosive device, any pornographic literature or
pictures. . . ."

Wilson and Chief followed the officers onto the plane.
They eagerly hustled for seats, obediently fastened their
belts, then along with every other Marine aboard glued
their eyes to the stewardesses. Never were three women
more rapidly stripped, ogled, and raped than by the lust-

ing minds of one hundred and sixty-five Marines on Flight 1400 to Tokyo.

"Good afternoon, gentlemen." The stewardess began her speech and Chief's lips seemed to move as if he were in a trance.

Ooh, that voice of yours is soft and wet honey, like you're licking me all over. But *gentlemen?* Are you bird-turdin' me, baby? We're nothin' but animals—*Grrrrr.*

Wilson glanced over at Chief and grinned in anticipation as a silent Indian, a cool professional fighter named Chief, metamorphosed into Randy Eagle, the Crazy Californian. He saw Chief's eyes follow the stewardess like a robot.

". . . Welcome aboard Pan Am's 1400 R 'n' R Flight to Tokyo. . . ."

Chief's lips moved hungrily:

Excuse me just a moment, miss, while I get *aboard you.* Yes, that's fine, now continue.

". . . Because our flight today . . ."

Oh, yes, *any* day's okay with me.

". . . flys partly over water . . ."

Here I come, *flying* right on down on top of you like a Phantom jet . . . divin' down *eeeeoowwwwww!* How was that for a landing, sweet skivvies?

". . . We are required by law to explain . . ."

Explain! Listen, doll, come over here and I'll *show* you a few things.

". . . the operation of the life jackets you will find under your seats . . ."

You want to get under the seat! Well, do you think there's room for both of us? Just squeeze on under and no-one will see, heh, heh, heh.

". . . Miss Furbarins the . . ."

Miss *Fur-Burger* is it? We must get out from under here now. What will the other poor passengers do if you don't go out and demonstrate the operation of the life jacket?

". . . in the forward part of the compartment . . ."

Yes, darling, your *forward compartment* is just delightful.

". . . Miss Harper in the center . . ."

Miss *Hair-Pie!* What? You want to get down here, too? But you have to demonstrate—Yes, I *know* you're dying for it, so just a quick one. Hurry up! Slide under here. Yes, that's it, baby. . . .

". . . And Miss Gintiano in the rear . . ."

No! Miss *Giant Jugs?* You, too? Absolutely not! A *ménage à trois,* you say? But I *promised*—besides you'll never fit—how can you slide under here with those—ah—protuberances?

". . . will now demonstrate . . ."

Oh, yes, let's demonstrate. Girls! No! Come back—I was about to explain my theory of—having a bit of trouble there, Miss Giant Jugs? You seem to be stuck on your protuberances. Here I'll just push them around a bit—what?

". . . The life jacket is placed . . ."

Who will I watch? Who will I watch? Gotta hurry, gotta decide—Miss Fur-Burger, I think. Angle of vision is very good. Little hazy on Miss Hair-Pie. A fucking giant's head blockin' Miss Giant Jugs. Okay, lucky you, Miss Fur-Burger, Screaming Sky is now homing in!

". . . over the head in this manner . . ."

Yes, here I am, Plastic Man, disguised as a life jacket slipping down over and around her neck. She doesn't realize who I am. Doesn't suspect a thing. Ohh, that perfume. Ummmmm—she's a little sweaty in the pits though—only natural with all that runnin' up and down the aisle. And now, Plastic Man disguised as a life jacket drops down. *Right on her boobs!* Ohh, so nice and warm and she still doesn't suspect my true identity. Nice, soft boobs—wait—what's this? Feels kinda *funny* here—kinda like—a *Hong Kong Bra?* Je-sus Christ! What kinda shit is that?

". . . Then the straps are pulled in this manner . . ."

Owww! God, girl, take it easy—you're pulling on my—owww!

". . . and fastened . . ."

Oh, no! I can't move. I'm trapped! Wrapped, I mean, ahh, now what?

". . . To inflate the jacket, you simply jerk this . . ."

No! No! Don't jerk that! Anything but that!

". . . If the life jacket fails to inflate, you simply pull out this tube . . ."

Is she gonna do what I think she's gonna do? Yes, o yes, she is!

". . . Place it in your mouth . . ."

—mmmmmm—

". . . and blow . . ."

O yes.

Now if you don't mind, a little hum-job might be nice. Music is so pleasant, don't you think? My request? Well, something that goes through several octaves would be appropriate—ah, do you know *"Un bel di vedremo"* from *Madame Butterfly?* Yes, but you can't hum it—oh, that's a *shame.* Well, something lively and spirited then—let's see—"Dixie"! You know it! *Great!* And then after that, "Yankee Doodle"! Must keep a sectional balance you know. Hmmmh—Hmmh—Hummmh—hmh—hmmmmmh—hmh—hmmmmmmmmh—hmh. Splendid! Well done. Now "Yankee Doodle."

". . . Now the girls will . . ."

No no no *no!* I have another request—wait!

". . . demonstrate . . ."

The well-greased circular motions of your fragrant honey pots.

"You know, Sally, it's *incredible* how attentive those guys are. Nobody *ever* listens on the stateside runs."

"Would you like a magazine, sir?"

Hey, it's Giant Jugs! No magazine—just pop your big boobies out and lean over here so I can put my face right between 'em and play motorboat. *Brmmm—brmmm—brmmm!* No, wait! These jugs are big enough to play speedboat! *Browmmmmmmm!* Maybe even for—can it be possible? *Mississippi Paddle-Wheeler Steamboat! Bra-loom, Bra-loom, Bra-loom, Bra-loom!* No, sorry, not quite. But the speedboating was nice. *Browmmmmmmm!* "No, thank you, miss." Thanks anyway, though.

"Would you like something to drink, sir?"

It's Hair-Pie! No, what I'd like is for you to quickly drop your knickers and sit on my lap for a fast furious fuck. "What do you have, please, miss?"

"Well, we could give you coffee, tea, juice, or milk."

Milk? How 'bout I just suck on your titty to see what comes out—Eggnog? Ovaltine? Carnation Instant Breakfast? "Is that fresh milk, miss?"

"Yes, it is. We took it on in Tokyo."

No, on second thought you can just slide your skivvies off and sit on my face for the rest of the trip. "I believe

I'd like a glass of fresh milk, please, miss. I guess I haven't had any since I was home in San Francisco."

They finally got through the R 'n' R Center briefing, which amounted to a lecture on: "Do something on R 'n' R that you can write home about."

Wilson wanted to go with Chief, but a brother had persuaded him to go to a Soul Bar, so they agreed to meet in the morning.

"You understand, Chief?"

"Hell, yeah, man, I'm an Injun remember—no sweat—split, man—like fly. I'll see you in the morning."

Wilson sighed in relief.

In front of the R 'n' R Center where the buses let them off, small Toyopet cabs were buzzing into position, revving their motors.

They were called Kamikaze cabs because all the drivers were said to be Kamikaze pilots who didn't make their big trip during the war. "Hey, Kamikaze cab," Chief yelled. A tiny Toyopet roared up and screeched to a halt in front of him.

The driver was a squat young man with 1958-style Elvis Presley hair and sideburns. He wore large black sunglasses, and a cigarette hung from his lips, Bogart-fashion. He smiled wickedly and hunched over the wheel. The cab shot forward and dived into the traffic and suddenly cut in front of a large truck. The truck driver yelled something out the window. The driver was yelling back when he saw the light. The cab slammed to a stop halfway across the intersection. The light changed and the cab peeled away, dragging another taxi. The Bogart-cigarette burning slackly at his lips, the driver swerved to miss a bent old lady crossing the street. He grinned and swung to the other side of the two-way street to pass a line of traffic.

"Give 'em hell," Chief shouted.

The driver turned back to him. "Damn right, man. Fuck 'em all. Let it all hang out."

Hey, this guy speaks English better'n me; Chief grinned.

"What your name, Joe? Mine Ringo."

"Just call me Chief."

Four Hondas thundered by, racing. They weaved in and out of traffic, passing everything, their young riders lying flat on the seats, their long black hair wind-plastered to their heads.

Chief smiled, leaned back in the clear-plastic-covered seat and took a deep breath. The past six months slid away from him. He began combing his hair down his forehead and over his ears.

"At last," he murmured aloud as he took out the red band and tied it around his forehead. He slid over and looked in the rear-view mirror. He twirled his head, making the hair fly in all directions. Finally he took out a plastic flower and stuck it in the band. "All right, Ringo Baby. How 'bout that?" The crazy grin spread full across the face and he laughed at his reflection.

Ringo was half turned around, staring, and suddenly jerked back, spinning the wheel to avoid a bus. "You GI?" he asked doubtfully over his shoulder.

"Nope. I'm Injun," Chief sang back. He looked once again in the mirror and frowned remorsefully. Still too short in back, but I'd never get away with any more.

Ringo shrugged and shook his head. *Americans*.

"Now listen, Ringo. First, I gotta get a good hotel. The best. You know, near where the action is."

"I know."

"Then I gotta buy some clothes."

"I know. I numbah one guide, Joe." Ringo was studying the Chief in the rear-view mirror.

"Hey, Joe, you smoke?"

Since he was sitting with a Marlboro in his mouth, Chief cocked his head inquisitively. "Smoke?"

"Sure, Joe—*you* know—grass, pot, weed, mah-ree-wah-nah."

"Well, Ringo, I just might be interested. Like turn me on to it right now, man," he said chuckling, remembering the stern warnings they'd had not to bring pot on R 'n' R. Even had a shakedown search before they got on the plane.

"I take you now. Okay, Joe? No sweat. Very cheap. Good stuff."

"Well, okay, but just a look." Look, hell! I'll just focus my burning eyeball rays to light it, and then with super-powerful lung action snuffle all that smoke up from a distance of fifty feet. But I gotta be *cool*. Could be a trap. This guy might take me to some spot, call his buddies, try

to roll me. Nobody gettin' my ging, not my R 'n' R ging.
Just keep cool, watch and be ready to duke it out.

The cab wormed its way into Tokyo. The city was steaming in the late afternoon sun. Traffic jams, construction
projects, the rat-tat-tat of jackhammers. The taxi plunged
down a street clogged with people. Its horn stiff-armed a
path. It twisted into a tight dark alley and stopped.
Peeled, postered walls held the cab in their grip. Ringo
squeezed out.

"Five minute, Joe. You wait here, okay?"

"Yeah, sure." O Jesus, now what am I into? I'm just a
Goddamn *prisoner* here. Where can I go? Well, it'll take a
hell of a lot of those little fuckers to get my scratch. I'll
bash their fucking gourds. I don't care how many. . . .

"Hey, man."

Chief jumped as an old man stuck his head in the window. No, maybe he wasn't old, but he *looked* old. Time-
less, like Chinese always look. The skin hung loose on his
bony face like a gunnysack half-full of shelled corn. He
cracked open the rear door and slid in. Ringo squeezed
back in front and turned in his seat to watch.

Chief started sweating and moved closer to the other
door, but the old man smiled and pulled out a package of
Winstons.

"Winstons? I don't want Winstons." He turned to
Ringo, "What is this? I thought you said . . ."

"Ah, so, Joe, look, look"—Ringo pointed to the package. The old man ripped open the pack and took out one
cigarette; smiling from ear to ear, he held it for Chief to
see. The open end had been twisted closed into a little tit.
However, from the outside of the package, it looked exactly like a regular pack of Winstons, right down to the
cellophane wrapper. Even when the top had been removed
in the normal fashion, only the butt end of the filter tips
could be seen. Chief's eyebrow arched. In Vietnam, marijuana cigarettes were sold individually or just loose in a
plastic bag.

He took the "Winston" and sniffed it. Instantly Ringo's
hand shot out with a flaming lighter. Chief felt one moment of caution, then sucked in gingerly. The cab filled
with the sweet pungency of good marijuana, and a slow
grin spread over Chief's face.

"There it is! Okay, Ringo, tell him it's a deal." He

reached for his wallet and stopped, kicking himself mentally for being so careless. "One minute."

Chief took the pack and carefully emptied it until he
had counted twenty cigarettes and saw that they all had
rolled tit-ends. He sniffed each one.

While the Chief's eyes were down, Ringo and the old
man exchanged a glance of new respect, but when Chief
looked up, their faces showed only mild contempt and in-
sult. Chief saw their looks and his face slipped back into
the Indian mask.

"Very good," he said and again reached for his wallet.
The two faces smiled broadly.

The cab rolled on and Chief drew deeply, inhaled and
held his breath, letting the smoke go to work. He held it
as long as he could, then dribbled it out in little puffs. He
finished the Winston without bothering to roach it and
leaned back against the seat, his head resting loosely on
the cushion. Nothing yet. Well, I do feel happy, he
thought. But I've been happy ever since I got on the
plane. He lit another. Ringo eyed him closely in the rear-
view mirror.

"Go a little faster, can you, Ringo?"

"Sure, Joe, I know."

Chief sat in the middle of the seat and stretched his
arms out on top of the backrest. He turned his head till
he could see out the rear window.

Ahhh, this is it. R 'n' R. I *am* happy. Everybody is
happy. His mind felt light and gay. Yes, he was light. His
wings were out. Let's fly.

The taxi rolled down the runway. Forward on that
throttle, back on that stick—lift off! Yeah! Raise those
wheels. Good. Smooth. Great day for flying. Back on that
stick. Now banking. Banking left. Smoothing out. Yes.
Now sharp bank right. Leaning. Coming in. Coming in
too fast! Reverse engines! End of runway! Stopped. We
made it. Great flying, Ringo, landing just a little ragged
though.

"Hotel, Joe."

"My name?" "Yes, name." "Register?" "Sign line one,
please." "Sign name?" Christ, this is ridiculous—Joe, isn't
it? No, Chief—no, *SS Eagle*. Silly of me, just a little confused by the extremely bright lights in here. "Address not
necessary. That's good. Pay now? Five days? Fine."

Clothes—must buy clothes. Over there. Shop? Yes, I see it. Beautiful lobby you have; you're welcome yes, yes, first trip to Tokyo. Oh, yes, I *love* it here. Colors, fine colors, in here yellow red orange blue luscious. I could just eat 'em all up. Yes, trousers, please, and a couple of shirts. Oh, yes, these are beautiful, I'll take them, no don't wrap, yes, your English is very good, I understand it perfectly, can you understand mine? It seems a little different than usual. *Christ, gotta be cool, I must be talking crazy and they'll know. Must be against the law here, too.* Oh, yes, and I'll take some of those and those and those and those—several pair. I didn't bring anything with me and I must change sometime, right? Ha Ha Ha. Change? Oh yes, money. I forgot. *O God that was a stupid thing to say, Jesus man, get hold of yourself. I am acting weird, I know I am, and everybody can tell. Smooth be smooth. Mmmm,* room not bad with kinda glowing pink walls. Now get outta these duds, throw 'em off all off, throw 'em in a drawer—outta sight—throw 'em away, throw the Corps and everything away. Now completely naked and born again. *Shower-Power!* O say can you see by the lemon-yellow light an unbelievable all to myself hot-and-cold-tiled-floor-silver-nozzled shower. Yow! Zinging, zapping, penetrating my bod with needles needles needles! Lather up with slick-warm-thick-great-for-rub-bod-soap so sweet smelling and clean, but clean, man, I'm in Clean City! And now, for a hold on Root City!

Walk carefully now. Paid cab? Yes. Pick way, sidewalks crowded. Keep your balance. Don't bump anyone. Football game! I'm running with the ball. Blockers ahead, sweeping forward, twisting, swivel-hipping, bouncing off a would-be tackler. Stay behind the interference. O God, no! A whole bunch of the other team coming this way, sweeping for us. The whole line coming for me, the backs, too. The whole bench, even the refs. *Block 'em! Rock 'em! Sock 'em!* Going all the way ninety-nine yards for a score! Yes, friends, it was a great game, and again, led by the brilliant running of Cannonball Joe, South San Francisco High has just defeated the Trojans of Southern Cal, the fans are going wild!

Christ I must be grinning like an idiot—"STOP"—*compose those features, man*. And here we have a bright flashing pure, burning green and white neon—Mano's Disco.

That is the *in* club, yeah. We'll just go right into orbit there.

Music! Follow that music! Faster! Faster! O great sounds! *Bam-bam, boop-boop, bob-bop.* My feet starting to dance. Now my bod's dancing, too! Now my head's dancing! *Bam-bam, boop-boop, bop-bop, stop feet . . . Stop bod . . . Stop head. . . .*

Christ! that's better. I gotta be cool. Outta control there for a minute. Lucky no one saw me. Now just push open the door and . . . O my Jesus, Mother of the Great Wind and Stars, it is Heaven! Angels everywhere! Hundreds of them! So beautiful. And lights, thousands of floating, drifting, soft lights, flowing over everything. Ahhhhhh. Flashing lights! *Bam-bam, boop-boop. No. Can't* let that get started again.

Coming toward me! Closer. Is it? It is! An angel! *Dum-da-dum-dum.* Dragnet theme swelling to a crashing crescendo! Sailing toward me with the lights drifting and playing all over her, pink dress, long black hair, Waikiki-brown skin, cuddly-cute angel face, fire-engine red lips, and general alarm tongue. Waves of perfume preceding her, coming toward me rising up like a Waimea Bay thirty-footer, towering over me, rising, I'm on that wave. Here I go soaring . . . flying . . . falling. My twelve-foot, four-stringer Hobie Big Gun with shark's-fin skag bites into the wave. Hang ten, we're over the top, sliding down, Waimea roaring like a thousand freight trains! Spray in my face, sweeping forward. The Malibu Kid! Plummeting down! Too sharp! Curl braking! Off-balance! Falling! Wipe-out! Washing to shore.

"Like to sit down, Joe?"

She knows me. No, I'm not Joe. Am I?

"Like to sit down, Joe?"

I am a little dizzy. "With you?"

"If you want me."

Ohhhh, I think I'm gonna pass out! "Lead the way."

"Follow me, Joe."

Looks like a sock stretched tightly o-so tightly over her bod, a pink knit sock—a minisock. A sock dress. Don't women have dresses they call socks? Or is it smocks? No matter, it's what's under it that counts. Under? O great squaw of the mountain. Can it be? Is it possible? Surely not! But is it? *It is!* There is absolutely nothing in any way, shape, or form under that sock except Waikiki-brown smooth-as-a-baby's-ass skin!

"Empty booth over here, Joe."

Here I go again—soaring . . . flying . . . falling. Pink snow. Soft snow. Soft-pink-powder snow. Buckling on my fiberglass Head skis over my Lange boots, adjusting my cool-ray Polaroid goggles, digging poles in, thrusting jaw forward. Balancing on her shoulder, pushing off down her front slope over the soft-pink-powder. O no! Misjudged the slope! Too steep! Straight down! Shooshing out of control! Dip ahead! Rise. Jump. Off the ground! Flying! Falling! Poof! Thank God—soft landing. Pink powder snow is very soft. Whassis? I seem to be stuck. Some kind of crevasse, everything pink, everything warm. Amazing the snow doesn't melt. Squeezing me. Lot of swinging and swaying with a kind of bounce-jiggle thrown in. Swing-sway, bounce-jiggle.

"Here we are, Joe—you like?"

"Oh, cozy little booth, huh? Just for us two alone. Ha Ha Ha." *O God, what a stupid thing to say, that was. I'm talking like a hick. Be smooth, man.* Be your usual smooooth cooool self. Smooooth . . . cooool.

"Smooooth, cooool."

"What you say, Joe?"

"Ah . . . oh, nothing." *Jesus Christ, get hold of yourself, you dumb ass.*

"You want drink something?"

"Sure. A tremendously tall cold beer."

"You buy me a drink, too, Joe?"

"Oh, yeah, sure."

"Thank you."

Now we're getting in there—gotta turn on old Charm City.

"You very nice, Joe."

She likes me! My God, I think I'm falling in love with her—no, that's ridiculous. No, I think I really am. "Listen, beautiful girl. Tonight we are going to drink together to celebrate a new life and my absolute, overwhelming happiness."

"Okay! Be happy together! I get drinks. Wait minute."

My girl. She is just so fine and I am so happy. So

happy, in fact, that I can hardly keep from: "Hee Hee Hee—Ha Ha Ha—Ho Ho Ho!" *Wait, gotta stop that insane laughter.* Hee Hee. Ho Ho.

Stop!

Christ, I was almost hysterical and out of control and everybody's lookin' at me. They're watchin' me, and they know and they're gonna report me, and I'll be taken away—Waaait-a-minute—I don't think they are watchin' me. In fact, they're actin' kinda crazy, most everybody in here looks outta control. I wonder if they're . . . all smoking. . . .

"Here's drinks, Joe."

Oh! *Startled me!* My girl, she's so wonderful and I'm so happy. "Beer looks cold."

"Yes, very cold beer for very hot boy."

"This is very good beer, miss-ah-oh, o-no, I forgot your name. I'm sorry."

"I don't tell you name yet, crazy man!"

O God, that was stupid. Crazy, she said. She's noticed. She knows. Gotta be cool.

"My name Sayu."

"Sayu. It's a beautiful name. So light, so soft. Sa-Yuoooo. Just like it's floating on fresh seabreezes. Sa-Yuooo Ahhhh."

"Thank you. Very nice talk. What your name?"

"My name?" *Oh no, don't let it happen again!* Joe? No. Chief? No. Randy? This is ridiculous. "Hee Hee Hee—Ha Ha Ha—Ho Ho Ho!"

"Why you laugh?"

"I know this sounds crazy, Sayu, but just for a moment I couldn't think of my name, when I know perfectly well it's . . ."

"You crazy?"

Get hold of yourself, dammit. "No, Sayu. I'm just kidding. My real name's Eagle, Screaming Sky Eagle. For a while it was Randy Eagle, but sometimes people just call me Chief. It's funny."

For one second the girl looked at him as if he'd gone stark-raving mad. "I like Joe." She shrugged. "Easy remember."

"Okay, my name Joe."

"You buy me another drink, Joe?"

"Yeah, sure." Beautiful dark eyes she has, like soft, warm pools you can dive right in. I'll just zap her with the old-Evil-Eye-Eagle Single Whammy! Heh Heh Heh Heh, I'll turn it all the way up to a Double Whammy! Staring deep, actually projecting my whole self out of me across the table plunging into those dark pools, zapping deeply down down down—oh no, here we go again—flying . . . soaring . . . falling.

"You like dance, Joe?"

Dance? Yeah man, dance. Listen, Sayu baby, get Chief stoned like Joe's stoned now and turn him loose on those wild sounds and set out there with him one wild, hair-flying, bod'-shakin' chick. And put them both on the floor directly in front of those big Sony amps with the Crazy Lobos Filipino Band—three guitars, organ, drums, sixty-six model Beatle duds, and a good driving shoutin' sound—and, baby, you gonna have an EXPLOSION!

'Cause Chief's gonna turn the concentrated focus of his blasted mind on those sounds; and the sounds are gonna travel pure and free and beat on his eardrum, which bangs 'em out on his anvil, then his stirrup leaps up and spurs into his auditory nerve, which shoots all this crazy commotion, whambo-zambo, right into his brain!

"Come on, Joe, dance."

And Joe, or Chief I mean, no Joe, let him be Joe. Oh, oh! He's not Joe anymore because he is dancing. He has become his great hero read-it-in-World-Lit-I-saw-the-flick-twice-and-read-the-book-again Zorba! He's gone dancing madly, his arms flowing, his torso jerking, his whole bod' leaping up and down, and his head bouncing like Sugar Ray in his prime using it as a speed-bag. Outta sight!

Sayu! Under that pink sockdress her beautiful free breasts are doing wild dance of their own, bouncing, leaping, whirling like twin props on a P-38 gone mad!

Now go with Concentration-Free-Communication-Dance —arms and bod' flowing with the waves of sound, and head bouncing with the beat, legs and feet leaping into a fantastic communion with the music. And now, the greatest test of all—incorporating and harmonizing and unifying all. Yes, all of the people on the dance floor, thereby dancing with everyone and everything in this whole universe and rolling all our strength and all our sweetness up into one dancing ball.

Soaring . . . flying . . . falling. . . . Dance, everybody
dance. *Bam-bam, boop-boop, bop-bop* Dance feet . . .
Dance bod' . . . Dance head. *Dance. Sock it to me,
Sayeeooo!*

Chief woke slowly and blinked at the bed. He was
alone. He had no idea where he was or how he had got
there. Gradually he focused and studied the room. The
huge wooden wall-to-wall bed dominated the room. Its
headboard was a maze of shelves and drawers. On the
shelves rested a Hitachi clock-radio, a small electric fan, a
Toshiba transistorized TV set, a ticking alarm clock, a roll
of toilet paper, and a large framed photo of Sayu and the
other bar girls. They wore kimonos, serious faces in rigid,
stylized poses. They were standing in front of a painted
backdrop of a bright-red Buddhist temple. Blooming
pink-cardboard cherry trees arched over their heads.

In the drawers he found a pile of individually wrapped
prophylactics, a box of Tampax—regulars—several Japanese film and romance magazines, a book of *Peanuts*
comic strips in Japanese, the book *Speak English in Three
Days,* and a stack of letters postmarked Rapid City, South
Dakota.

Sayu came in, made a face, and began stripping off her
stockings.

"Why you fight, crazy Chief?"

"Huh?" He blinked.

"Talk, drink, dance, boom-boom. Numbah one. Fight
no good. Numbah ten." She unzipped the back of her
dress, drew it up over her head, and flung it on the side of
the headboard.

"What're you talking about?" Chief began to frown,
trying to think back.

"Why you like black GI? Black GI numbah ten? You
crazy."

"Oohhh." Chief pressed his head as the remembrance
came back to him. "Black GI. Fight," he murmured. One
by one the details came into focus.

Sayu had to stay at the dance hall until midnight, so
Chief had gone next door to a small bar—The Hot Pants.
Somehow Wilson had found him, arriving with two other
Marines who had come on the same R 'n' R flight—a Chi-
cano named Ramos, and a big-boned dude from Boston

named Hickland. Chief glanced around immediately when he saw Wilson because The Hot Pants wasn't a soul bar. Chief shrugged; Wilson was like that. But he had to grin when they sat down and he saw Wilson's head.

"Where'd you get the shapeup?" Chief asked at once. The hair just above the temples of Wilson's forehead had been shaved with a razor to make the hairline recede slightly on each side. A single line, a sixteenth of an inch wide, had been cut straight from the left forehead toward the back. The hair was trimmed and combed away from the line. On the top and sides the hair had been brushed up and cut off flat.

"Downtown," was all Wilson said.

They had several quick drinks and even the waitress eyed Wilson coolly, but Wilson ignored it all. Then Chief noticed that four sailors were watching them contemptuously.

"You know them fuckin' swabbies over there are startin' to piss me off," Chief drawled casually.

"Cool it man. No sweat," Wilson said. But Chief heard the tension in his voice.

"Yeah. They kinda piss me off, too," Hickland added, seeing Chief's intent.

"Ah, to hell with 'em. *Christ,* you guys. They're fucked up, drunker 'n' shit." Ramos sighed.

"Les take a walk and see if we can find a little fun," Chief said, glancing over at Wilson.

The four exchanged a sly conspiratorial look and began to slip from the booth.

With Chief in the lead, they weaved down the narrow passage that led to the foyer and the door. Chief pushed it open. "Rain, it's raining."

They stepped back in and leaned against the wall. "Jus' wait here for a while."

Inside the bar the four sailors paid their bill and drunkenly disentangled themselves from the small booth and the girls who were coaxing them to stay.

"Nothin' happen here, honey. Place has a *bad* odor." One of the sailors drained his glass, held it at arm's length, looking at it, and let it crash to the floor.

Mama-san shouted something in Japanese and slid heavily off her stool at the bar.

The sailors reeled across the dance floor and entered

the passageway. They stiffened as they saw the four Marines leaning against the wall.

"Wha' was 'at noise we heard in there?" Chief drawled at the first sailor.

"Dropped a glass, boy," the first sailor said.

"Go back in an' pay Mama-san for it," Chief said. He pushed himself away from the wall, his hands hanging loosely at his side, blocking the exit.

"Well, ain't this a colorful bunch," the sailor mocked.

The four Marines were now arranged shoulder-to-shoulder facing the four shoulder-to-shoulder sailors.

"Tell the jungle-bunny to go in and sweep it up, and we might pay." The sailor motioned toward Wilson.

"Go-back-in-an'-pay, you swab jockey," Chief said, punctuating each word with a finger jabbed into the first sailor's Adam's apple.

"Get your fuckin' hands off me, jarhead!" the sailor said, knocking Chief's hand away from his throat.

"Take him!"

In a blur of motion Chief grabbed the sailor's tie and yanked him over to Wilson, who spun him around and kicked him hard. The sailor spiralled into the bar and crashed on a table.

Out of the corner of his eye, Chief saw a huge sailor on his left swing for him. He didn't have time to duck or move but, with cat-quick reflexes, jerked his head just a fraction. The fist tore past his ear and the big exposed body lurched after it. Chief, in a crouch and too close to punch, turned sharply into the man and snapped up his right knee. The knobby bone drove squarely into the onrushing groin and the sheer momentum of the sailor threw Chief back on his butt. The sailor hung motionless for just a second, his face frozen in surprise. Then he screamed a sickening yowl and folded to the floor, puking uncontrollably.

From the floor Chief saw the others fly into one another. He scrambled to his feet, but when he was halfway up and off-balance, someone slammed into his ribs. He reeled back and crashed into a sliding partition. The thin Japanese paneling gave way in a splinter of wood straps and tearing of paper. Chief fell through into a dark hallway as he heard the police whistle.

Again he leaped to his feet, this time looking frantically

for an exit or a place to hide. A figure came running down the hall out of the darkness, and Chief instinctively grabbed a piece of the wood paneling for a weapon.

"Chief-san, Chief! No, no, no." It was Sayu. "Police come. No fight crazy man. Police take you Monkey House."

Chief's eyes darted up and down the hall, alert, not knowing yet whether the girl was helping or if he should run.

"Chief," she shrieked. "Come with me. Hide, my house."

He heard the stomp of the MP boots charging in the front door just beyond the partition he had crashed through. "Les go!" He grabbed her hand and they ran off down the dark hall.

"Thanks, Sayu," he said, sitting in the bed watching her undress.

"You crazy—smoke, drink, fight, pass out."

"You're right—crazy." He reached for her.

"No." She pulled away. "Take bath first." She sniffed her arm and crinkled her nose. "Skin stink." She turned around, reached behind her back, unhooked her bra, and threw it in a bamboo basket. "Clothes stink." She peeled her panties down to her ankles, stepped out of them, hooked a toe in the elastic band, balanced on one foot, and kicked the panties across the room into the basket. "Home run!"

Chief reached for a cigarette and wondered why she had saved him.

He couldn't remember what happened to Wilson, except that later he turned up with a chick called Suzie-san. Sayu had seen her but said nothing at the time.

"How 'bout we take a bath with Suzy and Wilson."

Chief thought he saw just a flicker of the haughty look Charlene's mother used to have. Then her face fell serious and impassive, as if she too had put on a mask.

"No can do," she said flatly.

He looked at her curiously, "Why, Sayu?"

She said nothing for a minute. "Okay, Chief, I like you. I tell you. You no be angry?"

"No," he said, putting on the Indian stone face.

"Your friend black; I not go with black GI."

"I see." He nodded, showing no emotion through the Indian mask.

"Black GI very dirty—stink."

Chief thought a minute and then said evenly, "Well, the idea was to go take a bath. Then we'd all be clean."

She looked disdainful and sniffed.

"The other girl, what's her name, Suzie-san, didn't seem to mind. I thought Orientals liked black men."

"*Japanese* not same as Orientals!" Her eyes blazed.

"Okay, okay, I'm sorry." He smiled quickly. "But what about Suzie-san?"

Sayu tossed her head. "She no good. Besides Suzie-san go with black man for money."

For *money?* Chief thought. "I don't understand," he said softly.

"Japanese girls go with black GI because they will buy many things. Girl can get black man to buy presents for her. They will buy clothes, jewelry . . . anything."

"But. . . ."

"Black man will pay more and buy more presents than white, especially if girl go with him every day—no butterfly. But good girl no like black man. You watch, same girl go with black man all time."

"I see, I see." Chief stroked his hairless chin. From the closet she drew two crisp, clean, cotton kimonos, wrapped one around herself, and threw the other to him.

"C'mon, crazy man." She smiled. "Take bath, forget fight, forget black man!"

They padded down the hall outside her room and turned in at a door with a kanji character burned into the brown wood.

Inside was a sunken bath, its wooden sides already brimming with steaming hot water. "*O'furo,*" she said, "Japanese hot bath." The whole floor was tile and sloped slightly toward a drain in the middle. A single copper faucet stuck out from one wall. It was a cold tap and was covered with condensation from the hot room. Under it several plastic pans and basins lay empty and waiting. Sayu turned to a small cracked mirror stuck to the wall and lifted off her wig. Then she stripped off her long false eyelashes and scrubbed the heavy makeup off her face. She untied the sash around her waist, took off her kimono, and hung it on the wall beside her wig. She turned to face him.

Sayu, the sultry siren of the Disco, sexy and steaming in low-cut dress and engineered bra, had disappeared. In her place stood Sayu from Hokkaido, a pale, rather plain, slender girl just out of her teens.

"You look very pretty, Sayu," he said in a soft voice. "Very pretty."

She filled one pan with cold water and scooped hot water from the *o'furo* with another. Chief eyed the steam rising from it and gingerly stuck a toe in. He jerked it out. "Damn, Sayu! I'll never get in there. Impossible!"

"Oh, yes, easy. Feel very good. First wash, wash all over then rinse, then soak in *o'furo*."

"It's too hot. Look at my toe, it's red."

"No, no. Ease in very slowly."

Chief looked dubious.

She moved toward him and began untying his kimono sash. "Take this off," she said in Japanese, "we're going to become clean."

Chief jumped back and looked around a little embarrassed. A dark room was one thing but. . . . "Sayu, somebody could walk right in here."

She laughed and grabbed the kimono.

"Hey, give me that." Chief's hand shot toward her, but she danced away. He saw Sayu standing, hands on hips, absolutely nude, her eyes laughing at his embarrassment. "What the hell—when in Rome—" he half-murmured. The dark eyes narrowed with anticipation.

"Bath now, Chief-san," she said, pushing him gently toward a stool.

"Okay baby, wash." He sat, closed his eyes, and relaxed in anticipation.

She mixed the pans until the water was warm, then poured it over him. The water ran out the drain in the floor. She lathered a sponge with tinted-green soap and started rubbing it around his neck and face. She moved on down, finding and scrubbing every inch. Lifting his arms, she worked the sponge into his armpits and down the ribcage and around and around on his stomach.

Chief's mouth spread in a thin crooked line. The corners turned up in a contented smile. His eyes would have closed, but they were driving into every inch of the pelvis moving directly in front of his face.

She tugged him to his feet and bent quickly to swish the soap over his thighs and then carefully up into the dark tangle of hair. As he stood, she squatted in front of him and worked the sponge around and around until his loins were hidden in a mass of soapsuds. She dropped the sponge, and her fingers encircled his genitals and rotated gently outward with a slight pull. She carefully took each testicle in her fingertips and lightly rolled them in her cupped hand. Then she reached through his legs, her hand turned upward and her fingernails scratching along the bottom V of his cheeks, between the dark skin where his legs met and forward to the bottom of the baggy wrinkled skin where the little weights swung down. Again and again her hands plunged in and raked back as if she were beckoning someone toward her. Chief moaned with pleasure and leaned forward from the waist, resting his arms on her two shoulders, his legs automatically spread wider from the knees.

Secretly delighting in his pleasure, Sayu slipped to her knees and leaned her body into him. She pressed her cheek against his soggy stomach. Slipping one hand firmly between his legs and curling the other one around his hips, she ran her forefinger straight down his spine into the tight crevice. Chief's easy sighs gave away to harsh breathing. Her thumb came up and replaced the finger, drew circles on the bottom of his cheeks, and slowly penetrated until it ground against the tight sphincter muscle. Chief rose up on his toes in exhilaration, and his whole body began to rock rhythmically.

He reached to move her head but she darted away, giggling softly. Gently she pushed him back to the stool. He sank down weakly and leaned against the wall for support, his eyes half closed.

The slippery wet sensation of her sudsy fingers lulled him into a steamy sexual stupor.

"Yiiaaaiii!" Cold water had suddenly sloshed over him from head to foot. Chief flew off the stool and lurched forward, his fist coming up by reflex. The cold water splashed to the floor; his breath sucked in with a gasp. He glared at Sayu, his fist opened, and sagged.

"Why, you, you . . ." His dark eyes spewed white-hot

sparks, but Sayu's head rolled back and she laughed. Chief glowered, lunged for her, and she threw the pan at him. He ducked but slipped on the sudsy floor, sprawled and fell at her feet, legs and arms outstretched.

"Oh Chief-san, you so funny." Her naked little body shook with giggles and laughter as Chief glowered. Soapsuds showered down upon him. Instantly the rage melted and a lecherous grin replaced the scowl.

You little vixen bitch, he thought. This was just what he liked. Two copper arms shot up and steel hands clasped on her thighs. He jerked her into the air and down on top of him. Rolling over on top of her, he crushed her mouth with his. Her hands started to beat on his back and then relaxed and flowed to his neck.

After the pounding, he felt her fingernails dig into him and her mouth push up against his. When he sensed her distraction, his free hand groped for the cold water tap nearby. As he felt her relax, he turned the tap to full, sprang up and shoved her hard. She sailed under the stream head first. Her fanny slid on the soapy tiles, but Chief held her ankles, guiding her under the water jet as it ran the length of her body. She gasped, then sputtered as the water hit her face and moved on down her body. Like a shot, her upper body came up off the floor head first, but Chief held her ankles firmly. The water blasted right down onto her stomach and hips. Her eyes went wide as saucers, and she started to struggle, but she couldn't get any traction on the slippery surface. Then with a final shove, Chief slid her across the floor like a hockey puck. She grabbed for something to stop herself, but there was nothing she could do. She kept on sliding and flopped right into the steaming *o'furo. Splosh!*

"Yeoww!" Her scream rent the whole building as she exploded back out of the water. Steam rose from her lobster-red skin as she hopped about. Chief doubled over in hysterics.

"Goddamn you, Chief, you motherfuckin' son of a bitch, you dirty cocksucking bastard." Her Oriental composure was gone and she quivered with rage. Chief's laughter slowed and turned to amazement as the American curses rolled out of her mouth in perfect Marine slang.

Then slowly and finally, in a compulsive burst, Chief grinned.

"Come on, Joe, let's go *o'furo*. Slowly this time. Slowly."

He eased down onto the waist-high massage table, his body still bright-pink from the hot water. Warily he sensed her scurrying around, and then he felt her hands flutter over him coolly. His nostrils tingled as a mint-rose scent wafted over him.

Her hands began a staccato chop on his neck, shoulders, and back, and then turned to a sharp *plop, plop, plop* as she interlocked her thumbs and used both hands as one. Chief began to relax. Her fingers probed into his neck and shoulders, massaging the ropy tough muscles. Slowly he melted into the table.

She worked gently at first, but then the probing fingers began to dig harder. She seemed to pull individual muscles right out of his back, then kneaded them individually back and forth before driving each one back in, crushing the bone on the way down.

The pleasure was very near to pain, but the total effect left him breathless with delight. "Take it easy, baby." But she steamrolled on down the small of his back, cracking all the vertebrae as she went. Then her strong fingers worked their way down the coppery arm, rolling the muscles back and forth like pieces of clay putty.

My God, he thought, I've never felt anything as good as this.

The probing fingers spread the knuckles of his hands and gouged into his palm. Then she drew each finger back, stretching the tendon and sliding her hands over the skin. Chief drooled in exasperation and delight.

His body reeled and floated on a cloud. The only sensation was that of her moving, probing hands. The hands slid down and began to work each toe as they had done the fingers, then up the heels and into the calves. She kneaded the sinewy tendons and worked along the backs of his thighs.

She thought how some men spread out like blubber and their fat muted the pleasure of her fingers, but Chief's dusky copper skin stretched silkily over the muscles, not an ounce of fat.

She attacked his lean, hard cheeks and felt the muscles flinch to her touch. Suddenly, without warning, she hopped to the table and carefully placed a dainty foot on the narrow waist.

"Oohhh, Christ a'mighty, you'll break me in two." But she trotted on, ignoring his protests, walking up and down his back. Finally, she stopped, and Chief felt his body go limp in relaxation. It had hurt, but now it felt as if his whole being was a loose string. "Ahhhhhh."

He rolled over at her prodding and lay on his back, glancing down at himself. It lay shriveled and limp like a fat wet noodle. He quickly raised his eyes to hers and began to wonder just what she was going to do. He wondered how he had lain naked under the fingers of this naked girl and not been conscious of sex. She read his glance and smiled mischievously.

"I like you, Chief-san." She leaned forward and pinched the aquiline nose. "Cut off nose and you be same as Japanese." She glanced down at the wet noddle and whispered in his ear. "You like Sayu, Chief-san?"

"Yeah, baby, I love you," he breathed, his free hand slipping from the table and groping for her thigh.

"Me love you, too, Chief, give you one *toxon* good time."

I wonder what this is going to cost me, he thought.

She lowered her mouth to his chest, and as her teeth scraped along his breast, he no longer cared.

Her lips and cheek brushed him and then her pink tongue darted over his nipple. Again and again it zipped, licking broadly this time. His breath began to come in little jerks. Her head moved around in small circles as the mouth was parted in a tiny *o*. The breath came hotly on his wet nipple, as the mouth closed on him. His nipple hardened in a minute erection and her teeth nipped the edge and then the tip. Jerking her head up and looking down, she laughed throatily. "Other one, too, Chief-san?"

"Yeah," he murmured weakly.

Slowly the mouth worked its way down the trunk and stomach. Her tongue darted teasingly into his flat navel, and the lips whispered. The mouth kissed its way around the stomach, back and forth from hip to hip.

I don't believe this, Chief thought. Is she really going to do it? His breath was ripping in and out now, wildly. Her mouth went over to the flat of his hip, her long hair falling across his middle, sending quivers of sensation through his already worked-up body. He shivered; his buttocks' muscles bunched and his pelvis surged upward.

The hot mouth swooped down to his knees and started up, kissing little circles on the insides of his thighs. Chief's whole groin twitched rhythmically as her head groped between his legs. Her lips pulled and bit at his skin, going upward.

"Go, on, Sayu, go on." He panted heavily.

His legs spread automatically, instinctively. He couldn't have stopped them. His whole body seemed to flow into his groin as it arched upward toward that searing mouth, and his upper body slipped to the edge of the table and he pulled her over tight next to his head and shoulder. Her mouth kept on searching. He felt the hot breath flow down on him.

"Yes, yes, go on, do it. Oh, yes, yes, yes. Do it! Go on, put your mouth on it." His heat flowed to her and her legs scampered up onto the table beside his head. He could feel her muscles quivering as she lay stretched out beside him.

"Go on, go on," she said in Japanese.

Profession gave way to passion and her head rammed between his legs. Her tongue licked him and her hands dug under him, shoving him tighter against her face and throat. Crazy with lust, he lifted her hips and pulled one leg across and over his head. He pulled her squarely down on top of him, one thigh on either side of his face. Then he buried his face upward.

My God, she's wet. This little whore is actually hot for me. Holy Christ.

They both went wild, bucking and arching and twisting frantically. Feeling his tongue, she clamped her mouth over him tightly. Then his head rolled back and he grimaced as if in pain. His mind and body were beyond anything but reacting to the sucking torrent on top of him.

She pressed her fingers into the little spot below the scrotum which augmented his size, the other hand cupped and rolled the heavy weights directly under her mouth. With a rush he erupted, his every fluid pounding upward into that sucking mouth. Her teeth never touched him but her tongue pressed down, circling tightly, licking and searching.

He squeezed her thighs to his chest as if to push his very self out of his erupting volcano.

Hot and thick, his blood, bones, and muscles flowed into the sucking cavern. Her mouth lingered, seeking the last drop, and then abruptly she spun and put her face next to his. A little surprised, he held her loosely as he felt her throat press against his ear; suddenly he heard the gulping swallow. His mind staggered.

Wilson

The door burst open and Chief hurdled into Wilson's room screaming.

"*Hooo-oop.*"

Wilson jumped straight up about two feet, snatching the cover up to his chin. "Hey! What's the . . ." Recognizing the Chief, he sank slowly back, nervously eyeing the hall through the open door even though it was the last day of their R 'n' R. The girl took a quick glance and burrowed back under covers.

"How 'bout it, Wil. Good stuff?" Chief sprawled into a chair, grabbing a bottle of whiskey and kicking the door shut. He wore shorts, his neck scarf, and the gold bracelet.

Wilson's grin flashed and he looked over at the mound of covers beside him. Only long black hair could be seen flowing out from the sheet. "There it is."

Chief laughed lazily and lit a cigarette. *There it is* could refer to almost anything, but it usually meant good. "How 'bout another hotsie bath?"

"No thanks. With you along one's enough." Wilson grinned wanly, remembering the way the two of them had taken four girls into the bath and Chief had dumped a box of laundry soap into the hot water recirculator.

"Hey man, I forgot to ask. How'd you ever get away from the MP's the other night?"

"Simple." Wilson grinned. "The head of the MP detail was a soul brother; he put all the squids in the clink."

Wilson sat up and stretched. The smooth brown skin rippled against the white sheets that had slid down to his hips. "Pour me one, too, Injun." Wilson motioned to the table. "Need to get rid of this head."

"Scotch whiskey, eh?" Chief said, going to the table. "Pretty fancy shit for a jungle-bunny grunt."

"Why, you fucking red heathen savage"—Wilson had a split second of surprise—"least I don't smoke peyote."

"Yeah, but you'd smoke anything else," Chief said, handing him the glass. "*Corporal* Wilson."

"Thanks, *Sergeant* Eagle." Wilson grunted and took a swig. Lieutenant Hawkins had put Chief and Wilson up for promotion after the big fight.

"I'll wait till I see the chevrons before I count the dough."

"Hey, man, you get the gun for the Lieutenant yet?" Wilson asked abruptly, realizing this was their last day.

"You better believe it. I went yesterday." Chief chuckled, his eyes twinkling mischievously.

"Yeah? No shit? Where is it? What's it like?" Wilson said excitedly.

"In my room, and it's beautiful. Just like he asked for. A twelve-gauge Browning automatic shotgun, lightweight model."

"Wow, I gotta see that! Where'd you get it?"

"At the big Navy PX outside Tokyo in Yokohama; I took the monorail just like he said. I even got some money left over."

"Think you can get it back into d'Nam all right?"

"Oh hell, yeah. Be no problem getting anything *into* Vietnam. They never check going in. Everything you'd want to keep outta somewhere else is already *in* Vietnam. Dope, diseases, bugs, you name it. Getting *out* is the problem."

"You're right, man." Wilson laughed. "That's some weapon. Think the Lieutenant will cut it down?"

"Think?" Chief arched an eyebrow. "Is the Pope Catholic? Is pussy good? Is the Top a two-faced bastard? . . ."

"Okay okay." Wilson laughed. "Man, I don't know, seems like Lieutenant Hawkins sure has changed. 'Member how green and stubborn he was when he first came?"

"He ain't changed," Chief said and cockily flipped his cigarette out the window. "He just didn't have the benefit of all my good training before."

"Aw your ass. Next thing you know he'll be a crazy, blood-thirsty Injun like you."

"Oh now, Robert Wilson, how can you talk such trash? You know I'm fighting for a just and lasting peace so that the freedom-loving peoples of South Vietnam can have an elected democracy and live without fear of Communist aggression." Chief spoke with utmost piety. "Or that's what it says in the *Stars and Stripes*." Chief held his palms up in a gesture of wide-eyed innocence.

Wilson grunted and snatched the bottle from Chief, then took a long straight swig as if to clear his ears. *"Waugh!* Should be beer at this time of morning, but it's okay, better'n that Colt Forty-five shit we get in d'Nam."

"It's afternoon, dipshit, and time to get going. Can't miss any good R 'n' R time. Hey"—Chief stopped, his glass midway to his mouth—"did you find out yet?"

"Find out what?"

"If it's really sideways. What else?"

"Awww . . ." Wilson looked away, his face flushing. "No, too dark."

"Well, let's find out now man, 'fore we go." Chief's face was a huge leer. He leaped up and headed for the girl under the covers.

"Hey! Not now!" Wilson sat up quickly and reached to hold the blanket down. But Chief flipped up the cover and yanked a bare ankle.

"Hey, girl-san! Wake up!"

The form under the cover yelped but wrapped the cover tighter and tried to burrow down. Chief shook the leg as if it were a dustrag. The quilt flew aside as the bare leg came out kicking. The girl reared up, grabbing at the quilt with one hand while the other hand arced through the air for the Chief's face. He ducked just as the long, catlike fingernails swung past, missing him by an inch.

"Get that crazy GI out of here," she yelled at Wilson while furiously kicking free of Chief.

But Wilson was too astonished to say anything.

"Hey, girl-san, hey Suzie-san," Chief said while jumping out of the range of the claws, "your big friend here says you aren't enough for him. He say you get tired too quick and he want *two* girl-sans tonight."

"What?" She turned the wrath to Wilson.

"No, no, no, I didn't say that. Goddamn you, Chief."

"*Now!*" Chief shouted again. "We shall solve the an-cient mystery of the Orient."

Too late the girl saw the Chief leap onto the bed. In a flash he swooped down and grabbed both her ankles. Abruptly he jerked them up, tumbling her head and shoulders to the floor. His powerful body strained, and each muscle seemed to jump out against the glistening coppery skin. His arms spread out wide into a *V*-shape, an ankle locked in each hand. And the girl's legs, now spread wide made an equal *V*—upside down, each tapered leg sweeping down to the little tuft of straight black hairs. She struggled and pitched, but Chief held her firm.

"At last. Wilson, *look*." Chief was yelling as loud as he could, still standing ramrod straight.

Wilson's eyes were popping like two doorknobs as he stared down. The girl's screams rose in pitch. Wilson stared as if in a trance and Chief rolled his head back in a mighty chant. *"The great riddle is solved. Look. Look. Oh, whole wide world, look. Oriental pussy is* not *sideways!"*

Indian Song

As the eventful hour neared, Chief, Wilson, and the two buddies, Hickland and Ramos, sat drinking steadily. "Know wha' we oughta do?" Hickland said, looking at his watch. "Buy coupla bottles and sneak 'em back onna plane."

"Damn good idea. Keep ole R 'n' R goin'."

"Hide 'em in our socks. Jus' walk right up the fuckin' ramp."

"C'mon, you fuckin' drunks," Wilson said. "We ain't got much time. Finish the beer and les make it."

They lurched out into the streets, their arms around each other, their free hands waving like some multiwinged bird trying to take off.

"Taxi, taxi! Whoa, boy, whoa up there."

"Christ it's just a pony. Too small—I can't ride this one."

"Get in dammit. You ain't the Lone Ranger."

"Whiskey, whiskey, boy-san, we buy. You know?"

"I know," the driver said. He eyed them warily in his

mirror. They were silent again, jammed in the back seat of the small car. Their eyes looked, but it was difficult to tell what registered on their brains. They had the desperate air of criminals trying to escape.

"Bread. Who's got bread?"

"Gotta have bread, gotta buy booze, gotta drink up, gotta keep our party goin'."

"Cough up. Everybody."

They fumbled through their pockets and dumped two thousand yen, two dollars and fifty cents, and a few odd MPC into Chief's hands.

"Now you go buy all the booze you can."

The taxi stopped in front of a combined bar-bottle shop and Chief struggled out.

"An' hurry up dammit. We only got a few minutes."

Chief disappeared inside the bar.

"How come you gave him the bread?" Wilson asked. "He's so fucked up he can't even talk."

"Got a funny look on his face, too. Weird. Like he's not even here."

"Naw, he's jus' thinkin' 'at's all. An' I s'pose you dudes ain't fucked up, huh?" Hickland said.

Chief walked up to the bar. The part of his brain that dealt with things like twenty minutes until R 'n' R ended, planes leaving, court-martials, brigs, rules, and regulations switched off. "Gimme beer," he said to the waitress. He stuck the handful of money in his pocket and sat down at a small table. The beer came and he drank it down. "More."

The waitress brought another. Across the bar a group of Japanese men in Levis and T-shirts were drinking sake from tall water glasses. Chief stared at the bottle before him and slowly peeled off the wet label. He spread it carefully on the table and smoothed out the wrinkles. He studied it for a while and then took another long drink.

"Where inna hell is he?"

"We gotta hat up. Not much time."

"Plane's gonna leave."

"Missing a movement—tha's some bad shit, man."

"C'mon les get 'im."

They stormed into the bar.

"What inna hell are you doin' there, Chief?"

He didn't look up.

"Look at him drinkin' up our money."

"He's fuckin' paralyzed."

"He's inna 'nother world."

"Get those bottles'n les get our asses outta here."

Hickland, Wilson, and Ramos went over to the bar and began trying to make the waitress understand what they wanted.

Chief pushed his chair back from the table, stood up stiffly, and walked outside. He saw the waiting taxi and got in the empty back seat.

"Go," he said in a low voice.

The driver turned.

"Go," Chief repeated. His watery eyes stared blankly. "Go!"

The driver shrugged his shoulders and started off down the narrow street.

At the bar each of the three had a small bottle of whiskey in his hands. They turned to Chief's table.

"He's gone!"

"With the money!"

"Find him!"

They ran outside and saw the taxi pulling away. Through the back window they saw Chief's head roll on the seat top.

They started running down the street, yelling and waving their hands madly. "Stop, stop!"

"Come back here, you asshole!"

In the bar the waitress looked up. "Hey, they didn't pay!" she said in Japanese. She went outside and the sake drinkers followed.

The waitress saw the three drunks running down the street.

"There they go!" she shouted.

She began running after them and the T-shirted men joined in the pursuit. One of them was brandishing a large, empty "Typhoon Fifth" sake bottle.

The taxi slowed at a crowded intersection, and Wilson caught it. Hickland and Ramos ran up, panting and puffing.

"Are you crazy?" they yelled, piling in.

"We got no money, we're late, and the fuckin' plane goes in fifteen minutes, you stupid shit-for-brains!"

"R 'n 'R Center! Driver, R 'n 'R—you know?"

The driver nodded and the cab stated rolling again.

Chief stared at them blankly, smiling the strange, distant smile.

"He's crazy!"

The pursuers saw the cab pull away.

"Stop them! Stop that taxi!" the waitress cried. "Stop them!"

"Stop them!" the sake drinkers shouted. "Stop them!" passersby echoed.

Shoppers, storekeepers, whores, Mama-sans, bartenders, strollers, merchants, seamen, pimps, a couple of sailors, poured into the street and took up the chase.

"Stop them! Stop them!"

In his mirror the driver saw a horde of screaming people running down the street—coming after *his* cab! He tried to accelerate, but the streets were narrow, crooked, crowded—

"What the hell's all that noise back there?"

All but Chief twisted to look out the rear window. He just stared straight ahead.

"Jesus Christ, it's a mob! They're after *us!*"

"Step on it, driver! Get us outta here! R 'n' R Center, dammit get to the R 'n' R Center. Go. We'll be safe there! Go, go, go."

"Lock the doors!"

"Move it! Go!"

In a moment the cab was surrounded by a mass of people. An angry sea of faces pressed against the windows. Kicks and blows were raining on the cab in a driving beat. The driver was shouting.

"Whatta they want for Chrissakes?"

The face of the waitress appeared in the sea. She was beating on the window, pointing.

"Him, him! They want him!"

Chief was sunk down in the seat, still smiling the far away smile, oblivious of the tumult.

"Money! Money! They want money!"

"We didn't pay!"

"Give 'em the money!"

Chief didn't move.

"Take it away from him!"

Wilson frantically searched Chief's pockets, pulled out the roll of bills.

"How much?"

"Who cares? Give it all to 'em!"

The sea of faces was pressing harder against the windows. Noses and mouths were grotesquely distorted. The drumming on the sides and roof continued. The driver was holding his head in his hands.

"Stick it out the window! Stick it out the window!"

Wilson rolled his window down a crack and pushed the money out. The waitress grabbed it and waved it triumphantly in the air. The crowd cheered. Chief just smiled. The cab drove off.

"Lookit that silly-ass grin on his face. He don't even *look* human!"

"Thank God, we're outta that. Now R 'n' R driver, *Hayaku*, hurry up! Go."

"That crazy Indian don't even realize we're talkin' 'bout him. He's in another world."

Chief sank lower in the crowded seat. Low growls began rumbling deep in his throat. Suddenly he sprang up, grabbed the driver by the throat, and began biting at his neck. The driver threw his arms into the air. The cab swerved.

"Grab him!"

"Pull him off!"

"Hold him down!"

"Christ, he is crazy!"

The driver brought the taxi back under control. His hands were shaking on the wheel. He drove faster.

"He's growlin' like an *animal!*"

"The driver's scared shitless!"

"Whatsa matter with you, Chief?"

Still growling, still wearing the fiendish smile, Chief lunged again, broke away from Wilson, and bit at the driver's throat. The cab ran off the road and onto the sidewalk. Pedestrians scattered, screaming.

"Throw him down!"

"Sit on him!"

"Dammit, can't you hold him?"

The cab careened back onto the street.

"He's Dracula!"

"*Both* of you sit on him!"

Chief's growls got louder. "*Aararrrrgh.*" The driver, pale as a sheet, began tearing through the traffic like a demon.

"Take it easy, Drac, babe. We'll getcha some blood, man!" In the tiny taxi Chief was shoved against the door. He lay partially on the seat and partially on the floor, as Wilson and Hickland sat on him.

"Listen to him growl!"

"*Aarrrrgh.*"

"No sweat, driver, we got him now."

The cab driver leaned forward and put the pedal on the floor.

"You know what happened," Wilson said, "He's gone back to being an Indian."

"Indian, hell—he's reverted to an *animal.* He thinks he's back in the caves or the jungles or somethin'," Hickland said.

"He's a Neanderthal!"

"Yeah, Mr. Neanderthal, give us a growl."

"*Aarrrrgghooooo!*"

The taxi streaked through the heavy traffic, using both lanes, ignoring red lights.

"Go, driver, go! Go, go, go!" they chanted.

"Or we'll let DRAC loose on ya'. Yahoo!"

The cab rounded the corner of the last street. The R 'n' R Center loomed ahead. In front of it one hundred and sixty-one Marines were getting on buses to go to the airport. Immediately behind those buses a new batch of one hundred and sixty-five had just arrived on R 'n' R and were unloading and filing into the center.

The taxi tore down the street and skidded to a stop in the only open space—near the curb and right in front of the center. The rear door flew open. Chief fell out onto the sidewalk. Wilson, Hickland, Ramos, lurched out after him, using him as a welcome mat. The whole crowd stopped, then crowded to see. There was a lone cheer, then several hundred Marines began cheering and clapping. Some lieutenant began shouting angrily.

There is a standing order for all U.S. forces throughout Vietnam that no personnel returning from R 'n' R shall be assigned any duty within twenty-four hours after arriving back in Vietnam.

VIII

Cordon at Gio Linh

Wilson

As his rotation day approached, Wilson worked ever more diligently on his short-timers' calendar. Never was time calculated, bisected, and dissected more precisely. His mind became an intricate chronometer, ticking off the seconds until he would go back to the real world. He worked on the calendar on his helmet cover as though it were a computer blueprint. There were no weeks or months on this calendar, only descending columns of numbers in baroque boxes. The numbers had started in the hundreds and ended with one.

Elaborately Wilson marked off the sixtieth day with a magic marker. Just fifty-nine days and a wake-up, and I'll be home, he thought cheerily. For a long time he gazed at the numbers, then he began to carefully add a new space after the last box which contained the number one. He drew the new box bigger than the others and decorated it with flowers and whorls until it resembled an elaborate rococo frieze. In that last frame he printed one word—SYLVIA.

The Chief had gone straight to the bush after R 'n' R but Wilson was a "short-timer" now—less than two months to go before he rotated. He tried to get a job in the rear at Quang Tri: clerk, supply, mailroom, mess hall, driver, anything would do. Usually a man who has served his whole tour in the bush will "get some slack" at the end. But Top Goresuch said they needed men in the field. Wilson noted, however, that most of the guys who worked in the rear were white; the only brothers in the rear seemed to be sick or wounded.

Sighing wistfully, he put aside the helmet and headed for the slop chute. He walked reluctantly down the dusty road knowing Carlysle was back in Quang Tri and sure to be around the slop chute. Wilson wondered what Carlysle was doing in Quang Tri. Word was he'd started a riot in

the Ten Shaw area in Da Nang, had been in the brig, and
was now up for yet another court-martial. If only they'd
let him alone, Wilson thought, he might lose some of his
hate and fire.

"Wilson"—Carlysle's voice was low, as the tall handsome man came out of the makeshift beer hall. Wilson
looked up sharply and their eyes met in a hard stare. Solemnly they gave power.

"When did you get back?" Wilson asked flatly.

"About a week ago. Got outta the brig."

"Where?"

"Da Nang."

Then it was true. Wilson wondered if the brig time
counted on his tour. "How much time you got?"

"My time's up. I done served my time. I's supposed to
go home this week, but they got me on hold."

"Because of the brig time?"

"Yeah, man, I'll be doing bad time. Bad time, you hear.
They say that time I done in the brig don't count on my
thirteen-month tour."

"I hear you're up for another court-martial."

Carlysle's bony face began to shake. The muscles in his
neck stood out. "Wilson, I tell you. I'm gettin' fukked
over; they're trying to make me go back to d'bush. But I
won't. I done served my time in d'bush. They say bush or
court-martial. Well, I won't go."

Wilson looked away sadly. It was the same story.

At that moment an officer in pressed, clean utilities was
walking through the Delta Company area. First Lieutenant Jim Ragland had just been assigned as the executive
officer of Delta Two-Seven. Now, as he walked, he was
popping choppy, crisp salutes in return to the enlisted
men's equally salty salutes.

"Square that cover away, Marine," he barked at a man
who had his utility hat slouched down on the back of his
head. The man sullenly put it forward and saluted in
silence. Ragland popped another salute and strode on. As
he was about to turn into the company office, he saw Wilson and Carlysle half a row away.

Wilson's back was turned, but Carlysle saw the officer.
He stared indifferently and made no move to salute.

"Hey, Wilson, gotta sky up." Carlysle's eyes flicked.

"What . . ." Wilson turned at Carlysle's glance.

"Marine," Lieutenant Ragland hollered. "You, Corporal."

"Me?" Wilson pointed to himself.

"Yeah, you, come here."

Wilson looked around toward the group at the slop chute. Carlysle was gone. Wilson frowned and went toward the officer, saluting sharply. He had never seen this officer before.

"You the man who has just been promoted and came back from R 'n' R?" Ragland asked coldly.

"Yes, sir."

"A squad leader in the Second Platoon?"

"Well, I was. Yes, sir."

"You have been requesting a job in the rear."

"Ah . . . well, yes, sir."

"Come inside, I want to talk to you."

Wilson followed him. They went into a cubicle and the officer motioned Wilson to sit.

"What's your name?"

"Wilson, sir, Corporal Robert Wilson." He kept wondering who this new officer was.

"Okay, Wilson, I want to set you straight right from the start. I'm the new exec of this company, and there's going to be some tightening up."

"Of *Delta* Company, sir?!" Wilson's body started. The words were out before he could think.

"Of course, what company do you think, Marine?" Ragland was plainly annoyed.

"Oh, I—I'm sorry, sir," Wilson stammered quickly. "I was just surprised. That's very good, sir." *The executive officer.* The words whirled through Wilson's mind. That meant he was going to be above Lieutenant Hawkins. Hawkins would die.

"Well, that's all right." Ragland relaxed and smiled. This was a good Marine—polite. "As I was saying, Corporal, you have a good reputation. I've checked your record book, and your platoon commander seems to think very highly of you."

"Thank you, sir," Wilson said. Is this ding-a-ling going to take over our company, he thought. At least Calahan had his shit together in combat, but everyone wanted Hawkins to take over when Calahan left.

"Now, Wilson, I don't know how the situation was in

Da Nang or on R 'n' R, but I do know that some of the First Division units are having a lot of trouble and we don't want any of that here." He paused and looked sharply at Wilson. "If you know what I mean."

A tremor of caution went through Wilson. "Ah . . . I think so, sir." He nodded politely.

"That man you were with," Ragland leaned forward.

"Lance Corporal Carlysle, sir?" Wilson frowned slightly but kept his voice polite.

"*Private* Carlysle," Ragland spat.

"Yes, sir." Wilson knew now to keep his mouth shut.

"He's a troublemaker." Ragland looked straight at Wilson. "I want you to stay away from him."

"Sir, I was just . . ."

"Look, Marine, this is for your own good! Keep clear of that man and his kind. He's a racist and a troublemaker. You have a good record and I want you to keep your nose clean. You get in with him and you'll get in trouble."

Wilson's body froze. He opened his mouth to speak. And slowly he realized he couldn't. He wouldn't any more tell this Chuck than he could tell Carlysle.

"You *did* ask for a job in the rear, didn't you?"

"Yes, sir." Wilson forced a smile, unable to believe the words.

"Well, what I'm saying is for your own good."

Desperately Wilson started to speak again. But experience had taught him; he shut his mouth and agreed politely. "Yes, sir."

"Good." Ragland smiled genuinely. "You look pretty squared away to me. I want to see you stay that way. That's all."

"I certainly will, sir." Wilson nodded respectfully once again, came to attention and went out.

Hawkins

Almost two months passed before First Lieutenant Jim Ragland joined the company in the bush. And perhaps that was only because Delta was assigned to a big cordon operation at Gio Linh. The tiny hamlet and outpost was the northernmost U.S. position in South Vietnam. There was a tower from which one could see across the Ben Hai

River, which was the center line of the DMZ. Just on the other side of the river was a North Vietnamese camp. On a clear day the large red flag was visible; with binoculars it was possible to distinguish individual men moving about. Gio Linh was the only place in all Vietnam where you could see the enemy before he shot at you.

The purpose of the cordon was to search the hamlet and a nearby refugee camp for VC. The whole Marine battalion joined with an ARVN regiment in surrounding the area. Later the Vietnamese police would search it. Of course, there was a headquarters area for interrogation, briefing the brass, and so on. The Second Platoon of Delta was assigned to guard the headquarters, even though it was already within the cordon perimeter.

For Hawkins the duty was just a pain. Calahan made everybody shave their mustaches and get haircuts. The men rebelled and started getting Mohawk haircuts. Calahan had a fit. All for the brass.

"Lieutenant Hawkins?" It was Major Tolson.

"Yes, sir." Hawkins set down his beer and went over to the flap, blinking at the bright light that poured out around the Major's figure. Hawkins and Joseley had been nursing a beer stolen from battalion headquarters and discussing Ragland. The night was a dark sticky black, the way only Vietnamese nights can be.

"The Colonel is going to spend the night here tonight. He'll need a helmet. Run out and find him one from somewhere."

"Colonel Gaither, the regimental commander?"

"Yes, who else? Now move."

Hawkins hastened back to Joseley, oddly excited and pleased to be doing something personal for the regimental commander.

"Joseley, where can I get a helmet?"

"Mine, sir?"

"No, no. I've got to get an extra one for the fucking colonel."

Joseley looked blank. "Gee, I don't know, sir. Most everybody's only got one."

Hawkins' anxiety almost caused him to fume at Joseley's innocence. But slowly it dawned on him how difficult it might be to find one. "Well, you go around to our men and ask. I'll look around the headquarters area."

"All right, sir," Joseley said doubtfully.

Hawkins made his way over to the mounds of gear which surrounded the battalion headquarters and began to grope around. Jeeps, tents, bottles, C-rations, water cans, just about everything except a helmet. "Hell, there won't be an extra helmet around here. They'll only be back in the rear area. Maybe if somebody was medivacked . . . but nobody would get sick on this duty."

"Did you find one, Jose?"

"No, sir. Nobody's seen any."

"Damn. What am I going to do?" He began to fidget. "I *can't* go back and tell the Colonel that I haven't been able to get a helmet for him."

Joseley watched his lieutenant pace up and down, and then said gently, "Sir, if you really need one, perhaps some of the men could 'find' you one." Joseley gave a little laugh and looked away.

"Oh, no," Hawkins spoke crossly. "I can't take one from them."

"That uh . . . wasn't quite what the men had in mind, sir."

Hawkins stopped dead and looked at Joseley. He seemed to debate a minute, then chuckled. "All right, gimme my thieves up here."

Joseley hid his grin and ran off to get Sail and Davis. They came at once. Hawkins looked at the two grinning faces and kept his expression deadpan.

"Uh, did Joseley, uh . . . did Joseley tell you what I need?"

"Yes, sir" came the snappy reply.

"Fine. Now nothing but a helmet," Hawkins cautioned, trying to keep his face stern.

"Oh, you know us, sir." The voice was full of innocence.

"Yeah, that's just the trouble," Hawkins hesitated but decided he had no choice. "Okay, go to it, and thanks."

They disappeared without a sound and about fifteen minutes later Sail returned. Hawkins sprang up. "Get it?"

Sail handed him a rounded object.

"Outstanding." He felt for the strap. Even in the dark he could tell that it was a good one, a new helmet in good condition. "Thanks. Where's Davis?"

"Oh, he went back to his hooch. Don't need both of us just to bring this up here." Joseley gave a little laugh and looked away.

"Where'd you find it?" Hawkins frowned.

"Oh, it was just laying out by the road, sir. Somebody must have dropped it off the truck."

"You mean a truck that ran right by Hotel Company?"

"Yes, sir, that's what I mean," Sail said innocently. Hawkins couldn't hide his grin, but he said nothing. Then he smoothed his uniform and went to the big tent and opened the flap. The sudden light blinded him, but the Major merely gestured to him to take it into the inner room. Blinking in the bright light, Hawkins went into the side room and stood rigid at attention near the opening but no one spoke. He wasn't sure what to do. His eyes took in the three men. Two of them had silver eagles on their collar. One was Colonel Gaither, the other an Army colonel. The third man faced away. They paid no attention at all to Hawkins.

"We're just not getting any confirmed VCI out of this. We've *got* to have some results," Colonel Gaither spoke to the Army colonel.

"I know that, but this has been a VC area for years. We can't get any leads because the people just aren't talking," the Army colonel said.

"Look, Harley, both Saigon and Da Nang are watching this one. Christ, I've heard that Goodpaster may fly in here tomorrow. We *got* to produce some bodies, some facts, and some figures we can put on paper."

"You're right. We're going to have to put some more squeeze on, though I hate to do it."

Hawkins decided they must not know he was there. He tapped respectfully on the canvas wall. "Excuse me, I have brought a helmet for the Colonel."

Colonel Gaither's frosty eyes flicked up at Hawkins for a moment, then looked back to the other two men. "Set it over there on the table." He waved a finger.

Hawkins quickly put the helmet on the table and turned to go. He was halfway out the door when a deep voice whipped out and caught him. "Lieutenant!"

"Sir?" It was Colonel Gaither. Maybe they were going to ask him to stay. Ask the bush lieutenant how things really were. Hawkins saw the gray-white hair and square chin set fiercely; but the hard, frosty eyes had just the slightest twinkle. Colonel Gaither's face was an odd mixture of amusement and rebuke. Then Hawkins' eyes bugged slightly; the third man was Lieutenant Colonel Ryan, his battalion commander! All three were looking at him intently. He sensed something was wrong and a little sweat broke out on his upper lip.

Colonel Gaither spoke slowly. "Lieutenant, did you intend for me to wear this? Or maybe this is some sort of a joke."

"Uh . . . sorry, sir?"

The Colonel motioned toward the helmet. Hawkins glanced down, his eyes now adjusted to the light. He had felt it to be a good one. He had even smelled the inside and it had been new leather. But he froze in horror and his stomach flipped over as he saw the helmet. He gasped conspicuously. The helmet was indeed new. The cover was clean but across the front in large bold black letters was printed

FUCK YOU

"Oh, I'm *sorry,* sir. No, it certainly wasn't a joke. It was dark out, I couldn't see . . ." He snatched it up. "Please excuse me, sir; I'll get the Colonel another one." He turned and fled from the tent.

Sail insisted that they hadn't seen it either. It was too dark. It was lying beside the hooch of somebody in Hotel Company. Davis had talked to the man in the front and Sail had sneaked up from behind.

"All right, all right, I believe you. But I've still got to have a helmet, damn it. I'm just going to have to go through the whole platoon and find a man with a helmet without any writing on it. Then we'll switch."

But helmet after helmet had something on it. They were the natural bulletin boards of Vietnam: girls' names, cartoons, drawings, hometowns, peace symbols, flowers, calendars with days scratched off, every conceivable slogan and obscenity.

Carefully he examined each one. He wasn't asking; he just demanded to see their helmets. Each one produced a new pain:

EAT THE APPLE AND FUCK THE CORPS.
HO CHI MINH SUCKS.
DON'T SHOOT—I'M SHORT.
LOVE THY NEIGHBOR—KILL GOOKS.

Reluctantly Hawkins realized that his was the only one in the whole platoon without a marking. Solemnly and sadly he took off his own helmet and looked at the FUCK YOU written on the other one.

This time he placed his own unmarked helmet on the table. The Colonel only grunted.

He came back to his platoon CP and sat down slowly.

"You could scratch it out, sir," Joseley said cheerily, "until we can get some more helmet covers."

Hawkins didn't answer for a while but just stared. His mind was thinking of the cordon and the pacification operation he'd just seen being planned. He got up, put the helmet squarely on his head, and nodded at Joseley. "Naw, I think I'll just wear it like it is."

First Lieutenant Ragland

First Lieutenant Jim Ragland walked briskly up to the cordon headquarters and fired a salute.

"Good morning, sir." His voice was crisp and cheerful.

"Morning, Lieutenant." Major Tolson waved in reply. "Jim, the word is that we're going to have a high-ranking visitor this morning. All the way from Saigon. I don't know who, but I'd like you to check the security platoons and make sure all of our people in the area are squared away."

"I'll get right on it, sir. Some of them look like they need a little soap and polish."

Tolson turned back to his paper work.

Ragland saluted again and abruptly went out. He smiled as he walked down to the lines. He would bet ten dollars it was General Goodpaster who was coming. Ragland had been very much in the know when he had worked in Da Nang coordinating pacification.

He had served in several administrative positions and performed well. For the last six months he had helped coordinate the CAP, Combined Action Program, a pacification effort. He was convinced that pacification and Vietnamization were the only way to win in Vietnam. Unlike many in that field, he had applied himself diligently. But Ragland was a career man and command time was essential to promotion. So he had extended his tour for six months and requested assignment to a company. Ragland was a senior first lieutenant, but he knew that any captain would have priority for company commander. So he had checked carefully at division headquarters, pulled some strings and was assigned as executive officer to a company whose commander was short.

What luck, he thought, to be on a cordon op right off the bat. He'd square this bunch away fast. He checked the two platoons on the outer perimeter first. Saluting and a sharp appearance were essential to military command and discipline. If he had his way, all the men would wear regulation blouses whenever they were outdoors. T-shirts, even the green T-shirts, made for Vietnam, looked sloppy to him. One of the worst things for morale was a sloppy appearance. When he took over this company, Delta was really going to look sharp.

But as Ragland approached the Second Platoon CP, a tiny frown came into his eyes. Lieutenant Hawkins stood spread-legged, watching him approach. Ragland's practiced eye swept over the second lieutenant; Hawkins was as dirty as his men. Calahan had said the man was tough in combat, but he didn't look it. He looked clean-cut, except for the dirt and that shotgun. Ragland remembered Hawkins as an overeager lightweight, almost naïve. Yet now he seemed soiled and sarcastic. Probably thinks he's salty as hell, Ragland mused wryly.

"Hello, Chris."

"Hey."

"Where'd you get the gun?" Ragland nodded pointedly.

"Tokyo PX."

"It's nice, but not regulation, you know. Particularly sawed off like that."

"No shit."

The two men eyed each other mutely for a second, then simultaneously they heard the noise and looked up together. At first it was just a faint drone like a huge factory of humming machinery far off in the distance. Everyone stopped whatever he was doing. Out of the morning sky came the forefront of a great locust cloud. Tiny in-

sects whirred over the horizon. In the lead came two of
the shiny new Cobras, the latest all-fighter helicopters
equipped with rockets, miniguns, even automatic grenade-
launchers. They darted back and forth angrily, crisscrossing in the path of the oncoming swarm. Next, very low,
came a brace of armed Hueys, the door gunners leaning
out over their cocked machine guns, eyes sweeping the
ground, the Hueys barely above the treetops. They were
acting as targets, bait for the enemy snipers. Then, high
above, came the armada of helicopters. Bringing up the
rear were more fighter Hueys, the pilots with their fingers
on the rocket buttons.

"Hey. Here they come," Ragland shouted.

"Who is it?" Hawkins stared up, neck arching as the
cloud came closer.

The sky grew dark as if the cloud of locusts had blotted
out the sun. The locusts grew into giant whirring bumble-
bees. Then out of the center of the swarm the queen bee
circled and dropped, touching down at the very edge of
the LZ.

Suddenly all the brass of the cordon were lined up, brav-
ing the prop wash. Like rows of cottontails in the storm,
they were bent over and whipping back and forth.
Ragland was in the middle.

The rotor cut and the door slid open. And as if the
door had revealed a Jack-in-the-box, out popped a shiny
marionette, its M-16 stiffly at port arms, its chest thrown
forward tightening every razor crease of the immaculately
starched utilities. The square-cut, blue-eyed Teutonic head
snapped back and forth, giving the impression of diligently searching some unknown treeline for snipers.

A tall gray-headed man got out casually, and the shiny
Jack-in-the-box hopped in an anxious little bounce to a
position exactly four feet to his side. The casual gray-
headed man walked up toward the briefing room and the
marionette pranced a side-step to stay parallel, still at the
exaggerated port arms, darting about and looking intently
into all the bushes.

Immediately all the cordon brass rushed forward and
began a crisp ritual of saluting and eager handshaking.
The tall gray-headed man returned their salutes easily,
shook the outstretched hands quickly, and never broke his
confident, rapid stride toward the briefing tent. A stream

of lesser luminaries with various odd briefcases and weapons hastily followed their leader. Then, as the General sat down, the marionette did a little pirouette, snapped around, and faced abruptly to the rear, the M-16 still a supererect port arms.

Ragland pushed forward and his eyes fell on the collar of the older man's shirt—four stars. He felt a pleased tingle and stepped back smiling.

"Four stars! *Who* is that?" Hawkins' voice rasped crudely in his ear.

"That, asshole, is General Goodpaster," Ragland whispered indignantly.

"Oh."

The Vietnamese colonel stepped to the chart and began to explain the operation in simple but readily understandable English. He stated they already had five VC suspects.

"Have you gotten any good information from them?" the General asked.

The Vietnamese colonel talked on smoothly, his face in a wide smile. "They were captured early this morning, sir. They are being interrogated at this minute. We should have some good results soon."

"That's outstanding. This operation is somewhat of a showpiece and we have great expectations for it. I'm going to be looking forward to some real results," the General said.

The Vietnamese colonel smiled politely and went on briefing.

Colonel Gaither, however, frowned and whispered to the hefty, square-cut Army colonel, "Looks like we're gonna have to push hard."

"Yeah," the Army colonel answered, "if Saigon is on our back, we gotta put some figures on the board."

Ragland listened intently, then noticed Hawkins edging around the back of the crowd. Immediately Ragland went over and pulled him aside.

"Look, you better get squared away if you're going to hang around here."

"What?"

"Look at yourself. Look at your boots."

Hawkins' eyes went to his boots. They were rumpled and whitened from long use. He looked in the tent. Every boot gleamed bright.

"So," Hawkins said. "That's disgusting."

"So I suggest you do the same."

But Hawkins wasn't paying attention. He had just seen the rank on the collar of the Jack-in-the-box. "Look," he whispered urgently, "look at that." Hawkins nodded toward the Jack-in-the-box. "That general has got a *major* for a bodyguard. I can't believe it. That picture-poster phony is a *major!*"

"He's not a bodyguard; he's an aide," Ragland said disdainfully.

Hawkins shot Ragland a sour look and moved closer to get a better view. The major was young. Without insignia, he might have been a polished young buck sergeant, stiff at attention in full dress. Perhaps a show guard at the White House. "He looks like he wears pads under his arms to keep the sweat from staining his starchy utes," Hawkins said wryly.

"Aides have to dress sharp, you idiot." Ragland kept his voice low and glanced around the tent nervously.

"Okay, Ragland, if this guy is an aide, why is he carrying an M-16 and jumping around like that? He's acting like he wants everybody to know he's a bodyguard. It's ludicrous for a major to act that way."

"He happens to be your, as well as Captain Calahan's, superior."

"Well, I wouldn't want him for my superior." Hawkins' voice rose perceptibly. "Not in the bush."

Ragland's eyes flicked rapidly from Hawkins to the tent; he realized that a bad scene was developing. He had to get Hawkins away quickly. "Okay, Chris, he is a little put on." Ragland's voice relaxed warmly. "Come on. You ever seen a Cobra up close? Let's take a look while they're bullshitting." He took Hawkins by the arm and steered him toward the LZ.

Hawkins glanced back once, then strolled lazily toward the new fighter helicopters. "Look, Ragland, you've been in this pacification stuff. What's all this about? Are we getting anywhere?"

"I think we really are." Ragland spoke eagerly, relieved to have Hawkins away from the tent. "The HES ratings are way up. There are hardly any VC in the eastern half of the province."

"Yeah, but the VC are nothing. They run soon as you

fire. Wait till you fight the NVA."

"You miss the point. Our main job is to help Vietnamese help themselves, not do their fighting for them. You know . . . win the hearts and minds." Ragland added the last with a half chuckle.

Hawkins shook his head. "I don't know, Christ, I don't know. I've been riding up and down these roads now for a long time, but sometimes I think that half of the women in this country are whores and the other half take in GI washing or sell beer and pop and marijuana along the road. To them we're just big, ugly, and rich, and we're making all their women whores. Remember those girls you and Mel Northcutt got for me back at Cam Lo?"

Ragland nodded and looked away uncomfortably. "Chris, our role here is to neutralize the Communist infrastructure government, so as to allow the South Vietnamese government to establish itself. So far we've mostly been doing the fighting, but eventually we'll have to pull our troops out. Therefore what we have to do now is push the NVA out and destroy the local VCI sufficient for the local GVN to maintain their hold. Gradually we upgrade the areas from VC territory to GVN control. Hence the HES, Hamlet Evaluation System. It's a chart to map our progress."

"Ragland"—Hawkins' voice cut in quietly—"I haven't fought any charts yet. I've fought people and I suppose they're Communist people, and that's why I'm fighting them. But I'll tell you one thing: You don't fight a war for charts or neutralization; you fight a war for land." Hawkins' eyes drifted off to the north. "Land—some concrete object to take or hold—that's really what it's all about. That's what inspires men. If you're not fighting for land, you're just fighting to kill."

Hawkins

Nobody knows it, but Vietnam is really a beautiful country. The morning broke bright and clear over lush green rice fields ripe before the harvest. The sky was a deep crystal blue without a trace of smog. The cordon entered its fourth day, and the Vietnamese peasants were being herded in by the truckload. Hawkins watched with curiosity, but most of the men were long since bored and lay around eating, writing, mostly sleeping, and occasionally cleaning a weapon.

Suddenly a shot cracked out over the cordon area. Instinctively everyone dropped to the ground, crouching, hands darting for weapons. Anxiety faded to embarrassment as they realized it was just an accidental discharge. Hawkins' first reaction was relief that it wasn't in the Second Platoon. With all the loaded weapons, it was a common but dangerous happening. Then there was a cry of pain.

"Somebody's hit."

"Who is it?"

"Is he hurt?"

There would be other corpsmen there, but Doc Smitty picked up his bag and went over to see if he was needed. The others ran after him out of curiosity.

"Look"—Chief grabbed Hawkins' arm and pointed— "it's that new first lieutenant."

"What?" Hawkins felt his heart jump up, pounding ridiculously. They were about fifty yards away, but he could see plainly. It *was* Ragland. He was holding up his left hand and hopping about. There was blood on his arm.

"He shot his finger off with his forty-five," somebody yelled.

The group burst into raucous laughter.

"Hey! Cut that out," Hawkins yelled hoarsely, looking about quickly. He held his face stern, yet a delicious pleasure fluttered up inside him.

"You're in, Lieutenant!"

"One down and one to go."

"Hey, Lieutenant, we'll frag the Captain's hooch for ya."

"Hey, 'Tenant, how much you puttin' in the kitty on Calahan's head?"

Hawkins saw Joseley watching him. The little man said nothing but stood off silently with a slight, wry grin. It said more to Hawkins than all the shouts, and for an instant their eyes twinkled together.

"Reckon you got it now, Lieutenant. Sure hate to lose you though," Smitty drawled slyly.

"Won't be long, sir; this company'll be known as Hawkins' Heroes," Chief sang out in falsetto.

Unable to stop himself, Hawkins forgot his composure.

"Yeah, you Indian savage, and that means *you'll* have the platoon. Christ, everybody'll be carrying tomahawks." Hawkins yelled it loud and the laughter and hooting turned on the Chief.

It was silly, of course; Hawkins reproached himself. Ragland had planned to stay in the Corps and a thing like that could ruin his career. With oddly mixed feelings Hawkins turned from the scene and slouched toward his platoon CP. As he stooped to make his Irish coffee, he chuckled and his lips smiled. Better him than me.

Hawkins

Chief, Sail, and the squad leaders sat around the Lieutenant laughing. "This cordon duty is good shit, Lieutenant," Sail said with a glance at the Chief.

Chief put on his Indian mask and rolled his eyes.

"Yeah, you dudes are stealing the booze faster than they can fly it in here for the brass," Sanders said.

"Okay, okay," Hawkins cut in with a grin—"Chief, we're supposed to get some new men today. I think they came in on the last chopper. Go down to the LZ and see if the Gunny is going to give us any."

"Right on, sir."

"And see if you can get me some more shotgun flachette rounds," Hawkins yelled after the Chief.

"How them flachette rounds work, Lieutenant?" Sail asked.

"Great! Look here, I'll show you." Hawkins reached for the shotgun and jacked a shell out of the tube magazine.

As soon as Chief brought the gun from Tokyo, Hawkins had sawn off the barrel and about a third of the stock. At just under three feet in length with a shoulder sling attached, it carried easily in the jungle.

"Lemme borrow your knife." Hawkins' fingers guided the blade around the tip of the shell, slicing the plastic. The end came off and nineteen shiny razor-sharp darts dropped into his palm. Each was about an inch long and flared at the base.

"Wow."

"They also put them in artillery and mortar rounds. Their main purpose is to wound, not kill. The bigger ones can impale a man to a tree."

"Jesus, them is mean lookin'."

Sail took one and pinned it in his hat. "Platoon insignia."

"The only insignia I need is *short* insignia," Wilson chirped happily, taking a flachette and pinning it to his helmet cover on the box numbered eight. "I'm so short I can look a grasshopper in the eye."

"How much time you got?" Sanders asked, laughing.

"Eight days, man! Just eight days and a wake-up." Wilson held up his helmet and proudly showed the "short-timers' calendar."

"You got short-timers' fever all right," Sail said. "Somebody blew his nose this morning and you jumped in a foxhole."

They all laughed and Wilson just grinned. "Ole Top wouldn't keep me in the rear, but I still ain't taking nooo chances when I'm short."

"Hey, here comes Chief . . . *And look who's with him,*" Sail said darkly.

Their heads jerked around together, and Hawkins was fleetingly aware of a murmured hush. He looked to see Chief leading three men. Surprised, Hawkins recognized Sedgewick.

"Hello, Sedgewick," Hawkins said pleasantly. He didn't think much of the man, but he was glad to see an old guy back.

" 'Lo, Lieutenant."

"Haven't seen you since you were medivacked months ago. Are you all well?"

"Top said so."

Hawkins immediately noticed a surliness in his attitude he hadn't seen before. The bush would take that out soon enough, he thought. The second man was boot. All new gear. The third had obviously been incountry for some time. He was small and thin with light-brown skin and even teeth. His face was bony. Only in body was he similar to other blacks, with full, high-swelling buttocks which made his pants stretch tight. His waist and trunk cocked forward just above the hips, then swayed back upright at the sternum. The effect was distinctly African. His helmet was slung carelessly over his canteen and the head was bare. His hair seemed long and bushy and it spread in a brown, reddish-tinged arc. He wore a string of beads around his neck and sunglasses—the little rectangular kind the gooks sold. But it was the expression on his face that caused Hawkins to frown. He knew most old guys didn't like to go back to the bush, but this face was solid bitterness. Even through the sunglasses the eyes were hard and contemptuous. Somehow the bright even teeth seemed out of place in the bitter face. Although Hawkins had never seen him before, the man looked off deliberately with studied boredom.

After an awkward pause, the Chief spoke. "These are the new men, sir." His voice was oddly tense.

The Lieutenant took out his notebook. "Well . . . Names?"

"This man's boot. Name's Cooper. You know Sedgewick. And this other dude's been with us before, too." Chief jerked his thumb.

"This platoon?"

"Yeah, Second Platoon." Chief hissed through his teeth.

Curious, Hawkins looked at the Chief, then at Wilson, finally back at the new man. There was something wrong. The man must have been hurt quite badly to have been away from the platoon so long. "What's your name?"

For the first time the man looked toward the group. His eyes swung slowly around and fell upon the Lieutenant's face with hard contempt. Finally a single word spat from his mouth.

"Carlysle."

The Gunny

"Com'ere Carlysle." the Gunny called in his raspy voice. The Gunny knew Lieutenant Hawkins was away, and as top enlisted man in the field, it was his job to keep the shitbirds out of trouble. He knew he'd have to stay right on top of Carlysle because if the man caused a scene it might reflect badly on the company and on its gunnery sergeant. As he expected, Carlysle was loafing with some blacks from Hotel Company.

Carlysle walked over in silence and stared the craggy-looking man full in the face. "Yeah."

"You come back to the bush, eh, Carlysle? What happened to that court-martial you was suppose to have?"

Carlysle gritted his teeth. "I volunteered for the bush,

Gunny, and they suspended it." His face was aloof and hostile, speaking just civilly enough to get by.

"You mean they told you if you went back to the bush and didn't fuck up they'd let you out of it."

"Something like that, Gunny."

The Gunny contemplated him a moment, eyes searching.

"Well, listen to me, Carlysle"—the Gunny was careful not to say the word "boy," but he rolled the name out in such a way that it was loaded with contempt—"this is the bush, not the rear. Some say you do all right in a fight—I doubt it—but whatever, don't fuck up out here because I'll have your ass."

"I ain't done nothin', Gunny. Don't threaten me."

"You're on trial—if not in the rear—you are here, so square away and don't give me no trouble."

"I ain't lookin' for none, Gunny."

"That's good, because the first thing you're gonna do is get ridda that black T-shirt and them fucking hippie beads you got on." The Gunny pointed his bony finger at Carlysle's chest.

"I got a right to wear them!" Carlysle burst out. "What the hell, this is the bush, ain't it?"

"That's the order, Carlysle, no beads and no black T-shirts—put out by the commanding general himself," the Gunny intoned mockingly.

Abruptly Carlysle cooled. He spat casually on the ground and his voice was contemptuous. "Gunny, this is the bush; that order don't go here."

"You're a *Marine,* Carlysle—in the bush and out."

"Never been enforced in the bush before, Gunny."

The voice was cooly contemptuous, but Gunny knew Carlysle was furious. He held his fists ready.

"It starts *now!* And watch your wise mouth, *Private* Carlysle."

"How come the Catholics can wear crosses and chains and I can't wear beads?" Carlysle's face sneered slightly.

The Gunny's eyes narrowed to hard, round holes, and he thrust his face into Carlysle's. "You think you're gonna louse up *my* company, but you ain't. Now get 'em off right now!"

Carlysle's lips drew back across the teeth in a snarl. Gunny saw a sliver of rage and he waited. If Carlysle would just attack him, he would end all the trouble right now. His voice went tense. "You'd better get them off if you don't wanta walk point every fuckin' day."

Slowly Carlysle raised his hand and slipped the loop of beads up over his head. He turned his head away as if bored.

"Take 'em all off."

Carlysle took the small ones off his thin wrists. His face was a mask of contemptuous indifference.

"Get rid of 'em."

"I'll carry 'em. No law says I can't carry 'em in my pack, Gunnery Sergeant." As he held the beads, his hands were trembling, but he dropped the beads casually in his pocket.

"Yeah, you're probably stupid enough to carry the weight, but don't let me catch you wearing them. Now, Carlysle . . . get that black T-shirt off."

"Here?"

"Right fucking here, Carlysle." His voice fell to a low rasp.

Carlysle's eyes were burning holes as he jerked the shirt over his head. His bare chest glistened with sweat in the sun. "What are you going to do now, Gunny? Whip me?"

"I'll kick your ass if you don't watch that mouth."

"Just try, Gunny."

For a second they stared face to face, fists doubled, knuckles white.

"Don't tempt me. And don't wear any of that shit again." He jabbed a finger at Carlysle's face. "And I warn you, Carlysle, fly straight while you're around here. I run a tight company and you or nobody else is going to fuck it up. Now get over to your platoon where you belong."

Hawkins

As soon as he got to the CP, Lieutenant Hawkins cornered Joseley. "Who is that guy?"

"Which one, sir?"

"The soul brother. You know which one I mean."

Joseley's eyes flickered slightly. "That's Carlysle, sir," he said carefully. "I don't know him myself except that he's been here a long time. I don't know why he's in the bush now because he must be short."

"What else?"

Joseley wavered a second and then his face went blank. "I don't know, sir. They say he's been up for a court-martial, but you'd better ask Chief or Wilson."

Hawkins saw the wall come up. There was a limit to what Joseley would reveal about the men. But what was the reason? He wondered. Who is this guy? He had acted almost as if he were trying to provoke me.

At that moment he saw the Gunny coming toward him. Hawkins didn't like the Gunnery Sergeant, although he was an excellent NCO. At this moment he looked more than ever like a vulture. The deep narrow-set eyes and beak nose honed in on Hawkins. He had that "Honor-thy-officer" look, but Hawkins remembered the Gunny thought all lieutenants were shave-tailed punks.

"Afternoon, sir. Can I speak to the Lieutenant a minute?" The voice was syrupy, solicitous.

Hawkins half grinned to himself and braced for a snow job. "Sure, Gunny. What's up?"

The Gunny pulled Hawkins aside and lowered his voice. "This new man the Lieutenant's got, this colored boy."

"I got two black Marines today, Gunny—Sedgewick and another."

"Not Sedgewick, sir. The other one, named Carlysle." His voice was slightly annoyed. "The Lieutenant's gotta watch him. He's a troublemaker." The Gunny paused expectantly, but Hawkins waited impassively for him to go on.

"What's he done?"

"He's one of those black power racists." The voice was as though he were speaking of a snake. Again the Gunny paused, looking for a reaction. "He was with the Lieutenant's platoon a long time ago and got wounded, sir; and then he was on a ship and in NSA hospital. The past few months he's been at Quang Tri awaiting a court-martial."

"What's the charge?"

"They had a bunch of charges. Insubordination, disrespect to an officer, probably got a marijuana charge, too. But, *the Lieutenant knows*—he was a troublemaker." He spoke low, as if Hawkins were supposed to understand some hidden reason for the court-martial.

Hawkins understood perfectly, but he kept his voice

and face blank. "What's he done?"

"He's one of the ringleaders. Plotting. You know, trying to cause race riots and all that."

"Oh, I see." The Lieutenant scowled to show disapproval and the Gunny smiled.

"Yeah, they think he's one of those that threw the grenade under Gunny Cull's hooch over in Golf Company. But they couldn't prove it. I don't trust any of those plotting racist bastards."

"Well, how come he's out here now?"

"As I hear it, the trouble was they didn't have enough evidence for the big charges. So the Colonel gave him a break and said if he volunteered to go back to the bush they'd suspend his trial, pending good behavior for the rest of his tour. Actually, I think they just wanted to get rid of him. So we're stuck with him."

"So it would seem."

The Gunny looked at Hawkins keenly and his voice took on a slight edge. "Well, I thought you'd better know the story on him, Lieutenant."

"Yeah, thanks, Gunny. Glad you told me."

Abruptly the gunny saluted and started off but then stopped and spoke over his shoulder, "So you better watch him. Remember what he did to Gunny Cull."

Carlysle

"Wilson, what the fuck's the matter with you? We got an order to quit wearing black T-shirts and you sit there fukkin' with that calendar like you don't care none at all."

"Listen, Carlysle," Wilson snapped. "Sure I care. But they never said anything until you came along. Now the Gunny's on all the brothers' ass."

"That's 'cuz you never made a show of it. Everybody out here acts like they're trying to kiss the beast's ass."

"You better shut your mouth."

"You better listen to me, muddafukka. The brothers has got to stick together. You out here act like everybody's just big buddies."

"Carlysle, this is a bush outfit and you know it. The Chucks in the bush are uptight. We're united."

"United my fukking ass." His bony face became contorted. He spat the words out harshly. "The beasts will never unite with the black man. Ee-qual-ity. Shit. That's united? All the lifers and officers are beasts. The only thing the beasts understand is power."

Wilson fidgeted, then looked squarely at Carlysle, his voice cool but measured. "Carlysle, you're wrong. That talk about rioting and 'ruling over' is crap. There are plenty of Chucks who aren't beasts and the Chuck's officers aren't all beasts. Lieutenant Hawkins is one who ain't no beast."

"All officers are beasts, Wilson, even that fukking Lieutenant Hawkins of yours. And I'll show you."

He turned abruptly and walked off.

"Hey, wait a minute, Carlysle, where are you going?" Wilson called after him. Carlysle pretended he didn't hear.

Even back in the rear there was talk that this Lieutenant Hawkins had his shit together; but what really bothered him was that there should be an exception to his theory about the beasts. He'd just have to go talk with this dude.

Carlysle found the Lieutenant near his hooch, reading. Joseley was not there. Before he spoke, Carlysle caught hold of himself and put on the wheedling tone he sometimes used with officers. He stood looking down for a few seconds.

"Lieutenant, how about me speaking to you a minute?"

Hawkins looked up without expression. "Yeah, sure." He had seen Carlysle approaching.

"Lieutenant, I've been in d'Nam a long time and I been in d'bush a lot, too."

"Want a smoke?" Hawkins said extending his C-ration Winstons.

Carlysle halted as if slapped and his face wrinkled into a frown, but his hand reached for the cigarette.

"Go ahead," Hawkins said.

"Well, I figure we're here to fight, you know." Now that he had approached the Lieutenant, Carlysle didn't know exactly what he was going to say. He had been sure the Lieutenant would harass him immediately.

"Yeah?"

"So when a man's in the bush, it don't much matter

what he's wearing and it don't much matter if he's wearing the same thing as everybody else so long as he fights. Right?"

Hawkins cocked an eyebrow.

"Well, I had this black silk shirt and it was better than those issue shirts, and I liked to wear it." Carlysle paused, waiting for objection. None came.

"And I had a little necklace. It was sort of personal to me. Well, you know how it was, something that meant a lot to me. You know?"

"Yeah, I know."

"Well, the Gunny, he says I can't wear 'em. Now what's wrong with wearing them in the bush, Lieutenant?" Carlysle rolled his head triumphantly.

Hawkins sat silent, without moving and without expression. After a long moment he spoke evenly. "As I see it, nothing's wrong with that. Matter of fact, as far as I'm concerned you can wear a jockstrap and feathers if you want." The Lieutenant paused, his voice dry and terse, but Carlysle's face remained immobile. "However, I'm not the whole Marine Corps. Now the Gunny, he sees things the Old Corps way, more strict. And so he doesn't like anything that's individual."

"Well, if you don't care, how can the Gunny care? Tell me that."

"Oh, come on, Carlysle. You know as well as I do. He's the company gunny and the Captain likes him. And the Captain's going to listen to him. Something like that I can't interfere with. All you can do is wait until he goes away. Of course, if we're out with just the platoon alone, you can wear your black beret and black leather jacket if you want."

Carlysle knew he had taken the wrong course and shifted abruptly. "Lieutenant, I been in d'Nam almost thirteen months now and I got two Hearts. But I'm only a private. I should get promoted, but it always seemed to be something or somebody against me. What I'm saying is that I been here too long to walk point and that stuff. I should be in the rear now, but they keep fukking me up."

"Well, I'll put you up for Pfc," Hawkins said warily. "With your experience you'll at least be a fire team leader, so it won't normally be your job to walk point."

"Well, what if my fire team is gone or something?"

"Don't sweat it. If you been here that long you'll probably be a squad leader before you know it."

For a moment Carlysle glared, then shrugged contemptuously and stalked away.

"I got to get out of here," Sedgewick whined. "I can't go back to the bush."

"You only been back two days." Carlysle snorted sarcastically.

The two men sat alone, a few yards removed from the rest of the squad. It was just after dusk and they were eating their C-rations; Carlysle sat brooding over the Gunny, the Lieutenant, and Wilson. Sedgewick looked at the food and felt its dry tastelessness in his mouth. Then, with a quick surge of disgust, he flung it away from him. "I can't eat that shit." He spat. "That muthafuckin' goddamn Top. I had a good deal at Quang Tri, even got sent to Da Nang once for a checkup." He looked to Carlysle for an answer. But Carlysle only picked at his C-rations—wieners and beans—and ignored Sedgewick altogether.

"The doctor had me on light duty; I'm not supposed to be here."

"Yeah," Carlysle said, uninterested, "how's zat?"

"It's that muthafuckin' Top—he just calls me in and says I'm going to the bush—just like that. I said, 'Top, the doc says I can't go to the bush; I'm on light duty,' and he said, 'That ain't no good anymore—you're going!' That's all. Wudn't let me explain or nothin', Goddamn they'll fuck you over every time."

Carlysle continued to brood in silence.

"You remember when I had that real bad case of heat exhaustion?" Carlysle didn't move. "Carlysle, you remember when I came back," Sedgewick insisted.

"Yeah, muddafukka, I remember, so what?"

"Well, it fucked up my eyes. They was already bad and the heat did something else to them. I don't know what. The doc in Da Nang checked 'em, but he wouldn't do shit, just gave me some ole prescription. Shit! I cain't see." He began shaking his head and his voice took on a note of self-pity. "I'll get killed out here for sure; I'll never get out of here now. That cocksucking Top just ain't fair; he won't listen to the doc. I shouldn't even be here."

"Aw shut your mouth, Pimp. Nobody should be here."

"Well, you ain't got no business here either," Sedgewick said, piqued. "They fucked you over, too, didn't they?"

Carlysle thought bitterly that they *always* fucked him over. Although he agreed one hundred percent with Sedgewick, he felt in no mood to listen to anyone. In fact, he hardly heard Sedgewick's bitching.

"Damn, Carlysle, I gotta *do* something. I just can't take the bush anymore."

Carlysle thought how easy it would be to get out of the bush—that is, except for himself. Everybody in the whole battalion was against him. One false move and they'd jump. They had him. Anything he did would mean a longer time in Vietnam. But for Sedgewick, it would be easy. "Why you just don't shoot yourself?" he said absent-mindedly.

Sedgewick looked quickly to Carlysle, his breath catching. "What are you talking about muthafucker; I might mess myself up, then what?"

Carlysle brooded again. He was thinking of Wilson.

"Naw, that won't do, but I gotta do something. Maybe get sick," Sedgewick said slowly, but his mind was going wild with the idea. He had thought of just that thing hundreds of times, particularly when he was in the bush, but he'd never had the guts to do it. Yet if Carlysle would do it. He remembered the big hospital at Da Nang and smiled as if he were already there.

Suddenly Carlysle jumped up, a hard excited gleam in his eye. "All right, muddafukka, you want outta d'bush, I'll get you out."

Sedgewick stepped back. "Wha . . . what do you mean? How?"

Carlysle's eyes narrowed, and his lips pulled back in a snarl-grin. "Simple. We'll break your arm." His eyes bore into Sedgewick.

"Break my arm?" The sudden confrontation with a specific injury sent a flash of fear and uncertainty into Sedgewick. Sweat broke out on his upper lip.

"It's easy"—Carlysle's voice purred—"there's hardly any pain. It will heal perfect and it's guaranteed. *Nobody,* not even the fukking colonel, will send you to the bush with a big white cast on your arm."

"But . . ." Sedgewick sputtered weakly.

"But what? Are you chicken?" Carlysle exploded, his bony face thrust at Sedgewick's. "I thought you wanted out. I tell you the perfect way and you suddenly act like you wanna back down."

"No, but . . . but how?" Sedgewick was excited, but the thought of breaking an arm made his stomach woozy.

"Aw, forget it." Carlysle sat back down and picked up his C-ration can. His mind spun over and slowly his lips pulled back in a tight smirk.

As Carlysle sat back, Sedgewick looked at him nervously.

"No. Wait, Carlysle, I want out—tell me how."

"No sweat, you'll see." He looked away and slowly smiled as the pieces of his plan fell into place. "And I know just the man to do it for you."

"Who?"

"Corporal Wilson, your squad leader," he said deliberately and slowly, his expression more of a sneer than a smile.

"Wilson?"

"Yup, I believe that ole Corporal Wilson would be glad to help a brother."

"Aw, you're crazy, Carlysle. Wilson would never do something like that."

"You calling me a liar, muddafukka?" Carlysle swung back at Sedgewick viciously, his eyes blazing.

"N—no . . . no, Carlysle—Jesus, take it easy, man. I just said. . . ."

"I'm trying t'help you and you ain't done nothin' but act scared and back off and tell me I'm lying. Now you want out or not?"

"Yeah, Carlysle . . . but—" He was sweating freely now.

"All right, then just shut up and do what I tell you." Then his voice softened. "Now you *ask* Brother Wilson to help you and I'll go along and we'll just see."

"Okay, Carlysle." Sedgewick shrugged.

"But," Carlysle said evenly, *"you've* got to ask him."

Wilson

"Break your arm? What is this shit, Sedgewick?" Wilson spoke with furious indignation but was uneasily aware

of Carlysle standing behind him.

"Well, ah . . ." Even as Sedgewick faltered, Carlysle firmly shoved him forward. "Look, Sonny, I gotta get outta the bush, my eyes are bad, I can't see." His words tumbled out rapidly. He had told Carlysle it was crazy to ask Wilson; now he knew it. "That time I had heat exhaustion fucked 'em up, and, well, Carlysle said if I asked you."

Wilson looked quickly to Carlysle, and some of his wrath faded.

"That's right, Brother Wilson." Carlysle spoke for the first time, his voice sincere and open. But Wilson caught the hint of mockery. "We know you always ready to help a brother."

"What are you trying to do, Carlysle?" Wilson asked coldly.

As Wilson swung to face Carlysle, Sedgewick stepped back, relieved to be off the hook.

"You know what it is, Wilson," Carlysle said slowly. "This brother needs to get outta the bush, he's sick, he's on light duty, but Top fukked him over, now he's asking you for help."

"Shit! He ain't no sicker than I am."

"Well, Brother Wilson"—Carlysle's voice hardened a little—"maybe he is and maybe he ain't, but he's a brother and he wants out and he's *asking you* for help."

"So that don't cut no ice—I want out, too. Everybody wants out of the bush. What am I supposed to do? go around and break every black arm in the fucking company?"

Carlysle ignored the cut and swept on smoothly, "The doc had him on light duty, but the Top fukked him. All he's asking is for you to help him get back where he's *supposed* to be."

"So why ask me then? Why don't you do it, Carlysle?"

"Aw, man, you know they watching me every minute, but *you* man"—Carlysle cocked his head, thinking of a different approach—"you're a corporal now, you're a squad leader, and you're in tight with that lieutenant. *Least* you could do is to talk to the Lieutenant for Sedgewick and ask him to do something, maybe see the doc."

"Carlysle, no, that's . . ." Sedgewick started to interrupt, remembering what had happened before when he'd tried to request mast.

But Carlysle waved at him to be silent.

Wilson relaxed slightly. That was a hell of a lot different, but he knew Hawkins had his ass chewed by the Captain when he had taken Sedgewick up to request mast before; besides which, Lieutenant Hawkins was a lot sharper now than then, and Wilson was sure he didn't want to get the Lieutenant into this mess—true or not. "Yeah, I could do *that*, but it wouldn't work. I don't think you'd fool the Lieutenant. He'd probably send Sedgewick to the Gunny."

Carlysle didn't pursue it, but he had seen that he'd opened a wedge. Now there was room to maneuver. "All right, Sonny Boy," his voice cooed. "We won't do that; we'll just have to go back to the other."

"That's your business."

"True enough." Carlysle motioned to Sedgewick and started to leave. Then he turned and said, "Course you ain't gonna tell on us now, are you?"

"Shit, no, motherfucker." Wilson's anger flared. "What do I look like, some kind of stool pigeon?"

"I don't know, the way you in tight with the beast and all, I wudn't sure."

"Goddamn it, you better watch your mouth." Wilson stepped forward, unconsciously making a fist.

"Okay, Brother Wil." Carlysle stepped back, smiling, and put up his hands. Wilson had fast fists when he was angry. "Then why don't you just come on with us?"

Wilson stopped. He didn't really want to get into this, but it wouldn't hurt to just. . . .

"You don't have to do nothing, man—if you're afraid—but if you're together with your brothers, you can just come along, can't you?" Carlysle's smooth voice coaxed with just a hint of insinuation.

Wilson hesitated. Damn, how did he get into this, he wondered. He had only seven days to go. "All right." He sighed. "I'll come along just for company." He glanced around the hole and picked up his M-14. "Where you planning to go?"

Carlysle smiled to himself, but outwardly his expression was frozen. "I seen this place over back of where they bring the gooks in. Not too many people go there, and there shouldn't be nobody there at night."

They walked out past the battalion CP and down the corral of barbed wire. There was a half moon and they could just make out the way. They passed the ID check area and approached the interrogation huts. There was a light on in one of them, but it was toward the end. They moved into the bushes.

As they approached the huts, Sedgewick was more than a little nervous—he was scared shitless—but he could almost feel himself back in the rear. The thought excited him tremendously. There was that girl he used to get over by the road shops. He could still do it with his arm in a cast.

They moved off the path and pushed through the bushes into a little opening. Wilson leaned on his rifle and stood stiffly apart. The interrogation huts were about forty yards away, hidden by the bushes.

"All right, Pimp, you know what to do?" Carlysle asked.

"N—no." Sedgewick said.

"It's easy; you just wrap a shirt around your forearm . . . here." He took off his jungle blouse and his T-shirt, then he put the jungle blouse back on and wrapped the T-shirt tightly around Sedgewick's left forearm. "Now, sit down and lay your forearm on the ground. . . . That's right. Now, I need a couple of sticks or a smooth stone." In the dark he had to lean down to see.

"What for?" Sedgewick's voice was wobbly.

"Don't get shook, you'll see." Carlysle kept walking around bent over and, without looking up from the ground, he said:

"Brother Wil, ain't you gonna be of no help at all?"

"You're doing all right."

"Goddamn, man, I didn't ask you to do nothing but look for a rock. You can't even do that for a brother?"

There he goes again, Wilson thought. Why does Carlysle always have to make it a thing about the brothers? Wilson would do anything for his people, but this was stupid. "It doesn't have anything to do with being a brother."

"Well, what *does* it have to do with then?" Carlysle stood up and moved on Wilson.

"I told you, I just don't believe in . . ." He realized he hadn't told Carlysle anything. "In hurting yourself on purpose," he said doggedly, wishing he'd never come along in the first place.

"Hell, Wilson, he ain't trying to hurt himself; he's trying to *save* himself—trying to get outta the bush, where he's *really* likely to get killed."

"Well, fuck, where does that leave me? We're in the same squad together, and I'm still out here." Wilson's voice rose, but he forced himself to keep calm.

"I never told you to stay out here in the bush. Matter of fact, I think it's stupid that you're still out here."

"Look, Carlysle"—Wilson was struggling—"I don't like the bush either. Nobody likes it, but we're here and somebody's got to do it."

"Why? Why?" Carlysle pushed his face out, with his eyes bugging wide. "What reason have you got to fight the Vietnamese? Did they ever do anything to you before you came over here? Hell, no! But the beasts has done plenty to you."

Wilson was mad, but he knew that the argument was useless. "Come off that, Carlysle, that doesn't have anything to do with it."

"It's got everything to do with it. You name me one reason to fight the Vietnamese, and I'll name you ten why you should fight the beasts. But no, not you, muddafukka." Carlysle's voice grew intense and savage, his face tight. "Wilson, you fight for the beast. It's his war."

"I do not," Wilson shouted before he could control himself. What answer could he give Carlysle to that?

"Then who are you fighting for? You sure ain't fighting for the brothers." Carlysle's eyes blazed, and his face was thrust out at Wilson. "I said all along, and I said it to your face. You ain't with us. Ain't that right, Brother Sedgewick?"

Sedgewick, still sitting on the ground between them, was bewildered by the whole thing. He blinked and gulped. "Yeah . . . I uh. . . ."

"Shut up," Carlysle snapped, cutting him off, and looked back up at Wilson. "See, everybody knows what you are. You're a Tom. A fukkin' Uncle Tom!"

"Shut your mouth!" Wilson screamed. Nobody, but nobody, called him that. Rage piled up, and blindly he raised the rifle at Carlysle.

For a minute everything froze. Nothing moved. Not a sound. The moon glinted off the steel of the barrel, then Carlysle gently raised his hands, open and about chest-high; very slowly he stepped backward. For a second he'd been really frightened, and his eyes went wide, the whites showing plainly. Finally he spoke ever so softly, "Whoa, boy." He took another step backward. "Now you ain't gonna shoot me, are you?"

As soon as he'd done it, Wilson was flooded with shame. He lowered the rifle guiltily.

Carlysle watched the rifle, but as he saw Wilson's eyes droop, his voice flowed smoothly to bitter sarcasm. "Gonna shoot me. Gonna shoot a brother." Carlysle sensed that he had scored. His large white teeth flashed in the dark. "Well, Wilson, we won't bother you no more. No, sir, the brothers will leave you alone." Carlysle was careful, however, not to mention the word "Tom." "Won't ask you to help out no more."

As Carlysle droned on mercilessly, Wilson was torn. He felt the old argument ripping him apart. Why? Why? Why do you have to hate the white man in order to be black? To be in, to be respected. Oh, he knew Carlysle had done this just to get him to break Sedgewick's arm, which really meant just to go along with Carlysle. But it wasn't really Carlysle; if he weren't there, it would be someone else at some other time. The real thing was what did he, Robert Wilson, want. What was he supposed to be? What was he supposed to do in order to . . . in order to just live? All he wanted was to be accepted. As his rage drained, he felt weak, and he knew he was slipping. "I'm sorry, Carlysle." He lowered his eyes. "I just lost my head when you called me that. I'll help Sedgewick. You know I ain't for the beast."

Carlysle smiled. "Aw Sonny Boy, I'm sorry I called you that. I know you're with us. Ain't that right, Sedgewick?"

"Yeah," Sedgewick said numbly, still sitting and not really understanding at all.

"Well, let's get on with this," Carlysle said and again began to look for a rock.

"Here's one." Wilson stooped and handed Carlysle a smooth, flat stone.

"Thanks, Sonny," Carlysle said. He knelt down beside Sedgewick. "Now we just put it under your wrist, like this

. . . so's the middle of your forearm is just a little tiny bit off the ground." Then his voice lowered as if whispering a secret. "Now, we'll hit it right here in the middle with the rifle butt."

"Wait," Sedgewick cried out, starting to jump up. His face was creased and beaded with sweat. His eyes quivered white in the moonlight.

"Easy, man, your elbow's in soft dirt." Carlysle pushed him down. "It'll be a green stick fracture; bone will never even separate, but it'll show up on the X-ray."

"Sure?"

"Sure thing. Here, bite this piece of wood; it'll keep you from hollering and getting scared."

Wilson by now had rallied a little. "Look here, Carlysle, I'm afraid I might hit too hard; you better do it."

"Umph," Sedgewick took the wood out. "Yeah, Carlysle, you seem to know more; you better do it." His frightened eyes swept back and forth between the two men.

Carlysle frowned and looked down. He had already won the argument. The important thing was to make Wilson a real brother. "You got the rifle, Wilson, you go ahead there. Just take it by the muzzle and swing it like an ax. He'll be all right."

"I don't know." Wilson hesitated.

"If you do it, it will be sort of like a little ceremony, you know." His voice was crooning.

"Well . . ." Wilson felt the sweat running down his side. He saw Sedgewick bite the wood, distorting his face as his eyes whimpered upward. Slowly Wilson's fingers tightened around the barrel.

Hawkins

A half moon made just enough light for Lieutenant Hawkins to see as he walked around the cordon CP area. He was only half-checking the lines: if someone were to ask, he would have given that as a reason for being out. He really was just taking a walk. The night was pleasant, and it wasn't often he had the opportunity just to wander. Certainly he'd never had the chance at night outside a U.S. base. He borrowed a pistol, however, even though he knew the outer perimeter was beyond where he would go.

He didn't want to carry the shotgun at the moment. Too
many people always asked questions when they saw it;
and right now he sought solitude.

He walked on past the immediate area, enjoying the
night and the opportunity to be alone. He had to admit he
was curious, too. This cordon duty was really a change
and he felt like exploring. Casually he wandered past the
barbed-wire area where they kept the people pending pro-
cessing. Weird, he thought, how different it looked at
night. Concertina barbed wire was extremely difficult to
see in the dark, and he took care to keep his distance.
More than once, he had been cut on barbed wire. The cut
wasn't so bad as the inevitable jungle-crud infection which
got into it. He remembered Logan used to have disgusting
jungle-rot sores all over him. He remembered how he used
to make Logan wash at every stream, then run and catch
up with the column. It never did any good though. Hawkins thought about Logan calmly. He had no remorse. He
might have felt more if the man had been killed in combat. He had felt very badly at the time, but, what the hell,
he hadn't really known him at all.

Hawkins stopped abruptly. Without realizing it, he had
wandered over to the interrogation huts. Suddenly he
wanted to know more about them. They had told him to
keep away, but forbidding him to do anything always gave
him more desire to do it. Carefully, he moved closer. The
huts were dark, except for one, the largest. He saw the
light and wavered, but the temptation to investigate was
overpowering. Hawkins crept closer and examined the
building. It was plywood, like a Marine hooch, but with
no windows. There was a small slit near the roof which
the light poured through. There didn't seem to be anyone
around. He looked carefully; before there had been a
guard. Maybe something is wrong. He should check, he
told himself. After all, he was the head of the CP security.
He moved toward the hut, dimly aware that he shouldn't
but assuring himself that it was his duty. About ten feet
from the door, he halted. There were voices inside. He
heard the chow-ow up-and-down tones of Vietnamese, and
with a little shock he heard an American voice. It sounded vaguely familiar. As if hypnotized, he stepped closer
to the door, listening, wondering what he should do. He
was insatiably curious to know who was inside. Suddenly

he saw a figure lying in the grass. He jumped back, his hand jerking the pistol out. Then he saw it was a sleeping Vietnamese soldier, and he smiled openly, easing the pistol back with relief. It must be the sentry. Asleep, like all sentries. Hawkins looked around him. There was no one else. This was his excuse. He could go in and say he was checking the lines and had found the man asleep. He grinned and felt clever. Silently, he stepped past the man and reached for the door. Knock? No. Wasn't he the security officer? Just walk in. Besides if he knocked he might learn nothing. His stomach feeling a little giddy, he put his hand on the door. For a moment he thought of going back, then with a hard shove he pushed it wide.

Instantly someone screamed in a long shriek. A bunch of Vietnamese in tiger-striped suits jumped up, yelling. Two men drew pistols, glanced toward the back, and then rushed him. Just before the men hit the doorway, Hawkins heard someone yell his name. In those few seconds the whole room burned its way into his eyes. It contained six or eight of the Vietnamese in tiger-striped camouflage suits. They were the roughest, meanest-looking Vietnamese he had ever seen. Two of them had long split-bamboo canes in their hands. Two Americans wearing nondescript clothing were seated off to one side. One of them was hidden behind the other. It was the center of the room, however, which riveted his eyes. A Vietnamese man was hung by his wrists from the ceiling, stark naked. Connected to each testicle was a wire which led to a hand-cranked field telephone. The naked body was covered with long red welts.

During those few seconds, which seemed like an age, Hawkins couldn't move; but just before the two Vietnamese reached him, he came to his senses and jumped back. Then someone shouted in Vietnamese and the men stopped. Both stood glaring on either side of him, drawn pistols pointed directly at him.

"Hawkins! Hawkins! What are you doing here?" someone called from the inside and came running out.

It was Mel Northcutt.

Northcutt jerked his head at the Vietnamese and they went back in. As they put their pistols away, Hawkins realized he had almost been shot and felt a deep, frightening relief.

"Hawkins, what are you doing here?" Northcutt's face was angry and he shouted.

"Well, I . . . I have the security platoon for the cordon CP and I was checking the lines and ah . . . checking this area out . . . I saw this light and didn't see anyone so I came to check. I found this guard asleep."

Northcutt glanced at the guard, who was now standing very alertly at the door. He looked quickly around the hut. "Get inside," he ordered, taking Hawkins by the arm and leading him in roughly.

Hawkins felt his stomach trembling, but he kept his cool. Northcutt slammed the door with his foot and forcibly turned Hawkins away from the center of the room, facing him toward the door. Hawkins could see only Northcutt and the door.

"You're not supposed to be here," Mel said sharply. "Didn't they tell you to stay away?"

Hawkins grinned to himself. He had already seen everything he needed to in this room. For a moment he had been frightened, but now he saw Mel and he wasn't much more than anxious. "Yes, but I also felt it my duty to check the area. I saw a light and no one was around," he said defiantly.

Mel said nothing but eyed him intently. Hawkins began to feel a little apprehensive. "Look, Mel, I sure didn't mean to cause any trouble. I hope I didn't screw anything up. I just saw the guy asleep and you know, I thought . . . well, I thought I should investigate."

Mel's eyes narrowed and his face went harder than Hawkins had ever seen it. He continued to stare without speaking. The room was dead silent and Hawkins began to fidget. Damned if he was going to kowtow to this guy. He wanted a cigarette badly.

Finally Mel drew a breath and spoke. His voice was more precise and cold than it had been before. "Okay, Chris, listen closely"—he glanced over Hawkins' shoulder and gave someone a look—"you were *told* not to come here, but I understand about the sentry—at least I'll buy the story. Now if I didn't know you, I'd take you to your colonel, but as I know you I am going to assume you're intelligent enough to understand the situation and steer clear in the future. I shouldn't do it, but I will."

Hawkins nodded soberly. "Okay."

"What you've seen here—don't ask about and don't talk about. You know this is a war and we need information. Suffice it to say, no American took part in anything you saw. Do I make myself clear?"

"Yes."

"Okay, I want you to get out of here now, and don't discuss this. I'm not trying to threaten you, but I can go to your colonel if necessary."

"I read you loud and clear, Mel. There will be no problem. I am sorry for the trouble."

"Good, Chris," Mel smiled slightly and put out his hand. "Next time I see you, we'll have a drink."

Hawkins shook Mel's hand and smiled. The door opened and Mel propelled him out firmly.

The sentry, now very awake, eyed Hawkins coldly as the Lieutenant moved on in a self-satisfied daze. He thought he should be shocked, but he wasn't. He had had a peek into a completely different world that was tied directly to his world. Fascinating. What else went on? Who were all those people? What did Northcutt really do? His mind buzzed with the possibilities.

As he walked, he paid no attention to where he went. His mind was back in the hut, the scene clear in his eye. His feet carried him automatically. He was passing some bushes and for a moment, he thought he heard something, but he kept on.

Suddenly he did hear a cry in the night. *"Oaagh!"* He spun toward the sound, crouched, jerked out the pistol. Somebody *was* in the bushes! That was a real cry of pain! He felt the shock of fear run through him as he heard voices. That was English. He ran forward, pushing through the brush, stumbling in the dark. Just ahead. Was that voice familiar?

He burst into the little clearing, pistol in hand, and his eyes swept over three figures.

"What?" He stopped dead, recognizing Carlysle and Sedgewick but not comprehending the situation.

The three men heard the bushes rustle only a second before Hawkins came upon them. Instant panic. They jumped—to attack or flee—but the intruder was already there. They froze and could only stare wide-eyed.

Hawkins saw Carlysle holding a rifle. In the dark he did not recognize Wilson; his attention went to the man on the ground. Sedgewick was injured. Hawkins went immediately and bent down. "What happened, are you okay?" He saw him holding his arm, clutching it to his chest. "Your arm, what is it?" Gently he lifted the cloth, looking for blood. Sedgewick shrank back, eyes wild with terror.

Hawkins withdrew his hand and looked at the face. He stood and looked at Carlysle. "What's going on? What's the matter with him? What happened?"

Carlysle said nothing, and his face seemed to close like a trap. He backed up a step and looked darkly at Sedgewick.

Sedgewick spoke, still on the ground. "I broke my arm."

"Gooks?" Hawkins asked with growing awareness and discomfort.

"No, sir, just an accident."

Hawkins immediately felt the tension flow out at the news that there was no enemy. He stepped back and looked around, pistol in hand—still not aware of Wilson.

"What happened?"

"He fell, sir, broke his arm," Carlysle cut in smoothly.

"Fell where?"

"Oh—over at Hotel Company, sir. We was—ah—checking out the area and stopped for a moment to talk to some friends."

Hawkins looked at Sedgewick and saw the T-shirt. He saw the M-14 held in Carlysle's hands. He frowned. There was only one M-14 in the platoon.

He remembered their startled, frightened looks when he first came up, and slowly he began to realize what had happened. His voice was cool. "What did he fall from?"

"A truck, sir." Carlysle hesitated. "We was up on a truck-bed."

For a long minute Hawkins stood silent, looking from Carlysle to Sedgewick. He felt anger and dismay, yet disturbed and troubled by his own gut reaction. Negroes. No, he corrected himself; it wasn't race. These were just two bad eggs. Carlysle started to speak again, coming up with great detail, telling how it happened. Hawkins cut him off, the M-14 tugging at his mind. His eyes went around and fell on the third man.

"Wilson! Oh, Wilson." A feeling of disillusionment hit him like a blast. "Did you? Are you?"

Wilson looked down, but even in the moonlight Hawkins had already seen the shame and humiliation on his face. "Oh, no, Wilson, you're not. . . ." Hawkins' voice trailed off, and he felt the hurt welling up in him. He could only stare at Wilson sickly.

"Lieutenant, he ain't hurt too bad." Carlysle's crooning voice cut across Hawkins' thoughts. "If you want we can go over, and I'll show you what happened." He droned on smoothly, spinning out the story.

Suddenly Hawkins' shock and grief burst into anger. "SHUT UP!" he roared. He swung around on Carlysle, and the motion caused the pistol to raise naturally. He glared at Carlysle, then at Sedgewick. "How stupid do you think I am? It doesn't really matter to me what happened, but don't try to fool me!"

"Don't tell me to shut up, Lieutenant!" Carlysle said threateningly.

"Carlysle, don't!" Wilson yelled.

"Don't tell me 'don't,' Wilson!" Carlysle screamed. He dropped back and violently slammed the bolt, jacking a round into the chamber. He crouched and, holding the rifle in front of him with both hands, faced Hawkins squarely. "It don't matter what I do; they're all against us. This son of a bitch threatened me. Drew on me; you saw it. Well, I ain't taking it no more!" His mouth snarled and his eyes were blazing.

Hawkins was stunned at Carlysle's violent reaction. For a moment he was too amazed to move. Then as Carlysle glared, Hawkins became aware of the pistol in his hand. Neither man moved. Each stood in a tense half-crouch and stared at the other. Then a loud click broke the silence. Hawkins had released the safety of the .45 pistol.

Wilson stood back, watching the showdown in horror. He wasn't sure if Hawkins had raised the pistol to shoot or not, but it was his Lieutenant. Carlysle was wrong, but he was a brother. His eyes went from Carlysle to the Lieutenant. Neither of them was watching him. His mind was screaming for him to act, but he didn't know what to do. Then he heard the click. With two quick silent steps, he flung himself forward and snatched the rifle from Carlysle. He emptied the chamber and turned away, unable to face either of them.

Carlysle said nothing, but Wilson felt the contempt burning into his back.

Hawkins breathed a great silent sigh. He was almost dazed with both relief and disillusionment. Everything had happened too quickly.

"Well, Lieutenant, go on and get it over with. You can skip the speech on my rights to a lawyer. I've heard it enough already."

Hawkins looked at him and confusion flooded his mind. Carlysle was one thing, and Hawkins felt sorry that he had never had a chance with the man . . . but Wilson. Wilson was one of *his men*. He felt numb. "You don't leave me much choice, do you, Carlysle?" His voice was dry and creaky. Emotions rushed at him from every side. They were all jumbled in his mind, and he could only think of what he would have to tell Calahan. "Well, come on, let's go back to the area." He looked down. "Get up, Sedgewick."

Calahan

Calahan was livid. He sent the radiomen out and they were alone in the bunker. Only a candle burned. Hawkins stood at semi attention while Calahan paced.

"Who's the one that got himself injured?"

"Sedgewick, sir. He was with the company before but he got medivacked for heat exhaustion."

"Is that the nigger that wanted to go behind my back to see the major?"

Hawkins winced at the word. "Ah, Pfc Sedgewick is the same man that once requested mast, yes, sir."

"That's what I thought." Calahan spat and looked sharply at Hawkins. "I knew then he wasn't any good. That racist troublemaker was with him, too, wasn't he?"

"Sir, I don't. . . ."

"Was it Carlysle or was it not?" Calahan snarled.

Hawkins stiffened. "Yes, sir, Carlysle was there."

"Don't try to fool me, Lieutenant. I know niggers. That's just what a nigger will do. Most of them ain't worth a shit! They're lazy and they're cowards. They'll do anything to get out of their duty. Particularly to get out of the bush."

"Captain Calahan, I don't think it's reasonable to judge them all by one; every man is different."

Calahan's eyes bugged out and he jabbed a finger at Hawkins. Abruptly he spun around and went to his pack, picked up his lighter, and began thumping it into his palm. "All right, Hawkins, so you think niggers are good? You think they make good fighting Marines?"

Hawkins held to his silence. It was senseless to answer a question like that.

"Well, let me tell you something, Lieutenant. Who do you think are always the first ones to try and get out of work and particularly to get out of the bush."

"I haven't noticed any difference, sir."

"Then you're blind, Lieutenant. Blind." The lighter thumping increased. "The next time we go to the rear, you just go to visit the doctor and you ask him who's always trying to fake something. For that matter, you ask *any* doctor in all of Vietnam. When a company is about to go on an operation—or go anywhere dangerous—the aid station is lined up with niggers. All of them are trying to get out of going to the bush, and ninety-nine percent of them are faking."

"I don't believe that, Captain." Hawkins felt himself hating the Captain. Of course, he had heard this same thing dozens of times, but that didn't make it a fact.

"Well then, Lieutenant, you just *ask* any doctor who has treated niggers in Vietnam and see what he says. Just ask."

"Yes, sir," Hawkins said tersely. There was no point in arguing with that sort of thing.

Calahan glared a moment, then sat down. "All right, now tell me exactly what happened."

"I've told you what I saw, Captain. They didn't say anything."

"They said nothing?"

"No, sir. I gave them an Article Thirty-one warning. In a case like this, it was obvious the first thing I had to do was warn them of their right to keep silent and have a lawyer and all that."

"You . . ." Calahan started to speak and cut himself off, fuming.

"Captain, you know as well as I do that in a case like this one, I *had* to immediately give them a full and complete warning. Even if it was an air-tight case, if I hadn't warned them, any court in the Marine Corps would have thrown it out. And if they didn't, an appellate court would have."

"Yeah, you're right about that." Calahan stopped his thumping and looked abjectly at the floor. Slowly he shook his head.

"This sure ain't the Old Corps." A wistful smile crossed his face. "Is it?"

"Ah . . ." Hawkins was visibly startled. "I guess not, sir."

"All right, Chris, you will immediately begin an investigation of this. See if you can get a statement from the injured man before he goes back to the hospital." He paused with the lighter in midair and looked up sharply at Hawkins. "And let me tell you . . ." He held the lighter in his fingers, jabbing it toward Hawkins. "The findings and conclusions had *better be* that it was a self-inflicted injury and that it was done in collaboration with the other man. And you *will* recommend that they be court-martialed for malingering."

"Sir, what about the other man? Corporal Wilson?" Hawkins' voice shook.

"Well, was he there? Was he involved?"

"He was *there*," Hawkins said uncertainly.

Calahan looked away and stroked his chin. "Well, see what you find, but in his case there are extenuating circumstances in the past. He's a good Marine."

"But, sir . . . what do I . . . what do I *do* about. . . ." His voice faltered and trailed off.

Calahan saw Hawkins' face and sensed his dilemma. "Chris, he *is* a good Marine, isn't he?"

"Yes, sir. The best."

"Well, you wouldn't want to lose him, would you?"

"No!" Hawkins almost shouted.

"Then from what I have gathered so far, your investigation will clear him."

"But. . . ."

Calahan saw the indecision, and his voice softened as he lit a cigarette. "Look, Chris, sit down a minute and let me tell you a few things." He held out the pack.

"All right, sir." Hawkins sat on an ammo box and reached for the cigarette. "Thanks."

"You are a good officer; you've become a particularly good combat officer; but you have a lot to learn about the Corps. Now, let's look at this business. These men were away from their platoon and committed a serious offense, all of which could reflect strongly on you as their platoon commander as well as on myself as their company commander. We could easily be relieved for such a thing."

Hawkins flinched inwardly, and Calahan sensed that it had not occurred to the Lieutenant.

"A man has been injured, so a report will have to go up; some action will have to be taken. In other words, somebody has to pay. Quite frankly, I don't feel like being relieved. And you are a good officer, so I don't want to lose you. But as their immediate superior, you will probably be blamed. If you stick up for them, then you are involving yourself. Your leadership will be called into question. However, if the investigation shows that this was a deliberate act of one or two individuals, acting on their own, with specific intent to malinger, then that's a different matter. These men are known as bad apples. If you investigate, find them individually responsible, and recommend punishment, then you are acting as a proper commander would when one of his men transgresses the law. Understand?"

"Yes, sir," Hawkins said slowly. Yeah, I understand, he thought. Shit flows downhill.

"To put it in a different sense"—Calahan began thumping again—"whatever happens in a unit is the commander's responsibility. By checking the lines more thoroughly tonight, or having your platoon sergeant check, by knowing where your men are at all times, you might have prevented this."

Hawkins was annoyed but realized the Captain was right.

"Also," Calahan went on, "I think it was the same with that man who drowned way back when you first came. I felt that had you been more careful, kept a tighter control on your men, it might not have happened—but, anyway, we got out of that one."

Sitting silently, Hawkins began slowly to shred his burning cigarette.

"Furthermore"—Calahan's voice dropped and he poised the lighter—"by such an investigation and recommendation, you will rid your platoon of two individuals who will do it nothing but harm."

"And Wilson is cleared?"

Calahan shrugged. "Shouldn't he be?"

Hawkins

It was midnight by the time Carlysle came over to Hawkins' hooch, and the moon lit the area clearly. Hawkins had thought about Carlysle and Wilson, yet he still had resolved nothing in his mind. He motioned for Joseley to move off. Sitting on the ground, he and Carlysle looked at each other in silence, and Hawkins felt the hard defiance. "Carlysle, I'd like to help you out, but I can only push things so far."

"Yeah, that's what they all say, Lieutenant. 'I'd like to help you—but.' " His words were calm, with obvious hatred.

Hawkins frowned and knew he'd have to go lightly. "All right then. What would you do if you were me?"

If Carlysle was surprised, he didn't show it. He sat for a long minute wondering what the officer wanted him to say. "Lieutenant, you want a statement out of me? Wilson and some of them say you listen to the brothers. I don't buy no white man's act, but I'll tell you something." He wondered how much he could say before the Lieutenant cut him off. "You know why I'm in the Corps, Lieutenant? Cuz the judge said join or jail. Oh, he don't come right out and say it, but it was made real plain, believe me. And I was a fool—I went along with it. I been in the bush, Lieutenant; I been in d'Nam a year. I had one court-martial, served a month in the brig. Right now I'm doing bad time.

"Before that, I done my share of the fighting. I walked point. My squad leader was killed, so I got to be squad leader. Then one day a buddy of mine gets killed and I got to go to the rear to make a report. Identify the body. Well, baby, that's when it all started. But that don't matter, I still went back to the bush. I was in Operation Ford and Operation Auburn. I got two Purple Hearts. They *have* to give me those medals, Lieutenant, because there is a record of the wound.

"During Ford half the platoon got zapped, and I was the platoon sergeant. So I'm in the hospital; in the rear cuz I'm wounded. Do you think I get promoted? Shit no, I'm a 'troublemaker,' so I don't get no rank. So then I got to go back to the bush. You think by that time I might be squad or even a fire-team leader. *Hell* no! What am I doing? Walking point. Well, that's when I started to get wise. So the first thing I done was get sick. Then the shit began again. You know why I'm here now? Because they had me up for another court-martial for insolence. For *insolence!* Ain't that some shit? Then all of a sudden they don't want to court-martial me; they just want to break me. They want me to cry and grovel at their feet and be a 'good Marine.' And they want me to go back to the bush.

"So the colonel say: if *I* volunteer to go back to the bush, they will forget about the charges. Goddamn, Lieutenant, what kind of a law is that? Either I did the charge or I didn't do it. Who is he? Some kind of God to dismiss the whole case depending on how I kiss his ass? To me that says if they can forget about my case, they can just as well *not* forget about it, and they can just as well hang me. That's no fair trial. That's just them doing whatever they want to do. Oh, yes. The Great White Lords on High. What would I have gotten, maybe three or four months in the brig? Brig, okay. But I still would have been in Nam. And when I got out of the brig, I'd still be here. Still walking point. None of that brig time would count against my thirteen months' tour. I'll be doin' bad time. Who made up that rule, I ask you? Do the people in the world know about that? When I get out, I'd have to go right back out into the bush. So now they say all I got to do is volunteer for the bush, and they're gonna let me out of all that. Yeah, they got you by the balls. There's nothing you can do."

He leaned forward and the moonlight made his bony face even harder. "Well, I took the deal, Lieutenant, 'cause I was chicken. I gave in to them. I let them beat me down. Well, now I'm tired of givin' in. They beat me down over and over. They beat you down all kinds of ways. The black man ain't got no chance. Well, today I made up my mind. No more am I going to give in. I ain't gonna make no statement and I ain't gonna stay in d'bush. I'm through cooperating and getting shit on." He stopped and looked plainly at the Lieutenant.

But Hawkins kept his voice neutral. "I asked you before what you thought I should do."

"Ain't much you can do, Lieutenant, 'cept not make no investigation, and maybe send me to the rear."

The savageness of the thin man's words seemed to pass. "I done my time. It's my *right* to be in the rear. It's my right to go home. But you ain't got the authority to do either one of those on your own."

Hawkins took out a cigarette and tossed the packet to Carlysle. As the match lit Hawkins' face, Carlysle felt a strange desire to communicate with the officer. He was striving to use the preferred dialect, as many ghetto blacks did when speaking to nonhostile white authority. It was strained and unnatural, and interspersed with his own tongue; but the words began to tumble out in disarray as the pent-up emotions rushed to be expressed.

"Every time the brothers get together, they say we're plotting. Everywhere you go, the black man is second class. Even in d'Nam we're second class. Well, we're tired of it, and I'm going to *do* something about it.

"You say there's no prejudice in d'Nam. Well, shit. Just look who's got all the good jobs. Who's in the rear areas? Lieutenant, there ain't one black ass in H 'n' S Company. There ain't one black ass in battalion supply. You ever hear of a top sergeant pickin' a black man for a clerk? Hell, no, we're out where we get killed. Who's the one that walks point all the time? I heard you had a brother on point his first day in the bush and he got killed."

Hawkins remembered Banks and felt a stir of resentment, but he kept quiet.

"Okay, back in the world they say nonviolence. They say, no, you can't go there, that's private property. They say it's gonna take time. Well, how long's it going to take? How long we gotta wait? We done waited long enough. Now we're going to be strong. We're gonna riot; we're gonna burn. We're gonna have power."

"You think violence is the way?" The Lieutenant made his voice neutral, without condemning or accusing.

"It's the only way for us. Look, Lieutenant, back in the

world the beast don't give us nothing but violence. Everytime we do something, there's the heat, the fuzz, the pigs. They put us in jail. You think the black man's got any rights in the back of a paddy wagon?

"We're tired of being sold out again and again. We marched and we picketed and where do we get? Nowhere. We're still the same poor, segregated, shitty black man. Well, the white man owes us something and we're gonna have it. The white race has got to *atone* for what they did to the black.

"You hear all this shit about the Constitution, about black capitalism, about when we're going to get some decent homes, about when we're going to be equal. All that never comes. We just hear words, words, words. But we never get any action. I know. I live in what *you* call a ghetto, Lieutenant, the black people have got to have a guarantee; they got to have a guarantee from the white man that we're gonna have our rights."

"You telling me that the white man owes this to you? That he's got to give you these things?" For the first time Hawkins' voice rose, showing emotion.

"Lieutenant, the black man has been a slave for four hundred years. But the Constitution says that all men are created equal. That they are equal. Well, the white man runs this country and he runs the Constitution. If that's what the Constitution says, when is the white man going to give us our equality?"

For a moment a cloud covered the moon, and they stared at each other in a void, only their butts glowing and lighting their faces periodically. Finally, the moon broke out and Hawkins spoke, slowly at first, as if sorting his thoughts like bullets.

"Okay, Carlysle. You talked. I listened. Now let me talk and you listen. I ask you *why*. Why do you think the white man owes you anything? Why do you think he's ever going to *give* you anything? You say the whites have got to atone. Why? Maybe my great-grandfather had a plantation full of slaves. Does that mean I got to atone to you? Maybe your great-grandfather was a slave. Does that mean you got to be a slave to me? You hear about promises and no action. Well, I hear about *demands* and no action. No taking. The blacks demand their rights. They demand better houses. They demand more jobs. The

Muslims even demand a whole state. Well, you're right in that you have to *do* something. You've got to take action. You, I mean the black people. I agree you're poor, you're oppressed, you're denied the right to a decent life. But what is your answer? What are you—you black people—the ones being denied all this, going to *do* about it? You've been frustrated so long, now you think cheap violence is the only way. You want to rise up and smash what's holding you down, what's sucking your lifeblood. Well, I say do it. Go rise up and take what you want. If you don't, you'll never be free, and you'll always be the ball-less Uncle Toms you've always been. If you want your rights, you've got to take 'em. No man's never goin' to give 'em to you."

Hawkins was looking him straight in the eye, and he saw Carlysle's jaw tighten and twist.

"Go on," Carlysle said through clenched teeth, "how're we goin' do what you're saying?"

Hawkins slowed, his manner more calm now that he had seen Carlysle would listen. He spoke again, slowly, urgently, hoping that he would say the right thing.

"Before you decide how you are going to do all this, you gotta decide *what* you're gonna do. And if I hadn't come to the Nam, I would never even have thought there was any question about what you wanted. But I came to the Nam and I lived with the brothers like Wilson and Big John. And from the talk I hear there's at least three different goals that the blacks want. Some want to be equal with whites and coexist together in an equally shared America. But there are some who say that that will never work. Some want a separate black state. Elijah Muhammad of the Black Muslims demands a separate state for blacks. And there are some blacks . . ." His voice lowered and he looked directly at Carlysle. "There are some blacks who want to *rule over*. You don't find that in the newspapers, but there are brothers that want to be masters of the whites." Hawkins paused, but Carlysle didn't flicker an eyelash.

"The first thing you gotta do is make a choice. Which one of those goals do you want; to make that choice you're gonna need more than balls. You're gonna need brains." He flipped his cigarette into the dark.

"You want to rule over? Most men want to rule over whether they admit it or not. To be an officer in the government in those new black nations in Africa, you've got to have a white servant. You know, one where they can clap their hands and say 'Boy' and the white servant comes running. It costs them a fortune to be able to hire people like that, but to be anybody in Black Africa you've got to have it. But in America it'll never happen. It doesn't take much brain to see that the white man is just too strong. You might force him to share with you, but you'll never rule over him; it's just a fact of life. I know Cleaver and those dudes say the yellow world will unite with the blacks, and the white power of the U.S.A. and Russia are on their last legs, and the colored peoples of the world are gonna rule. But that's just a crock of shit. The yellow man doesn't like the black man. If you've been in the rear areas long enough, you ought to know enough Vietnamese to realize that. Haven't you ever found that the whore prices are higher for a black man, that black dudes can't ever get it from some girls?

"So how about the second choice—a separate state. This country tried that over a hundred years ago and the result was the most bloody war in the history of the world. And the South of 1860 was a thousand times stronger and more united than the black people in the U.S. are today.

"Or maybe you want a separate place somewhere in Africa, like Israel. Then you can all go over there and live. If you did that, you'd be poorer than you are now. No, that choice just isn't realistic either; but, as I say, you have to have brains to make that decision. Maybe you ain't got 'em."

"Yeah? You ain't said nothing yet, Lieutenant. The question is how are we gonna get this? You said yourself that the whites ain't never gonna *give* it to us."

"That's right, Carlysle, that's abso-fucking-lutely right. You've gotta *take* it. You can't just demand; you've gotta take or you'll never get it. Just like the Jews and the Italians and the Irish all took their rights."

"Now you're saying something, Lieutenant; only we're gonna have to take with guns and blood or we'll never get it."

"And I say you're a fool if you think that." Hawkins paused and lit another cigarette, but Carlysle said nothing. "Violence is only going to end with your being hunted down and shot in the streets. Do you honestly think the white man, who is a thousand times stronger than you're ever gonna be, is going to share what he has with you if you shoot at him and try to kill him? He'll kill you just as surely as he did ninety years ago after Reconstruction. Look what's happened to the Panthers. Your only way is to work from within the system; and it will take brains to do that. And it takes a real man to use his brains when his balls say different. Your way is to die."

Hawkins stopped and stared straight at Carlysle.

"Well, Lieutenant, I'll die while my brothers unite. Let's just say I'm the point man."

The analogy disturbed Hawkins and he shifted his eyes; but he was still caught in his rush of thought. "I'll tell you who your really powerful leaders are. They're men like Julian Bond, Carl Stokes, Thurgood Marshall, and Mayor Washington. Because they know how to fight. Where are the hotheads like Cleaver, Carmichael, Seale, Williams, and Newton—they are either dead, broken, exiled, or in jail. Why? Because the superior force of the white man broke them. I'm being a *realist*, and you'll answer by saying you're never gonna be an Uncle Tom. You're tired of kissing ass, and you want to be a man. Well, I say, look at Bond. He is the strongest among you. He alone really knows how to fight. But he works with the whites. He's not for armed violence, and he's a man.

"I'll agree it's better to die a man than live a slave. But it takes a man to know when to use his brains. I say it's better to fight with your head than with your ass. Bond is no puppet. Stokes is no Uncle Tom. They are their own men. They go along with the whites sometimes to help the final cause. But that doesn't castrate them. That's being realistic. Black power—hell, yes, I'm for black power. Black economic, educational, and political power. And even love power. That kind of power can work. Violence power—never. At the end of the violence you'll be gunned down in the street. You'll die in a pool of blood on the pavement, and the blood will flow down the gutter."

The two men stared at each other, both having said their fill yet solving nothing. Finally the clouds passed over the moon, and in the dark Carlysle got up. He turned to go, then spoke over his shoulder: "You're fulla shit, Lieutenant." And he walked away.

IX

A-Shaw Valley

1

Hawkins

He awoke, blinked at the light, and snuggled back into the warm security of the poncho-liner. The rubber lady had just enough air left to fold up around him like a little nest. His head pillowed on the flak jacket; he drifted sensuously. Army flak jackets sure make better pillows than the hard old Marine ones.

Then it came back to him with a cold thud in his stomach: Wilson, Carlysle, Sedgewick, Investigation, Court-martial. Aw shit. The remembrance crushed the lazy half-dream. He flipped the liner back and began methodically stuffing his feet into the boots. The thought of what he had to do to his own men sat on his back like a grain sack. But the CP group was bright and chipper.

"Mawnin, Lieu-ten-nant," Doc Smitty drawled, puffing on one of his wooden-tipped Tampa Nuggetts.

"Good morning, sir." Joseley said, looking up from the *Reader's Digest.*

He grunted at them, but the morning was sunny and clear and he had to smile. The men were sitting around shirtless: biceps, triceps, and tattoos all out for breakfast. Only the Chief was still asleep. He would wait until the last minute, then roll out, adjust his hat, and step off as if he'd been up for an hour.

Hawkins snuffled around and found his blackened cheese-and-crackers-can stove. He used a fruit can for a coffee cup, lit a heat tab, then fumbled for the flask of bourbon. In minutes, he had his coffee.

"Joseley, you want a sip?"

"Oh, no thank you, sir." Because Joseley always turned it down, he felt safe offering it. Of course, he only had to glance at Smitty.

"Why sure, Lieutenant, ah reckon ah would like some."

—"Delta One, Delta Two, Delta Three, this is Delta Six. Put on your actuals."— Joseley reached for the radio

and flipped the Lieutenant the handset. Joseley and the
Doc hunched forward. It was unusual for the Captain to
call all the platoon commanders on the radio in the morning. The corner of Chief's poncho-liner moved, uncover-
ing an ear.

—"Two here"—Hawkins replied and sat waiting for the
other platoon commanders.

—"One go."—

—"Three here."—

—"Delta One, Two, and Three, this is Six. I have just
received word from battalion there has been heavy contact
to the South. Several outposts have been hit. It may be the
start of a new Tet offensive. Pack up and stand by to
heli-lift out in thirty minutes. Over."—

Hawkins and the men looked at each other, stunned.
New offensive? Another Tet? The Chief just got up, pulled
down the floppy brim without a word, and began to make
his pack.

Hawkins keyed the handset.

—"Delta Six, this is Two. Interrogative, over."—

—"Yes, Two, go ahead."—

—"Did they say where we're going. Over."—

—"A-Shaw Valley. Six out."—

This time even the Chief looked stunned.

"Go-ud-Da-umm! The A-Shaw Valley!"

"Here we go again."

"The A-Shaw Valley."

"Man, that is some baad country."

"Happens every time, catch a little good duty and then
wham."

Everybody rushed frenziedly to pack and clean weapons. The air was charged with the excited, yet deadly serious anticipation that always preceded a fight. Waiting for
combat but away from it always made the men worry.
Later, when the enemy was close, their anxieties were a
different kind.

In the rush, the ugliness of the past night was forgotten.
Investigation, paper work, brig: they would have to wait.
Sedgewick had been medivacked, but Carlysle and Wilson
would have to come along on the op.

The company choppered to an area and landed cold.
The contact zone itself was too hot to land a helicopter.
Some Army unit had made heavy contact and had been

thrown back. The gooks were dug in on several hills, fighting from bunkers, and they weren't running. It looked as though they were going to make a daylight stand, rare anywhere in Vietnam.

Fox Company preceded Delta up the hill. They engaged the enemy in the afternoon and set up on a ridge without taking the main hill. That night they were overrun, and the gooks got inside their lines. Some of Fox Company had been scattered into the jungle. The remainder were hanging on only yards from the gook positions. They were both dug in so close that it was impossible to call in proper air support.

Delta went up after them at first light.

Tension jumped from man to man and squad to squad, as the word was passed with the quiet sinking anticipation that always came before contact. Nobody talked. Even the necessary commands were resented for breaking the silence.

The company moved through the high grass.

"I don't like this, Joseley. There's no cover here; you can't even hide in this grass."

"They can't slip up on us this way, sir."

"Yeah, but they can mortar the hell out of us."

In subconscious response to his own words, the Lieutenant spaced the men farther apart and wondered how long it would take to get their own heavy weapons firing back at the enemy mortar or artillery. Counter-battery fire they called it.

Little rolling hills stretched away to the bigger one where Fox had been smashed. Two larger ones rose around it. They were trapped. The gooks had picked a good spot; it was going to be hard to get air support in there, and even arty wouldn't be much good. The low grass bothered Hawkins; he felt exposed.

The company had been moving less than an hour when a solitary shot split the morning air. *BNOWP.* The men crouched and whirled automatically all along the line, bolts cocked and slammed home. "Sniper. Face outboard! Sanders put a fire team out the left flank," the Lieutenant yelled.

The column halted of itself. The shot had come from the right flank behind the Second Platoon. Hawkins could hear the First Platoon putting out Bloop rounds in the direction of the sniper; he beckoned to Joseley.

"What's going on?"

Joseley slithered over onto his knees, his face pale and white-lipped. Nobody was more cautious than Joseley. He always looked scared, but he would go anywhere. "Nothing yet."

"That's odd. Captain is usually on the hook right away." They squatted on the ground and stared at each other, waiting for some word. The whole company was on the same net, and the quickest way to find out what was going on was just to listen. The firing slackened. There was no more incoming.

—"Two, Two, this is Delta!"—

It was the Captain's radioman; his voice was tight and worried. Joseley held up the handset so they could both hear.

—"This is Two. Go."—

—"The Six has been hit. You'd better tell your actual to come down here right away."—

Hawkins' eyes met Joseley's. So many times they had joked about this call. Now nothing was spoken, Joseley's eyes said it all. Suddenly Hawkins knew he was holding the reins; he would step alone into the little circle of radiomen, and a hundred and fifty Marines and their wives and mothers would be trusting in him. But for a final fleeting second, he lingered. His hand went out and touched Joseley's shoulder.

—"Delta Two, Delta Two, this is Delta, do you read me?"—The radio crackled insistently.

—"This is Two actual, I'll be right there."— He stood and barked at Joseley: "Go find Chief; he's got the show till I come back."

"Yes, sir." He started to go, then took one final look back. "Good luck, Mr. Hawkins."

The Lieutenant turned and, without speaking, strode through the column without looking right or left but aware of the respectful stares of the men.

Hawkins found himself thinking that unhappily it was probably just a nick. He came to the company CP portion of the line and found a hovering cluster. He pushed into the circle, dropping his pack. One glance was enough. The head corpsman had cut the shirt away and was trying to stop the blood from pouring out of Calahan's shoulder.

"How's he going to be, Doc?" Hawkins boomed it out, jarring the whole bunch.

The Navy corpsman ignored the voice for an instant, then realization spread to him and he looked up with new deference. Professionally and confidently he gave the information, his allegiance instantaneously transferred. "No emergency, but we should get him out before too long. He could probably walk a little if he had to, but it's better if he doesn't. He's groggy now because I gave him morphine. The bullet entered the back of his shoulder bone and came out in front of his delt. Smashed his clavicle but didn't pierce the lung. I don't think an artery's been cut, but the bone ends could sever one if he moves."

Lieutenant Christopher Hawkins glanced across the prostrate body and looked into the hard eyes of the Gunny.

The Gunny's stare wasn't quite hatred but more a look of: "Those bars may make you *it* on paper, but I'm really going to run the show." For a long minute, Hawkins eyed the grizzled, hardened face. Deep sun wrinkles creased the skin around the eyes and a touch of gray flecked the hair above his ears, which was exactly the same length as the stubble of his chin. It made the Gunny look like an old man. An old man of thirty-four. Marine Corps old, but tough. He had the hunched shoulders of an old man, formed through years of standing at attention without straightening his body. He started to speak, and Hawkins knew it had to be now. This was his first battle for the company; later would be a thousand times worse. He had learned that from LeBlanc. The Gunny's words seemed to rush at him, and he felt the panic rising.

"Well, Lieu . . ."

"Gunny! Get this fuckin' mob unbunched!" Hawkins' voice thundered and he paused just an instant. But before the Gunny could recover, he plunged on. "Call a medevac and get me an estimate on how long it will take. And hurry the hell up!" Abruptly, he turned and went toward the radioman without waiting for an answer.

It was an act, a bluff, but it had to work. He pretended to be busy with his notebook before calling battalion. He could feel the eyes burning into his back. Slowly, deliberately, Hawkins unslung his shotgun, hoping the Gunny was with him. The stock seemed to creak in the silence, and then the words came. The big raspy bullfrog voice blasted over him like a Mac truck: "All right, God damn it, spread the fuck out. Get your fucking ass out there and provide some fucking security. Didn't you maggots hear your company commander? Goddamn it, *move,* you sons of bitches."

Hawkins' whole insides smiled, and he fought to keep the grin from showing on his face. He knew Joseley would be smiling, too. The confidence spread through him like brandy on a cold day. He could do anything. *He could even forget about the investigation.* He turned to the radioman and said softly, "Get me battalion."

"I want you to roll your tanks up on that little knoll and fire upon the main hill there."

Hawkins wondered if the Colonel would have sent out another company commander if he had had the chance. He had been told to connect up with some tankers and somehow two tanks ploughed to within less than a mile of the main hill before the sergeant in charge became too scared to go on.

"We'll be pretty damn exposed, Lieutenant."

"That's all right, just move up on that knoll and keep a slow steady fire on the main hilltop. We're going to be moving out under your fire, and no gooks are gonna come up on you."

"*What?* You can't move out while we fire."

"Why not? A tank is the most accurate weapon there is. You're not going to hit us, and we won't be anywhere near the muzzle-blast."

"But it's against regulations to fire with friendly troops in front." His face had a queasy look.

"How long you been incountry, Sergeant?" Hawkins asked him coldly.

"Two weeks."

"Where's your lieutenant?"

"He took the other tanks up the LZ; they wanted more protection there."

"Then you're in charge of these two?"

"Yes, sir."

"In that case, Sergeant, you're working for me. And right now you *will* fire a slow steady fire at that hill. Starting right now!"

"But, sir."

Again Hawkins unslung the shotgun with exaggerated slowness and held it ready but not quite pointing at him. "Listen, Marine, the next thing you say, you're gonna be a fucking private. Start firing! That's a direct order."

The Third Platoon had been on point, and right off they balked. Their commander, Staff Sergeant Allen, got on the radio and said the troops didn't want to move out under the tank fire. Hawkins swore to himself and felt the indecision. He wasn't sure of the company yet, but he was sure of the Second Platoon. He called the Chief and told him to get on point. Then he went up and got as many as he could into a group and began talking. "Look, you all know as well as I do that when you're in a foxhole or a trench and the incoming rounds are pouring in you're not going to get up and run around. What are you going to do? Look around and watch? Sit up and fire? No. You keep your nose buried in the dirt because the shrapnel is up on top and you don't want to get blown away. Well, that's exactly what I want. I want to keep the gooks in their holes. They got bunkers up there, and I want them to stay down in them until we can get right up on top of them. As long as they're rooting, they're not going to be up shooting at us. Now, we know where the tank is firing; the rounds are way over our heads. A tank is extremely accurate and we'll be well below and out of the line of fire. The idea is to keep the gooks down so they can't have a turkey shoot on us while we advance through the low grass."

He stopped and wondered how many understood him. They were young, really just kids, dirty and scared.

"As long as you're with us, sir, we'll go." It was Sail. His voice was slow, almost spelling each word. "We'll go to Hanoi with you, sir." The rest nodded with incredible intensity. The resolution in their eyes was cold granite. Hawkins glanced at Joseley and a secret smile went between them.

The Lieutenant stood tall and the pride was ringing in his ears, only his voice was a little thick. "Move 'em out, Chief."

The Lieutenant picked up his pack and the entourage of radiomen fell in with him. One for battalion net, one for the company net, and one for the arty and mortar net.

With all the antennas sticking up, they looked like a walking radio shack. No wonder the sniper got the Captain.

Hawkins took one step, dropped his pack and reached for the air mattress and the extra chow. If he was going to run the company, he had to be light—even the rubber lady.

"Do you want this?" He motioned to the radioman.

"No, sir, we all got rubber ladies." Hawkins looked up at him in disbelief, and it must have shown on his face because the kid stammered out, "We got them at the Rockpile, sir. When the company CP stayed in the battalion headquarters' area."

Hawkins shook his head. By this time he should have learned. The company CP men were better off than the platoon men. Even in the bush, the lowest snuffy gets the bad end of the stick. The higher up you are, the better off you are.

He tossed the rubber lady along the trail; somebody would want it. He had to be light. He had to think, and he knew he couldn't get tired. He was *it* now.

They humped through the grass, a long green snake, going up and down over the rises, the tank rounds swishing steadily above them. For a few minutes the hill would be in sight, then hidden. He called for the big 81-mm mortars on the backside of the hill. Even if those rounds didn't kill a single gook, they would make some people duck. Hawkins began to squint, though it wasn't a bright day. His mind was racing over all the thousand things he should do. It kept coming to Hawkins that someone on that hill was watching him, and when he could see the top of the hill, he got the feeling that whoever was in charge there was thinking, too.

Hawkins wiped his sunglasses. Fox was still trapped; one platoon had been completely overrun; the rest had retreated to a knoll at one end. But the gooks had continued their attack into the daylight. That meant that they were awfully strong, or else it was a decoy attack. Gooks didn't stay long in one area when you could get at them.

Hawkins requested air strikes on the gook end.

The Colonel denied the air. Hawkins wondered why, thinking he should have asked the reason right on the air. He knew he had to keep pressure on the hill. His whole mind focused on the coming fight, and his past fights—

and mistakes—were burning guideposts. Everything he had learned seemed to pour forth, and he realized what he would need just before the attack. Napalm.

"Delta Two calling, sir." The radioman said formally. Hawkins took the handset.—"Yeah, Chief."—

The company radioman looked shocked. Hawkins gave him a big grin. He had never believed in the radio code anyway. Six for captain, One, Two, Three, for platoon commander. Blue line for river, brown line for road. Always give the call sign. Never say proper names or slang. It's supposed to fool the enemy. The book says if you use slang or real names the enemy could intercept and send a false transmission by imitating your voice. Ridiculous, Hawkins thought. All it does is limit your vocabulary and make it easier for the enemy to learn.

The Lieutenant was answered by a chuckle. Chief felt the same way. —"We got a couple of dudes from Fox up here. Scared shitless, can't hardly talk. Must be part of the platoon that got overrun."—

—"Send 'em back."—

—"Comin' to ya . . . *Skipper*."—

It took about five minutes before they reached the Lieutenant. He'd never seen humans so afraid and relieved at the same time. They stumbled along and sat down wearily. They had on boots, trousers, and T-shirts. One had an M-16, the other an M-14. Nothing else. No ammo, no helmets, no canteens, no packs, nothing.

"You from Fox Company?"

"Yeah." The voice was a whisper and Hawkins had to strain to hear.

"The gooks run you off the hill?"

"Yeah."

Physically they seemed okay, although they looked odd with no equipment. But their eyes were unfocused and had no relation to their faces. It was as if their eyes weren't even there and one could peer into their heads; only inside the heads was all black.

"Did you come down off the hill in the night?" The man didn't speak, just nodded, and he kept looking about in a dreamy fog.

"How did you find your way?"

"Last night we just ran and hid till morning. Then we

started toward the road. When we heard the tanks, we moved toward them."

Having reached safety, one seemed to collapse, as if his last strength had been expended. The other spoke weakly as if it tortured him to talk. "It was awful; they were in on us before we knew it. They jumped right in on the hole next to us, with satchel charges . . . and . . . and . . . killed the guys in that hole . . . I . . . I looked, right over there at 'em. Then all of a sudden they seemed to come from everywhere. They rushed up from the side. I thought one even came from the back of me."

"Was yours the first hole to be hit?"

"I don't know. Just all of a sudden they were there." The man shook his head pitifully.

"Didn't you have any warning? Surely someone in the company must have heard them?"

He looked down and hesitated, then became more remote. "I don't know, sir. They just came. One minute nothing, then—*whoom*."

Lieutenant Hawkins couldn't believe what he was hearing. Obviously these two must have been asleep, but the whole company couldn't have been so unalert that no one gave any warning. Yet what else would account for their lack of gear. With just a mere shout, they could wake up and put on their helmets. Hawkins looked up to the mountaintop. Either someone in Fox had screwed up or these gooks were really good.

The two men gave Hawkins a better idea of where the gooks were in relation to Fox Company, and he decided to ask for the napalm. The Colonel raged. Why did he keep asking for all these different types of support? Didn't he have tanks and arty firing? At first Hawkins thought the Colonel must be crazy, then he remembered that Calahan was almost the same way. What the hell—did they want them to take the position with C-ration openers? Only much later did he learn that the Colonel was asking for everything; it just wasn't available. But he got the napalm.

Hawkins called the Chief and told him to get the air panels out. The large colored handkerchiefs of iridescent red, yellow, and orange would mark their position. They were on the same hill as the gooks now, but the closer the air support the better. The gooks would have less time to recover.

—"Chief."— He spoke into the handset.—"Make them stick the panels on their helmets, particularly the point fire team. They are going to lay napalm as we go up the hill. The pilots *have got* to see these panels, so they know where we are. You've got to keep 'em calm and for God's sake, make them put their heads down when the bombs fall. Don't let them look at the bombs. We will be too close. Six out."—He remembered Banks' Hill.

They crouched down and pressed against the dirt. Assault, hill, bunkers—the words filtered dimly to Hawkins. This was it. He found himself wondering how the pilots could see a colored handkerchief at 600 mph. The airplanes would be their last support; then they would be on their own.

The planes came over and the oblong tubes dropped end over end, struck and erupted. The bright red balls burst out and turned orange, spreading over the hillside. Then a huge cloud of curling black smoke rose up.

"Now! Up the hill. Move out." The top looked like a California forest fire. The curling black gasoline smoke was gone, but everything was burning and smoldering. They climbed, pulled, and strained up—up into the inferno. Ten minutes later the AO, the aerial observer, called. One of the multiple radiomen handed the Lieutenant a handset, pointing up to the little single-engine spotter-plane circling overhead to direct the jets. "Call sign is 'Red Dog,' sir," he panted. The Lieutenant took the handset but didn't stop moving. The two-seater plane seemed to drop right into the valley between the hills.

—"Red Dog, Red Dog, this is Northtide Delta Six. Over."—

—"Hey, Skipper! The gooks ran off the hill when they saw the planes; now they are coming back. Over."—

—"Red Dog. How many? Over."—Hawkins was startled to learn the fly-boys cared nothing for radio procedure either.

—"Christ, can't tell; they're swarming out of the trees on the backside of the hill from you. They're coming up like mad. Over."— Hawkins dropped the handset and reached for the company net. God, what a conglomeration of radios. —"Delta Two, Delta Two, put the Chief on."—

—"Go Six"— The reply was instantaneous. The Chief must have Joseley glued to his back!

—"The gooks are coming up the backside in force. We gotta get on top before they do. Over."—

—"Right on—we'll make it"—

—"Move out. Let's go. *Get* up that hill. We've *got* to get up that hill. Go."—

From the top, he could hear sporadic rifle shots and the crackling of the napalm fire. Behind, he heard the Gunny and LeBlanc lashing out at the other platoons, driving the men up. Then from up near the point came a series of wild shrieking yells—*aiee hoo woo, aiee hoo woo.*

They rose and fell in pitch, like a chant, electrifying the men into a determined frenzy. They threw themselves into the hill. A couple of the radiomen turned and looked at Hawkins with astonished faces.

"Apache war cries." He shrugged and grinned through the sweat.

He had used every supporting weapon and every tactic he knew, and it still came down to the infantry slugging it out; he hoped it wouldn't come to bayonets. If the gook reinforcements got up the hill first, they could roll over Fox and fire down point-blank.

Push on, push on. Think. Again and again Hawkins seemed to sense the gook commander. He could almost feel their private wrestle; then in a flash he saw it clearly. *The AO had said that more gooks were going up the hill than had run down. The little gook bastard knew we'd call in air, right on the top where his people had been seen. Then when we got up so close that our planes couldn't bomb, he'd rush the rest of his forces out of hiding. The planes probably couldn't hit them in that little gully any-way.* Then Hawkins remembered the 81-mm mortars, and the fight that it took to target them on the other side of the hill. *Ha. Right where the gooks had been coming from. If only the mortars delayed them just long enough for us to beat them to the top.*

He racked his brains. And for a fleeting instant he knew—*if we had Army Huey gunships, we could pin the gooks down when they are exposed coming up the back-side of the hill. A daylight break, the perfect setup for*

*chopper gunships. Well, forget it, Marine. You ain't got
'em—next war maybe.*

The Gunny's bullfrog voice cut through his thoughts,
but it wasn't mean and pushy now. It was coaxing, urging,
driving. Go. Go. Go.

Sweat was pouring out. Hawkins' lungs and legs ached,
and the men were all carrying more weight than he. Halfway up, he decided to drop packs and keep just the fighting gear. It was rough; elephant grass and jungle made it
all the harder. What could he say to them?

Threats, curses, and promises can't drive a man beyond
a certain point. Only the man himself can push beyond
that point—but the men knew. And they climbed. It was
one of those rare times when men transcended being men.

Go, go, go, climb, climb. Keep on pushing.

They boiled over the top, screaming confusion. The firing started. The gooks were still in the bunkers. The men
were diving into holes and scattering in chaos. He got
down in a crater and tried to think. Panic was rising. Fox
was gone, huddled on a knob on the far end, exhausted
physically, mentally, and militarily. Delta had the job
alone. The temptation to freeze up was enormous, but the
other fights came back to him as screaming lessons.

He pulled the radiomen in tight around him.

—"Gunny, take one mortar team and the Third Platoon, move past Fox Company, and clear the ridge in that
direction."—

—"LeBlanc, spread your platoon as flank security between Third and Second Platoon. Keep connection solid.
Make sure no gooks get between the units."—

—"Chief, we're going down the main section of the
ridge."—

Keep calm. Keep calm. The hill had a long narrow
ridge on top. Hawkins headed Second Platoon in that direction. That would be the hard part. He moved the company CP up behind the Second as the other platoons
strung out. Second hit the first bunker and faltered. He
felt the urge to go to the front. No! He was company
commander; his job was to direct and coordinate. But
visual control of Second Platoon was critical. He took the
radio and put it on his own back. It was too slow grabbing the handset from the radioman each time. He got
one of the new squad radios that could fit in his hand and

hooked it onto his collar. The shotgun was still slung over his shoulder.

He put two squads across the waist of the hill facing down the crest, the machine guns in the middle of the squads. Wilson's squad was back as flank security in reserve. He kept the First Platoon up tight behind and spread out on both sides of the hill as the Second Platoon swept down on the ridge in wedge formation.

The smoke kept stinging his eyes. He felt a tremendous urge to run away to fresh air. He sensed the monstrous danger and panic nipped at him again.

TaTowTowTowTow—a machine gun opened up. Bullets were flying everywhere.

Hawkins and Chief began to yank, pull, shove, the men into line.

"Get down, sir, you'll get hit," someone screamed.

"Move your ass over there with the rest of the squad."

"Get the hell over there on line."

Sssssssszzzzzt. Thud.

"CHI-COMS, look out!

WHOOMP.

"They're still in bunkers, get down."

He crawled and tried to maneuver the men with the radio. He was the company commander; maybe he shouldn't be up this far. With conscious effort, he reached under the helmet and rubbed his forehead, then hunched down and spoke, evenly and smoothly into the handset.

—"Sanders, Sanders, move up on the left. Over."—

—"Holton, Holton, come even with Sanders—keep it on line. Over."—

—"Sail, Sail, get those machine guns moving. Over."—

"They're not moving on the other side," someone yelled.

"Chief," he was yelling now, "get over and take the right side of the hill. I'll take this side. We'll work the guns together."

Slowly they took shape. The men slithered and crawled, hopped up, ran and slammed back into the ground. A fire team rushed forward, took a new position, and hit the deck. Then the machine guns would cover.

"Now, go. Go. God damn it, move!"

Everything was set. The men were in position; Hawkins knew if he could clear the bunkers before the gook reinforcements got to the top, he would have it made. But the drive stalled.

However much he screamed and yelled and kicked, they just inched along. The new men were petrified with fear. They were stalled, poised ready but stalled. He couldn't push them. They would move an inch, then shrink back. His brain clicked desperately. What does the book say to do now? *What now, Lieutenant?* Sometimes you have got to push and sometimes you have got to pull. Leadership means lead.

"Gimme a frag," he yelled, "Sail, open fire."

TaTowTowTowTow. The M-60 machine guns opened up.

He rose to a half-crouch and pulled the pin. His face contorted, throat bulged. He could feel the veins puffing out in his neck. His lips drew back over the teeth, and his mouth opened in a screaming yell.

"KILLLLL. KILL THE SONS A BITCHES."

Chris Hawkins lunged forward of the line, leaped into the air screaming, and hurled the grenade. He whipped off the shotgun and fired from a half-crouch. A jolt of electricity went into the men; like machines suddenly turned on, they charged. Their voices rolled in wild yells. Madness seized them.

"Kill—kill!"

Aagghhhiii! Crazy screams of no words, just frenzy. Hawkins bit his lip for control. Without direction, he had only a mob. He slung the shotgun back.

—"Sail, Sail, watch my signal to fire. Over."—

—"Sanders, Sanders. First fire team forward. Over."—

Without the call signs and code, the radios were working like clockwork.

Throw a grenade. Hit the deck. FIRE, FIRE, FIRE. Cover for the next team. Move. Run forward. FIRE. Throw a grenade. Hit the deck. FIRE. Keep those machine guns firing. Move forward a little bit at a time. Get Down! Run. Cover. FIRE.

They became frantic in the battle heat, but frantic with precision. It was the Marines on line: High Diddle Diddle Right Up the Middle! Hawkins didn't know how he seemed to know just what to do. Only later would he realize that he had practiced this dozens of times in officers' training school: First, gain fire superiority. Everyone fires a heavy volume until the enemy is forced to stop firing and ducks into his hole to avoid being hit. Second, fire and maneuver. One team opens up and fires to pin the enemy down as a cover for the other team. Then the other fire team rushes forward five to six yards, throws a grenade, and drops to the ground. Then that team fires cover while the first team rushes forward. Fire superiority to pin the enemy, inch forward, and blast with grenades.

Suddenly there was a cry.

"Here come the gooks!"

He peered through the smoke. Little dark men were bobbing and bouncing on the far side of the hill. The reserve force of gooks had made it.

Chief

"Bring the gun up!" Chief yelled.

Baraby didn't move.

"Ah ain't gonna make it, Ah ain't gonna make it." Fear had seized him; his face was pale. He struggled to move, but he was frozen.

"Come on up, the rounds are still over your head," Chief insisted. "Just lay on your stomach and crawl." The Chief inched back and Baraby saw him coming. Slowly then he moved forward on elbows and knees.

"That's right." As Chief turned back to the front, his eye caught a flash of motion: Gooks running up on the far side. Instantly, he spread his legs and braced his knees against the ground, the rifle coming up automatically. He squeezed off about six rounds and glanced back at Baraby. He halted abruptly and looked down. The rifle had seemed to fly out of his hand. His brow wrinkled in question. He turned to look for the rifle, puzzled that it should fly away. He stopped and scratched his head, unconscious of the battle around him. *That's kind of funny because I thought I had a good grip on it,* he said to himself. The rifle lay two feet away, unnoticed.

"Now why did I do that?" he said aloud. A warm wetness running down his back shook his thoughts from the rifle. *What's that? I must be sweating. I never sweat.* He was puzzled; his hand went up to his forehead and wiped

across his cheek down to his neck. His middle finger went
into the deep gash. The blood pumped against his finger,
pushing it out of the trenchlike wound. He jerked his
hand away in disbelief and just as quickly put it back, this
time cupping the palm tightly to the side of his neck. He
felt thick blood gush on his hand, but his mind didn't
comprehend. The blood ran down his forearm. *I'm hit.*
And the realization knocked him back as if the bullet had
just then thumped him down. His helmet rolled off and
the shiny black hair spilled out.

He lay back and his mind swirled into unreality. For a
few moments he lay dazed. He looked straight up at the
sky and everything relaxed inside him. His mind reeled off
to nowhere. He was in a tunnel of sound, but he heard
nothing, saw nothing but the bright sky and one cloud. It
was a fluffy white could, not a very big one. He drifted
into a contented dullness. *Stop the bleeding, stop the
bleeding, stop the bleeding,* heard in a thousand first-aid
lectures, sounded somewhere in the mist. Abruptly his
mind swung back to reality. He checked his neck again.

Yes, I'm hit, stop the bleeding! Now he functioned,
unaware of anything but himself. His left hand clamped
the side of his neck, the fingers gripping the sinewy cords
in back for pressure. His other hand searched, reaching
for the battle dressing in the flak jacket. The jacket was
too big and the hand couldn't reach it. He rolled on his
side, struggling, and finally yanked it out. His teeth ripped
open the brown waxy paper. All the while he kept the
pressure on the wound with his left hand. As he rolled to
get the dressing, the blood ran across his face in rivulets.
He placed the bandage and clumsily tied it under his opposite armpit, then put his hand back on the bandage for
pressure.

Funny, he thought, he didn't feel anything; it didn't
hurt. He gripped his neck and felt himself begin to drift.
Drifting, going down. Suddenly it blasted to him. *I'm
gonna die!*

At the thought, a jolt of tension revived his body.
Maybe he'd faint first. He felt sleepy but no pain, and the
warm dullness came back. Well, if this is dying, he didn't
need to be afraid. There's no pain, it's just like going to
sleep or fainting. If it ain't gonna hurt, why should he be

scared? It's just like going to sleep; only he was losing a lot of blood. It will be just like going to sleep and not waking up.

"Chief's hit!"

"Corpsman!"

The words seemed to come from a great long way off. Yeah, where is the corpsman? he thought. "Corpsman." He half sat up and looked around; nobody came. He wondered slowly why the corpsman wasn't there, then lay down again and thought about dying.

But one man had heard the cry. Wilson ran back, calling and looking frantically. "Chief, Chief." Then his eyes saw the tiny body. He flung himself to the ground, and hovering over the little Indian he saw the blood. "Oh, Chief, Chief, Chief, it's gonna be all right."

Anxiety gripped him and he was on his knees in the dirt, head bent over to hear the soft voice, almost like kneeling to pray. His hands reached down lovingly. "It's all right, Chief, you'll be all right," he cooed. "Let me see the wound." Wilson cradled the head in his lap. The long brown fingers smoothed the hair and delicately touched the cheek. His senses came to him and he whipped out his battle dressing. "Hang on, Chief, hang on. Don't let go. You're gonna make it." And then gently but firmly he raised the Indian's back and slipped the gauze strap under, hitching it up tightly above his neck.

"Tell me when it's too tight."

Chief smiled. "It's okay."

Something made Wilson look up; he seized his rifle and fired a few rounds at the flank. "I've got to get you out of here, Chief." Baraby and another man hovered nearby. "Set up a base of fire into that treeline in the flank," Wilson yelled. "I'll carry you on my back, Chief."

The men started pumping rounds toward the treeline.

"No, I can run."

"No, I'll carry you."

"Yes, I will, I can make it." Even in his weak state, Chief's battle instincts controlled him. He pictured himself perched on Wilson's shoulders. Wilson would have to stand to carry him that way. The Chief had never been that exposed since he'd been in Vietnam. "I've got all this heavy gear on, flak jacket and all. You'll never get me onto your shoulders."

"All right, I'll carry you in my arms!"

Chief frowned inwardly. "Okay, but I don't think you can make it; you got all your gear and mine."

The cover firing slowed after the initial burst, and the gooks were flitting closer. "Chief, let him carry you, we can't sit here all day!"

"Okay."

They poured on the covering fire again, and Wilson put one arm under Chief's shoulder, and another arm under his leg. The other leg dangled. Wilson ran two steps, and both fell crashing to the ground. Simultaneously they started to laugh. Wilson cursed. He had too much gear on. Chief laughed. It all seemed ridiculous, lying in the pile. It was as if they weren't even in combat. They both thought of that day in Tokyo when they had been drunk and naked together in the *o'furo*.

Wilson grinned at the Chief. "Can you make it?"

"Yeah."

"Let's go—sure you can make it?"

"Yeah."

"You ready?"

"Okay. Let's go!"

They sprang from the ground, hopped, stumbled, and ran back toward Fox Company, toward safety. Chief stumbled, and they both fell into a little crater.

The bandage had slipped, pulling the wound open wide. The blood spurted out. Wilson pulled Chief to the ground. "Take it easy, man; let me fix it back." The loss of blood and sudden exertion drained the Chief. He flopped over and lay back, his face white even under the sunburn and natural copper.

"I'm dizzy, Wil, I'm gonna pass."

Immediately, Wilson seized his wrists; he felt nothing. Fear darted into his eyes. He put his head on the chest and sighed with relief as he heard the thump-thump. Got to get him back where they can give him some blood.

He threw off his own flak jacket, frags, canteen, and ammo, and ripped off Chief's 782 gear and gathered up the body. The head flopped back as soon as he lifted it; Wilson staggered awkwardly. He put one hand under the head, and held the head against his biceps; then gathering up the legs, he lifted again. He sprang forward. He ran. It wasn't far now, there were corpsmen back near Fox Company. Churn, churn. Stretch, stretch. Run, run. Chief's body sagged and the weight pulled on Wilson, but the smooth muscles strained on.

Like back in high school. Coming out of the turn in the 220. Turn your head from the slant. Straight forward now. Dip a little bit. Pour it on! Wilson heard the crowd roaring. The muscles rippled, wavered, and pulsed under the weight. His knees lifted like pistons pounding across the ground. There's the knoll; Fox is behind it; they got some blood there. He cradled the body tighter to his chest and pounded on.

He turned the corner as a mortar landed ten feet directly behind him. Corporal Robert Wilson's body slammed forward, taking the full blast of the shrapnel.

A helmet bounced once and rolled along the ground. Like a spinning top, it quivered slowly to a stop. There was an ornate pattern of boxes and numbers on the helmet—like a dice table. SYLVIA —it said.

Hawkins

He saw them darting over the hill, slipping into the holes and bunkers. The men saw it, too, their firing slackened, and a couple turned to run. Hawkins pictured a horde of gooks charging the hill, and he too caught the urge to bolt. In a split second the urge could spread through all the company. One panicky man could stampede the rest.

"Hold your ground!" he screamed.

Somebody began firing rapidly. A gook that had popped up was ripped in two. The panic stopped; both sides seemed to belly down like a tiger crouching to spring. Hawkins twitched for ideas; he must keep up the momentum of the attack. He looked back and was surprised to see the whole bevy of company CP taggers-on: radiomen, mortar teams, bodyguards. They were clinging to the ground, looking at him as though he were crazy. *The company commander had a 60-mm mortar team.*

"Mortars up," he yelled, scrambling back toward them.

Two of the team crawled up, wild-eyed. "We can't fire. A grenade hit Grimes and the base plate was blown away."

"Where is it?"

"I don't know," he cried in desperation.

"Can you use a helmet and fire it freehand?" Hawkins rasped.

"Ah . . . sure!" The mortar team leader almost laughed as his confidence came back. He grabbed off his helmet and sat down, putting the helmet on the ground between his legs, the open end up. He put the mortar tube in the helmet and held it at an angle toward the gooks with his bare hands. He eyed the distance and the angle for a moment as the other man readied the shell. "Fire," he yelled and ducked his head. The other man dropped in the round. *Poop.* The Lieutenant held his breath, watching. *WHOOMP.* It landed about twenty yards from the end of the hill.

"All right," Hawkins bellowed, "All right. Lay it on 'em."

The mortar man grinned and made a little Kentucky windage adjustment as the other man began steadily dropping rounds in the tube. The rounds fell at random on the back of the hill.

Hawkins crawled among the men. They were holding but ducking. The gooks were gaining fire superiority. Rounds were whipping in. Suddenly Hawkins threw back his head and began to scream: rebel yells, wolf howls, bear growls, curses, everything. The men tensed in surprise.

In a flash the frenzy was picked up and the air became a crazy football stadium of yells. Only they were curses and howls and every sound utterable by the human throat. The enemy firing slowed. "KILL."

"GO." The Lieutenant shouted out, but no one heard. They surged forward in perfect battle order. Charge, fire, hit the deck, screen, cover, grenade, fire, go, stop. Yell.

On such little threads a battle hangs. A unit that panics will flee and be cut down. But a charged-up assault will keep right on going—even to the last man. Once in a final assault control is almost gone. Iron discipline helps, but it's really the spirit that makes it.

The Lieutenant bit his lip and pounded his helmet to control himself. Use the radio. Talk to the squad leaders. Check the other platoons. Maneuver your men properly. *Keep control.*

They moved forward in a frenzy, firing like mad. Still the NVA didn't fold.

There was a scream for corpsman. Hawkins looked back to the right. The Chief lay in the dirt, blood spurting from his neck.

For a split second Hawkins gaped, then something snapped. He shrugged off the radio pack and flung it to the radioman hovering behind him. "They killed the Chief," he screamed, his hands jamming cartridges into the shotgun. He charged straight forward, the stubby gun blazing. He was oblivious of everything except the need to kill what had killed the Chief. A gook panicked and ran from his hole. The Lieutenant shot him on the run. *"Die, Fucker!"*

Hawkins stood over the body and smashed the butt down. Again and again he raised and slammed the gun. Forgetting everything he stood against the sky, clubbing the dead body as the gooks crept closer. Then from nowhere someone knocked him to the ground. He rolled by instinct and a man leaped over him, fired calmly, and killed a gook not ten feet away. In another second the Lieutenant would have been dead.

Hawkins looked up and saw the bony, caramel face, hard and defiant as always. But for the first time there was just a hint of a smile.

"Take it easy. Lieutenant. You're doin' great; you're practically taking the hill single-handed. Don't lose your head now. We'll all get killed."

Their eyes met—blue and black. Carlysle was right up in front. He'd been the one delivering all that firing before. Standing alone, almost forward of the line, with the battle swirling around them, the two men looked at each other, then out to the gooks. Their gaze swung back and locked. Finally, the Lieutenant spoke. "You wanna take the point with me?"

"Let's go, Lieutenant."

Tomorrow, next year, they might be killing each other. But for that moment, they were brothers in battle. Not soul brothers, but brothers in soul.

Chief

"Pull that body in line with the others."

"What difference does it make if they're in a row—they're dead."

"I don't know, but the gunny said do it that way."

"Think they'll get that amtrack up here?"

"They'd better. We'll never get enough choppers in here to get all those bodies of Fox out."

The sun dropped even with the horizon, making a red fireball, and the men squinted to look for the big armored personnel carrier.

"Hey, I hear it!"

"Yeah, that's gotta be it. Can't see it though."

"Get 'em ready, wounded first, then the bodies."

The ramp door dropped open and the Chief sat up painfully. He lifted the glucose bottle off the stick and carefully wrapped the arm with the tube in it to his side. Bent over like an old man, he limped into the amtrack. He sat down at the back and waited.

The men outside loaded the others on. Some with stretchers, some by slinging the man between them in ponchos, some by lifting them under the arms with their shoulders.

"Hey, what happened to the little guy with all the blood? He's got a glucose bottle going."

"He walked in by himself."

"He can't do that."

"Let him go, we ain't got time!"

The door clanged up and only a little red light glowed.

There was a corpsman in the amtrack. "How do you feel?" he asked.

"Okay, I guess, a little weak."

"Let me take that needle out; won't do any good the way we're gonna be bouncing." He took the bottle, and saw the soaked shirt; an expression of amazement and concern crossed his face. He eyed the bandages. "If that starts bleeding, let me know."

"Okay."

The little motor whirred again, and the door descended mechanically, like an automatic elevator door. It clanged on a rock and the whirring stopped. This time the stretcher-bearers dragged on lifeless bodies. The last rays of the sun stabbed in briefly.

"Gotta move back."

"There isn't room," the corpsman protested.

"Sorry, Skipper says we got to get the bodies out."

"We'll have to stack 'em up . . ."

"Well, make it fast; we got to get out of here in a hurry."

They began dragging in more bodies, hurrying, not bothering to use a stretcher or a poncho. They just lifted under the armpits and dragged the heels; heads rolled back and dangled loosely, mouths agape.

"Okay, move it."

The little motor whirred and the door ascended, cutting off the soft twilight. The machine clanged to life, and the whole inside began to vibrate. The floor pitched and bucked. Chief braced his back against the wall and felt the blood flow again. It seeped down to his pants, wetting his thighs.

"Hey, Doc, give me another bandage."

The corpsman held the ceiling tightly with one hand and stepped over the shadowy bodies. He strapped another bandage in place, directly over the other ones, so tightly it squeezed the others like a sponge. The blood oozed out. The machine bucked on, and then stopped once more. Chief was dimly aware of thudding noises and shrapnel striking the amtrack body. The little motor whirred and the door clanked. More bodies were dragged on. This time they raced to pull them in anyway possible— by ankles, wrists, feet; the heads dropped down to the dirt, dragged along like sacks of wheat being towed and bounced over the ramp. They had to stack the dead ones like cordwood until the pile was three feet deep.

Whir—Clang—the dull red glow—and the machine bucked on.

The dizziness came again as the glucose energy was used up. The tough little body rocked and toppled over. Chief stared at the red light, his mind seemed to sway, a redness came over him, and he swam into a sea of red mist. Hs body was miles and miles away. He was swimming lazily in the Red Sea. A red sun shown down.

The corpsman swore and watched him tumble. He was helpless to do anything but hold on.

At last the bucking and pitching stopped. The door clanked open. Chief became aware of a rhythmic thumping. It was dark. He tried to get up, and his mind swam up out of the sea into the mist. Dimly he was aware of arms lifting and dragging.

"Take it easy," the corpsman yelled.

"Skipper only gave us a few minutes to load. Gooks still got an active mortar up there. They'll get the range in no time."

Chief lay down on his side, his head against the hard floor. The stack of bandages built up from the side of his neck pressed against the floor, squeezing the bandages even tighter. Chief could feel the thumping now. He was in whatever was thumping. The thumping got faster and became a roar.

As the chopper ascended, he faded into unconsciousness.

Bright lights pried open his eyes and brought him back to alertness. There were stretchers now and many hands lifted him quickly and gently. He lay back flat and watched, his face pointing straight upwards. He saw the wires in the top of the chopper. They moved. Then there was more light. A doorframe passed over his eyes, and he could see up into a large room. The ceiling moved. He could see fluorescent lights hanging down from the ceiling. A man in a loose green gown moved over him, glanced at his tag and motioned toward the wall.

It was a hospital. I'm gonna be okay, Chief thought queerly. He lay rigid on the canvas stretcher. He must lie still, so it wouldn't bleed. Don't move a muscle. He concentrated on stillness. His mind wasn't flowing now, and he lay still for what seemed like hours. Then he began to grow misty. He wasn't sure if he was conscious or not. Dully he felt the blood flow down his neck. It made a little pool where his head indented the canvas, but still he lay motionless.

The pool built up, and he felt it trickle down his back and wet his buttocks. Don't move. Got to lie still or it would bleed more. But where are they? Must be some guys hurt worse than he was; they gotta take care of them first. Maybe they forgot him. Should he call out? No, others must be hurt worse.

The blood collected in a pool around his buttocks and

slowly began to drip onto the floor. Chief's mind began to slip again, and the fog crept up. He went swimming, swirling, and swimming down, down, down. He was just barely aware of the blood dripping, dripping. Almost subconsciously he felt it coming up to his ears. Something made him struggle to move his head, but now it was stuck. He relaxed and drifted off. The fog came back. It was the fog at the Laotian border fight. He could see the flare overhead. Slowly the flare descended and went out. He wondered dully why they didn't fire another. Blackness now.

Footsteps approached; he heard words. His eyes opened again; a face peered down.

"Hey, this guy's bleeding like a stuck pig." The words cut through the mist.

"Jesus, look at that hair. He a Marine?"

"Hey, he's dripping through to the floor. Doctor! Better check this one."

Another face came and peered down. It was an older face with glasses. "Get him in there right now."

Hands reached to move him, but the head stuck to the canvas. The blood had dried and glued his hair to the cloth. Chief saw a hand coming toward his forehead. The hand grabbed his long hair.

"This may hurt, but there's no other way."

The hand yanked, and the Chief felt his head wrench free. Blood ran onto the floor and splashed on the man's green gown. Chief saw the ceiling move again. It seemed to lurch and then he saw the bright spotlights coming. Now the spotlights were all grouped in a bank directly over his face.

A masked face readied a needle. "Count to ten and let me know if you feel dizzy."

The doctor swabbed and inserted a needle. "Okay, start counting."

"Ten . . . Nine . . . Eig . . . Hey, hmmm. . . ."

Hawkins

The napalm had stunned the gooks in the bunkers. The mortars held off some of the replacements. The screaming whipped the men to a frenzy, and Carlysle and the Lieutenant made the point of a wedge as it slashed into the gooks. Together they were a team of demons leading a pack of wolves.

"Kill the son of a bitches."

"Kill 'em, kill 'em."

"KILLLL."

"DIE YOU BASTARDS."

Carlysle covered and Hawkins tossed in a grenade. Then Carlysle slipped in the back and slaughtered.

A piece of shrapnel caught the Lieutenant's eyebrow and the blood flowed down the side of his face. He had to wipe his eye to see, but it kept on flowing. Carlysle took a chunk in his shoulder, and blood ran down his arm mingling with the sweat and dirt.

Zzzzzzzsst. THUD. "Look out! CHI-COM."

Hawkins jumped back, tripped, rolled, and slammed into a hole, the fragments nipping at his forearm. He looked back through the smoke, his jaw thrust out and teeth bared. "Fucking bastards."

He jerked his head, flipping sweat and blood like a wet dog shaking himself. A dark figure swayed up in front of him like a target. Eyes wide, he tore forward as a full-back, finger pumping on the automatic shotgun. At *last* they were visible, not shadows in the jungle. He fired and dropped, running and dodging, throwing grenades into bunkers, working with Carlysle as a team.

And all along the line the men worked in teams. Crazed with the kill orgy, the whole line leaped forward with utter savageness, keeping perfect fire and maneuver battle order. They charged into the bunkers screaming, killing everything in their path.

"Go, go."

"KILL—KILL—KILL."

Lieutenant Hawkins lay on his stomach and wormed behind a dead gook for cover. They were almost to the end of the hill, but there was a narrow hole right at the edge. There was a gook in there who kept holding them off; and Hawkins couldn't get a grenade into the hole. He motioned to Carlysle to the left. "Put fire right in his hole—I'm gonna charge him. Don't quit firing until I'm in."

Carlysle jammed a fresh magazine in the M-16 and put one between his teeth. Hawkins loaded the sawed-off

Browning full and cocked one leg up to push off. His head lay sideways on the dirt, his hands ready to push off.

"Now," he screamed. Carlysle half-rose and poured fire around the top of the hole. Hawkins felt his hands pushing down and he sprang. He charged low, firing from the hip. He saw the dirt puffs flying up all around the hole as Carlysle pumped round after round. It seemed to take forever to cross the short space. He knew Carlysle's bullets were getting closer, whipping right by his side. Then the gook popped up and saw an insane animal with streaming blood covering half the face. There was a white eye-hole in the red mass and an open snarling mouth. Hawkins saw the snout of the gook's AK just as Carlysle's bullet creased his helmet snapping his head back.

That was just enough of a delay. Hawkins jumped in on top of the gook, boots crashing down on his shoulders and stomach, thrusting him back into the bottom of the foxhole. He jammed the muzzle of the stubby shotgun into the gook's mouth as if it were a bayonet, pulling the trigger again and again. The full blast of two twelve-gauge shells blazed out. The head exploded, splattering bits of bone and globs of brain. It was as if someone had hit an overripe cantaloupe with a sledgehammer. The gooey parts of the brain stuck in the stubble of Hawkins' beard as he ducked down and looked out over the rim. They'd made it to the end of the hill.

"Come on up"—he swung his arm in a big arc. The men struggled forward like gladiators slashing with swords. They came in a savage dance of killing and fell into the last holes, firing down into the treeline. And they fired over and over into the warm bodies.

Carlysle thudded down beside the Lieutenant and stood on the gook's frayed neck stub; for the first time they stood erect and looked at each other. The hill was theirs.

Almost imperceptibly the combat tension slipped and in its place a wild exhilaration mushroomed. Men literally jumped at each other as the brotherhood of victory blazed in their eyes.

"We won! We won! We did it!"

"We Goddamn did it!"

Men were yelling, shaking hands, pounding backs, hugging each other, and firing captured AK-47's in the air. Even Carlysle laughed aloud, and slowly Hawkins grinned, the brains globules dripping from his beard.

"Carlysle." Hawkins spoke the lone word and slowly extended his hand.

Amidst the yelling the two men looked deep at each other for a long moment, the Lieutenant's hand reaching out. Carlysle's eyes flicked down to the open hand, and for a second there was a smile, then the lips hardened and the whole body swayed up to its full height.

"Ain't no way, Lieutenant." He shook his head from side to side, then turned his back and climbed out of the hole.

Hawkins stood staring after him until the hysterical glee of the men swept everything away, and a great caldron of joy bubbled up around him. The intense kill-craze lust of the battle erupted into the unbelievably sweet joy of victory. As there is no greater sorrow than in defeat and death, there is no greater joy than in battle victory. *No greater joy in all the world.*

"I got that one."

"Hell, you did; I got him."

"Did you see that fucking gook's chest split open?"

"Yaahoo."

"Hey, look, here's a Crispy Critter, a napalm-fried-gook."

Sail picked up a gook machine gun, tried it once, then rolled his head back and let out a yell as he fired a solid stream straight up into the air until the rounds ran out. *"Yeeeaaaaghhhooooo."*

Leaping, dancing, hopping with glee, the men went wild, absolutely wild with joy. Hawkins looked around, and for that moment the joy of battle victory blazed in every eye. Every one.

2

Hawkins

The morning was clear. From the hilltop Hawkins could see down the side of the mountain. The jungle green blended into the lighter green of swaying elephant grass, which swept down to the rolling golden hills below. His eye caught a sparkling mountain stream in the distance. All was bathed in a brilliant tropical sun. It didn't seem possible that they had come over those hills just yesterday. But the burned-over top and the poncho-shrouded forms told him it was true.

Carlysle helped Hawkins wrap Wilson's body. Not a single word passed between them, but on some silent signal they went together with the poncho. Like pallbearers the whole squad carried the body to the LZ and put it on the chopper. Hawkins and Carlysle walked behind in silence. Just before the chopper left, Hawkins took the wallet and once again looked at the picture of the girl; he thought of the letter he would have to write.

For other men who died, they felt a sadness, but it was remote. Contacts and friendships are so brief, so casual, that unless two men are in the same platoon or the same squad they are but passing acquaintances. In d'Nam the roster changes everyday.

After a while Hawkins saw Joseley trudging up the hill to the high part where the company CP was. Hawkins smiled and felt the bond between them. But Joseley fidgeted and was a little awkward. Hawkins thought maybe he was embarrassed or shy to be hanging around the company CP. Finally Joseley stopped in front of Hawkins and looked away with a little frown as if uncertain of something. "Lieutenant . . . ah . . . the men got together and sent me up to talk to you."

Hawkins saw the purpose in the face and knew the men wanted to ask for something. They had sent Joseley as their speaker. "Yeah?"

"Well, sir, the men would like to know if it's okay if they put up a flag."

For a moment Hawkins didn't understand. "A Maine state flag?"

"No, sir." Joseley stiffened. "The United States flag."

"You got one here?" Hawkins didn't comprehend.

"Yes, sir, several of the men carry them in their packs all the time."

Hawkins lit a cigarette and looked away as the impact flooded over him. "You know," he said slowly, avoiding Joseley's eyes, "that we're not supposed to do that."

But Joseley looked straight back. "Yes, Chris, I know that."

Hawkins looked down at the dirt on his boots, conscious of waiting stares of the whole CP group. Then he knew it had to be. "You're Goddamn right, you can." He felt an odd pressure behind his eyeballs. "You can put it right here on top, and I'll hold the formation myself."

"That'd be good, sir."

It was just a little flag, and they tied it to a long bamboo pole with the wire from a C-ration carton. They dug a hole for the pole and got some rocks to brace it. Everyone on the hill stopped to watch the preparations. Then, when all was ready, the company had to wait a couple of minutes while they adjusted the rocks.

The whole company spread across the hill, standing together in squad formations. Some of the squads were beside their holes; some came up closer to see better. They couldn't get too bunched up because the gooks could still mortar them, but the men all stood very straight wherever they were. The "color guard" signaled they were ready and the Lieutenant swelled his lungs for the parade-ground command.

"Comm-paanee Ten HUT."

The color guard pushed the pole upright and quickly adjusted the rocks to hold it. As soon as it was flying, a breeze rippled the red, white, and blue cloth. Hawkins' hand snapped up, his fingers just touching the steel rim of the helmet. For a second he held the salute, watching the flag, then he dropped his arm and did an about-face. Again he filled his lungs for the command, but for a long minute he stood poised, looking at the troops spread out around the hill: dirty, ragged, and in a motley array of Marine, Army, and NVA clothes. The squads were spread around in a rough circle, but every man was rigid at attention. Some had brought their weapons up in a rifle salute; others had their arms cocked in the crooked, salty salute of the grunt Marine. Hawkins felt a tight knot begin to squeeze on his lungs and creep in behind his eyes. For a second, he was afraid he would choke up, but he saw their faces—hard, strong and smiling proud.

"Reaaady HOO."

Then the ceremony was over and they went back to making coffee and cleaning rifles; and as they sat around the tales began to grow. But even as they joked, they could feel the flag over them. The bright colors waving against the sky caught the eye, and every now and then a man would look back up to see them once more.

By afternoon the avalanche which always descends after a big battle began to hit company. First came the supplies; ammo LAAW's, grenades, mines, and even B-rations arrived by the pallet load. The men eagerly swooped up the new stuff, but it seemed ironic to get so much *after* they had really needed it. Hawkins, however, ordered case after case of LAAW's and led the men out for practice. As usual, several of the LAAW's they had carried for a couple of weeks didn't work. Hawkins vowed he would never be caught again with old ones so long as he was company commander.

They stood on the edge of the hill and fired at the trees below. Then they brought up some of the captured RPG's and fired them for comparison. They decided the American rockets were more accurate long range but that the Communist-made ones were as good or better at ranges up to forty yards. A few of the old men scoffed at both and maintained neither were as good as the old 3.5 rocket-launcher bazooka.

As they were firing, a helicopter descended. Hawkins was surprised to see an Army captain and a Vietnamese Special Forces major alight. He had been told to send an example of all captured weapons to the rear, but no Marine brass had yet come out to inspect personally.

The Army captain looked over the weapons casually and poked around the bodies. He frowned and conferred with his Vietnamese counterpart. Finally he turned to Hawkins.

"Lieutenant, what we are looking for is insignia. The unit you fought appears to have come from the North only recently. We were hoping to get some of the rank markings while they were clean and new but . . . ah . . . the bodies seem to be . . . ah . . . devoid."

"Well, Captain, the men like to pick up souvenirs, you know. Did you have something specific in mind?"

The captain frowned, "I'm after anything that shows unit or rank—belts or the star-and-wreath pin that officers wear." He paused and looked around intently. "We would particularly like the little round pin that has the picture of Mao Tse-tung on it."

"Yeah, I've seen all of those at one time or another." Hawkins nodded. "You want to see some."

The captain's eyes lighted and he glanced at the Vietnamese major. "Do you have some now?"

Hawkins laughed and lifted his jungle shirt, showing the big brass buckle with the star. The captain bent forward, looking closely and smiled. "Oh—I have seen similar ones but smaller; the ones that big are rare."

"Some of the men have nicer ones. This one's a little beat up, but it's got sentimental value for me."

The captain straightened and smiled sweetly. "Lieutenant, I certainly wouldn't want to take *yours*, but perhaps you could get—ah—an extra one from one of your men, one that came from this unit."

Hawkins looked at the captain sharply and felt the growing disgust. "I don't know exactly what they have, but let's see what we can find." He called for souvenirs, and shortly a parade of objects was shown to the Intelligence officer. His eyes glistened as he eagerly jotted in a notebook, then he took out from his pocket a little camera, a half-frame PEN, Olympus 35-mm, and photographed each item. There were silver stars which indicated junior officers. There were pin-on buttons and emblems which designated officers in general. The pins were made of red-enameled metal with a raised star, three-quarters encircled by rice or wheat stalks. Only one of the little pins with Mao's head could be found. The captain was obviously impressed with what he saw. "Lieutenant, your men have some excellent examples here. We would certainly like to take some specimens with us."

"Captain, the men don't really like to give them up once they have fought for them." Hawkins eyed the man coldly.

These damn Marines, the captain thought, shifting uneasily, never cooperate. "Lieutenant, we really need to just get some specimens." He lowered his voice confidentially. "You see, we are trying to reproduce them in Saigon."

"Is that right?" Hawkins was immediately intrigued. "What for?"

"I can't tell you any more than that," the captain said airily.

Hawkins thought a minute, then struggled not to laugh in the man's face. If you told me that much, you might as well tell me all. It isn't too hard to figure it out, he thought. "Okay, Captain, if we run across any extras, I'll sure try and save them for you," he said.

"Lieutenant"—the captain scowled and stressed the juniorness of the word—"perhaps you don't realize the importance of Intelligence work. We *need* some of those insignia."

I'll bet you do, Hawkins thought. Take it to the office, show it to the CO and then put it in your own seabag. He almost said it aloud, but something held him back. "Sir, as I said, if you'll give me some time, I'll try and get some for you."

The captain's face reddened. "Look, Lieutenant, I don't think it's necessary for me to have to see your CO. It would be easier if you'd just produce them now."

Hawkins looked down at his boots and felt a part of his mind forming the old lines of reason, smoothness, and conciliation, and suddenly he was disgusted with that part of himself. He sniffed and spat loudly to the side. "Captain, I may only be a second lieutenant, but I'm the company commander of this outfit, and right now I rule this hill." He paused and spread his feet wide. "And none of my men are going to give you anything that they own—unless they feel like it and unless you got the cash to pay for it."

The captain glared, then turned abruptly for his helicopter. Just before boarding, he turned to Hawkins. "We'll see about this, *Lieutenant.* I'm flying straight to headquarters now."

Hawkins just laughed and turned away.

The Intelligence captain was gone only about ten minutes when another helicopter landed. After the supply choppers and the Intelligence man, Hawkins was beginning to wonder what else would come. It was three reporters—two Marines working for the *Stars and Stripes,* and a civilian. The Marines were shiny, bright enlisted men, a young staff sergeant and a buck sergeant, clean-cut and conscientious in nice squared-away utilities. Hawkins decided they were the Yes, Sir—No, Sir—Three Bags Full,

Sir type. The civilian, however, was hefty, even plump, compared to the lean Marines. He had heavy sideburns, and his hair was long at the back of his neck. He spoke very little but looked around carefully and let the two Marines do the talking. When he saw the flag, he stopped a moment and gazed up, then jotted something in his notebook. Hawkins watched them from the CP and decided they could come and find him.

The Marines immediately wanted numbers and body counts. Hawkins lay on his back and told them calmly that he didn't know, but they could ask Sergeant LeBlanc, who was counting and burying the gook bodies now. After they had taken what facts and figures he could give them, the sergeant asked politely, "Sir, what is your reaction to the announcement that U.S. troops will be withdrawn soon?"

Hawkins chuckled to himself. "Well now, North Vietnam is a small country and only has so many men. We've killed so many that pretty soon they just won't have any more to send, therefore pretty soon the war will have to be over. I hear they are down to teen-agers and old men now." He grinned broadly and the two Marines seemed disappointed and wrote nothing, but the civilian reporter jotted a note. Then they wanted Hawkins to describe the battle. He snorted but was secretly pleased. However, when he told them about the napalm, they looked at each other sheepishly.

"Ah—I'm afraid we can't use that, sir."

"You mean they don't let you mention napalm in the *Stars and Stripes?*"

"No, sir."

"Well, that figures," Hawkins said. "It does sort of mess people up."

The two Marines appeared relieved. The civilian reporter had yet to say anything.

"Come on, I'll show you what it does." Hawkins stood and slung the little shotgun over his shoulder. He saw them stare at it and paused to light a cigarette. He knew he was showing off and he flipped the match arrogantly, noticing the civilian reporter jotting in his notebook again.

Hawkins led them to the far edge of the hill and walked down to a charred figure. The reporters gasped and Hawkins delighted in their reaction.

"This is what we call a Crispy Critter," he said.

The Marines were mutely respectful, but the civilian eyed him darkly. Hawkins gazed down at the gook. The body looked like a piece of steak that had been charred completely black, but it was plainly a human figure. It was draped grotesquely over a stump. The head seemed to be looking up as if begging. Hawkins took the cigarette from his own mouth and deftly inserted it between the charcoal lips. The Marines gave a short, polite laugh, but the civilian's face had become a mask of cold indifference. Hawkins appeared not to notice but merely grinned and waved at one of the men who had stood watching. After leading them back to the CP, he flopped in the dirt and lit a heat tab to make some of his C-ration Irish coffee.

"Sit down and take it easy." He waved them grandly to be seated. "Sorry I can't offer you a Martini, but I guess you get that back in the rear anyway."

They didn't reply to the barb but squatted uneasily. Hawkins started the coffee with exaggerated deftness, enjoying their stares.

The civilian spoke for the first time. "Lieutenant, that's not an issue weapon you have there, is it?"

"Nope," Hawkins said, continuing with the coffee, "that's my own private baby. It's a Browning automatic; cut 'er down myself."

"Aren't shotguns outlawed by the Geneva Convention?" the civilian asked.

Hawkins leaned to his side, closed one nostril with his thumb and blew his nose onto the ground. He wiped the remains from his scraggly mustache with the back of his wrist and then eyed the civilian coolly. "That's what I've heard, but I reckon every Marine company in Northern I Corps carries a couple of them. Course they're all pump type, government issue, not an automatic one like mine."

"Are shotguns good in the jungle?" The reporter's voice was open and passive.

"Tremendous," Hawkins said with eager gusto. "They are great on point or at night on an LP."

"Tell me, Lieutenant"—the voice was still neutral—"why do *you* carry the shotgun?"

"I told you because . . ." Too late Hawkins saw the trap and cut himself off. Who was the civilian prick anyway? "Because it's a good weapon, that's why," he finished lamely, hoping the reporter would drop it.

But the reporter bore in. "Lieutenant, I've been told that a company commander and even a platoon commander are not supposed to shoot. Their job is to direct the fire of others. That's why only a pistol is issued." His voice had become sharp.

Hawkins remembered immediately that he himself had said and believed that very thing several months ago. His jaw twitched and he cursed the reporter for reminding him, for even knowing such things. He rationalized that it had been a long time since he had had an intelligent verbal scrap. And he tried to ignore the mushrooming disquiet within himself. "That's true, but we fight NVA up here, not chicken-shit VC, and most officers carry a rifle for extra self-protection."

"I see," the reporter intoned. "When you got the gun, had you already been in combat and felt you needed more protection?"

"That's right," Hawkins said tersely.

"One more question, Lieutenant." The reporter's voice became insistent. "Did you personally participate in the assault on the bunkers or did you just direct?"

Hawkins was conscious of the Marine reporters picking up their notebooks. He scratched his beard uneasily. There was a moment of silence. "Why, ah, no. I was just on the . . . I was mainly directing mortar fire and maneuvering the platoons." He glanced quickly to see if the radiomen were listening.

"Did you fire your shotgun?" The voice was pleasant again.

"Well, I had to shoot it a couple of times," he said uneasily, hastily lighting another cigarette.

"Oh, come now, Lieutenant, don't be modest." He leaned forward and spoke directly into the Lieutenant's face. "From the way your men idolize you, I think you must have been right up there in the thick of things."

Hawkins saw the trap of the dilemma clearly and he was acutely aware of the Marine reporters jotting furiously and the radiomen listening. "I do my job, that's all." He looked away and puffed the cigarette heavily. The reporter saw his prize escaping him and suddenly his voice became harsh and accusing. "Lieutenant, I think you like to get in there and fight, don't you? You like to get right in there and smash heads, *don't you, Lieutenant?* And your men idolize that, don't they?"

Hawkins' eyes narrowed to slits, but he forced a carefree laugh. "Well, now, Mr. Reporter, if you keep on like that, I might have to *get right in there* with you."

There was a burst of laughter and Hawkins smirked in satisfaction. The civilian reporter, however, merely shrugged and stood up.

Shortly a helicopter came and the reporters left. As he watched them go, Hawkins let out a deep breath and shook his head to forget about the monster he had just glimpsed within himself.

But he couldn't forget. The words circled and came back to him again and again. *You like to get right in there and smash heads, don't you, Lieutenant?* Hawkins picked up the shotgun and looked at it vacantly. He'd killed with that, but he couldn't possibly feel remorse. It had to be done. Kill or be killed. *Enjoy? . . .* He remembered the first gook he had killed. It seemed so long ago, yet it was only a few months. Instinctively his hand flicked the safety and hefted the weight of the gun. Maybe he did like it. Was that wrong? Direct your men. He had led the men, but he had also directed. And they had followed. The words echoed from some long ago training, *Follow me.*

At length Hawkins stood and slowly looked around the hill. His hill. His company. His men. *Your men idolize you.* The thought made a little glow swell up from his chest. Maybe he had bashed heads, yelled, and everything else, but he had led. He had planned and thought and won. He'd won a company. Not a company like his father's company, but maybe his company was better than his father's.

Eventually, even the Colonel made a visit to the hill, but this time Hawkins was forewarned as the battalion radio crackled and the word came out. As soon as he heard the chopper, Hawkins went down to the LZ and stood waiting. It wasn't a sleek Huey such as had brought the Army men and the reporters. Instead, two old Ch-34's creaked over the horizon, almost Korean vintage but everybody liked them because they were "fun." It was like flying an old World War One open-cockpit bi-winger. They trembled and shook and would carry only three or four passengers, but it was real flying!

Hawkins had the ground crew waiting. They donned their shirts and put the cards and dice away. As the birds approached, the company helicopter support man popped a yellow smoke and the lead chopper dropped to the mountaintop perch. Just as it touched down, Colonel Gaither hopped out, held his hat, and ran from the prop wash. The bird quickly roared again and took off because the threat of enemy mortars was still great. The regimental sergeant major, Sergeant Major MacIntyre, and the new battalion XO, Major Tolson, and an assortment of others piled out from the second helicopter. Delta Company stood and gawked.

As the wash receded, Hawkins stepped forward smartly and shook the Colonel's hand. No one ever saluted in the bush because of the possibility of sniper fire. "Good afternoon, sir," he said crisply.

"Good afternoon, Lieutenant. This is Delta Company Two-Seven and you are Lieutenant Hawkins, correct?"

"Yes, sir, that's correct."

"Well, Lieutenant, I was most grieved to hear about Captain Calahan, but in his absence you've done an outstanding job."

"Thank you, sir."

"Incidentally, you will be pleased to know that Captain Calahan is going to be all right."

"That's wonderful, sir. Where is the Captain?"

"He's on the *Repose* right now, although I believe they will send him to Japan for recovery. But I'm really here to congratulate you, Lieutenant."

The entourage had moved up and stood in a semicircle behind the Colonel. Hawkins stood very tall and proud. "We monitored your battalion and company radio net during the fight, and I think you did an outstanding job filling in for Captain Calahan."

Hawkins felt one fleeting wince, then beamed. "Thank you, sir. The credit should really go to the men; they are the ones who did it."

"Indeed they did and I will commend them suitably." Then the Colonel paused and looked sharply at the Lieutenant, although he had been looking straight at him before. Hawkins saw the change in expression and mentally crossed his fingers.

"Lieutenant, haven't I seen you somewhere recently?" The Colonel's face was slightly quizzical. Hawkins flushed and felt his stomach drop. For a second he considered saying no, then he realized he had *the* helmet on.

"Ah—sir, I think we . . . met . . . ah . . . a few nights ago at the Cordon Operation."

The Colonel looked blank for a second, then his eyes flicked to the Lieutenant's helmet and he laughed, "Ah yes, you're the Lieutenant who brought me the helmet."

"Yes, sir." Hawkins felt his ears burning.

"Well, how 'bout that." The Colonel chuckled and then dropped the matter. He spoke another minute or two, then stepped back as Major Tolson and the others came forward to congratulate Hawkins and shake his hand. Each of them said something of praise. Just as Colonel Gaither stepped back, however, he noticed the flag flying on the peak of the hill. A slight frown passed over his face but Hawkins, smiling and beaming and shaking hands, failed to notice it.

Then the Colonel asked to tour the hill and be briefed on the fight. He shook hands with the Gunny, Staff Sergeant LeBlanc, and Staff Sergeant Allen, and with random others as he went along. He listened closely as Hawkins explained his tactics. As they passed the lines, the men stood silently watching the two go by. Hawkins watched them from the corner of his eye and he read the pride in their faces.

"Lieutenant, I had word that most of your wounded are doing well and clamoring to come back to the company. That's the kind of spirit we like."

"Thank you, sir." Hawkins smiled. Abruptly his face darkened and he felt the knot come up in his chest. "Sir, did you hear of a man named Eagle, a Sergeant Eagle?"

"What happened to him, son, was he wounded?"

"All I know is that he got hit, but after it was over, nobody could find him."

The Colonel heard the catch in Hawkins' voice, and he turned to the Sergeant Major who trailed behind. "Get that name and check on him, Sergeant Major."

"Yes, sir." The Sergeant Major nodded and turned to

Hawkins, taking out a pen and notepad. "How was that name again, sir?"

After about forty-five minutes the Colonel called for the helicopters to come back and as they appeared on the horizon, he turned and shook Hawkins' hand again.

"Lieutenant, there is one more thing I want to say. Your battalion is, of course, short on officers, but not so short that we would put a second lieutenant in charge of a company." Hawkins stiffened and felt his heart sinking. "That would cause no little consternation to other officers in the battalion who are more senior than you. You understand, I'm sure."

Hawkins' face darkened. "Yes, sir, I understand." He tried to keep his voice normal.

"However, I know that you are soon to be a first lieutenant, and a good combat leader is hard to find, so I'm going to recommend to Lieutenant Colonel Ryan that he keep you on as company commander of Delta Company." The frosty eyes twinkled their brightest.

"Oh, sir"—Hawkins' face lit like a basketball flare—"that's great. I . . . I mean, gee, thanks, sir."

The Colonel smiled and looked up as the chopper started to descend. "So I want you to get Delta ready; and in a couple of days you'll be moving out of here and we'll find some more action for you."

"Great, sir." Hawkins grinned. "Oh, who will be taking our place here?"

The chopper got louder and just a trace of annoyance passed over the Colonel's face. "It will be a one-way lift, so we'll provide a couple of gunships for security while your last men are getting out."

Suddenly Hawkins was alarmed. "Sir, *someone* will be coming up here, won't they?"

The Colonel frowned. "No, Lieutenant."

"But, sir, do you mean . . . well, we can't just *abandon* the hill!" He was shouting now to be heard over the noise of the chopper.

Normally, the Colonel would have rebuked him for such an outburst, but he remembered that this was a special day for the Lieutenant and he had come to congratulate him. "Lieutenant, you let us worry about the strategy," he shouted against the noise.

"But, sir, we took . . ." His voice was lost in the roar

of the motors and the prop wash. The Colonel turned sharply and boarded.

Hawkins stood and stared after the Colonel numbly. The pilot, seeing that Hawkins had been speaking to the Colonel, waited for him to turn his back. When he didn't, the pilot shrugged and gave full throttle for takeoff. The wind increased and bit into Hawkins' eyes and pushed the tears back across his temples. As the bird lifted, the blast increased until it pushed him backwards. He staggered, almost falling, then Major Tolson caught his arm and pulled him around and held him until the bird left.

"Chris, what's the matter? Are you okay?"

"Huh?" He looked at the Major blankly, then straightened up and wiped his eyes. "Oh yeah, I'm okay. Wind got me."

The Major looked at him curiously. "You didn't get hit in the fight, did you?"

"No, no." Hawkins shook his head as if in a stupor, then swung sharply to the Major.

"Major"—Hawkins touched his arm—"they're not really going to abandon this hill, are they? I mean after all we did."

"Well, I guess they are." The Major frowned and looked around. "Christ, who would want to keep this God-forsaken place?"

"Oh, yeah, I guess so." Hawkins nodded and looked off. Then he realized the Major was watching him and he spoke firmly. "Yes, sir, that's true, nothing here."

The Major relaxed and gave a short laugh. "You better get some sleep, Chris, you look a little tired."

"Yes, sir, I will." Hawkins straightened and gave the Major a smile.

"One more thing, Chris, I must mention before my chopper lands." His face became serious and he stepped closer to Hawkins, speaking softly. "That flag—you know we can't fly the U.S. flag without the Vietnamese flag."

Hawkins just stood looking woodenly at Tolson. He started to protest but ended by nodding his head weakly.

"Look, I know how you feel, but the Army's in on this Op with us, and there's no telling who will be coming up here after what you've done."

"Well, you're right about that," Hawkins said ironically.

"Listen, the news of this fight is all over I Corps. You

may have one of the highest kill ratios this year." The
Major was looking intently at the Lieutenant, wondering
at the melancholy. "You are being put up for all kinds of
medals, and you can put anyone from this company up
for a Star—or, hell, anything; and I guarantee it will go
right through."

Something clicked in Hawkins and he looked the Major
in the eye, "You sure about that—*anybody?*"

"Anybody that fought here yesterday, no sweat at all."
Hawkins looked away and down to the Second Platoon.
His eyes squinted slightly and his jaw tightened. "There is
somebody I want to put up. I want to put him up for a
Silver Star." The voice was low and tense.

"Sure thing. Just give me his name and I'll start the pa-
perwork."

"His name is Carlysle."

Major Tolson fished for a pocket notebook. "Spell it."

Hawkins looked up to the flag and distinctly spelled
each letter.

"Got it." Tolson snapped the book shut. "Look. This is
big. It wouldn't surprise me if General Stillwell or even
Walt flew in here; so you gotta get rid of that flag." He
smiled, seeing the Lieutenant nodding. "You know how it
is, that crap about how we're asked here by the Vietnamese, thus we're not operating on our own, so we don't
fly our flag by itself. You know. It happened during
Tet—in Hue. Remember the guys felt the same there, they
fought and died to take something and they felt real
proud. Hell, there were American flags flying all over;
well, they had to take them down there, too."

"Yeah, yeah, I remember."

"Here comes the chopper. You explain—the men'll understand." He bent against the wind, starting to run, then
flung back, "And congratulations again, Hero."